What the critics are saying...

"This wonderful paranormal story is just great. A great read, hot sex scenes, interesting and fast moving story line...All in all an enjoyable read." ~ *Mon-Boudoir Reviews*

"Liddy Midnight's erotic lovemaking scenes are breathtaking, using imagery from nature to display the wind sprite's many talents. Cyrus is a hero to fall in love with." ~ *Fallen Angel Reviews*

"What a unique world she creates in her stories...one which is hot enough to keep the reader yearning for more. Cyrus and Drey are such individuals, each with great powers of their own. And the details of the passionate love scenes, so inventive and imaginative!" ~ *Paranormal Romance Reviews*

4 stars "Small Magick is a delightful, stimulating, romantic fantasy with a twist. The relationship between Drey and Cyrus is passionate, sensual and definitely hot...I love how the author portrays Drey's world as a simple, medieval, small town village where everyone knows everyone's business...I also enjoyed Ms. Midnight's writing style. She made me feel as though I was traipsing around the meadows feeling the sun and breeze butt naked. I hope to read more from Liddy Midnight." ~ *Just Erotic Romance Reviews*

"Liddy Midnight has penned a tale that is fascinating and blazing hot." ~ *Romance Reviews Today*

"Liddy Midnight has brought to us an enticing new book of magic in the Dark Ages. You will simply fall in love with Drey's cat, Mousebane...I highly recommend this book to anyone interested in magic." ~ *Coffee Time Romance*

4 stars "The description of the different types of mages has me diving off on tangents trying to figure out what would happen next. Although I was on the right track, Ms Midnight kept me wondering right up to the last word. Ms Midnight cast a spell on me while I was reading. It was one I was loath to break." ~ *eCataromance*

"With complex characters and a fast-paced storyline, the latest from Ms. Midnight has a very unique concept, and is executed quite well...A wonderful way to heat up those winter weekends, FIRE AND ICE by Liddy Midnight is sure to keep the cold at bay!" ~ *Romance Reviews Today*

"An erotic fairy tale that keeps the reader at a slow burn..." *Thea Devine, best-selling author of SEDUCTIVE, SINFUL SECRETS and SECRET PLEASURES*

4 stars "Ms. Midnight weaves a story of passion and adventure as Brand, Trina, and her newly found uncle Juhan begin their voyage of getting Trina back to her people. The quest is not an easy one...For a well-rounded book full of action, adventure and hot sex you will not want to miss Fire and Ice. I know I am glad to add this book to my collection and I think you will be too." ~ *Just Erotic Romance Review*

LIDDY MIDNIGHT

Elementals 1

ELLORA'S CAVE
ROMANTICA PUBLISHING

An Ellora's Cave Romantica Publication

www.ellorascave.com

Elementals 1

ISBN # 1419954113
ALL RIGHTS RESERVED.
Small Magick Copyright© 2004 Liddy Midnight
Fire and Ice Copyright© 2005 Liddy Midnight

Edited by Brian St. James
Cover art by Syneca

Trade paperback Publication March 2006

Warning:

The following material contains graphic sexual content meant for mature readers. *Elementals 1* has been rated E–rotic by a minimum of three independent reviewers.

Ellora's Cave Publishing offers three levels of Romantica™ reading entertainment: S (S-ensuous), E (E-rotic), and X (X-treme).

S-*ensuous* love scenes are explicit and leave nothing to the imagination.

E-*rotic* love scenes are explicit, leave nothing to the imagination, and are high in volume per the overall word count. In addition, some E-rated titles might contain fantasy material that some readers find objectionable, such as bondage, submission, same sex encounters, forced seductions, and so forth. E-rated titles are the most graphic titles we carry; it is common, for instance, for an author to use words such as "fucking", "cock", "pussy", and such within their work of literature.

X-*treme* titles differ from E-rated titles only in plot premise and storyline execution. Unlike E-rated titles, stories designated with the letter X tend to contain controversial subject matter not for the faint of heart.

About the Author

ꝏ

Liddy Midnight lives, loves, works and writes in the woods of eastern Pennsylvania, surrounded by lush greenery and wildlife. Although raccoons, possums, skunks and the occasional fox eat the cat food on her back porch, she's no more than half an hour from some of the finest shopping in the country. Situated in this best of all possible worlds, how could she write anything other than romance?

Liddy welcomes mail from readers. You can write to her c/o Ellora's Cave Publishing at 1056 Home Avenue, Akron OH 44310-3502

Also by Liddy Midnight

ꝏ

Ellora's Cavemen: Dreams of the Oasis I *(anthology)*

Fire and Ice and Small Magick are also available separately as E-books through Ellora's Cave website.

In Moonlight *(anthology)*

Transformations *(anthology)*

By Liddy Midnight writing as Annalise

Equinox II *(anthology)*

Venus Rising

Contents

Small Magick

Fire and Ice

Small Magick

ॐ

Chapter One
The Dark Ages

ᔰ

Drey poked at the turned earth around the young plants and grimaced. Large clods stuck together like so much clay. 'Twas the same everywhere she'd tried to place her garden. This piece of land would never produce an abundant harvest; the soil was too pale, its texture too heavy.

She should be able to work a spell to better its quality. *Should* be able to, but couldn't. She sighed and rubbed one hand across her face in frustration. There were so many things beyond her meager abilities. Dissatisfaction settled over her, an all-too-familiar emotion. She'd seen her grandmother light a bonfire built of wet wood with naught but a glance. Her late mother, 'twas said, could command the waters of a river to change its course. Born into a family of powerful mages, how had she alone come to lack Talent?

"No matter what I do, this garden will never grow lush and green like Aunt Ingreth's. Her entire valley has naught but rich, dark earth. If I had her Power, I'd be able to make this valley fertile, too." She tried not to sound petulant. After so many months of dealing with her shortcomings, she still found it difficult to accept her limitations.

"Mrrp," her cat Mousebane replied, rubbing around her ankles. He dove across a furrow after a beetle, disturbing the neat row.

"Mousie, you're not helping. Henck took the time to lay this plot out nice and square. I'd like it to stay that way." She wiped a stray wisp of hair off her forehead, which was promptly pulled free again by a gust of air. She tucked the end into the top of the plait. It sprang right back, thanks to the stiffening breeze.

Another thing she couldn't manage. Her sisters influenced the wind and the rain, so why had she no such ability?

Pushing herself up off her knees, she sought the bench by the shed that housed the chickens and her mule. As she unlaced her boots, she looked out over the garden. The patch wasn't large but she could take pride in the work she'd done. In the few hours since dawn, she'd planted the onions and several neat rows of turnips. The herbs she'd transplanted yesterday and watered well had begun to recover, turning their wilted leaves up to the sky.

She slipped off first her boots and then her knitted stockings, draping them over the boots. Her labors had produced a fine sheen of dampness over her skin, despite the cool spring morning. Leaning back, she hiked her skirt up to her knees. Tucked up to the north wall, the bench provided a sheltered seat with a view. She shifted her shoulders into a comfortable position and tried to relax the tension that always filled her when she contemplated her limitations.

A wonderful vista stretched before her. Beyond the garden, a path wide enough for a wagon led down from her holding, winding around pastures and stands of trees on the lower slope of the mountain. She followed the path with her gaze, to where it met the road that went across the valley to where the village still lay in shadow.

'Twas clear the hamlet had begun as not much more than a cluster of huts on the shore of the inlet. Larger homes and shops marked the growth of the past decade, as trade improved and fishing became more profitable.

Every dwelling had a large garden behind it. The buildings farthest from the docks were tiny cottages, sitting amidst large plowed fields. Farming wasn't a profitable endeavor, not with the heavy, hard soil of the valley. That thought skirted dangerously near her earlier concerns and she resolutely directed her attention away from it.

She'd heard rumors that, when the village was first established, a mage had built the cottage she now lived in. No signs of previous residents remained, at least none she'd found. The door hinges had needed repair and the mattress had rotted away, but little else about the snug house had needed to be replaced. The shelves beside the hearth had been bare of crockery and everything bore a thick layer of dust but she'd found nothing beyond what one might expect of a long-abandoned cottage and no clue as to who might have once occupied the space. She'd found no remains of a garden, either, despite searching for a patch of ground that might yield better earth.

Henck had set up a space for her to compost table scraps and asked her to bring some nice, fat worms from her aunt's garden when she next visited her family. He promised such things would help but he warned 'twould be slow, mayhap take more than a year to improve just her tiny patch of garden.

If only she could somehow make that soil more fertile.

If only she commanded more than the small magick she had.

There was no escape. She had to face it head-on. Like the twisting paths in a tangled forest, all thoughts returned to one point. She was a fraud.

Had she somehow inherited her father's lack of Talent? Whoever he might be. Her family never spoke of him. Might their dismissal of him be rooted in his unsuitability as a mate for her mother?

Such speculation was futile. What had been, had been. There was no changing it. She was what she was.

Drey let the thought go and rested a moment, enjoying the warmth of the sun and the majesty of the view. The wind picked up a bit, tugging at her plaits and her hem. She turned her face up to the sun, reveling in the cool breeze as it washed over her. The Goddess had blessed her in many ways. She tried to keep the good things in mind and not dwell on what she didn't have.

Mousie ceased his digging and came to stretch out at her feet.

"Now I know why you like to laze around in the sunshine. After working hard, this feels good." A gust picked up her hem and bathed her thighs in a refreshing current of air. Drey tucked her skirt down before she reached out with her toe and tickled his large, snow-white belly. "Of course, you'd not know what hard work is, now, would you?"

The fat cat settled on his back, cocked his feet and looked at her, upside-down.

"You're going to go to sleep, aren't you?" She smiled and nudged his stomach. "What about the mice in the shed? What about the crickets in the garden? There will be crows gathering to eat my young plants, too."

Mousie merely blinked once, slowly, before shutting his eyes.

Drey had to chuckle. "It'll serve you right if I bring home a kitten to do the work you're too lazy to do."

That earned her a brief glare and a long-suffering sigh.

"I've never seen a cat that can convey as much emotion as you can with a single breath."

A loud purr rumbled up from the depths of his chest. A tiny yellow butterfly flitted about the cat's feet before alighting on his belly. Drey chuckled again as the fur there rippled and the insect took off.

"We may not have such good soil as Aunt Ingreth has but we certainly have more breezes." She clutched at her hem again and laughed at the rising wind's efforts to tug it free. A gust picked up one of her socks. It tumbled a few feet, end over end, before landing across Mousie.

He catapulted as if someone had pinched him, landing on his feet a full yard away. Drey took in his wide eyes and huge tail and had to laugh harder. "I've never seen you move so fast! Now I know you could catch mice if you wanted, you're just too lazy. Your secret is a secret no longer, my fat friend. Get to work!"

The cat glared at her and stalked off. The effect was ruined by his immense girth, which gave him more of a waddle.

Drey doubled over with mirth, while the wind kicked up tiny dust swirls across the garden.

"Mum?"

She turned to find the butcher's eldest daughter, Mara, dropping a quick curtsey. She suppressed a groan. What would the villagers think of her once Mara reported to her mother, and her garrulous mother told everyone else, the local mage had been sitting alone in her garden, laughing like an idiot? The villagers had welcomed her upon her arrival last spring but Drey knew folk. Men or women, they all loved to gossip and gossip about someone who was still considered an outsider was the best sort.

"Aye, Mara?" She hoped the blush she could feel creeping up her neck and face wasn't as noticeable as it felt.

Mousie intervened, rubbing against Mara's hem. The lass bent to run a hand along his back. The cat rolled over and offered his belly. Mara ignored him, straightening and turning her attention once more to Drey.

"I've come to watch your animals while you're away." When she didn't respond, Mara looked uncertain. "My da said you'd need me a day early this week and that I was to stay for a few days."

Drey leapt to her feet. "Thank you, Mara. Let me show you the little you need to know."

Dear Goddess, she'd completely forgotten this was the day she'd planned to visit her family. She hadn't given it a thought since she'd discussed her trip with Mara's father. Fortunately, the lass had come early. There was plenty of time to toss a few things in a basket, make the hike to her childhood home and arrive before her many nieces and nephews licked the platters clean.

* * * * *

The sun was at its zenith when Drey crested the hill. She set her basket down and paused a moment to look out over the valley. The familiar setting of her childhood spread out before her. Her heart lifted. After a year on her own, she was home.

She'd often climbed the apple trees by her gran's cottage, fished in the brook and hauled water from the well. She'd learned to smoke the bees into drowsiness and collect their honey from the old hives that still stood near the orchard.

From the wagons clustered about the cottage, she'd wager her three sisters had already arrived, along with their husbands and numerous children. Some neighbors must have come, too, for there were far too many vehicles for her family alone.

Drey lingered, watching the bustle below and savoring the anticipation of gossip and good food. Aunt Ingreth would most likely open the last of the winter stores for this gathering. The entire family would crowd around the trestle tables the men were even now dragging out and placing under the trees and eat until they were in danger of bursting.

She'd missed her large family, both the chatter and the shared quiet moments. Although she loved her little cottage and the valley she'd moved to, in the seasons she'd been gone, she'd found herself lonely at times.

The wind that had accompanied her from her home picked up, teasing wisps of hair loose and brushing them across her face. She laughed, swiping at the errant tendrils with both hands. A sudden gust plucked at her skirts, almost twirling her around as the light wool and linen belled out around her. Cooled a bit beyond comfort by the air rushing over her legs, she let go of her plaits and slapped her gown down. Her hair flew free of its confinement. She gave up. Snatching up the basket, she let the wind take her where it willed, tugging at her hair and whirling her down the slope that led to the proper road below.

A chattering throng came to meet her, Aunt Ingreth striding ahead of the rest. The little crowd's talk subsided to whispers and they parted to let her sister Jenny come forward. Jenny's husband Robert followed closely enough to keep his arm around his wife. Drey looked into his anxious eyes for a moment, then focused on Jenny's drawn face.

"Drey, it's so good to see you." The words came out in a thread of sound. If Drey hadn't been listening closely, she'd have missed them.

Her heart ached and she wished she could echo the sentiment as they embraced. Her youngest sister looked decidedly unwell. The dark circles around her eyes dipped down onto her cheeks. Her thin arms felt like sticks. 'Twas then that she realized Robert was providing more than encouragement; he was keeping his wife on her feet.

Drey held her hand up and everyone quieted. Aunt Ingreth herded the children off to the kitchen. The adults, with sympathetic glances at Robert and Jenny, began to drift away. Robert tugged on the shawl Jenny held, moving to drape it around her bony shoulders. Jenny shook her head once and whispered, "I'm fine."

It was clear she wasn't fine. Drey's stomach tightened painfully. She'd last seen Jenny at the harvest celebration, when she'd been great with child and glowing with health. How could her vibrant, vivacious sister have turned into this weak slip of a woman in such a short time? "What is it, Jen?"

"The twins. I've not been right, not since they were born."

"Early in the winter?" Jenny nodded and Drey continued. "Were both the births normal?"

"Normal enough." Her short answers, not much more than puffs of air, were far from normal for anyone in the family. Speaking, even a few words, was clearly an effort.

"They came early?"

"Aye." Robert answered as he rubbed his wife's shoulders.

"But not too early?"

Jenny shook her head and Robert grunted.

With each answer, her dread grew. Drey took a deep breath and closed her eyes. Setting aside her concern, she concentrated on her sister, extending her senses through their joined hands, up along Jenny's arms, visualizing the body in front of her in her mind. A pattern of light and shadow took Jenny's shape, shifting and settling as Drey examined each part of her beloved sister.

The vibrant glow of health was absent. Her sister's form was faded, pocked with dimness in places. Her head. Her lungs.

Unless something changed, her sister would only worsen. If she worsened, she would soon die.

With reluctance, Drey opened her eyes. She had to figure out what was causing this weakness. "Were you fine before the births?"

Jenny looked at Robert in mute appeal and raised a trembling hand to his cheek. He nodded and she closed her eyes, resting her head on his shoulder.

"Aye. She had no trouble. It wasn't her first and the lads were small, as twins are wont to be. In the weeks after, she failed." Drey thought she saw the glint of tears in his eyes before he ducked his head.

"Who does the cooking and cleaning?" There was a lot of work to do, looking after a home and five children, two of them newborns. Drey could imagine that alone would exhaust most women.

"We've had a kitchen lass for two years, since little Ingreth came along, and my Maeve's been grand. She's stepped in like a grown woman, picking up what Jenny cannot. I help when I can."

A young stepdaughter's help, however well intentioned or skilled, and the odd moments a busy husband could spare were not the solution Jenny needed. Drey had discovered that maintaining her own cottage, even living alone, was more work than she'd anticipated. There were always chores: animals to tend, mending to be done, meals to be prepared—and she was only one person to look after. How had Jenny managed as long as she had, with only one servant to help her?

"How is your business?" Drey really wanted to know how his finances were but to ask outright would be rude, even for family.

"Fine. Much better than previously. We've recovered from the fire in the tavern. I just hired on another clerk and the old brewery—you may recall I have a quarter interest in that—is profitable at last. The mild winter helped increase both travel and trade, after the good crops last year, you know, and—what's that?" Robert looked down to see Jenny release her grip on his shirt and hold her finger across her lips. "Oh, lass, you're right. She's not interested in my business but the money. I'm doing well, better than most." He folded his wife's hand in his and rubbed her lips lightly with his thumb. Looking back up at Drey, he said, "She's my life. I'd spend every last copper I have to heal her."

"I know you would." Drey looked at Jenny, smiling in the circle of his arms. "How's your milk been?"

"Flowing well," Jenny managed.

"Is it enough to satisfy them both?"

Jenny glanced uncertainly up at her husband, who answered, "Aye, so it seems. They do begin to cry again before she's uncomfortable with the fullness but we figured that was a bonus."

A thin cry came from the direction of the wagons, quickly joined by another. Jenny flinched at the sound. One of Drey's cousins hastened to gather up two bundles from the shady end of the largest cart. The cries increased in volume.

Drey eased the shawl from her sister's fingers and caught a running child. "Here, laddie, take this to her."

He looked where she pointed, to her cousin shushing the twins, then darted over, dropping the shawl across the woman's shoulder on his way by. As the three of them watched, she wrapped the babies in the soft wool, bounced them a little in her arms and the cries subsided.

"You're not ready for them again, are you?"

Jenny jerked her head to the side. A tear trickled down her cheek. Or had it come from Robert?

"It's not the blessing you thought. Two babes are harder on the body than one, even in the womb. You may think of them as easier because they're smaller from the start but there are two of them. I suspect Jenny's never recovered from the birth and nursing two babes is keeping her so weak she can't heal."

Robert pressed her closer. His voice shook. "Will we have to choose?" Drey understood his pain, for they'd lost their second child and only son to a fever in his first winter. He didn't want to lose one of the twin boys but she knew he would make that sacrifice to keep Jenny alive.

"Not if you hire a wet nurse. You live in a bustling town. Find a woman—or even better find two—to help you. Look for someone who's just lost or weaned a babe or has an abundance of milk. I suggest you also hire more help, at least a maid and a cook. A full staff of servants would be better, at least until Jenny gets her strength back.

"Meet this problem from both sides. Give the twins another source of milk and give Jenny as much time to heal as you can. Have Aunt Ingreth and Gran make up some tonics to help her restore her strength and keep the larder stocked with meats and cheeses. Jenny, you may nurse your babes if you want but don't force it. You must eat what you can manage, as often as you can, and sleep as much as possible."

Drey did a few quick mental calculations. "Mayhap Edwina can help us today." She raised her voice to call her eldest sister. "Edwina! Edwina!" Around the yard, heads turned and she called again.

After a moment, Edwina emerged from the deep shade behind the cottage. Drey eyed her sister's plump form, assessing the possibilities. They looked good.

When Edwina drew close, Drey merely said, "Jenny's not got the strength to nurse her twins. Can you help?"

Edwina's face broke into a grin. "Aye, I've not yet weaned my youngest. To tell the truth, I've been trying to cut back on Carrie's nursing but she's not convinced it's for the best. I'd be happy to feed your squallers while you're here." She patted her belly and winked at Jenny. "That means I can eat for four at the table today. I've helped in the kitchen since dawn and it's a fine feast that's being dished up. Gran and Aunt Ingreth have outdone themselves."

Drey watched as Jenny's eyes followed Edwina across the yard, to the woman holding the babies. When Edwina began to unlace the ties of her bodice, Jenny closed her eyes and sighed, her body sagging with relief.

"Thank you, Drey." Robert reached out and clasped her shoulder in a firm grip. "I didn't know where to start. Thank you." His voice broke. "Little Jen, I'll get you something to drink right now."

She watched him sweep Jenny off her feet and carry her to a seat in the shade. Now that Robert knew what to do, his wife would recover. It seemed to be mostly common sense but then many men lacked that very thing.

The ability to assess an individual's strength or illness was all her own and Aunt Ingreth had often assured her it was nothing to dismiss as ordinary. Drey decided she may not wield great Power but she did have small magick. Sometimes that was enough to make a difference. Right now, for Jenny and Robert— as well as their twins—it certainly had.

* * * * *

Jenny had already begun to look less fragile and better rested after only two days with Edwina sharing the burden of nursing the twins. Her voice was stronger and her pallor improved.

The change in Robert was plain as well. He'd laughed for the first time since the twins were born, Jenny'd confided to Drey. Her last sight of them just before she left was of a relaxed and smiling Jenny nestled against her husband, secure in his love, their sleeping twins rocking in a large cradle at their feet.

As she left the last meadow behind and entered the hills between her childhood home and her cottage, Drey admitted to herself that Jenny and Robert shared the kind of devotion she wanted.

With what kind of man might she find that deep, lasting love?

Slipping the basket onto one arm, she nestled it in the crook of her elbow and pulled her little panpipe out of her pouch. She absently whistled an old tune while she pondered those odd and fascinating creatures, men. Certainly her perfect mate should have a sense of humor. Intelligence, definitely. A handsome face? Possibly, but she'd met those with fair faces and unpleasant temperaments. She had no desire to share her life with a hard-hearted man. Character outweighed appearance. She listed what she regarded as virtues: independence, thoughtfulness, a willingness to work hard combined with good skills, self-confidence and fidelity. Definitely fidelity.

The wind rushing down the mountain whirled her skirts around her ankles and lifted the ends of her plaits. She turned her face up to the sun, blowing softly into the pipes while her fingers coaxed a lullaby from the reeds.

Courage. Strength. Tenderness.

When she ran out of virtues, she thought about physical characteristics. There was such a variety to choose from!

She'd always been attracted to lean men. Stefan, the man who'd loved and then left her last fall, had been somewhat beefy and perhaps his desertion was all for the best. Her childhood friend, Gerda, had preferred stocky, solid men and indeed, to no one's surprise, she'd wed one.

Giving her mind free rein, Drey began to consider men's looks. There was the blond lad who traveled with the players and that rangy ruddy-faced farmer's son. Although the latter lacked the player's training, he had an appealing, long-limbed grace. The fisherman Marc had such striking blue eyes. She tried to envision a rangy, blond-haired fellow with striking blue eyes and found it not much more difficult than the meditation exercises she'd mastered as a child.

Now, could she change the rounded chin? Make the cheekbones a little broader and more well-defined? She continued to amuse herself with the vision in her head, altering her imaginary mate's features while she piped and walked. The breeze continued to play with her hair, winding strands around her fingers as she moved them deftly over the pipes.

Would his voice be deep and rough or would he speak with the rich tone of the alarm bell in the village? She'd imagined three very different individuals, each one handsome — when had she decided she did want a handsome man? — and each one embodying her ideals, before she tried to imagine their touch.

What would it be like to be touched by a man who truly loved her? Stefan's touch had been thrilling. She'd thought she'd been in love with him but now she realized that what Jenny and Robert felt for each other was so much more. Stefan had never looked at her with such tenderness, had never caressed her with his eyes the way Robert did Jenny.

Which meant that the happiness she'd felt with Stefan was less than it could be. Now *that* took her breath away. Coupling with Stefan had been wonderful; what bliss would she find with a man she truly loved?

She found herself treading the path around the mountain above her cottage. Her shadow fell short on the ground before her. A small rock beside the path was where she usually chose to break her fast but the familiar view of valley and fields seemed too ordinary and flat for her today.

Mousebane squalled his *come-and-look-at-this* cry. Drey stopped on the path and looked around for the large russet tabby. Unable to locate him, she moved toward where she thought the cry came from, the slope above her. One hand holding the pipes, she wiped the hair out of her face with her other hand and squinted up.

"Mousie!" she called.

He cried again.

A gust of wind parted the grasses and she saw him, standing partway up the hillside.

Large creatures, perhaps deer, had tracked through the undergrowth to her right. The wind shifted the grasses this way and that, giving her glimpses of the trail. Mousie stood looking at her over his shoulder, clearly waiting for her to join him. The path wended around the looming face of the mountain above, defined by an occasional broken twig and flattened grass before it disappeared behind a clump of bracken.

The few times she'd tried to explore the mountain, she'd found naught but impassable slopes, crisscrossed by a few faint trails worn by sure-footed wildlife over steep terrain she couldn't manage. If the wind—and Mousie—hadn't revealed this trail, she'd have never found it. Curiosity, as well as Mousie's encouraging cries, urged her upward, so she set her feet on the path.

Chapter Two

ରେ

The track dipped and turned back on itself as it wound up the slope, finally delivering her to a pleasant hollow in the eastern face of the hillside. The ground sheared off at the edge of the little meadow. Exploring as close to the edge as she dared, she chose her footing carefully, keeping to what she hoped was solid ground and avoiding the gaps left by small rockslides. From here, she could see far across the valley. The river and its bustling docks in the village were visible off to the north, but not the sea. Neither was her cottage, tucked up against the mountain below.

A large, flat stone, warm and inviting in the bright spring sunlight, occupied the center of the clearing. Mousie sprawled across the center of the stone. She settled in beside him to partake of the treats her aunt had packed. When she opened the cloth bundle, she found a wedge of sharp cheese, a heel of bread, a small crock of beer and an almond scone.

The effort of her climb and the sun had warmed her, almost too much. She shed her woolen gown. Her boots and knitted stockings went next. Remembering the tumbling sock in the garden, she carefully set her boots atop her clothing. The drop in front of her was far too steep for her to chase wind-blown garments over the edge. She sighed, much more comfortable without the restriction and weight of the wool. Her linen shift clung to her skin, damp with perspiration from her exertions.

Plucking at the light cloth, pulling the hem up around her knees, she enjoyed the sensation of the cool air curling around her legs. The long, warm grass felt delightful around her bare toes. It took but a moment to untie and unbraid her hair. The breeze cooled her scalp, tossing her loose hair around her shoulders.

She spread the cloth and set out her feast. Sitting in the midst of nature's bounty, she couldn't possibly forget her manners. She took a moment to honor the four directions. When she addressed the east, the home of the wind, she felt the breeze pick up, bathing her in a gust that tousled her hair and whipped her hem up around her thighs. It quickly subsided, leaving her feeling caressed and blessed. The wind had definitely accepted her thanks!

For the first time, she decided that she might indeed be able to learn how to raise and wield the Power her female relatives managed with ease. It was interesting that the Power ran strong and sure in the women of her family, but not the men. In fact, she couldn't remember ever even hearing her uncles speak of magick unless it was with derision. The closest they came to practicing it was a hand gesture to turn aside the attention of someone they wished to avoid at the market or in the street. Gran and Aunt Ingreth had never discussed it but could this be a women's mystery, one men didn't share?

At Mousie's demand, she broke off several generous hunks of cheese for him. He hunkered down next to her, purring loudly while he licked the cheese wedged fast between his paws.

She ate while she pondered the different men she'd envisioned. She did want to find a man to love. Despite her wishes to continue her solitary studies, she knew it was past time for her to set up a household and begin a family. Unfortunately, that required a man, preferably a husband to help shoulder the load of work that came with a family. Stefan just wasn't the right one for her.

That left her with one question. How and where could she find the right man?

As she often did while thinking, she brought her pipes out again and played softly. The day was so beautiful, the first truly warm day of spring. Shoots of the earliest spring plants unfurled their tiny leaves in the sunshine. Birds twittered and flew back and forth above her in the few trees hardy enough to cling to the mountain. The breeze returned.

She turned to face the gently stirring air. Wisps of her hair danced about, just at the edge of her vision. Was it her imagination or did the wind pick up when she began to play? The warmth she'd raised while climbing to this wonderful place drained away under the wind's gentle caress. Her shift dried, giving her a pleasant chill, so welcome after the heat of her cast-off woolen gown. Gooseflesh crawled across her, puckering her skin and pebbling her nipples against the linen. The cool draft swirled around her, lifting her hair and tugging at her clothes.

She gave into the seduction of the breeze, turning to face the cliff and spreading her knees to let the air dry her everywhere. She lay back on the stone and lost herself in the notes she played and the sweep of the clouds across the blue, blue sky.

What a marvelous place! She could retreat here whenever she needed a break from her studies or her labors. The fact that no one could see her here was an additional attraction. She could mayhap bring her work and continue her exercises under the wide arc of sky.

Nay, on second thought, she'd rather keep this meadow as a refuge. This would be her secret spot, her sanctuary from the cares of the world. A sanctuary from thoughts of her shortcomings.

* * * * *

Drey opened her eyes and stared at the slender candle before her on the old, scarred tabletop. The wick remained white and cold, despite her repeated efforts to drag magick from within herself and light it. She rubbed at her forehead to ease the ache of futile concentration.

Toddlers often commanded fire in such a manner. Calling an element was the first step to controlling it, she'd been told over and over. Would she ever succeed in this simple task?

As if sensing Drey's break from her work, Mousebane jumped onto the table and rubbed his cheek on her chin. She scratched down the cat's back as he arched against her. A low, rumbling purr rose from him.

"Mousie, your mistress is a daft, thick-headed blunderer who can barely manage to keep herself together. Some mage I am! I've got a candle that won't light, a scrying bowl that shows me naught but my reflection and a fat cat that won't chase mice. If it weren't for the ills I can sense in creatures large and small, I'd believe I'm a false mage of the highest order." She sighed and rested her forehead against his flank. Despair would do her no good whatsoever. She resolved to make the best of what she had. "At least I can see what will help those in need and ease them with my herbs."

Her resolution to focus on her blessings evaporated. The prospect of never progressing beyond simple healing filled her with frustration and sorrow. She should be doing so much more.

"And I talk to my cat as if he were my child."

Mousebane gave her a sympathetic *meep* before he thudded to the floor and wound around her ankles.

Once more she took a deep breath and expelled it in a sharp sigh. Could it be she'd been going about this all wrong? Mayhap her aunt and Gran were wrong, that her Power did not lie within her, but around her. They'd taught her that Power was the same as a mage's will and that everyone—mage or no—created Power as they went about their daily tasks. Most did not recognize they had it, nor did they use it.

What happened to that Power, then? Did those who were not mages shed it if they did not use it? Might bits of Power linger in the corners and alleys, wherever it was ignored and cast aside, unused?

Mayhap she herself shed Power in this fashion, without being aware of it. She snorted. It certainly wasn't as though she'd ever managed to use it.

Closing her eyes and spreading her awareness through her cottage, she sought out leftover, ambient Power wherever it might have come to rest, questing in corners and under furniture.

To her amazement, she readily found strands that glittered and shone in the shadows. Her breath caught in her throat. Had she possibly solved her problem?

Gathering up the few glittering strands she found, she braided them together. A soft tingle spread through her as she worked. Stretching her hand out, she made a fist as if grasping reins. The threads of Power quivered in her grip.

Fastening the image in her mind, she cocked her wrist. Holding her breath and opening her eyes, she summoned the image of a small flame as she extended her fingers and released the gathered Power in the direction of the candle.

A thin thread of smoke spiraled up from the darkened wick.

Her heart leapt. She'd almost done it!

Her near-success renewed her determination. Convinced she'd stumbled on something new and important, she steeled herself and once again spread her awareness out, beyond the walls of her cottage, into the surrounding countryside.

She felt nothing. No glittering threads, no small shining pools, no signs of lingering Power where the proper conditions and combinations of activity and elements might bring it forth.

'Twas as though she had used up whatever ambient magick was available in that first, feeble attempt.

Closing her eyes, Drey concentrated more fiercely. No matter how long it took, she would succeed! Knowing now what Power felt like in her hand, having felt the slight tingle and shiver of its presence, she could still taste it. That first sip made her thirst for more.

This time she sent her call out beyond the vale where her cottage lay, down into the valley. She sought the glittering filaments in the village and the fields, in barrows and byres, wherever nature and the folk's activities might have left it. Faint echoes of Power remained around the river, lurking under the docks and near the wells, but that was all. She found echoes but no gleaming threads or strands, nothing she could use.

Having scoured every nook and cranny of the valley, she finally opened her eyes and admitted she'd been wrong. The ache in her head intensified, bringing tears to her eyes. Surely she wept from pain and not the bitter taste of defeat.

Absently she reached down to stroke the back of the tabby stretched at her feet. Her talent may indeed be limited to seeing people's illnesses and knowing what would heal them.

Mayhap her aunt and Gran were mistaken, that she had no talent for magick. Mayhap she merely had common sense in abundance and used that to help others. Mayhap all her years of study and effort had been spent, in essence, chasing rainbows, with naught to show for all her effort. She found that prospect almost beyond bearing.

However, even if her skills were limited to employing common sense, then she should make use of them. To heal her headache, she needed a soothing tea.

Rummaging among the aromatic bundles of herbs hanging from the cottage's rafters brought her a little peace. Here she was comfortable, here she was confident in her abilities. Clinging to that thought, she found the fragrant tea did little to chase the bitter gall of failure from her throat.

Her gaze kept returning to the candle on the table, proof of her inadequacy. Finishing the tea, she could no longer bear the confines of her cottage. Gathering up a few bits of food, she left.

Without thinking about it, she found herself on the trail up the mountain. The sounds of her world surrounded her — the chirping of birds, rustling leaves and the distant plaint of a crow. Reaching the meadow, she crossed to the flat stone and sat down. Here she could almost see forever. Indeed, out beyond the village, far off where the hills parted, she thought she could see the silver gleam of the sea. Turning her face up to the sun, she let the gentle breeze caress her, washing across her aching temples and toying with her hair.

This was where she truly belonged, outside, among the creatures of the mountain. Here she found a measure of peace.

High above, a huge hawk floated in a lazy circle. She watched it idly, just enjoying the sensation of warm sunshine and gentle wind. What must the great bird feel, soaring aloft as it did? What did the world look like from that height?

She tried to envision the valley as if from above, the village laid out much as she could see from here, a scattering of buildings along the tracery of roads and paths. Hedgerows and woodlands would be dark patches among the green of pastures and planted fields.

The wind subsided and the grasses stilled. The faint trickle of water intruded on her thoughts.

Was this the source of the clear stream that welled up in a spring at the base of the mountain? She'd found it tasted just as good as the water from her well but was far too cold for bathing.

She swung off the stone and followed the sound across the meadow, to the side opposite the cliff. There she found water trickling out of the stone face and into a small pool. No out-flow from the natural basin was evident, so the water must seep through a crack down into the mountain again. She dipped a hand in and found it numbingly cold, even icier than the water from the spring.

Tracing the edge of the meadow, she found a break in the undergrowth near the path down the southern face of the mountainside. There she discovered a patch of blackened earth. A suspicion formed in her mind. She pulled aside the weeds that obscured most of the hearth, revealing a ring of stones to contain the fire.

Surveying the area from that point, she could see the meadow formed a circle. The cliff anchored one point of the compass.

Air.

Opposite it lay the pool.

Water.

Here was a hearth, long-abandoned, aye, but once used frequently, she'd wager.

Fire.

Across the meadow, she also wagered she'd find another sign of previous use.

Earth.

In the center stood the flat stone.

An altar.

How could she have sat there and eaten her meal several weeks ago, oblivious to what she now saw so clearly? From the looks of the overgrown hearth and the absence of ashes, no one had used it for many years. Surely long enough that knowledge of this place and its significance had fallen from local memory.

Rumors of the mage who'd built her cottage sprang to mind. Finally, some evidence that those stories might be true!

Excitement bubbled up within her, and joy that she had discovered something on her own. Finally, dusting off her hands, she decided she could not pass up the opportunity presented by the natural circle.

Her feet fairly danced down the trail as she returned to her cottage and gathered the things she'd need. Candles and coals from her hearth. Her little cauldron. A handful of seeds, both herbs and flowers. An antler she'd found in the yard when she'd arrived. The clay cup she'd made years ago and decorated with designs she loved. Her two ritual knives: the athame and a little belt knife. Her mother's oak wand.

In no time at all, she stood back at the stone altar in her meadow.

Her race first down and then up the mountain path had warmed her beyond comfort. She unlaced her gown and pulled it over her head, folding it neatly beside the altar. Her boots and thick stockings followed.

She debated about her shift for a moment before deciding, why not? No one could see her, so she shed it as well. The sun on her bare skin felt unfamiliar and yet decidedly right.

The breeze rose again. She lifted her heavy hair off her neck, stretched her arms up and turned, letting the air waft over her and dry the perspiration on the back of her neck, under her arms and between her legs. She spread her limbs, reveling in the sensation of total freedom. How wonderful this was! With no one to watch her, she could wallow in the novel sensation of nakedness to her heart's content.

The image of Jenny in Robert's arms came back to her. What would this freedom be like if she had someone to share it? She could readily imagine the ecstasy of joining with a lover here.

Which of the men she'd imagined would he be? They would stretch out together in the soft grass, taking their time to explore each other's bodies while the wind and the sun bathed them in warm caresses. She longed to see just how soft the grass really was and caught herself as she sank to her knees.

Was she daft, that she should lose herself in fantasies, when she had this wondrous circle to celebrate? She pushed all thoughts of men from her mind.

Drey began at the northern edge of the meadow, where she found a thick stone slab. Clearing away the choking weeds took but little time. She spent another few minutes rubbing moss away to reveal a star inscribed on the surface. There was a little indentation below that and there she poured her seeds.

She envisioned the seeds sprouting, bringing forth life from the earth. With a shaking voice, she began, "I bless these seeds and stone, that they may be fit to dwell within this circle of light." She thought the engraved star filled with light for just an instant.

At the little natural basin filled by the trickle from the mountain, she dipped both hands into the icy water. "I bless this water and basin, that they may be fit to dwell within this circle of light." This time, she was certain the water flashed silver.

She had cast circles in her cottage, in a field she liked and with her family but never had she seen such an acceptance of her blessing. Excitement tempered with awe quickened her breath.

She next gathered a few sticks from under the bushes and trees and dry grass from beneath the new shoots. Piled in the old hearth, these easily kindled when she dropped a coal among them.

The fire warmed her outstretched hands. "I bless this fire and hearth, that they may be fit to dwell within this circle of light." A crystal-white flame blazed suddenly in the heart of the fire, then disappeared.

The eastern direction puzzled her. There was no sign there had ever been a symbol there, no evidence of a manifestation of the element. Mayhap it had gone over the edge in a rockslide in the time since this circle was last used. Finally, she found a stone with a dimple on top, filled it with a few pinches of herbs, dropped a little coal in and set it near the cliff's edge.

She held her hands above it. "I bless this scent and air, that they may be fit to dwell within this circle of light." As the fragrant smoke began to rise, she smiled. What would the wind do to acknowledge her blessing?

Instead of rising to the sky, a small cloud of smoke gathered just above the stone. As she watched, it grew in volume. The mass then formed a column and rose to wrap around her hands until they were completely engulfed. The ball of smoke hovered there.

After a moment of thought, she spread her hands apart, mentally pushing the smoke out, dispersing it to the wind. Sheer joy bubbled up inside her and escaped in laughter that followed the smoke out across the valley.

As she turned back to the altar, a breeze caressed her cheek, flowing down across her shoulder and between her breasts. A shiver ran through her. She felt that the element of air was special here, and perhaps that was why there was no anchor for the east; the altar faced that way and, in a sense, the whole circle was devoted to air.

Circling the slab, she laid out the items she'd brought. Satisfied that she'd placed her tools on the altar properly, she walked once more to the edge of the cliff. Holding one arm out, with her fingers pointed at the ground, she walked the perimeter of the circle, clearing her mind of everything but her gratitude for the lovely day. In each direction, she called upon the spirits to attend her.

When she reached the cliff's edge again, the circle snapped closed with an audible click.

Never had she heard that before! Drey continued back to the altar, to call upon the Goddess and the God to join her in celebration of her newfound sanctuary. She had no purpose in this ritual, other than thanksgiving for finding this special place and joy in being alive.

Gone were her thoughts of wielding Power. Forgotten were her frustrations at bungling even the simplest of magickal tasks. There was nothing she wished to accomplish, so she resolved to send the Power she raised back whence it came, to the mountain and the sky.

And raise Power she did. She closed her eyes, feeling the energy rise within her. The sun warmed her. The earth cooled her feet as she turned beside the rock, facing each direction and bidding the spirits farewell and thanks. Her arms outstretched above her head, she released the Power she'd raised.

A gust of wind buffeted her as the circle dissipated and a thud shook the ground.

The hair on the back of her neck rose as a decidedly male groan came from close behind her. Her eyes snapped open. She whirled to find a man sprawled beside the altar stone.

He stared up at her in silence, blinking brilliant sky-blue eyes.

She stared back, taking in his pale blond hair and high cheekbones. His face was long and narrow, with sweeping curves that improved on her imagined men. Each breath he took drew her attention to the pleasing contours of his chest. Muscular, but not too much so.

Desire flared within her and she had a fleeting thought that now she could test the softness of the grass. She shook her head, turning her attention from that glorious expanse of pale flesh. He shifted and she focused on his feet. His large, strong-looking feet led to long, rangy legs. Long, rangy legs led to —

She swallowed hard and stepped back a pace.

He was *naked*!

She groaned in frustration. Holy Mother of all. Never before had she shown any indication of Power. Now, somehow, she'd conjured the man she'd decided was perfect. He was none of the three she'd envisioned but a combination of all she'd considered. A very appealing combination.

"Are you hurt?" His voice echoed the clear note of the alarm bell, not the husky rasp she'd imagined.

He still lay there, staring at her. When she drew in a breath, his gaze shifted, dropping below her chin. The light in his eyes changed as he surveyed her body. No longer showing shock, his face lit with what she could only describe as hunger.

Sweet Goddess, she'd forgotten she was naked, too.

* * * * *

The young woman stood over him, glowing in the sunlight. His fingers itched to stroke her creamy skin, to see if it would be as soft under his fingers as it looked. Her dark hair tumbled about her shoulders, several strands dancing over her breasts in the breeze. Ah, her breasts were truly beautiful, rounded enough to completely fill his hand, he'd wager. As he watched, her nipples contracted. His eyes narrowed and he fixed his attention on her breasts. A jolt of something, a *feeling*, the likes of which he'd never before experienced, passed through him with a shiver.

"I should ask if you are all right."

Her voice rippled over him, causing another shiver. His groin tightened.

Her eyes were as dark as her cloud of hair. "Where did you come from?" She dropped to her knees beside him.

Her new position put her marvelous breasts on a level with his eyes. Almost close enough for him to take a taut nipple in his mouth. He wanted to do just that, suckle and tease her until she melted into him. She took another breath and those hard nubbins rose and fell, inviting him to lean forward just a bit and taste them. The effort of resistance robbed him of speech. Wordlessly, he pointed to the sky.

She looked up and frowned. When she met his eyes again, he read confusion there, mingled with her own desire.

"I don't understand."

He was certain she didn't. He had detected a delightful innocence in her during her casting of the circle, a blithe unawareness of her abilities. Nonetheless, the reason she'd bound him was clear.

Desire for her surged in his blood, gusting through him with each breath he took. He was aware of every fiber of this mortal body being focused on her, from his hands that itched to explore the textures of her skin to his rampant cock that he could barely control. From the look in her eyes and the scent of arousal that surrounded her, he wasn't the only one craving more than a kiss.

She put out a hand to his cheek. The tingle that spread through him from her touch was mirrored in the widening of her eyes. He turned his mouth into her palm and kissed her. The lingering taste of the herbs she'd burned for him was smoky on his lips.

Her sharp intake of breath told him just what he needed to know.

The desire that racked him also held her in thrall.

He drew her to him with an arm about her waist, transferring his mouth to hers as he did, swallowing her gasp as their skin met and slid in a delightful friction.

She tasted of sunshine. He gave in to the urge to stroke her, running his hands over her ribs, tracing the soft contours. Her body was nothing but silk and swans' down beside him, arching into his hands, rising to meet his touch.

The soft globes of her breasts invited him to knead and explore. He discovered that her breasts did exactly fill his hands. The tight nipples peeked out from between his knuckles, repeating their invitation to taste. She had summoned him here to give her pleasure, had she not? He could do no other than oblige her. He bent his head and took one taut peak into his mouth.

She thrust against him with her hips and moaned. Her hands grasped his head, threading through his hair to anchor him in place.

The nipple he held tightened between his lips. He lightly nipped with his teeth, once, twice, before tightening his grip to pull gently but firmly, until the weight of her breast lifted off his hand, suspended from the nipple caught in his mouth. Her breath came faster, inspiring him to seek more ways to please her. Almost of its own accord, his tongue swirled across the tip of her nipple.

She jerked and cried out. Her fingers clenched and pulled at his hair.

He opened his mouth and the tight peak of her breast popped free, shining wet in the sunlight and bobbing with her uneven panting as she fell back with a helpless groan.

How odd these mortal bodies were. Merely tasting her, pleasuring her, had made his balls tighten. How could he feel her arousal so keenly in his belly?

He shifted his weight, moving so he could see all of her. The earthy fragrance of her arousal rose from her cleft, where her legs had been pressed together. He inhaled the scents that surrounded them. His head filled with the combined aromas of her heady womanly essence, the clean smell of the grass crushed beneath them and a sharp musk he realized came from him.

His breath came faster. When he stared into her wide, dark eyes, felt her shudder against him, his body reacted with a tingle along his spine and a shiver across his skin. What magick was this, that linked them so? His eyes narrowed. What else had she done to him, in her summoning spell?

His suspicion was lost in sensation as she pulled his lips to hers. Unbidden, his tongue swept inside the wet heat of her mouth to caress hers. By all the gods and goddesses, she tasted better than he ever could have imagined. Her hips moved against him as they kissed, slowly at first and then with greater urgency, inciting unrivaled sensations that streaked through him to pool in the growing hardness of his cock.

He wanted to shove his cock deep into her cleft, ride her until he exploded inside her. The insistence of that desire shook him; he had witnessed mortal couplings before but never had he imagined the unrelenting need and promise of release that now buffeted him.

She stroked her hands down his back, following the continued tingles that raced in tiny flashes of lightning up and down his spine. He wanted the magick of her touch on him, everywhere. He wanted the hot velvet of her mouth on his nipples, on his skin, everywhere. He wanted to taste her, her breasts, her fragrant mound, her mouth, her skin, everywhere.

When she traced the line of his jaw and ran her hand down across his chest, clouds of lust began to gather within him, piling one atop another in a growing storm. Her fingers feathered across the tip of his nipple and sparked a full bolt of lightning, a sizzling charge that blasted through him. As if he had not shaken and trembled beneath her attentions, she continued on, stroking him lower and lower. The heat of her touch scoured his nerves, further sensitizing his skin.

Who would have thought he'd feel each caress, whether across his inner elbow or his stomach, all the way to his toes?

Her breath came faster, in time with his. His need spiraled, growing as she met his touch with hers, mewing softly as he stroked her belly and inner thighs, wringing a growl from him when she wrapped one hand about his raging cock.

He rolled atop her, instinct bringing his knee between hers to part her thighs. He explored the soft curls that adorned her cleft with his fingers, finding dampness that grew to slick heat under his touch.

Her fingers played up and down his shaft, pressing below the head and bringing forth a small spurt of his seed. Wonder of wonders, that he didn't spend himself right then. Why did not mortal men expire with the joy of this? He suspected he might, if he did not satisfy the thrusting urge of his cock, and soon.

Prying her fist from around his cock, he laid her hand on his shoulder and applied himself to readying her for his entrance. He suckled at her breasts, moving back and forth between them while his fingers teased her, tracing her wet folds and entering her weeping channel to stretch her just a bit, until she pounded on his shoulders and cried out.

She grasped his head in a fierce grip. "Now! Please," she pleaded.

He obliged her, sliding his cock into her slick heat in one thrust.

The clasp of her hot, tight sheath almost undid him. He stilled for a moment, gathering the strength to resist, to prolong this incredible sensation as long as possible. Here, in this mortal body, he found more exhilaration than a raging tempest, more powerful joy than the rush of a tornado.

"Ahhhh," she keened softly. "You are perfect."

He twitched his hips forward, planting his cock a little deeper. Her eyes widened and he grinned.

"Sweet Goddess!" Her channel clamped tight along his entire length.

He could feel an inner ring, very small, pressing against the head of his shaft. He shifted slightly, causing a little friction there, where they met deep inside her.

Her hips bucked beneath him and she cried out wordlessly. Her hands fluttered across his torso, clenching into fists and then opening. He captured her hands in his, spreading her arms out to the side and pinning her spread-eagled on the grass. He drew in a sharp breath at the way her breasts rose in invitation.

'Twould be churlish to disregard that invitation, when she had gone to the trouble of summoning him to pleasure her. He dipped his head and tasted first one nipple, drawing the tight nub into his mouth and swirling his tongue over the tip before going on to the other. While he repeated this, leaving each puckered point gleaming in the sunlight, he again rubbed the head of his cock over that circular ridge deep inside her.

She cried out again, pulling unsuccessfully at his imprisoning hands and thrashing her head back and forth. Her eyes were closed and she clasped him even tighter with her inner muscles, until stars danced in his vision.

"Sweet Goddess, indeed," he ground out on a harsh breath. "Never have I known such pleasure existed. Never."

She opened her eyes and fixed her glazed stare on him. "Nor I," she whispered.

Slowly, he began to slide in and out, relishing each inch, the contrast of pressures in pushing and pulling. Lowering his head, he captured her lips with his. Her tongue swept into his mouth, her panting breaths mingled with his, and he could no longer hold back.

With a cry, he increased the tempo of his strokes, finding she matched his rhythm with her tongue. While she thrust in and out of his mouth, he drove his cock in and out of her impossibly tight channel. Her hips rose to meet each thrust he made. Their breathing grew labored and then stopped for several heartbeats. She abruptly broke their kiss and turned her head. Her teeth sank into his shoulder as she clenched around him, once, then twice.

He thrust into her more deeply than he thought possible. That tight ring he'd been teasing opened to seize the head of his cock in a grip that was intense pleasure, bordering on pain. His back arched as he fought its grasp, wrenching free as his release struck him with incredible force. He roared with the intensity of the sensation, curling his toes. The thunder that shook his frame roared up to explode in his head. The rush of his cum spilled forth, filling her with pulse after pulse. It felt as though his essence was being poured into her.

Winded and drained, he collapsed atop her. His head fitted comfortably and naturally into the hollow of her shoulder. His cock pulsed once more before returning to its soft state and slipping free.

The young woman in his arms murmured and stretched. He rolled to her side, freeing her from his weight. His new position also gave him a good vantage point from which to admire her.

Dark lashes lay against her plump cheeks, rosy and damp from their exertions. Her face was full and kind. She was a siren; a sorceress who'd conjured him to adore her body. He reached up and ran a finger around the contour of her ear.

She shivered several times before she opened her eyes and gave him a lazy smile. He grinned back, completely enchanted with her. Adoring this beauty was no chore.

"What is your name?" he asked.

Her smile faded at the question. "Mildread, but my friends and family call me Drey."

Already he missed her smile. It warmed him inside, just as her touch heated his blood. "I suppose I now count among your friends, do I not?"

Her eyes closed for a moment and an emotion he couldn't read flashed across her features. "I have shared nothing like this with anyone I know." Her voice was low and husky. Just those few words sparked desire in him again. His cock stirred to life.

"And you do not know me." She nodded at his statement. "Call me Cyrus."

"Is that what your family and friends call you?"

"I have no family, or friends, other than you."

One of her brows rose. "How can that be? Everyone has family of some sort, somewhere, and everyone has at least one friend."

"Everyone but me." He ran his hand up her thigh, feeling the lean strength beneath the softness. "Your skin feels as good to me now as it did when you played your flute."

Her mouth dropped open and her eyes grew round. "What?"

A smile tugged at this mouth. She was adorable when she was confused. He stroked a few wisps of hair behind her ear. "Your hair, as well." He pulled a handful of the fragrant cloud up to bury his face in it. "Mmm...soft as thistledown. It smells nice, too. Like honeysuckle and wild roses, with a hint of the sea."

"I've never seen you before!" she protested.

"Aye, but I've seen you, often. And touched you." He continued his explorations, stroking across her neck. "And heard you. You play those little pipes of yours well. I loved it when you shed your garments and bared your skin to me. Few others have so dared. The last time, you kept your shift."

She stared at him in horror and shook her head. "Nay! There was no one else here. You can't have seen me!"

He smiled at the memory of her boldness, both then and now. "Oh, but I did." She was both siren and child, a mixture that drew him, made him long to test the extent of her knowledge. What would make her eyes open wide with surprise, as they did now? For surely, though she had gaps in her knowledge, she'd known enough to Call and bind him.

Chapter Three

ℬ

Her eyes narrowed with suspicion. She had been alone in this clearing, alone in the circle. She *knew* that, as sure as she knew smoke rises and water flows downhill. Alone on the mountain but for Mousie—unless this man had concealed himself to spy on her. "Where were you hidden?"

"I wasn't. What need have I to hide? There is no joy in that. I brushed over you, tickled you here." He slid a hand across her shoulder. "And here." He stroked a fingertip down to the tip of her breast. "And here."

He traced her nether lips, parting the soft, dark curls with his hand. "I liked this place best of all. You're not only soft here, you're fragrant and warm."

A horrible suspicion began to form in her mind. Nay, surely 'twas not possible. How could it be? Not possible for most, but especially not for her.

Her heart faltered. She covered her face with both hands and moaned. "Great Mother preserve me, I've summoned a wind spirit."

"One who is more than willing to do your bidding, fair one. Shall I pleasure you again?" He moved his fingers, slipping one between the slick folds to test her readiness. Her juices, mingled with his thick semen, coated his hand. "You are more than ready, as am I."

"Nay!" She pulled away and leapt to her feet.

"Then, if you have no more need of me, send me back." He eyed her with hunger writ clear across his features. His cock stood erect, ready to serve her will. She looked away, unwilling to believe what she had done, despite the evidence before her.

"Summon me the next time you're ready for more love play. I will eagerly await your Call."

She jerked back to face him. "What?"

"Did you not summon me in mortal form to please you?" He scrambled to his feet and stood beside her. "I assure you, I too found it pleasing. I've not experienced the joys of mortal lovemaking before. No one before has Called me for this service or bound me in this form. I thank you, for I did indeed enjoy pleasuring you."

"You *are* a wind spirit." Sweet Goddess, how had she managed to summon him?

"Aye, so you said before and so you were right."

'Twas too fantastic to believe. A giggle burbled out of her. She, who had no abilities beyond her small healing magicks, had somehow bound a wind spirit, who—or was it which?—had then made amazing love to her.

She began chuckling softly and soon was roaring with laughter. Her knees buckled and she sank into the grass again, hugging herself and howling until tears ran down her face.

Her wind spirit lover paced and huffed. When minutes passed and she didn't stop, he ceased pacing and knelt beside her. "Are you well, Drey?"

The instant he touched her, she sobered. Her laughter subsided with a final hiccup. Wiping the tears away, she sat up and regarded him seriously.

"I'm a mage of little talent. I failed this morning at the most simple of tasks, one most children have mastered almost before they can talk, and now you tell me I've not only conjured a wind spirit but also bound him to human form. I'm not capable of such a deed. You must be mistaken."

He drew himself up. "I am never mistaken. I felt your presence before you moved into your cottage. I've seen many come and go, most little more to me than a ripple in time. You impressed yourself on me immediately. You possess more Power than you know."

She barked another laugh and felt ready to sail off on more gales of hysteria. "I have no Power. You are mistaken, even if it's for the first time."

He shook his head and gestured for emphasis. "You may have yet to grow into it but there is Power in you nonetheless."

She ran one hand through her hair while she thought about this. He couldn't possibly know what he was talking about but she didn't feel right contradicting him again. "Then go away and let me study for a few more years. I'll summon you again when I know what I'm doing."

"Fine." He closed his eyes, wondering what the transition would feel like. His arrival in mortal form had been much like a gust of wind slamming into the hillside. "Go ahead."

"With what?"

His eyes shot open again. He watched as she rose to her feet once more, waving her hands toward the cliff's edge.

"Just go back to the clouds or the spirit world or wherever you live."

"You brought me here. You must send me back."

She gaped at him. "How do I do that?"

A sinking sensation began in his stomach. Her continual denials were beginning to sink in. Mayhap she was correct and did not know how she had conjured him. Nay, the ramifications of that did not bear thinking about. Holding his patience on a thin thread, he explained, "You reverse what you did, undoing the conditions in your spell."

"I cast no spell. You just," she spread her hands helplessly, "fell from the sky."

He frowned at her. "Wind spirits do not simply appear in a man's form. Some mage, a powerful one, must summon them, Calling and binding them to his or her will. Once the spell is written, 'tis a simple thing to reverse it, freeing the spirit."

"I wrote no spell! I can't even light a simple candle! How could I summon a wind spirit?" she shouted and began to cry.

He was helpless in the face of her tears. Share pleasure with her he could but his nature was not such that he could deal with mortal troubles. Besides, he would not expect her to be able to command fire. "Wind and fire are not the same element. You play your flute with a talent beyond most mortals. Your affinities lie in other realms, not those of fire."

"And how do I train myself to use those, er, those affinities?"

Did this little fool know nothing? He blinked in shock and worked to control his reaction. "Who did you the disservice of setting your feet on the path to learning the art of magick but abandoned you before teaching you anything? You must practice."

"My aunt and my grandmother. They sent me here, to unlock the secrets to my Power on my own, as the women of my family have always done." She sniffed and wiped her cheeks. "And what will you do while I'm training? How long will it take?"

He revised his opinion of her. She knew *less* than nothing. He'd believed it to be common knowledge that the magickal arts were either as simple and as easy as breathing or else they had to be wrested from one's soul by force. Clearly she and her lineage fell within the second group. "Perhaps years."

With dismay, he realized that he might have a lot of time to experience life in this mortal body. He turned his face to the sky as he felt the weather change, a subtle alteration in humidity and temperature that, hours earlier, would have sent him racing to bring clouds and rain to the valley.

What *would* he do while she trained?

Her face fell and she sniffled again. "Are you stuck until then?"

He had not considered his plight.

Her inexperience sentenced him to the possibility of years in mortal form. *This* mortal form. The thought itched under his skin. Already he longed to soar among the clouds, to dance across the countryside as freely as he'd always done.

"Aye. Stuck I am, indeed."

* * * * *

Once more Drey paused in her efforts to recreate the ritual she'd performed to summon Cyrus and rubbed her aching head. If only she could unlock the secret! The key remained stubbornly hidden in her mind.

Three times they had returned to the meadow and three times she'd cast the circle. Each time she'd felt the completed circle snap into place, each time she'd felt suffused with less Power than she had the first time and each time Cyrus had remained beside her, still in mortal form, when she released it. Something was different but she couldn't figure out what.

She needed her aunt's advice, and Gran's, too, but she daren't approach them for help. They were the ones who'd insisted the key to unlocking her talent lay deep within her and that only she could tap that well of Power. She couldn't imagine their horror at her having summoned Cyrus and locked him in a man's body. Cyrus was right about her being the only one who could free him; she knew that much from her studies.

Only the mage who wrought the spell could undo it.

Or the death of that mage could.

Nay, she would not even consider that a possibility.

If only she could figure out how to produce and control the Power she needed. Drey glanced over at Cyrus. Had she not known his true nature, she'd have never suspected he was other than mortal. An old linen tunic of hers, cut wide for winter layering over heavy wool, fit him well enough. A pair of braes hugged his long, muscular legs. When she discovered Stefan had forgotten them, she'd intended to cut them down for herself. Her dislike of plying a needle had put the chore off again and again. 'Twas a good thing, for it meant she had clothed her guest without resorting to borrowing garments and giving rise to gossip.

Cyrus dangled a bit of yarn for Mousebane. The fat old cat pretended to ignore him, washing an immense paw while covertly eyeing the frayed bit of wool on the end. In a moment or two, she knew, he would no longer be able to withstand temptation and would pounce.

Mousie was helping Cyrus explore various sorts of play. They both were making more progress than she was with her studies. She'd not been able to raise the slightest bit of wind, either to move the tuft of wool she'd torn from the end of the yarn or to flutter a candle flame. At Cyrus's urging, she'd given up trying to light one. He claimed that moving the flame was within her abilities and accomplishing that simple task would please her no end.

Cyrus chafed under the restrictions imposed on him by his current form and knowing this fueled her urgency to become a true mage. She must work harder and learn to use the Power he said she possessed. She had to send him back. He didn't deserve being trapped in a mortal body.

"You need a respite from your efforts," Cyrus said, looking up from the squirming cat, now wrapped in the length of yarn. "How do you expect to accomplish anything when you're strung as tight as a bow? Come, let me help you relax."

He held out his hand to her. The tender expression in his eyes was more than she could resist. No matter that her shortcomings were the reason he was trapped, he did not hold a grudge or blame her.

"Aye, I'll come with you. Where?"

"I thought your bed but mayhap you'd prefer a different bower?"

"Such as?" She mistrusted the wicked glint in his clear blue eyes.

"Hmm…the open field beyond your garden? The day is lovely and I would see you garbed only in sunshine."

"Nay!" Drey tried to untangle her fingers from his. "Nay! 'Tis too open. We would be on display; anyone passing by could see us."

He retained his hold on her and pulled her closer. "You mortals have such odd notions about perfectly natural things. Do you not know that you all look the same? And that you all—every one of you, young and old—seek the pleasures of the flesh from time to time? Why do you hide yourselves away, like thieves stealing a moment of joy in defiance of their neighbors?"

"We need our privacy, Cyrus. Though you may find us so, we do not all look the same. Some of us are thinner than others, others more plump. Some have long legs, some short. Women are very aware of their—ah—those features that set them apart from men. Or, actually, those features that draw men to them." Lights and lanterns, she was blushing! "You yourself have complimented my appearance and my scent; does that mean your compliments are lies, for I am the same as all mortal women?"

"Ah, no. You are different." He released her hand, only to capture her face by cupping his hands on her cheeks.

"How different?" Held as she was, she could only stare into his eyes. While she watched, the deep blue lightened in color and became threaded with silver.

"I have never encountered another mortal whom I have the urge to kiss or to bury myself in." He tilted her face to his and gently brushed his lips over hers. "You alone stir me. Do you see?"

She pressed against him and returned the kiss, threefold and more. Rubbing her hips against his cock, she teased, "I can feel how I stir you."

Through the layers of cloth, her heat burned him. He felt his cock stir and stretch. "Ah, yes, my beautiful mortal, you can certainly feel my need for you. I feel it the more strongly, though."

He shuddered as she continued to tease him, grinding her hips against him and then retreating when he thrust forward. Thunder, but she felt right in his arms. He cupped her bottom with both hands and lifted her against him.

"Forget the field," he whispered. "I think the table will serve us well."

"The table?"

"Aye. It appears to be just the right height," he explained as he edged forward, backing her onto the tabletop. For a moment, her weight pressed his hands into her softness. He squeezed her gently and then slid free. It took him no time at all to sweep her study aids out of the way.

Her mouth formed a silent "O" and her eyes widened. He captured her lips in a quick, deep kiss. She melted into him as his tongue explored her mouth. She slid forward, coming to rest with her crotch against his, wrapping her legs around his hips and pulling him closer. Desire spread through him, giving rise to an urge to sink deeply into her heat. His cock grew harder.

With a groan, he released her long enough to push her shoulders down to the table. She regarded him with a small smile as he unlaced her garments and pushed them down to bare her breasts and trap her elbows at her waist.

"Oh, you are truly not like other mortal women. You are much more beautiful." He lowered his head and took her nipple in his mouth. "And you taste wonderful." Sucking and tugging gently with his teeth, he listened to her soft cries and felt his own need grow.

Giving his whole attention to the task at hand, he gently tortured her with his lips and tongue until she whimpered. He lifted his head to feast his eyes on her, enjoying the sight of her breasts swollen with passion and topped with tight nipples glistening from his kisses.

Cradling her face in his hands, he brushed his lips over hers. "I want to taste you in every way. I want to knead your breasts until you beg for mercy. I want to fill you with my cock. I want to hear you cry my name as you shatter around me." He stared into her wide eyes. "May I?"

"Oh, aye, please do," she breathed.

He kissed her gently once more. Lifting his head, he admired her womanly curves as he slowly straightened. Her full breasts were adorned by wide areolas tipped by dark nipples, tight now with passion, quivering with each breath she took.

"You, too, stir me as no other has," she whispered.

Cyrus lifted her skirts and ran his hands up her thighs. He stroked the soft skin of her inner thighs. That soft skin led him to a nest of springy curls. Parting the hair, he dipped two fingers into the moisture he found hidden between the plump folds of her labia. His cock jumped within his braes, eager for release, eager to replace his fingers.

Keeping his eyes locked on hers, he lifted his finger to his mouth. The heady aroma of her arousal caused his head to spin and fueled the urgency of his jerking cock. He worked to quell his own ardor while he licked her juices and shuddered at the sweet taste of her desire. "You taste divine."

She struggled against the gown that pinned her arms. "I want to touch you."

"Next time," he promised. "If you want to help, hold this." He stuffed her hem into her hands, pushing the cloth out of the way as he knelt before her.

Her dark thatch partially hid her cleft. He breathed in the scent of her, musky and rich. Drops of moisture glinted on her nether lips. Spreading her thighs, he leaned forward and parted the curls. He thrust with his tongue, sucking her sweetness as he delved into her wet heat.

"Ahh!" Drey keened and jerked her thighs beneath his restraining hands.

With ease, he held her in place while he feasted on her. He lapped from one end of her plump lips to the other, ending with a swirl around her firm pearl. Pursing his lips, he suckled hard on the hardening little bud.

She writhed on the table. When he sensed she was near her peak, he resumed stroking her with his tongue.

The third time he sucked on her, she cried out, beating her heels on his back and releasing a flood of incredible sweetness into his mouth. With delight, he drank deeply, reveling in the nutty flavor of her climax.

When she finally lay limp and sated, he stood and shucked his braes. Catching her gaze and holding it with his, he stroked his hands down her thighs one last time before stepping closer. The tip of his cock nudged her curls. Taking his cock in his hand, he circled the tip around her clit. Once, then again.

She closed her eyes and whimpered. "Don't tease me anymore! I can't stand it."

He circled once more and rubbed the tip down her cleft. The friction of her curls across the sensitive head made him jerk his hips, seeking to plunge into her. He increased the pressure, squeezing the cheeks of his ass together to resist while every fiber of his mortal body screamed for release. Glittering promises of ecstasy sparked through him, making the hair on the back of his neck stand up.

Dipping his cock a little deeper between her lips, he gathered some of her juices and stroked again, slowly, top to bottom. The lubrication only increased the intensity of the sensation. With an effort, he restrained the urge he felt to plunge into her in a frenzy of lust. This time was for her pleasure, not his. He paused, the tip of his cock poised at the entrance to her passage.

He reached up to take her breasts in his hands, ignoring the surging need to penetrate her. Rubbing his thumbs over her nipples, he asked, "Are you relaxed yet, my dear one?"

"Not completely." She gave him a lazy smile. "Mayhap you could help me a bit more."

"It will be my pleasure." With one jerk of his hips, he thrust his cock deep into her hot, wet grip. "Yours as well, I hope."

Her hips rose to meet him. "I believe we can count on that."

He withdrew and thrust again. Her tight sheath, primed by her first climax, grasped him firmly. He had to work to move against her tight grip. Each pull was agony on his part, fighting as he was against his own approaching climax. Each thrust sent him closer to the edge of that precipice. He leaned over her, distracting himself by tonguing and sucking her nipples as he massaged her breasts.

She tossed her head back and forth, moaning his name.

Her climax began with shivers that squeezed him like a tight fist. The third thrust into her tightening channel brought stars before his eyes. The celestial vision spread through his body, tingling from his toes to his scalp. As he continued to thrust into Drey's taut heat, the tingle centered in his cock and balls before he exploded within her. Her spasming womb milked the last of his seed from him as he collapsed atop her.

"Please, free my arms—I want to touch you," Drey gasped.

"Certainly, sweetling." Cyrus lifted his weight off her and balanced on one arm. It took but a moment to free her hands. He put a finger to her face and traced the curve of her cheek. "You take my breath away."

She ran her hands over him. A small smile played around her mouth. "I want to return the pleasure you just gave me." Her hand dropped to encircle his soft cock.

He shuddered and drew in a quick breath. Her spark touched off a surge of desire but his cock only jerked once and remained as it was. "Another time. I am spent. You have sucked me dry."

Her eyes lit with mischief. "Nay, 'tis not exactly what just happened but I will suck you dry soon enough."

The delighted anticipation in her laughter echoed his. He helped her rise. With a few quick movements, he set their clothing to rights.

"Will you return to your studies or will you walk with me? I'd love to see you clothed only in sunshine."

That knowing glint was in his eyes. Drey sighed. "I need to learn how to send you back to your world."

"Are you so eager to be shed of me? Come, let us enjoy the day. Mayhap I can give you a taste of my world."

How could she resist his offer, accompanied by such a tender smile? She rose on unsteady legs and took his hand.

Chapter Four

🕭

"Show me your world first," Cyrus said.

And so she did, playing her pipes when she wasn't describing the time she'd seen a magnificent stag posing in this clearing at dusk or where the best wild honey could be gathered. They explored the foot of the mountain, finally coming to the waterfall at the head of a broad stream that flowed away from where they stood, meandering through the fields until it reached the river just above the village.

His interest in the physical world was as enthusiastic as that of a child, always touching, tasting and examining. Only once did he remark, "This is so different from what I know of the world from my natural form."

She found herself taking a new interest in her surroundings, merely from watching him enjoy textures and colors. Shades of blue, silver and gray shifted in his eyes, reflecting his curiosity and satisfaction. She felt she would never tire of being with him.

"Shall we sit here for a while?" he asked, indicating a fallen tree in the shade. They sat above the pool that had formed at the base of the falls, Drey playing and Cyrus tapping his feet in time. Finally, he nudged her. Once he gained her attention, he had to lean close and raise his voice above the splash of the water. "Keep playing, and watch!"

Sunlight slanted through the trees, lighting billows of mist at the base of the waterfall, setting them aglow. Drey's fingers faltered and she almost dropped the pipes.

Sinuous, hazy figures moved through the mist. She blinked several times but they remained as she first saw them, veiled by the fog. Were they indeed spirits of some sort, moving in time to her tune?

"Water sprites, dancing on air!" Cyrus chuckled. "You brought them out to play, you and your talent with your pipes."

Almost a dozen of the water spirits or sprites played in the foamy cascade of the waterfall. They were more slender than mortals, tall and willowy and ever so graceful. She would never have mistaken them for mortals had she seen them under other circumstances.

'Twas difficult to watch the figures and play but somehow she managed to continue breathing and directing her hands to do her will. They watched the sprites until Drey's fingers tired and her breath grew short. The figures were visible for a heartbeat after the last notes rang out, then they vanished.

"Oh, that was amazing!" Drey caught up Cyrus's hand in hers. "I had no idea one could ever see such beings. Did you call them?"

"Nay, as I said, your playing called them forth." He brushed back her hair and caressed her ear. "You do wield magick."

"How did you know they were there?" A hundred questions tumbled about in her mind, each striving to be voiced next. "When do they dance like that?"

Cyrus chuckled. "I know them because wind and water are two sides of the same coin, as you might say. We are bound together, in both tides and tempests. Who do you think fans the mist into such displays?"

"The wind spirits?"

"Aye. My brethren." The clouds in his eyes swirled and darkened. "I have done such many a time, tossing the water sprites this way and that. 'Tis a game we all enjoy."

Drey's delight over the water sprites evaporated in a wave of guilt. She bit her lip. Cyrus had been so generous with her, showing her things she'd never imagined, and 'twas her fault he could not fly free. Having just seen water sprites, she had to believe him when he claimed she did command some magick but she knew it to be small and insufficient to restore him to his rightful form. "I do wish I could send you back to your world. I just don't know how," she whispered.

"I understand." His expression was bleak for a moment and then he straightened his back and smiled. "At least for the time that I am here, I can share such things with you. Few mortals have witnessed what we just saw."

"And for that, I thank you." Drey raised a hand to his cheek.

He responded by slipping his arm about her and drawing her close. She fit well against his side. The curve of his shoulder might have been made for her head.

She settled against him with a tiny sigh of contentment. Cyrus laced his fingers through hers and moved until his cheek rested atop her head. Aye, they fit together well.

Every time she touched him, she felt more than contented, she felt a *rightness* that she'd lacked with Stefan. Every time she looked at Cyrus, her heart contracted a bit. That had never happened with Stefan. There was no comparison between the emotions the two men evoked in her. Stefan had been right for that point in her life but, while he had excited and pleased her, she had not ever envisioned living with him for many years, nor had she wished to.

Sitting here in Cyrus's embrace, a deep and abiding calm stole over her but she knew his touch could take her to the heights of ecstasy. That combination, of a presence both soothing and sensual, was a new experience. A welcome and comfortable new experience. She wanted it never to end, she wanted those years and years of living together.

Was this what Jenny felt with Robert? How could it be? Cyrus was not mortal. He was not like her; he could never be like her. Why did she feel this *something* while she was with him? Why did she long to spend her life with him? Mentally, she shook herself. She should be worrying about sending him home, not pining over their lack of a future together.

"Even I have never seen precisely what we just saw. The world looks different through mortal eyes." Cyrus rose to his feet in a fluid motion. "Come, let us continue our walk."

Drey took his hand and let him pull her to her feet. He kept hold of her hand and tugged her along. "I know of a grove I want to show you."

The way led through dense woods, away from the cascade and the stream. No path existed—they had to push their way through bracken and detour around brambles until they reached a glade filled with sunshine and wildflowers. Colorful spring flowers nodded in the gentle breeze.

Still holding her hand, Cyrus pulled her into the center of the clearing. Humming, he began to dance, drawing her along with him.

Drey pressed against him, into the warmth of his body. He certainly felt mortal, as warm and as solid as anyone she'd ever touched. Where their bodies met, she was aware of him as she'd never been aware of any man. Every part of her being responded to the song he hummed.

She found herself loath to leave him when he pushed her away to twirl her into a sequence of steps unfamiliar to her. Then he pulled her back against him and she settled once more into his embrace. They whirled and swayed together as the tune wrapped around them.

Finally, he slowed and stopped, pulling her into a tight embrace. His hard cock pressed against her belly through the layers of garments he wore.

The mood shifted from dreamy to sensual in a heartbeat.

Drey stretched up on tiptoe to whisper in his ear. "Did you not promise me a chance to give you pleasure?" She placed her hand over his shaft and squeezed. He arched into her palm and gasped in a breath. "It feels like you've recovered from your exertions."

His eyes darkened. "Indeed."

"I would like to see you clothed in sunshine once more." She looked around, sucking on her lower lip, and considered the contours of the glade. When she turned to him, she found he had his attention fixed on her mouth.

"Will you suck me like that?" His voice was hoarse with desire. "Will you take my cock in your mouth?"

What would he taste like? She licked her lips slowly. He followed the motion of her tongue. A surge of feminine power swept over her, followed closely by the urge to show him some mortal pleasures... 'Twas only fair, as he had been so willing to share the water sprites with her. "Would you like me to?"

He groaned. "Oh, aye."

She smiled as she took his hand and led him to a sunny area of short grass. "This should suit us."

He made as if to unlace her gown and she stopped him. "You first."

Under her direction, he stepped back and dropped his hands to his sides. She swept a glance up at him through her lowered lashes. He was holding his breath, waiting for her touch. With a small smile, she began to remove his clothing.

Each time her fingers slipped off the cloth and brushed his skin, he shuddered and moaned. The sounds cut right to her belly, dampening her nether lips in readiness for him. She found herself trembling along with him as she freed him from his garments.

By the time he was out of his shirt, the outline of his erect cock against his braes was well-defined indeed, and larger than she'd ever seen. When she reached for the ties at his waist and her knuckles pressed into the thin line of hair arrowing into his braes, his hips thrust forward. She found herself making the same gesture, eager for him to fill her.

Who would have thought that anticipation could be so arousing?

When she finally loosened the ties and his cock sprang free, he was panting and clutching her shoulders to keep from falling. She helped him lie back and bared him completely for her enjoyment.

The light hair sprinkled across his chest trailed down to point like an arrow at the nest of curls from which jutted his engorged cock. Sweet Goddess, he was beautiful! She stretched out a hand to touch him, tracing a finger along his ruddy shaft. The tip was swollen, dark like a plum, thrusting from its hood into her grip. She wrapped her palm around it, exploring the different textures. Slightly wrinkled here, there ridged with veins that pulsed beneath her touch and velvet soft across the head.

A drop of his seed glistened at the slit. She dipped a fingertip into it and he jerked his hips again. Looking into his eyes, she brought her hand to her mouth and licked her finger clean. She tasted a hint of salt and him.

His mouth hung open and his eyes were glazed with passion. "Sweet Mother, do not tease me so."

She licked her lips, finding the taste of him lingered. His eyes followed the motion. That wonderfully potent woman's power grew inside her and made her smile. Who knew there were so many ways to wield power? This was not magick but 'twas power nonetheless and exciting in its own way. "You took your time exploring me. Are you so eager for me to be done with touching you?"

"Nay, I am eager for you to taste me fully." His head fell back and he gasped out the words.

'Twas a heady feeling, knowing that he hungered for her touch. Instinct told her that she alone could bring him to this state of helplessness. Her excitement increased at the realization. She leaned forward to run a hand across his chest. Her breasts shifted against the soft linen of her chemise, pebbling her nipples into hard points. She moved again, just to feel the delicious jolt of lightning that streaked from her nipples to her womb. The motion released a flood of liquid to pool between her legs.

Who would have thought that giving pleasure could be so arousing?

Rising, she teased him deliberately, taking her time in unlacing her gown. She held his gaze, willing him not to break eye contact, leaving him striving to follow her actions with his peripheral vision. Aye, he knew what she was doing, for when her bodice fell to her waist, baring her breasts and revealing her taut nipples to the warmth of the sun, he whimpered.

"Please!" His voice was harsh with strain.

"In a moment," she soothed. "I want us both to be naked."

"Aye. But hurry. I am fair to bursting with need."

She pushed the gown down and stepped out of it. Wearing naught but her short boots, she carefully folded all their garments, turning her back on Cyrus to bend over and place them carefully on a nearby stone. She peeked at him between her knees before straightening and was pleased to see his attention riveted on her curves.

And he thought he was close to bursting now?

A smile played about her mouth. She turned to face him and squatted to unlace her boots. Her knees spread wide, she treated him to an unobstructed view of her cleft. As she bent to one side to remove her footgear, she felt the curls part and cool air wash across her wet folds. The earthy fragrance of her arousal enveloped them both.

Cyrus gave a strangled cry.

She placed her boots alongside their garments before returning to kneel and take him again in her hand.

Cyrus growled in the back of his throat. His cock, harder and thicker than she'd ever seen it, leapt in her grasp.

Acceding to his wishes, she bent over to lick across the plump head, feeling his slick seed spread under her tongue. The taste was more intense than before and she reveled in it. This was his essence. Another large drop welled up from the slit and she lapped it up. He was hot velvet under her lips, the soft texture of an expensive weave she'd once fingered in the marketplace.

She turned her attention to exploring the shaft, running her tongue down into the nest of pale hair while she rubbed the tip with her thumb.

Cyrus moaned and thrust upward with his hips. He implored her, "Hurry!"

She held his hips still by sitting on his legs. He shuddered and growled, bucking against her in a futile effort to hurry her along. Feminine power sang through her veins, a delicious counterpoint to the Power she raised when she cast the circle. Both were strong; both were undeniable in their appeal; both were part of her.

She traced the slit and the rim of the head where it joined the shaft. When she dipped her tongue into the hole at the top of the slit, he moaned and threaded his hands in her hair, holding her tightly. She opened her lips and sucked his cock inside, widening her jaws to encompass the large head.

"Ah, sweet Drey, you feel so good." He sighed. "Take all of me, please!"

She laved the head with her tongue, scraping her teeth gently across the sensitive underside. The clench of his hands and the hitch in his breath told her when she found a spot or a touch that drove him wild. He thrust with his hips, almost fucking her mouth as his hands moved her head where he wanted her. She twisted and turned until she found a position that let her take him in deeply, until the soft tip nudged the back of her throat and she could only breath between his thrusts.

Taking her time, restraining him with the simple expediency of her weight, she lapped and nipped and suckled until his cock was pulsing beneath her touch. When the stones in his sac retreated, she readied herself for the spurt of his seed.

The force of his climax unseated her. He thrashed and jerked in her mouth, shooting pulse after pulse down her throat. She swallowed as fast as she could, exulting in his musky, acrid flavor.

He lay as one dead, limp and spent. The only sign of life she could detect was the slight rise and fall of his chest.

She stretched out beside him on the soft grass, watching him as he recovered his strength. When at last he opened his eyes, she voiced her opinion. "I think mayhap you were not completely recovered from the exertion of pleasuring me this afternoon."

He grinned. "Never underestimate the abilities of an elemental. Give me but another hour or so and I'll show you what I can do."

"Will you, now?"

"Aye." He drew her close, wrapped an arm around her and breathed into her hair. She melted against his warmth. "You feel perfect, soft and warm."

"So do you." She found herself unaccountably shy, ducking her head. After all they'd shared, why was she reluctant to face him? To give herself something to do, she began to relace her clothing and boots.

He stopped her, turning her to him and lifting her chin. His blue eyes, now free of clouds, were tender. "There's no need to hide from me. You summoned me; we have no secrets."

Except for the fact that she might be falling in love with him.

Except for the fact that she was torn between helping him return to his world and keeping him here with her, forever.

How could she consider imprisoning him, keeping him bound to mortal form? That was no proper sentiment for a lover. Love shouldn't be selfish but she found herself wishing nonetheless that they could stay right where they were, as they were.

To hide her confusion, she buried her head in her chemise. When she emerged, she was composed enough to raise her head and look him squarely in the eye.

"I thank you for your compliments."

"They are nothing more than the truth." He bent to pull up his braes. "There is nowhere I'd rather be at this moment, other than here with you." He spread his hands out to indicate their surroundings.

She turned to survey the glade. The sun had passed its zenith and lengthening shadows took over the western half of the clearing. She turned and took his hand. "Thank you for showing it to me. This is lovely. I had no idea any place like this existed in these woods."

"I know. This is one of those hidden wonders mortals have yet to discover." Cyrus drew her into his arms again. "Thank you, sweetling, for showing me another mortal wonder."

She smiled and ran her fingers through his silky hair. The silver strands tangled, ensnaring her hand as he had ensnared her heart.

Dear Goddess, what was she to do?

Love him, her heart said.

Free him, her head responded.

She couldn't do both. Certainly not at the same time. Mayhap she must be content to love him now and free him when she could.

* * * * *

Together they set out, hand in hand, around the mountain. When they reached the edge of the fields cultivated by the villagers, he sat with his back against a stile and pulled her down to sit beside him. He freed her hand and bid her, "Play for me, please."

Putting her pipes to her lips, she blew a few random notes before beginning a lively jig.

"Watch," Cyrus instructed.

He turned his face up and whistled a note almost beyond her hearing. She raised a brow in inquiry and he gestured to the field in front of them.

At first she saw nothing out of the ordinary. A lone yellow butterfly flitted among the early flowers at the edge of the field. A few bees droned back and forth. Another butterfly, this one white, joined the first. Before long a whole cloud of them began to gather, pouring in from all corners of the valley. As she played, the colorful mass danced and swirled in time to her music.

Cyrus gestured again and the butterflies broke into two groups, one mostly yellow and one mostly white. They twined around and flowed through each other in a brilliant pageant.

Drey could contain her delight no longer. She found she couldn't both play and laugh. Laughter won. As the music ceased, so did the synchronized display.

"Thank you!" She managed to gasp when she gained control of her breathing enough to speak. "That was truly lovely. I've never seen anything so beautiful."

"I have."

She turned to see shining in his face the same tender, deep affection that Robert wore when he looked at Jenny. Her heart echoed the feeling.

Dear Goddess, she'd found the one she'd wished for, someone she could love enough to build a life together with. Her breath caught in her throat.

She'd found him in a wind spirit, not in a man.

Chapter Five

ഇ

"I think you should try to release me."

Drey's heart plummeted at the thought. She was still torn, for she both wanted him to stay with her and yet knew of his impatience to return to his normal form. Since it was her fault that he was trapped, how could she refuse his request?

"Let's go up to the meadow," she agreed with an inward wince. She had no confidence she could return him to his natural form but she owed it to him to try.

The noon sun warmed her shoulders as she walked in front of him on the path. The willow basket containing her candles and cauldron and herbs banged against her legs with every step. Her heart thumped in her chest, as much from trepidation as from the climb. What if she failed again? Even worse, what if something went wrong and an unforeseen disaster occurred? Her haphazard history with working magick did not make her confident she could send her lover back to his own world.

Cyrus dawdled behind her, trailing the length of yarn. Mousie still chased it, although the fat fellow was huffing and puffing by the time they reached the meadow and her circle.

With a heavy heart, she laid out the items on the altar. Then she took up her athame and began to cast the circle. As she went through the now-familiar routine, she tried to keep her thoughts on Cyrus and his plight and how he might feel as a free spirit soaring across the vast sky. She imagined so well she also felt a longing to take to the air. The cliff called to her, begging her to leap and let the currents bear her aloft. She shook off the urge and set about her task.

And so she closed the circle, again both hearing and feeling the snap of it springing shut. Approaching the altar, she began the chant she'd been working on. She took a deep breath and hoped she'd worded it correctly.

"All unknowing I wrought a charm,
Meaning you and no one harm
Now may you in your own form fly
Returning to your world, the sky.
An I will, so mote it be."

She finished with a flourish and turned to point at Cyrus as she broke the circle. There was another audible pop.

Her basket soared aloft and disappeared.

Cyrus began to chuckle as the Power of the circle dissipated. "An impressive display but it's still not quite right."

"Will I ever set you free?" she wailed. She swept the altar contents into her skirt. It would be a long and uncomfortable trip down the mountain with her hem hiked high.

Mousebane came to bump his head against her knee. Cyrus came to place his arm about her shoulders.

"You're getting closer. At least something made it to the sky."

She turned to regard him with a solemn expression. "You're making the assumption that my basket is now winging through the air. It may have gone elsewhere or become something else."

He pondered that for a moment. Indeed, he'd not like to be turned into a clod of earth or a tree but becoming a bird wouldn't be a terrible thing. "At least you raised the Power. I felt it. You must have as well. That's a big step in the right direction."

She shrugged, clearly unimpressed by his logic. Together they trod down the mountain in silence while he sought something to say to lighten her mood.

Drey put her tools away with a heavy heart. She had just set her small cauldron in its place on the shelf when a timid knock sounded at the door.

"Come!" she called.

Mara stood in the doorway with one arm around the shoulder of little Lysbet, Wentil's youngest daughter, from the outermost holding in the valley. The tiny lass stood in the doorway and twisted her hands in her skirt. Tears ran down her cheeks.

"I found her crying in the lane. She lost her way," Mara explained.

Drey stooped and spoke to the child. "Lysbet, what's the matter?"

"Please, missus, will you come? Me mum is took real bad." Lysbet hiccupped. "She was fine last eve but, this morning after we broke our fast, she fell in a heap. Me da's put her to bed but she's pale and breathing quick like and can't speak."

Before the lass finished, Drey rose and went to gather together herbs and a few pots of unguents. She lifted down a new basket and filled it.

Cyrus came to stand next to her. He took the basket after she tucked a cloth over the contents. "I will accompany you."

She blinked at him. Mortals were outside his ken. Why should he care about Lysbet's mama? She kept her tone low, to avoid being overheard. Thus far, Cyrus had not come to the attention of her neighbors. "I will appreciate your company but what can you do to help?"

"Perhaps nothing. Perhaps much. In this form, I am the stuff of magick, am I not?" He too spoke softly as he regarded her with a steady, clear, blue gaze. "You may have need of me. In that case, I would prefer to be at hand."

"Aye. Mayhap you could be of help." She didn't understand just how but then she didn't yet know what she would face. She admitted to herself that whether he could provide help was immaterial; his company was always welcome. "Come," she said, taking Lysbet's hand and heading out the door. "Lysbet, Mara, this is my friend, Cyrus. He is going to come with us."

Lysbet ducked her head and tightened her grip on Drey's hand.

"'Tis nice to meet you, sir. I'm worried about Lysbet's mama but my da's waiting for me." Mara said, heading back toward the village. She called over her shoulder, "Good luck, and may the Goddess guide you."

Drey acknowledged Mara's blessing with a wave while her thoughts raced ahead of them. What could have taken Betsy so suddenly? Two days ago, Drey had passed by their holding on her quest for wild herbs and moss. Betsy had paused in her labors long enough to exchange a greeting. The woman had looked as she always did, bustling about her chores. She'd had a tired smile but who wouldn't with seven children, none of whom had yet seen ten summers? Her color had been good and she'd moved normally, giving no sign of any pain.

Betsy was the strong glue that held her family together. Her husband Wentil never smiled or had a kind word for anyone. He was a hard man and a harder worker. Word around the village was that, in his business dealings, he was exacting but unfailingly fair. He cared for the fields and any business that had to be done, leaving everything else to Betsy.

They turned away from the village, hastening toward the foothills as fast as Lysbet's short legs could carry her. It wasn't until the slopes rose around them and concealed her cottage that Drey realized Cyrus easily kept pace behind them. She gave herself no more time to consider his presence or her response to it; she only knew it was comforting not to be entirely on her own.

In short order, they reached Lysbet's home at the convergence of two streams. The large, tumbledown cottage had clearly once been owned by more prosperous folk. Drey clung tightly to the railing of the footbridge and picked her way carefully through a maze of loose boards and gaping holes. The stream wasn't deep but a dunking would only delay her. How long had Lysbet wandered before Mara found her?

Betsy lay wheezing on a pallet in a corner of a dark, airless back room. Wentil sat clutching her hand, staring intently at her. He ignored his children, huddled in the deep shadows. Their frightened eyes were huge in their pale faces. Drey's heart went out to them. Their mother held the family together, often by sheer force of her will. Their father, hard worker or no, appeared to be of little use in a crisis.

Flinging open the nearest window to let in more light, she winced when one of the shutters crashed to the ground outside. Cyrus took over and wrestled open the other window in the room. Spring sunshine streamed in, brightening the worn blanket that covered Betsy and highlighting the dust and clutter in the corners.

Drey shot him a grateful look before moving to examine Betsy. Wentil never acknowledged her presence. Betsy's pallor was bad and her ragged breathing echoed in the room. The air hung heavy with the smell of fried onions and old apples. With a sinking feeling, Drey sat across from Wentil and clasped Betsy's hands in hers.

She closed her eyes and concentrated.

Betsy's ample form took shape in her mind. Drey's apprehension increased as she noted the large dark areas in the chest and head. While she watched, they spread.

Her potions and herbs would be useless against the *wrongness* that began in Betsy's head. She had seen this before.

Wentil still had not given any sign he knew she was there. Turning to face the children, Drey prepared to give them the bad news. She found the words stuck in her throat. What would happen to this family without their anchor, their support? Casting about for something to say, some way to ease the blow, she found that instead she had picked up the basket and clutched it to her like a shield.

Cyrus came up behind her and placed a hand on her shoulder. "Is there aught to be done for her?" he whispered.

"Nay," Drey breathed. Although Wentil gave no sign of hearing their conversation, she was loath to distress him or the children until she had no choice. From the looks of them, they already knew the situation was dire.

He gave her shoulder a squeeze. "Then make it appear that you are trying. I will help." Prying the basket from her numb fingers, he opened the cloth she'd tucked on top and began laying out her herbs and pots.

With an effort, she forced her mind from speculation and to the task at hand. Doing something, anything, was better than dwelling on the situation. In action she found an anchor for her roiling emotions. Grief for her friend, and this family, gave way before a determination to do what she could to help Betsy, however futile it might be. "Lysbet, fetch me some clean water." The lass jumped to do her bidding. "You," she pointed to the biggest lad, almost Lysbet's height but more sturdy in his build. "Find me a brazier. With coals."

Cyrus touched several of the pots in turn and asked, "Which shall you need?"

"It makes little difference." She kept her voice low. "Herbs and potions can only prolong this state, not ease or cure it."

"Perhaps if you tried some magick?" he suggested softly.

She twisted her fingers together. He was making her face her fear head-on. Dear Goddess, what she wouldn't give to be able to do just that. "I have none to try!" The words came out in an anguished murmur.

"I disagree."

She glanced up, her jaw set, ready to argue. Then she saw his face, filled with compassion and encouragement. Her angry words died before they reached her lips.

"You summoned water sprites with your pipes." He placed his hand over hers. "You summoned and bound me. You may not control or command it but never say you have no magick."

She closed her eyes against the hot prickle of tears. Might he be right?

Lysbet and her brother returned just then. Instructing them on where to put the pan of water and how to position the brazier gave her some time to recover her composure.

Once the items were settled to her satisfaction and the children huddled once more with their siblings, she took his hand again. Since he had brought the subject of magick up, mayhap he had an idea of what might help. Linking her fingers through his, she asked, "What do you suggest?"

"Perhaps if we work together, or if you play your pipes, we can effect a change in her. What did you do, when you first took her hand and closed your eyes?"

"I don't have my pipes. I left them on the table." Drey groped for words to explain how she knew what ailed Betsy. "I built in my mind an image of her, a vision of her body that shows me her well-being. A healthy person's image shines bright silver. I can tell from the glow, or dimness, what parts of her are affected and sometimes I can see specifically what the cause of the illness or pain is. This is centered in both her head and her chest."

"Then you might try to envision a change in that image, the dimness turning brighter or disappearing altogether, leaving only glowing silver." Cyrus tightened his fingers on hers. "I will support you, sending strength into you."

Hope sprang to life at his words and she tamped it down. Why should she succeed now, when she never had before? Biting her lip, she decided she had to try. If she never tried, she'd never know.

"All right. Lend me what strength you can."

She closed her eyes once more and summoned the image of Betsy as she had seen it moments before. Immediately the head of the image darkened, driving the dim glow of failing health down to almost total blackness. Fear lurched in her belly. The progression was swifter than she had thought. Betsy had not much time — or life — remaining.

Taking a deep breath, she prayed for strength. Was it her imagination or did she feel something flow into her from where Cyrus held her hand?

The sensation intensified, becoming a tingle of Power. She relaxed a little and the flow increased. Gathering her will, she forced the image in her mind to change. The black filling the head lightened. She pushed against the darkness, willing it to depart, willing the glow to return.

To her amazement, the shadowed areas gave ground to her effort. She pushed again. The chest began to glow with health once more but the head did not yield beyond the first change. Again and again she tried, battering her will against the darkness in the image, but to no avail.

When she opened her eyes, she had a headache and sweat was dripping from her face. Her shoulders slumped with fatigue.

"Look." Cyrus directed her attention to her patient.

Betsy no longer gasped and wheezed. The furrowed lines of pain between her eyes had softened.

Drey gently squeezed his hand. They'd done it! With his help, she'd managed to do something. Not cured the illness but definitely made a difference. She met his eyes, seeing the relief and satisfaction she knew mirrored her own. "Thank you," she whispered. He had no reason to care what happened to Betsy or her family, yet he had encouraged and aided her. No matter that he was not mortal, he was a good man. "Thank you so much!"

One final time, she closed her eyes and viewed Betsy's form. This time she could detect no change, no further encroachment of the illness. She felt she could leave her now, although she would have to return to check on her later. Mayhap another day, when they were both strong, she and Cyrus could push the darkness back a bit more. She hugged that hope close. She'd never seen anyone who could effect any improvement for a victim of this particular ailment. Until now.

To prevent anything from draining Betsy's health, Drey warded the room. She quickly sketched sigils of protection around the windows and the door, tracing a circle that joined them all. When she drew the circle closed, the air in the room shook with a slight vibration, so low she was barely aware of it. Had Cyrus's love, and his faith in her, begun to open up her abilities? She had never felt the wards take hold before.

Mayhap she did have Power but then, wards were a simple ritual. Healing Betsy would take more than small magick.

She grew even more determined to find the key to controlling and commanding Power.

Wentil never moved when they gathered up her things, spoke to the children about how to take care of their mother and departed.

The following morning Drey and Cyrus returned to discover that the wards had held and the children had done their jobs.

Their mother was unchanged but her surroundings had undergone significant change for the better. The corners were clean and free of clutter. Every window in the house had been thrown open and no stale smells clouded the air. Wentil no longer sat in a silent stupor by his wife. Although he only grunted in greeting, he was busily oiling the hinges of the shutters. Drey noticed he had already repaired the broken ones and restored them all to their proper positions.

Betsy lay in her sunlit room, breathing easily. No sign of the illness marred the woman's chest when Drey assessed her condition. Even with Cyrus aiding her, Drey found she could make no further improvement in her patient's health. The darkness lodged in Betsy's head stubbornly remained. Drey was disappointed but felt stubborn herself. She was determined she would win this fight.

* * * * *

On market day, Cyrus accompanied her down to the village to sell her herbal concoctions and buy supplies. He wandered off to watch a group of children play while she dickered with the miller over how much coin he wanted to grind her grain.

"Drey! How are you?" An older woman in a worn woolen gown approached from the direction of the river.

"Anice! I'm well." Drey found herself swept into a hug.

"How's Betsy doing? I heard about her falling down like that. Gerta and her daughter went over this morning with some fresh bread and sops. Her poor wee ones. How that Wentil will fare, having them all and the crops to care for, I don't know. He's a harsh man, he is." Anice shook her head and made a sign against the evil eye. "None of us knows when it will be our time."

"Nay, we do not. I saw her last evening. She's holding her own." Drey began walking. "I'm at my wits' end to find some way to help her."

Anice patted her shoulder. "Now, lass, don't worry. If anyone can, 'tis you."

A farmer's wife hailed them as she trudged past.

Drey returned the greeting before facing her friend once more. "How are your children?"

"Wild as ever. The little ferrets are getting faster every week. I can barely keep up with their antics." Anice wiped perspiration from her brow.

Drey could well believe her friend had trouble managing her brood of five boys. Fortunately, her husband was a valued member of the community. Good smiths seldom found themselves without food in the larder or a roof over their heads.

"We've not seen you for some time. Are you progressing with your studies?"

"Slowly, but I'm learning. Soon I'll be able to slow your children down and make your housework do itself!"

They shared a laugh over the old joke between them. The second time they had sat down together to chat over a cup of Drey's most soothing tea, Anice had confided her hate for keeping a house up, especially sweeping and baking. Drey had confided her dislike of sewing and the two had grown to be good friends in the years since.

"Have you met the other mage?"

Drey stopped in the middle of the path. "Other mage?"

"Aye, he's taken over the cot up in the hills at the river head. 'Tis said he's a real powerful man, in the service of the king himself! He was here early this morning. Not so old as I expected," Anice sniffed. "Having seen him, I pay little credit to the rumors of his abilities."

"A *man* who's a mage? I've never heard of a male mage." Drey could hardly breathe for excitement. Mayhap this man could help her find the key to unlocking her Power.

A mage trained elsewhere might know methods her family didn't.

Anice sniffed again. "Evidently they exist. We've only been blessed with females but I can't see why a man can't raise Power as well as a woman." Anice shrugged her ample shoulders and plopped onto a bench beneath a tree near the town center.

"Is he still here?" Drey craned her neck, trying to see above the villagers milling around between the stalls. "What does he look like?"

"Not what I expected, even if he were older," Anice snorted. "Middling height and dark, with a brisk manner. Too friendly. Seems to me as mages ought to be more dignified and distant from us others."

"Anice, we're not freaks or lords, we're just like you," Drey exclaimed. "How can you say that you expect a mage to be different?"

"I know you're just like us. We know you. You needn't impress us and we needn't bow to you. I just think a new mage, especially one who works for the king himself, ought to stand on his dignity, wear finer clothes, dripping with gold and gems. If we're to be living close by a royal servant, we ought to get to see a treat when he comes around."

Drey shook her head. "Anice dear, there is no difference between a royal servant and you or any of the villagers, other than who pays you and where you work."

"No difference at all?" Anice sounded vaguely disappointed.

"None," Drey responded firmly.

Anice drew in a sharp breath and clutched Drey's arm. "Now, that's what I call a treat!"

Drey followed the direction of her gaze and found Cyrus laughing with a group of children. He pretended to be a fisherman, unfurling a shawl over a young lad as though it were a net. He did look a treat, dressed in her second-best tunic and a pair of leggings, his eyes shining that cerulean blue.

If she acknowledged him, Anice would pester her with questions for hours. Now that she knew there was a male mage for her to meet, she had an even longer list of tasks to accomplish. She pretended ignorance of Cyrus, asking, "Is that the mage?"

"Nay, didn't I just tell you he's middling and dark? Yon lad is tall and fair." Anice couldn't tear her eyes off Cyrus. "Very fair."

Drey spied a stranger of average height who paused at one of the stalls to look at the merchant's wares. His stocky form was bundled into a heavy cloak, its hood thrown back to reveal closely shorn dark hair and a neatly trimmed beard. The wool of his garment was fine, dyed in rich colors.

She nudged Anice, directing her attention away from Cyrus. "Is that the mage?"

"Oh, aye, that's him. He's called Kelsh." She turned her attention back to Cyrus.

Drey knew Anice wouldn't miss her as she slipped off, working her way around the fringes of the crowd. She saw the mage was examining the fine leather gloves and pouches Unter made. She kept going, until she could approach the glover's stall from the other side.

The mage Kelsh was bent over to examine a pair of heavy leather gloves, displayed with matching jesses. Did he keep falcons? He looked to have the wealth to indulge in any hobby or pastime he wished.

As she'd seen from across the market, he was sturdy in build. From here, she could clearly see his face. He frowned down at the glove, seemingly lost in thought. She sighed. Another man with beautiful lashes. Other than his compelling dark eyes, his features were nothing special. He was good-looking, but in a rather ordinary way.

Certainly nothing like Cyrus. Cyrus. She was doing this for him, to atone for imprisoning him as she had. She owed him not only for that, but for all the pleasure he had given her and the wonders he had shown her.

She took a deep breath and returned to her study of Kelsh. The hand that stroked the leather with a firm touch was square and capable, the fingers clean and the nails neatly trimmed. All in all, she approved of what she saw. She decided she could do this; she could ask this man to help her.

She took another deep breath and, before she lost her nerve, boldly stepped up, waiting to gain his attention until he turned and almost walked into her.

A smile transformed his face, turning him from ordinary to handsome in a single moment. His dark eyes were truly beautiful, lit as they were now with warmth and pleasure. "Ah! You must be Mildread."

Drey thought that Anice should see him now, for he did look every inch the courtier as he took her hand and bowed over it. "Please, call me Drey."

His broader smile took her breath away. "Drey, then. You must forgive me for not making your acquaintance sooner. I should have come to see you when I learned I was not the only mage in the valley. Several of the villagers described you well and now I have found you." He took her arm in a firm grip and drew her along with him through the market.

Her reply was lost in the jostling of the crowd and the noise of the hawkers as they made their way to the tavern. There they tumbled into the sudden quiet of the interior and groped through the dimness for a table. Drey could barely make out the unlit candle and plate covered with the previous patron's leftovers. The wick flared to life, and she realized Kelsh had done it with but a twitch of his finger.

She wanted that Power so much she could taste it.

He must have read the hunger in her gaze, for he looked her in the eye. Before she could glance away, he'd trapped her eyes with his. She couldn't move as he lifted both hands to frame her face.

"You are frightened. There is no need."

She swallowed, hard. Somehow, his assurance only fed her fears.

His dark brows rose. "You cannot control your Power," he stated.

"I have no Power to control." Did even this man, who purportedly knew so much, think she was other than she was? Tears pricked at her eyes.

"No, lass, you do indeed have great Power. You just haven't found it yet." He released her, shaking his head. "When you do find it, aye, it will be something wondrous to behold."

Words stuck in her throat, words she needed to force past her lips. *You can do this,* she scolded herself. *Just open your mouth and speak!*

He looked up and cocked a brow at her.

"Can you help me find it?" There! She'd said it. She grew faint at her temerity. How could a mage who worked for the king possibly find the time to help her, who was little more than a weak hedge-mage?

She couldn't read his expression. He examined her for an impossibly long moment before replying. "What do you want?"

The words now poured from her on a single breath. "My only training has come from my aunt and my grandmother and they sent me off to study on my own, claiming they no longer had aught to teach me." She swallowed again, a hard-won clearing of her throat before she did the boldest thing she'd ever done. "I'd like to become your apprentice."

"Well," he said mildly.

The barmaid approached and he ordered. "Ale. For both of us?"

Drey nodded. The wench flounced off, leaving her awash in disappointment. He'd all but rejected her.

He tented his hands and regarded her over the fingertips. "That is an interesting proposal."

Mayhap he hadn't rejected her, at least not outright. Could he be toying with her? Her earlier fear returned, threatening to choke her. In the candlelight, his eyes were impossible for her to read. She gripped the edge of the table with both hands. 'Twas all she could do not to bolt from the tavern.

Two tankards appeared out of the tavern's gloom and were plunked down on the table. She felt rather than saw the wench disappear in a twitch of skirts.

"And what am I to do when you find your wings and leave me behind in the dust? By your aura, you may prove to be at least my equal. What do I gain by training someone who may prove to be more than my equal, mayhap even my replacement?"

"Anything you wish." As soon as the words leapt from her lips, she wanted to call them back but 'twas too late.

A gleam came into his eye. "Done. I'll ask for my payment when the time comes." He drained his ale, tossing the tankard and a few coins on the table and left. Three paces away, he turned back. "Be outside my cottage at dawn, the day after tomorrow. Plan to stay for two days."

Drey sat nursing her ale for a long time. Sweet Goddess, she'd been rash. What had she done?

It was the height of foolhardiness to agree to, nay to *offer* him, future payment of whatever he might ask.

What if he wanted a child?

She knew nothing of him. In their brief conversation, she had not sensed any darkness in him. What if he was not a servant of light? Aye, he served the king but she knew naught of kings' concerns. Would a king necessarily require integrity and honesty from those in his employ? She'd heard disturbing things of kings who would pay any cost to hold their thrones and of mages who practiced the black arts to ensure their masters' continued supremacy.

What if Kelsh wanted her life?

Chapter Six

ಣ

When she met up with Cyrus again, he'd already loaded the sack of flour on her mule. The other supplies she'd bought were in a heap nearby.

"Have you finished visiting with your friends?" he asked.

She nodded and bent to organize the pile. Some they would carry and some would be loaded on the mule. Cyrus tried to start several conversations but she merely shrugged. They made the trip home in silence.

After the evening meal she sat down and faced him. "I've learned there is another mage in the valley," she began.

"And what of it?" He shook his head. "You summoned and bound me. You are the only one who can free me."

The resigned look on his face strengthened her resolve. No matter what price Kelsh might ask of her, she would pay it, and gladly, to give Cyrus what he longed for. "I know that. However, I can't figure out how to do it and I don't want to take forever to reach that point. You deserve to be freed now."

"So keep studying." His voice was flat. His clear blue eyes turned to pale gray.

By now she could read his thoughts and emotions well enough. How did he know she was going to tell him something he wouldn't like? She took a deep breath. The words came out in a rush, not at all the way she'd planned and rehearsed on the way back from the village. "I've asked to become his apprentice. He agreed."

Cyrus sat and stared at her with a dumbfounded expression. "What has he said he can do for you?"

"I didn't tell him about you." The words tumbled over themselves in her haste to explain. Sweet Goddess, she was making a mess of this. "He told me I do have great Power but I haven't learned to tap into it. I asked him if he could help and he said he would."

"At what price?"

She turned her face away, too embarrassed to reply. She'd hoped he wouldn't ask the very question she'd avoided thinking about.

"There's always a price, Drey. What is his?" He put a finger under her chin and gently turned her to face him. "Well?"

"He will tell me when it's time."

Cyrus exploded from his seat. "What?" He crossed the room with angry steps and whirled to face her. His eyes darkened to the swirling gray of a storm cloud. "You made a blind bargain? Never do that, least of all with a mage! You know nothing of him! Do you realize what he could ask of you?"

With her heart pounding in her chest so loudly she thought surely he could hear it, Drey drew herself up to face him. "Aye, I do. Anything he wants."

"How could you agree to that?"

"How could I not?" How could she make him understand how much she wanted to do this, for him? The words burst from her, the anguish that had been locked within her finally breaking free. She pounded her fist on her chest. "I'm the one who bound you against your will. I'm the one who's so stupid I can't undo it! I'm the one who has to watch you suffer, knowing you long to return to your world." She paused to dash the tears from her cheeks.

"I'd do anything to set you free. I love you," she whispered brokenly, admitting what she'd suspected for days.

"And I you. Ah, sweetling, how can you be so foolish?" He came back and gathered her into his arms. "I'd never cost you so much."

His lips met hers with a sweet tenderness that almost broke her heart. Nay, that would come when he left her for good, to return to his own world. For now, she'd take what she could of him and rejoice.

She twined her arms about his neck and pulled him closer. Opening her mouth, she invited him in with a soft sound. He obliged and tenderness became entwined with ardent possession. She reveled in the familiar taste of him, the flavor that was his alone, that whispered, *Cyrus*, to all her senses.

In perfect harmony, they shared the task of disrobing, tangling their fingers together in the laces of her shift. Cyrus chuckled as she paused to kiss him before the soft linen passed over her head. The fabric held the unforgettable sweet smell of her cleft. When her face appeared, he captured her lips on a sigh.

He held back as he had not before, loving her with the seductive curl of a gentle breeze rather than the tempest that she knew lay beneath the surface. She arched into him, seeking the pleasure of skin against skin. His fingers feathered across her, followed by the slightest breath of a kiss. She shivered, feeling the answering rise of desire and passion within her, pulsing hot and heavy. His heart answered the rapid beat of hers but his touch remained as soft as the sigh she gave as he found her most sensitive places.

His tongue barely touched her nipple before he sucked in a breath, cooling the drop that lingered on the tip and wringing a gasp from her. Lightning streaked from there to her other breast where he repeated the sweet torment, fanning a tempest to life.

Desire raged within her as his fingertips, tongue and lips skimmed over her skin. He paid attention to every sensitive spot he'd discovered during their time together, kissing first her ear and then her neck before moving back to her breasts. Each kiss was followed by a swift lick of his hot tongue and a soft puff of cooling air. The effect of the contrast between heat and cold astounded her, as every inch of her body came alive as never before.

The slightest touch on her neck, her breasts, her belly called forth ever stronger gusts of passion. He moved over her skin slowly, until she was fairly beside herself with the relentless sensations. She clutched at his hair, his shoulders, the blankets — when had they reached the bed? — to keep the buffeting gale from tearing her apart.

When he at last parted her thighs to delve his tongue deep into her nether curls, she lost hold and found herself swept out of control, into a pelting, driving torrent of ecstasy. Cyrus never stopped touching her as he shifted to replace his mouth with his cock, pressing into her. He filled her in a relentless, slow surge, giving her time to feel his entrance, the stretching of her tight passage. Scorching gusts blew through her, a flood of escalating turbulence. She found herself rising on the wind, ever higher, ever more taut, until he began to move within her and the storm broke. A flood of ecstasy rushed over her, wild and hot. Lightning flashed within the cloud of bliss, sparkling delight that howled through her again and again.

"Cyrus!" she cried. As she tightened about him, she felt the flow of his seed fill her. His roar of release was the last thing she heard before rapture blinded her and she fell into darkness.

* * * * *

At dawn two days later, Drey stood shivering with cold outside the mage's small house. 'Twas far grander than her tiny cottage, with a tiled roof rather than thatch and a second story, where she had only one room and a curtained sleeping alcove — not even a loft.

The door creaked open, giving her a glimpse of the empty hall and four doors on the first floor. Steep, narrow stairs rose at the far end.

"Come," the mage's deep voice called from somewhere inside.

Before she set foot in his house, she hesitated. She regretted the foolish offer she'd made him but she couldn't think of a way to undo their bargain. Mayhap she could talk a village merchant out of an agreement but not a mage and certainly not one so much more powerful than she.

Screwing up her courage, she swallowed and placed a foot over the threshold.

Nothing happened. There was no clap of thunder, no bolt of lightning from above or explosion from within. She crossed into the hall, chiding herself for her flight of fancy.

"Welcome to my home." The words floated softly from the shadows in the front room to her right. "Be blessed, as I am by your presence."

The formal greeting flustered her for a moment and she groped for a suitable reply. "You bless me with your welcome and your hospitality."

"Good, good, glad to see you're punctual." Kelsh strode toward her, down the hall from one of the back rooms.

Drey glanced into the shadows to see what device he used to throw his voice. She saw only the dim forms of chairs and small tables clustered around a fireplace.

"Come along, we'll be working in the largest shed today." He led her out the front door and around the house. Four outbuildings formed a square beyond a tidy kitchen garden. Merv, one of Anice's boys, was enlarging the planting area, breaking through clods of grass to turn the winter-hardened ground. His breath gusted white in the morning chill. He looked up from his work and nodded to her.

Today Kelsh wore a lighter cloak, also of fine wool, embroidered about the hem with all manner of birds. She admired the craftsmanship even while she was amazed at some of the creatures flying around the hem. Who had ever seen such odd birds?

Before they entered the outbuilding, he shrugged out of the cloak and she saw that he wore the normal surcoat and long shirt as every other man she'd met but his were made of bleached snowy linen and rich wool the color of a bluebird. The neckline splayed open, revealing several curls of dark hair on his chest.

The building proved to be lined with worktables and benches. She recognized herbs she worked with herself, hanging in bunches from the rafters. Rows of bottles and jars and crocks and bowls of various sizes lined the shelves that ran around the walls above the tables. Through the thick glass of the tiny window she could see a distorted figure where Merv worked his shovel in the garden.

Her master turned to face her, waving a hand to indicate the room and its contents. "This is where I now work. I'm sure some of these supplies and tools are familiar to you. Even if your aunt and granny are the weakest hedge-mages, they'll have taught you something of herb craft and mixing unguents."

She bobbed her head, unsure of just how an apprentice ought to act. Should she speak up or let him do all the talking?

"I prefer not to do all the talking."

Her head jerked up. Had he read her thoughts?

Kelsh continued, apparently unaware of her surprise. "You may ask me any question you wish, just do not be surprised if sometimes I do not answer. Or I may not give you the answer you seek."

He righted a mortar that lay on its side. Catching up a cloth, he wiped the remains of a few leaves out of it before he placed it beside a pestle on the nearest shelf. "These work areas are designed to keep necessary tools and substances within easy reach. I know where everything is and you must not move anything without my order or approval. When you use something, be sure you return it to its proper place."

Drey eyed all the devices and containers. Some she'd never seen and others she recognized but could guess no use for. "What do you want me to do?"

He pointed to a set of shelves near the door. "First, before you can be of any use to me, you must read those scrolls."

She gaped at him. Read? How was she to learn if she didn't *do* anything, only read? Trial and error was the only way she knew to master any task.

"You can read, can't you?" he asked sharply.

"Yes, of course."

"Then get started." He softened his command with a smile. "You have several days of reading ahead of you. Use the table under the window while there's daylight. You are to get through half of them today and the other half tomorrow."

"What then?" she managed to ask.

"We'll discuss that after you've finished."

She seated herself, picked up the first scroll and began. When the sun set, he brought her two lamps and she read on. There were philosophical treatises on magick, line after line of spells from all over the world and crabbed notes scribbled on some recipes for healing potions and lotions. Some she could barely decipher, so old and faded was the ink, on thin vellum brittle with age.

Different hands had penned them all, with different styles of wording and reasoning. Some authors drew her readily into their arguments and stories; some wrote convoluted prose that was a trial to slog through.

She read far into the night, finishing the last one he'd set out for her just before midnight. She stretched her aching back and rubbed her sore eyes. Another large box awaited her attention in the morning, stuffed with scroll upon scroll upon scroll, she saw with a grimace. She rose on trembling legs and leaned over, stretching those muscles, too.

She turned to leave the shed, seeking Kelsh and instruction on where she should spend the night, when she stumbled over a pallet laid out on the floor. Three heavy wool blankets were folded on it, with the small brazier that warmed the building pulled to a close but safe distance. She hadn't even heard him, or whoever had made up her accommodations, creep in and then out. It must have taken several trips, or several people, to put all this in place.

Still in her clothes, she gratefully sank into the softness of the pallet. He must have filled it with something other than straw, was her last thought as she adjusted the down pillow before she slipped off to sleep.

Before dawn, she was awakened by a loud knocking on the door. Kelsh entered, with a large pot of tea and scones. He cleared a table of its tools and clutter and spread their breakfast on it.

"Now, tell me what you have learned from the first batch of texts," he ordered as he poured steaming fragrant tea into two heavy mugs.

While she munched on the raisin cakes and sipped her cooling tea, she tried to consolidate the information she'd gained from the texts into a coherent summary. Despite her best efforts, she knew she rambled all over the world and all over the topics of medicine, magick and art.

He said nothing about being displeased or pleased with her response, just motioned her to continue her reading once they'd finished their repast. She picked up where she'd left off.

Today's reading went more easily than it had the day before. She found her eyes racing over the scrawling writing, rapidly taking in the meaning and absorbing the details when they seemed necessary.

She finished several hours after Kelsh brought their evening meal. Once again, he'd left the pallet and blankets for her, along with a final scone on her pillow. The lamps had burned out just before she finished, leaving her in the dim light of a single candle.

Restless once she'd worked the kinks from her spine and legs, she prowled the room, reading labels and examining the contents of some of the containers. She knew enough not to open those holding unfamiliar substances. Some containers were made from the clearest glass she'd ever seen, permitting her a good view of the contents without risking inhaling some dangerous dusty herb.

One held an item she dared not touch, not even through the bottle. Within the glass something moved, writhing in odd colors when her hand came close. As she drew back, she thought she glimpsed an eye, one without a proper pupil, slit like that of a cat. After that, she didn't reach for any other bottles or jars.

Under one of the tables she found a small box of scrolls.

Should she read them? He'd told her to read them all but these had not been with the others. Had she come across something she'd be better off ignoring?

Curiosity got the better of her and she dug into the box, selecting the thinnest and most fragile of the lot. Taking it to her table, she unrolled it with care. The ink glowed strangely in the failing light of the candle. She leaned closer and saw it was pure gold.

The wielder of the quill had a lovely hand. The script flowed beautifully across the page. She followed it with ease.

The text addressed the question of success in love. She read of trying too hard to hold what one prized, of trying so hard that one drove one's goal away to the point of never reaching it. She read of holding with open arms.

It might as well have spoken directly to her about her magick.

Could magick be like love? Was she unable to tap the well of Power within her because of trying too hard? Had she thrown up barriers for herself simply by wanting too much? Had she always bound herself with her ambition, limited her achievements by the intense need to be like her aunt and Gran?

She thought about the first time she cast the circle in her meadow. She'd worked simply for the sheer joy of it, the wonder of discovery fresh in her mind, leaving herself open and ready.

That was when she'd called and bound Cyrus.

That was the only time she could think of that she'd not worried if she was doing it right, that she hadn't tried to do anything in particular, that she had let herself go and had rejoiced in an act of celebration.

Relief flooded through her, relaxing her. For the first time in her life, she could contemplate magick without feeling a knot between her shoulder blades or tension building in her belly.

With that relaxation came the realization of great fatigue. She yawned and stretched once more. So many sleepless nights, spent both worrying about Cyrus and enjoying his company in her bed, were taking their toll on her.

Working to control the nearly irresistible urge to keep yawning, she rolled up the scroll again, retying it carefully with the ribbon before she returned it to the box. Tomorrow she would examine her newfound knowledge, the treasure she'd been seeking.

Tomorrow she would return home. To Cyrus.

Tomorrow she could begin working on the spell to send him back to where he belonged.

Tomorrow she could begin dreading his departure.

Chapter Seven

ဢ

Kelsh awakened her before dawn with a hearty knock on the door. Once more, they feasted on scones and tea while he questioned her on the knowledge contained in the scrolls. Under the close scrutiny of his intense gaze, she answered to the best of her limited ability, unused to forming opinions of such complex and diverse ideas, let alone articulating them to a stranger. Where she would have answered her aunt or Gran quite readily, putting forth her perception of how the ideas put forth by the various writers connected and collided, she found speaking to Kelsh's expressionless visage to be unsettling, to say the least.

Finally, he pronounced himself satisfied with her progress. "You show an innate ability to synthesize and define the arguments of the greatest philosophers the world has given birth to. However, can you guess what pleases me the most?"

"That I read all the scrolls within the allotted two days?" she queried hopefully. Making his deadline had given her great pride in her reading abilities, as well as proven to herself that she wasn't a completely daft blunderer.

"Pick up this scroll," he ordered, tossing one of the smaller ones before her on the table. "Tell me about it."

The writing had been penned by some parsimonious scribe, who'd packed as many words on a page as was humanly possible. He—or she, Drey quickly amended her automatic assignment of the male gender to the writer—had squeezed every letter close to its neighbor, barely preserving the integrity of each.

"Aye," she began, "I remember this one. The writing is as cramped as can be, as if the scribe knew there was little more vellum to be had and needed to lay out the text in only one sheet."

"Look at the words. Read them aloud to me."

Drey cleared her throat and quashed the fluttering in her stomach. Opening her mouth, she stammered, "Ah...ah...ah..." and nothing more came forth.

Finally she confessed in wonderment, "I cannot."

"Do you know why?" His dark eyes bored into hers.

"Nay, the words make sense to me but I cannot say them."

"That is because they are in a dead language, one you have not encountered before. This is written in a language of the ancients, one long lost to human tongues."

Drey gaped at him. How could she understand words she'd never seen before? Surely he must be jesting with her.

"You wished to understand them and so you did." He grinned at her, an unexpected flash of bright teeth against his black beard. "I told you that you were capable of great things." He waved a hand at the shelves of scrolls she'd spent the last two days reading. "Most of these are in languages foreign to you. I set you the task to evaluate your suitability to me as an apprentice. You have passed the first test, with ease and better than I had hoped. Now go home, think about what you've learned and return here in three days. Be prepared at that time to assume the full duties of an apprentice."

He quickly gathered up the crockery and crumbs from their meal. "From that time on, I will expect you to prepare our meals, in addition to other tasks I will set before you. I can guarantee it will be interesting, having new worlds opened before you, but you will work harder than you ever have worked before."

Kelsh cocked a dark brow at her. "Your arrival is timely. I've just sent my cook to look after a friend who is ill. I hope your cooking skills are up to the task. I feed all my workers. That's two gardeners, the stable lad, a kitchen drudge, the fellow who does my spinning and weaving, two guards and a courier who is sometimes here. With the two of us, that's ten.

Occasionally one or more friends or associates of mine will come for extended visits."

She opened her mouth to ask about provisions. He forestalled her with another wave of his hand.

"The larder is well stocked. You will find whatever you need." Balancing the tray on one hand, he herded her out the door. "Your mule is in the stable. Egan has him bridled and ready for your departure." At her questioning glance, he continued, "I prefer a household that runs smoothly, which means I am in command. Now go and return in three days."

Drey found her mule contently grazing outside the stable. She poked her head into the building to thank Egan but found it empty save for another mule and the horses, a dappled gray and two blacks. Shrugging, she swung onto the mule's broad back and turned it downhill toward the bustling village and the river.

Mousebane greeted her warmly in the shed tucked against the side of her cottage, ignoring the rustling of what must be rodents in the hay.

"I'll be adding a friend for you soon, one I hope will take the duties of a cat more seriously than you do," she told him as she knelt down to give his neck and cheeks a good scrubbing with her knuckles. "Lazy fellow." He stretched under her attentions, putting his shoulder down and rolling onto his back to offer his belly for the same treatment. She kneaded the incredibly white fur he exposed. "How you can keep so clean, I'll never understand." He gave a little meow and writhed in ecstasy. "Of course, you don't do anything to get dirty, do you?" she chided him before straightening.

Cyrus met her at the door to her cottage. "I didn't expect to see you before nightfall." He hugged her to him. "I was concerned about him letting you go at all."

She smiled at him, grateful that he wasn't still angry with her. "Relax, my love. He's a mage, not a monster."

Chapter Eight

ॐ

"He's a man. That's reason enough for me not to trust him." Cyrus nuzzled her neck. "You smell a bit different." He inhaled close to her skin. The rushing air cooled her enough to cause a shiver. "Like spices."

"Oh, Cyrus, it's incredible! He's got the biggest workroom I've ever seen, filled with all manner of herbs and tools and exotic things. I can learn so much from him." Drey slipped from his embrace and grabbed his hands, pulling him into the cottage. "I actually read scrolls in different languages!"

He gave her a tolerant smile that didn't quite reach his eyes. "What else did you do?"

She babbled on about Kelsh's unorthodox teaching methods, of how she'd discovered so many different voices and ideas in the scrolls. He let her go, until she rambled to a halt.

"So, what did you do whilst I was gone?" She arranged her skirts about her on the stool.

"Oh, I did a little of this and a little of that. Mostly I missed you."

His lopsided smile touched her heart. He'd had naught to do but miss her, whilst she explored new worlds and new skills. He'd been alone but for Mousie, tending her cottage and livestock, no doubt dwelling on his predicament. And here she was, bubbling over with all that she'd seen and done. How selfish could she be? "Did you spend much time on the hill, listening to the whispers of the wind?"

"Aye." He avoided her weak smile. "I asked them about your friend the mage."

"And?" she prompted. Her smile fled. There was more to this conversation than she had expected.

"They cannot find any memory of him, any indication of a past."

Although his words sent a chill through her, she protested, "He's newly arrived. Mayhap his studies have taken him far afield, to lands you and your fellow spirits wouldn't know."

"We wander all over the land, in its entirety. I myself have swept across mountains, fields and oceans, eventually finding myself back where I began. If he's studied anywhere on this earth, we would know him. Who was he before he came here? *Where* was he before he came here?"

"How can that be important?"

He regarded her with serious eyes. "You must tell me. You're the one who made a blind bargain with him. His identity and his past might tell us more about what he's likely to ask for the price of training you. He could be a creature of the light but he could also be a creature of the darkness."

"I believe I would feel it if he served the darkness," she scoffed. "There is no taint or stench of evil about him."

"Then he feels normal? There are some old and powerful beings who are able to mask their true natures, both dark and light, from others, even those with Talent such as yourself. You never have an odd feeling when he's near?"

She hesitated. "Aye, he feels somehow different from the mages I know but, never having encountered his like before, I have no idea how the presence of a male mage should feel. He trained elsewhere, so I would expect him to have a different command of his Power."

"I see by your eyes that you're not sure. I hope I'm wrong but you are better off keeping a close watch on him."

Dismay filled her. She'd never been good at dissembling. "The man can read my thoughts! How am I to shield my—or rather, your—suspicions from him?"

Cyrus shrugged. "Don't. Let him know you wonder about his past. Would that not be normal on your part? If he has nothing to conceal, he'll satisfy your curiosity. If he explains nothing, you'll then know to watch him closely."

She stared at him, digesting his reasoning. "That's sound. He could have any number of reasons for leaving his past behind. Let him decide if he's to tell me or not."

A sizzling and crackling from the fire snagged her attention. A frying pan sat on the edge of the hearth, with steam rising from its contents. She jumped up with a cry. "Have you prepared sausages and onions?"

He had. He'd also prepared their bed, strewing it with small, fragrant, early roses.

She took the time to savor her favorite meal and then went eagerly into his arms.

"Don't you have exercises to do, before you go back to your master mage?" Cyrus teased.

"Nay, he only wants me to consider what I've read." She plucked at the ties of his braes. "Oh, and to return to him prepared to cook for his entire entourage. Now that I've passed his test of reading the scrolls he'll not be waiting on me any more! 'Twill be the other way around."

Cyrus growled and tugged at her sleeve with his teeth. "How'd you like me to wait on you for a while? While you've been gone, I've been thinking of a few things we could try. Want to come out and play with me?" he breathed into her ear, following the words with a flick of his tongue.

Without haste she drew her gown up and over her head. Undoing the ties at her neck, she loosened the chemise until it dropped to her waist. Standing before him half-naked, she delighted in the hunger on his face. Cupping her breasts with both hands, she held them up for his appreciative inspection. "I'd rather stay in here and play. How about you? Will you insist on going out there by yourself?"

"What are my choices? Hmm... I could be here with you," he touched her lightly with one finger on her shoulder, "or I could be out there, in the sunshine, with all of nature to keep me company." Shivers ran through her as he trailed his touch from her shoulder to the hollow at her neck to her other shoulder and back again. With each pass, he dipped lower and lower. She arched forward and up, seeking his touch on her breasts. He held her off, lazily tracing invisible lines of excitement across her skin, taking his time, drawing out the tension as her nipples tightened in anticipation.

"All in all, I'd prefer to have *you* out there, along with all of nature. However, I will make the sacrifice and remain inside here, with you." At last he touched her where she longed to be touched, lightly flicking a fingertip across the pebbled peak of each breast. At her indrawn breath, he looked up and their eyes met.

The tenderness in his gaze stole her breath. This was what she'd been missing with Stefan; this was what Robert shared with Jenny. Her vision blurred as hot tears gathered in her eyes and rolled down her cheeks.

He caught one on his finger. "You weep?"

"Only with happiness. You bring me joy."

"Then I but return the favor, for you are the most beautiful and intriguing mortal I have ever beheld." His eyes narrowed in sly humor and he gathered her up in a tight embrace. "And the only one I've held."

She smiled into his dear face. "Ah, my love, you are the best gift I could ever receive. I cannot tell you how happy I am that I summoned you and, at the same time, how I am saddened to have bound you." She began to cry in earnest, sobbing as the tears came.

He rocked her gently. "Hush, I know. Do not think of sadness. Here, with me, today, there is only joy."

In perfect harmony, they moved together, skin against skin. Not willing to wait any longer, not long enough to permit them to cross to her soft bed, he stripped her skirts from her and laid her back across the table.

While she watched, he tore off his braes. Impatient to possess her, he left them pooled around his ankles while he parted her knees and slid her closer. With one hard thrust, he claimed her. She arched up to meet him with each thrust, matching him stroke for stroke, clawing at his back, pulling him ever closer. His mouth took hers and he possessed her with his tongue and his cock, alternating thrusts of each, seesawing through her, in and out, in and out.

The tension he'd begun with his fingertips escalated, sucking her into a maelstrom of sensation and emotion. Ah, but he felt good, filling her, embracing her. Each time he surged forward, she welcomed him home with a parting of her legs and a relaxing of her inner muscles to ease his way. Reluctant to let him go, she squeezed his cock tightly in protest of his withdrawal.

"Ah, love, you are more than I could ever have asked for," he panted into her mouth as he drove into her once more.

Emotions assailed her, robbing her of the ability to respond in speech. She dove headlong into the feelings, reveling in their conflicting tugs. So often, she'd longed for such a chance at true happiness but having it was much more complicated, richer and a greater challenge. Desire spread through her, desire and the need to let him know she agreed completely. Regret that she had left him alone. A tenderness she'd not experienced before, mingled as it was with the poignant knowledge that, wonderful as Cyrus might be in his mortal form, he was hers for only a short time.

She suckled at him, encircling his tongue as she encircled his cock, grasping as he pulled back, welcoming him as he thrust in again. By the Goddess, this was ecstasy beyond deserving. She'd been so occupied with her first days of mage-study that she'd barely had time to realize she'd missed him while she was gone but now the scent and the feel of him consumed her. She longed to somehow merge with him, to become one in truth with this man—or whatever he was—who had crept into her heart. He had become a part of her, a necessary element in her life.

How then was she gladly to bid him farewell? How was she to bear watching him return to his ethereal form?

She shied away from the thought, seeking refuge in feeling—feeling the magick dance over her skin, tingle in her toes, throb in her breasts and shiver up her spine. She turned herself over to the welcome weight of his body, the substance of him in and around her, the sheer ecstasy of sensation he gave her as she climaxed. She clenched his cock in a tighter grip as her womb contracted. He surrounded her, filled her and carried her with him to the skies.

* * * * *

When she returned to Kelsh, she found him already busy at a cluttered table in the workshop. Before him lay a scroll, held open by the weight of several small clay jars. Around the scroll were scattered various tools and containers, some holding dried leaves, some oily liquids. His fingertips were stained olive green.

"Ah, just in time. I have several passages I want you to translate for me into other words. Your Talent will guide you. I need to be able to make sense of them in light of what I have available here to make the potions."

She hung her cloak on a peg and came to look over his shoulder.

He waved her to a stool at the next table over. "One is a cure for persistent coughs. The other will require the one who drinks it to speak only truth."

Her heart leapt within her. He was concerned with healing! Did she dare ask him about Betsy's malady? Aye, she would dare, she decided. This matter was important enough and he had instructed her upon her arrival to ask what questions she would.

"Have you come across anything to help a woman struck suddenly with a brain problem?"

"Describe her symptoms." He set down the jar he held and turned to face her. His attention remained riveted on her as she spoke.

"She has bad color, far too pale. Her breath comes quick and shallow. She lies, eyes closed, unaware of her surroundings. A feeling of wrongness in her head."

His eyes gleamed with interest. "What do you mean, a *wrongness* in her head?"

She hadn't anticipated trying to explain how she knew what was wrong with Betsy. She took a deep breath. "When I close my eyes, I see a darkness has settled over her head."

"And what do you see the rest of the time? Nay, do not bother trying to explain." He pursed his lips. "That is most likely a tumor, or mayhap a swelling in the brain. I have seen mention of it in several places but no one agrees on the proper treatment. Some claim the skull must be opened to release the evilness within, ofttimes repeatedly, and others say hot compresses are effective. They do not say where one is to apply the heat, however. I myself have never seen anyone recover once afflicted to the point of losing their senses."

Her disappointment must have shown on her face, for he laid a hand on her shoulder and said, "You must be asking because you know someone who has been stricken. I'm sorry. If I think of something more useful, I will tell you."

Drey tried to smile. "Thank you. I thought you might know of a treatment I had not come across."

He gave her shoulder a squeeze. "You learn much when you first realize how little we know. Your Power comes with responsibility. The work we do here in this workshop, and work done by others in sheds and lofts like it across the land, will help fill the gaps in our knowledge. Someday we will be able to help those stricken like your friend."

His words rang with sincerity. Emotion clogged Drey's throat and she could only nod her understanding and agreement. If Cyrus had heard this declaration, he'd not think Kelsh served the darkness.

How could *she* have suspected Kelsh was capable of employing the black arts? Her tension and concerns about working with him had sprung largely from Cyrus's objections. She had not yet found a way to ask her master about his past. Mayhap she should trust her instincts and cease worrying about his past.

"Work will take your mind off your cares, at least for now." He picked up the little jar once more and turned his attention to the workbench.

In this, too, he was right. Drey pulled her thoughts away from Betsy and her family.

Pen and ink awaited her, with a stack of clean flat sheets of vellum. She picked up the top sheet, marveling at the pristine whiteness and smooth surface. Every trace of hair had been scoured from the hide. 'Twas truly the work of a master craftsman. The pages before her alone must have cost a small fortune. With a new respect for the contents of the building, she surveyed the shelves again. There were more stacks of such vellum, and row after row of glass jars and bottles of all sizes and colors. She'd never seen so much wealth in one place.

"Here." Her master mage swept the tiny jars off the splayed scroll and thrust it at her. "Begin with this. There are others, should you need to clarify anything." He jerked a thumb at a table across the room, which held a box of dusty, wrinkled scrolls and twists of paper.

So began her first day of work as a mage's apprentice.

She found that as long as she didn't try to read aloud, she had no trouble deciphering the gist of the passages and precise definition of the words she read. She did need to seek clarification in some of the older scrolls for help in identifying the proper identity of herbs as well as proper measurements but quickly found what she sought.

As midday approached, he reminded her of her kitchen duties and shooed her on her way.

The kitchen also reeked of many coins well-spent. Rows of gleaming copper vessels hung above neat worktables that shielded basket after basket of supplies. She found a row of huge crocks in a low cupboard holding ground barley, oatmeal, and white flour so fine she wondered who'd ground it. Surely not the miller in the village, for he had never achieved this sort of artistry for anyone else.

The kitchen drudge was Rose, another of the older children from the village, who quickly proved to be well versed in the kitchen's layout and contents. With little fuss, they managed to turn out a substantial meal of oatcakes, sausages and onions. Why shouldn't her first meal here be her favorite?

It proved to be popular with the assembled staff as well. More than one of the men bowed respectfully to both the mage and Drey, offering their compliments and thanks for the meal before they returned to their chores.

Cleaning up was left to Rose. Drey returned to her translation duties, grateful for an extra pair of hands in the kitchen. The work to maintain such a large household was much easier with several people working. She spared a thought for Robert and Jenny, who must surely be recovering nicely with the weight of her household chores shared with a cook and a maid or two.

She finished her translations shortly after their meal break. Kelsh then set her to reading a new text, one that outlined exercises designed to help tap into the Power in one's self. She found that, while the meditation exercises her aunt and Gran had taught her were the foundation, these instructions carried her deep into her soul, revealing the sources of magick she'd been seeking.

Aunt Ingreth and Gran had tried to show her the ways they knew of mining magick from deep within. Drey found Kelsh's methods opened doors for her, revealing the magick that was hers, magick that was an integral part of her, and showed her how to build on her store of Power, how to draw from but not exhaust it.

She found she had a lot of magick within her.

Chapter Nine

℘

As she worked, she discovered more and more ways to tap into her Power. More and more places she could find it.

But the text cautioned that this sort of magick must not be used lightly, for it carries a price: whatever she used would sap her physical abilities, weakening her until she had time and rest to recover her strength. Mages with this kind of Power had to be careful with it, husbanding this resource as a miser hoards gold.

There were also descriptions of techniques and exercises to increase internal magick, to help the depleted mage recover more quickly. She memorized those, for who knew when she would have need of them? Should Kelsh set her to practical exercises, using her Power to learn control, she might have need of restoration rituals sooner rather than later.

Her interest in learning by reading before trying quickened. Perhaps in some of these older scrolls she might find references to elemental spirits. She'd conjured one from the air. Might there be also those of fire, earth and water? What were the water sprites she'd seen, mayhap water elementals in another form?

Kelsh had more translations for her to do, once he saw she had a neat hand and a facility for summarizing the information in the texts. Most were topics in which she had no interest and the rest of the day plodded by.

The evening meal taxed her abilities, for Kelsh requested a roast but waited until late in the day to make his wishes known. She knew to cut the large haunch into smaller roasts, to cook it more quickly, but they still ate late in the evening, once the pork was no longer pink. She learned from that to plan her day around the cooking tasks required to place the food on the table in a timely manner.

By the end of the following day, the kitchen was running smoothly and Drey felt capable in both her roles, as cook and as apprentice. She'd translated almost a dozen texts, from ancient languages she knew nothing about, into modern words and script. She found it quite odd that, when she merely glanced at the writing, it would be totally incomprehensible to her but when she focused on it, the strings of characters would resolve into words that made sense.

In the evenings she practiced the simple exercises Kelsh laid out for her.

The first evening she could barely keep her eyes open and he sent her early to her pallet. While she slept, he pulled out a small locked box hidden behind the jars on a high shelf. Unfolding the scraps of vellum within, he read and worked on them at one of the tables on the far side of the room. His labors produced various odors and mists that wreathed the room and enveloped her while she slept.

That night, her dreams were troubled. Monsters stalked her, some wearing familiar faces. She fled into a bog, where the mud sucked at her feet, threatening to pull her under the scummy surface. Bushes and twigs clawed at her garments and hair like grasping hands. The mist thickened and swirled about her. In the darkening eddies she saw sad women's faces with hollow eyes and gaping mouths that shrieked, "Free us, help us, avenge us."

She jerked awake to total darkness, her heart pounding and her shift damp with sweat. The mage had left. No moonlight penetrated the thick swirled glass of the window. No sound came to her. 'Twas as if she were alone in an empty world.

It took her some time to still her racing heart and relax her clenched fists. While part of her mind went through the routine meditations to center and ground herself, she examined the dream. The individual components she could understand. The mists undoubtedly represented the new endeavor she had undertaken: the future, shrouded in uncertainty. Whatever chased her, she couldn't decide. Lust? She'd certainly felt that with Cyrus and perhaps it indicated a character flaw she'd not expected.

Would she find herself throwing her body in a sexual frenzy at any attractive man, hungry for the ecstasy she'd discovered with her air spirit? She had trouble believing that, for her earlier sexual partners had left her comfortably satisfied but not panting after a repeat of the experience.

Kelsh himself was quite attractive, yet she felt no pull of sexual attraction toward him. When he touched her, as he did frequently in their work, her body did not respond as it did to a mere look from Cyrus.

Mayhap she had only a predilection for those who were not mortal. She might find herself conjuring elemental spirits, one after another, trying out the different skills of air, fire, earth and water. Now *that* she could see happening. She smiled into the darkness, wondering if the stroke of a fire spirit's hand would raise the same heat in her as Cyrus could with a light touch.

The thought of Cyrus made her think of her pipes. He did so like to hear her play while they wandered the hills and fields. For company, she fumbled in her pack and found her pipes. Sitting up in the cold and dark, she trilled a happy child's tune, bright notes to counter the remnants of the dream that pressed heavily on her mind.

As she piped, a paleness appeared in the air before her. Swirling dots of light danced in time with her music, growing until a tiny ball of fire pulsed at eye level. It lit the room with a cold, white glow.

Magefire!

Amazed, she abruptly stopped playing to examine what she'd done. The magefire faded and winked out. She put the pipes to her lips and played again, envisioning Power flowing from her into the air.

A small ball of fire again appeared, this time a little larger and brighter.

When she ceased playing, it once again disappeared.

She could not manage to sustain magefire without the music.

Disappointed, she stopped trying and found the effort had both tired her and given rise to a headache. Settling the pipes in her bag, she snuggled into the blankets and began the restoration exercises. As the ache behind her eyes eased, she slipped into sleep, satisfied with what she had learned.

* * * * *

A commotion in the yard disturbed Kelsh's studies late the next morning. "Come." He left the shed with a curt bark over his shoulder to Drey.

The stable lad and Merv each struggled with the reins of several horses. Beyond them, a large, richly garbed man was pacing up and down before three guards. His companion, a tall, dark man dressed in black, greeted Kelsh warmly, striding forward to shake hands.

He clasped Kelsh's hand in both of his. "Well met, friend Kelsh. Our lord sends salutations and his wishes for success."

The mage clapped his shoulder. "That is good news, Gregor. I look forward to showing you what I've accomplished."

The other man cleared his throat and stared hard at Gregor.

"Ah, I forget myself." Gregor did not look at his companion, remaining focused on Kelsh. "This fellow is Lord Roland, who is charged with assisting us."

Kelsh sketched a brief bow in the lord's direction. "I am honored to offer you my hospitality." He turned back to Gregor. "How long will you stay?"

"A few days, no more. Time enough to learn what you need and determine the best way to acquire it." Gregor spun and caught Drey staring at him. "And who is this?"

"Drey, my apprentice. She came to me recently. I believe I mentioned her in my last missive." Kelsh waved her forward and laid a hand on her shoulder. "She has proven to be of great help to me. Should you need a scribe's service during your stay, you will find she has a beautiful hand."

Gregor's hard eyes assessed her, scrutinizing her face before sweeping across her body. Drey felt that look, an unpleasant tingle just under her skin that lingered long after he'd followed his host and Lord Roland into the cottage.

"We'll be five more for meals now," Kelsh called out before the door shut.

Gregor held so much Power he fairly glowed, even in the sunlight. Drey spent much time considering his presence and how he fit into the work Kelsh was doing, or might be conducting, for the king.

From what she'd seen, Kelsh was attempting to improve on a number of innocuous spells and unguents. The majority of them were for healing. Perhaps the king suffered from a lung complaint or aches and pains. Word of the doings at court rarely reached the village, so she had no way of knowing if there were rumors concerning the health of anyone in the royal family.

What might he need that required the assistance of a very powerful mage and a lord?

The succeeding days brought no answers. Kelsh spent his time closeted with his guests, only emerging for meals and to fetch scrolls from the shed.

Drey was asked to translate several texts and to write out one dictated letter for Gregor. That message concerned travel plans, arranging a meeting in a fortnight at a port she'd never heard of. While she scratched the quill across the vellum, she paid little attention to the words she penned. Gregor's intent examination unnerved her.

She was certain he never looked away from her and his cold, black eyes never blinked.

* * * * *

The morning after the two men left, she asked for and received permission to visit Betsy. To her surprise, Kelsh continued, "I would like to see this woman myself. May I accompany you?"

"Aye," Drey said, although her heart sank. "I am grateful for your attention." She'd hoped to use this visit to tap her newfound Power and mayhap heal Betsy. She would feel awkward trying to do so in front of Kelsh. What if she should fail?

He spent quite some time going through the contents of his shelves, selecting a few bottles and jars, picking up many and discarding most. In the end, he chose to take only three and those he carried in his pouch.

Drey carried her basket, with her usual stock of unguents and herbs. Kelsh did not offer to carry it for her, as Cyrus had.

Wentil no longer sat by his wife's bedside but worked the field near the cottage. He acknowledged their presence with a curt nod and kept weeding. His harsh voice reached them as he castigated one of the four children who worked beside him. Little Lysbet risked a brief wave to them but did not cease her labors.

Betsy's children had been recalled to their usual chores, clearly giving up on the household tasks Drey and Cyrus had set them to. The interior of the cottage was, if anything, more squalid than before. Kelsh twitched his cloak away from anything he got close to and Drey could hardly blame him.

The youngest children were wreaking havoc by the hearth, putting together some kind of meal. Drey shuddered to think of what they were making. The stores she knew had been brought by some of the villagers would not last long and, without supervision, these tiny would-be cooks would most likely render anything they touched inedible.

Drey led the way to the back room and hastily dismantled the wards as she crossed the threshold. She wasn't sure what interaction they might have with Kelsh's Power or with whatever she herself might do to heal her friend.

Betsy appeared much the same as when Drey and Cyrus had left her after their last visit. Kelsh looked her over quickly before rising to face Drey.

"Her condition is exactly as you described. I am surprised to find her unchanged, if she has been sick this long. I can see nothing to be done for her. In general, those so stricken decline rapidly."

Drey hesitated to tell him what she had done with Cyrus's help, so she merely said, "I did not expect her to last this long myself. Is this a good sign—that she might yet recover?"

"I do not see how." He shook his head. "I know of nothing to be done in a case such as this. Her fate is in the hands of the God and the Goddess."

Drey realized his phrasing was so typical of a man. Her family had always put the Goddess first. The God lived and died through the cycle of the seasons but the Goddess was eternal. Should She not then come first in all things?

She could not bring herself to leave without trying to help Betsy, not when she might be able to cure her. Drey put a hand on Kelsh's arm and stopped him before he reached the door.

"Wait, please. I have something I would like to try."

He lifted a dark brow but returned to the bedside. "What do you think you can do?"

She licked her dry lips. "I...ah... I believe I can use the way I visualize her illness." Now that the moment arrived, she found her heart racing and her palms damp. She wiped them down the front of her apron. "If it works as I believe it might, I should be able to push back the wrongness in her head and restore her health."

"Interesting. Go ahead." He settled himself on a rickety stool.

Conscious of his gaze riveted on her, Drey seated herself by the pallet on the floor. She took both of Betsy's hands in hers and closed her eyes.

In a moment, she formed Betsy's image in her mind. It appeared as it had before, with a very dim light defining the head and the rest of the body fairly vibrant with the glow of health.

She turned her attention to the area around her, seeking out the ambient magick. This effort was much better than her first attempt, now that she knew how to open her senses to find what she needed. The years of occupancy by so many family members had left the cottage with piles of it. One by one, she gathered the gleaming strands, braiding them into thick glittering ropes.

These she forged together and thrust through her hands where she held Betsy's. She felt the tremble of the woman's hands in hers as the glow traveled up her arms, turning her image so bright it was hard for Drey to keep her attention on it. The mass of magick moved slowly to her shoulders and on up. The dark wrongness slowly gave way before it, scalded by the radiance of Drey's Power. With one final push, she forced the last bit of dimness from Betsy's head. The image in her mind glowed clear and strong.

She had done it! Moreover, she had done it using ambient magick, without much cost to herself. Satisfied, she opened her eyes and grinned.

Betsy sat up, awake and alert.

Drey longed to cheer in satisfaction but Kelsh's presence stopped her. She settled for hugging Betsy instead.

Kelsh stared back and forth between the two of them, open-mouthed. Several times he tried to speak but failed. Then he blinked and exclaimed, "I have never seen anything like that! I knew you had Power but, by all that's holy, I never guessed you had that much!"

"Thank ye, missus." Betsy clung to her hand, tears flowing freely down her face. "When I told Lysbet to fetch ye, I knew ye'd help."

Drey gently pushed her back when she would have sat up. "You may feel strong, Betsy, but you've been ill for more than a week. You should rest a bit longer. Tomorrow will be time enough."

At her urging, Betsy subsided back against the lumpy pillow. She frowned. "A week! How—how are my little ones? Has—er—has my man managed?"

"All is well. Worry about that tomorrow." Drey patted her hand once more. "Wentil is weeding and the children are helping him."

She said nothing about the children's cooking efforts as she promised to visit again soon and headed to the door. The less Betsy knew, the more she would rest today. The more she rested today, the better able she would be to deal with household disasters on the morrow.

Kelsh interrupted her thoughts. "Have Rose make up several baskets of food this afternoon and send a guard to bring them here."

He stood in the kitchen, surveying the mess. The children had stopped their activity and stared at him. "Nay, have her attend him. She should spend the rest of the day here, instructing these brats in cleanliness and basic cookery."

Drey's heart lightened as she followed him out the door into the sunshine. She had apprenticed herself to a good man.

"You have too much Power to risk not controlling it. Who knows what you might do, unsupervised and untutored? Let me consider what I must add to your exercises this evening."

"Thank you for your instruction so far. I would not have found the key to accomplish this today without your help. You say you have never heard of anyone being cured who was afflicted as Betsy was. Can I do such a thing because I've always worked as a healer?" An unspoken question hung between them. *Or am I truly a mage of immense Power?* She both yearned and dreaded confirmation of her suspicions.

Kelsh frowned for a moment before answering. "It may be that. 'Twill take time to determine where your greatest talents lie. Most mages have an affinity for one thing or another. Your strength may indeed be the healing arts but I caution you to not be hasty. Do not seek to extend your efforts beyond your control. There is no need to put the cart before the horse. You are doing very well, better than I expected. Continue your studies and you will find where you are comfortable."

Pleased with his words, Drey walked along beside him in comfortable silence.

Her mood changed when they neared the path to her cottage. Cyrus stood in the lane, watching them approach. The set of his shoulders, indeed every line of his body, was rigid with disapproval.

She hurried to introduce the two men, mage and air spirit. How should she describe what Cyrus was, in and of himself, as well as to her? Should she invite Kelsh to her home for refreshment before they continued the trek back to his holding? The social obligations of having her master in her home were beyond her.

"Master Kelsh, this cottage is where I live and this is Cyrus." What more could she say?

The men shook hands.

Kelsh stumbled back a bit and paled. "You...you...you are—"

"Aye. That I am." Cyrus leaned forward. His blue eyes shifted to a stormy gray. A stiff wind sprang up, blowing the mage back another step. "You would do well to remember it."

The air crackled between them as the wind strengthened.

Kelsh straightened and pushed back, a narrow nimbus of fire surrounding him. The embroidered band on his mantle pulsed as if the flames were real. Drey blinked twice to clear her vision but they still leapt and swayed.

"I have wondered where you came from, what lies in your past," Cyrus said, his eyes locked on Kelsh's. "I have a better idea now. Do not harm her."

A particularly hard gust buffeted Drey. She pulled her skirts close and struggled to keep her balance.

"Or you will do what?" Kelsh smiled, his lips thinned with effort. He strove to maintain his footing and his fiery aura flared darker and wider. "You should keep in mind that fire consumes air."

"And enough wind can extinguish flame." Cyrus grinned. He widened his stance. The wind increased again. "I am willing to wager I command enough. Are you?"

Sweat broke out on Kelsh's brow. His cloak billowed out behind him, the embroidered flames around the hem seething as they flapped. He visibly struggled to gain control.

All at once, the fight went out of him. He relaxed and smiled. "Why are we arguing? I have no intention of harming Drey. She's the most talented apprentice I've ever seen. How could I benefit from hurting her?"

Cyrus backed down as well, although his eyes still glowed tempest-dark and the breeze persisted. Drey had the sense that the storm still threatened, out of sight over the horizon. "I have no idea how you might but then I do not know you and the ways of mortals defy logic. Remember that she is under my protection."

"I will not forget." He turned to Drey. "Perhaps you would like some time at home before you return to your work. I will expect you by suppertime. We will discuss your additional exercises after the meal." Before she could answer, he turned and strode away.

Cyrus drew her close. Together they watched him until he was out of sight.

"I still do not trust him."

She responded simply, "I know."

"He is too much of a cipher. Where did he come from? Who trained him? The answers are important."

Drey nodded. "I know they are—to you. I have seen more of the man in these last few days. He is compassionate. He's devoted to his work."

"I care nothing for his work. I care about you." He turned her to face him. Fiercely he gazed into her eyes. "Should he harm you, I will kill him."

A chill ran through her. Whom should she trust, the spirit who loved her or the mage who could teach her to harness and control her Power?

Chapter Ten

ಹಿ

She returned to her apprenticeship to find Kelsh closeted with guests. The dark man Gregor was among them. When she rode into the yard that evening, he stood amid the herbs. A shiver ran through her, for the morning sun shone brightly all about him yet he remained in shadow. 'Twas as if the light avoided him.

He constantly found something that required her assistance. One day 'twas a missive he asked her to pen, another he had a parchment to be translated. The texts were unremarkable, a description of his travels and a list of accounts at a large estate. She'd seen similar ones in the many boxes tucked away beneath the benches in Kelsh's tidy work shed. She acquitted the tasks quickly, to be out of his presence as soon as possible.

One day her master requested her presence in the great room after the noontime meal. She left Rose to finish cleaning up the kitchen and did as he bid. She found herself facing his assembled guests, including two she hadn't known were visiting.

A tall man with stooped shoulders and a beak of a nose had been in residence for several weeks, keeping mostly to himself. He carried an odd smell about his person, something Drey could not quite identify although she was certain she'd encountered it before. Stains on his fingers and robe indicated that he was some sort of alchemist, working on a formula for anyone, mage or no, to turn cheap metals into gold. He wore an absentminded expression, as if he were not quite sure why he was there.

"Come in, my dear Drey, come in." Lord Parren, one of Kelsh's most frequent visitors, answered her knock on the door.

With his ready jokes and friendly banter, he was the entire staff's favorite guest. He smiled and took her hand, leading her into the room. "Thank you once again for a delicious meal. I look forward to my visits here, for the table is always laden with delights." He showed her to a seat.

"Thank you, Lord Parren. It is my pleasure to serve you."

He lowered his voice and winked. "Don't tell your master but I sometimes go a little bit out of my way to stop here."

"I heard that, Parren." Kelsh chuckled. "I told Rose to prepare cold meats and cheese for our late meal, so don't bother flattering her to get a prime serving."

A movement in the shadows caught Drey's attention and she missed Parren's jest in response. The small, disheveled man who often brought a load of meats to the kitchen door almost blended into the woodwork, dressed as he was in shades of dark brown and dust. She wondered at his inclusion in this company of men who appeared to be his betters. He watched her curiously as Kelsh asked her to be ready to make notations as they spoke.

The self-important and well-dressed Lord Roland had claimed the seat by Kelsh at dinner and occupied that place here as well. He spoke continually to Kelsh and Gregor in an undertone, ignoring the others seated around him while Drey sharpened her quill and opened the inkwell.

"Parren, if you're done flirting with the help, we can begin." Gregor spoke in a dry tone, clipping his words. He was clearly in charge of this meeting. Surely it must be a meeting, for she could not imagine it could be other than planned. So many diverse characters would only gather by mutual and prior agreement.

The subtle tingle of the wards she had felt as she crossed the threshold confirmed her suspicions, for Kelsh only protected his rooms when he felt it necessary. Whether his intention was to prevent something from getting in or getting out was what she didn't know.

Kelsh spoke first, welcoming them all, but Gregor was the one who barked questions and controlled the order of presentation. What they discussed, Drey never knew. She hadn't felt the spell take hold but she was certain they bespelled her. How else could she be rendered unaware of what they said? Although she did write constantly, the words streaming from her quill without her volition, the sounds they voiced meant nothing to her.

Whatever the first topic, they were not all in agreement. Drey did not have to hear the words to tell that Lord Parren and Kelsh were at odds with the alchemist, the butcher and Lord Roland. Gregor appeared not to take a side, pitting the two factions against one another as tempers frayed and voices rose in anger.

Gregor watched her closely, appearing to pay as little attention to what he and his companions were discussing as she did. His eyes were strange, with no contrast betwixt the pupil and iris, totally black. That unwavering regard disturbed her. Once she glanced up and caught him wearing a curious little smile, one that looked as though he were anticipating a particularly nasty pleasure. The expression chilled her blood and made the hair on her neck stand up.

They finally reached an impasse and Kelsh introduced another subject, one on which they were of one mind. In short order, the details were agreed upon and Drey's services were no longer required.

She fled as soon as she was dismissed, to hide in the work shed and shake the lingering horror by playing a soft song on her little reed pipes. The song and thoughts of Cyrus soothed the upset caused by the strange mage Gregor. There was no question in her mind that Gregor was no servant of the light. She wished she could discuss with Cyrus the meaning of the gathering she'd just left but he would only remind her of the concerns he'd voiced before her apprenticeship began. He'd been wrong about Kelsh, as far as she could discern, but the frightening company her master kept was clearly what he'd expected. She owed him an apology.

What would she do without Cyrus? She'd come to depend upon him in so many ways. He was not only caring for her home and creatures in her absence, he cared for her. He was a calming presence in her life. He filled her with happiness and completed her in a manner no man ever had. In his company, she'd seen wonders and discovered unparalleled joy. She owed him far more than an apology.

No matter how great a void he would leave in her life, she owed him a swift return to his true form. She believed her apprenticeship to Kelsh, however little time she had spent here so far, had furthered her skills and confidence and unlocked that ability.

When her hands no longer trembled and she could write, she set herself with a heavy heart to craft the spell to return Cyrus to his natural state. What was appropriate to include, what would properly convey her intent?

The four elements were important and sky images. His mortal form had been sparked by her imaginings of desirable men. She wrote a series of words across a scrap of parchment.

Soar.

Eagle.

Returning him to his world would make his journey come full circle.

Symmetry.

What would best describe Cyrus? He was an elemental, a wind spirit. How did that make him different? She stroked the feathery quill across her lips and spent some time thinking about this. He was not mortal but did that make him immortal? She wasn't sure enough about that to describe him using that term. An incorrect reference might negate the spell at best and cause it to blow up in her face at worst.

A spirit. Not mortal. Called from the sky.

Not of woman born.

Perfect. Deciding what elements to include and what not to say soothed her frazzled nerves. Gradually she calmed enough to sleep. She filled several pages with notations before her eyelids grew heavy.

* * * * *

Her next respite from study and work came a fortnight later. Arriving home at dusk, she found Cyrus still disconsolate at his imprisonment, though he tried to hide it.

She could barely contain her secret. Tomorrow she would send him back!

He'd not only cared well for her livestock, he'd cleaned the cottage and weeded the beginnings of her garden. When she thanked him, he shrugged and said he'd been bored and needed activity of some sort. She found a pot of hearty beef stew simmering over the fire and flour measured out for biscuits.

A short time later they sat down together to enjoy the meal.

"Your precious Mousie has missed you. I often see him climbing the path up the mountain or coming down from there. I think he hikes up to the meadow to see if he can see you."

She gave a gurgle of laughter. "I can hardly credit him undertaking that kind of exercise, all for the missing of me. He considers it to be an extreme effort to climb the wall so he can soak up the heat from the sun and the stone."

Cyrus put out a hand, touching her lightly on the arm. "I've found my feet taking that path as well."

Their eyes met. She read sorrow mingled with desire. He, too, must be torn with conflicting desires. She could take care of one of them for him now and the other in the morning.

Drey pushed her bowl back and rose. "I've had enough for now. Come." Holding her hand out, she invited him to her bed.

Neither spoke as they shed their clothing. Drey paused to crumble a few sprigs of lavender on the bed. Cyrus knelt among the dried flowers to touch her gently where she stood.

"I have missed you." His fingers caressed her shoulder, moving up to cup her cheek.

She turned her face into his palm and kissed him. "As I have missed you." *As I will miss you*, spoke her heart.

His work in her garden had left him with darker arms, hands and neck where sunlight had tanned his fair skin. Where he had been slender and firm before, he had acquired sculpted muscle. His pale torso almost glowed as she ran her hands over his contours. She could feel the increased strength and power.

He sucked in a breath as her hands traced the flexing muscles, caressing and expressing her love for him with each touch. He caught her hand and brought it to his mouth, pressing kisses on each knuckle and fingertip.

"I never realized the work you do. Since I have experienced the rigors of housekeeping and caring for your garden, I marvel anew at your abilities. Mortals have lived thusly for so long and you must work so hard, just to keep your families clothed and fed. I now know this body was not made only for pleasure, although I find a different satisfaction in wielding a hoe or an axe." Turning her hand palm up, he lightly nipped at the base of her thumb. "I have calluses to match yours."

"But we are still very different." She was thinking of how his attitudes were still those of an elemental but he took her comment otherwise.

He grinned and moved her hand down to his cock. "Aye, and blessings on those differences. Enough of serious matters. I have spent hours in the care of your concerns. Now I wish to spend myself in you."

When she would have pulled her hand away, he arched a brow. "Do I not deserve a reward? You have been off playing at magick, while I dug up weeds and carried your great beast of a cat up the mountain."

"Oh, you did not!" She gasped and slapped his shoulder. "Do not spoil him so! He will expect it and grow even fatter, until he must be carried everywhere!"

Cyrus shrugged, looking a bit sheepish. "He commands me and I must obey. Much like his owner."

"Hmph. There is still a question of who owns whom here, although I do try to keep the upper hand."

"Upper hand, lower hand, it's all the same to me, as long as your hands are on me." He lay back and stretched out with his hands behind his head. They both stared at his rampant cock, jutting out of the pale curls between his thighs. He twitched an unseen muscle inside his belly and the head bobbed in her direction. "Now tell me, what is your pleasure?"

"You appear to be awaiting *your* pleasure," she complained with a laugh.

"Nay, 'tis not so! I am yours to command." His mouth turned down in a pout.

"Do not gripe so. I command you to kiss me."

"Where?"

"Everywhere!"

They came together in heat and tenderness. The desire to create the best of memories infused them both with bittersweet passion. When one moved, the other responded instinctively.

He took her at her word, beginning with laughter to find the most unlikely places she would expect to be kissed. The top of her head. The soles of her feet. The point of her elbow. Her laughter changed to sighs of delight as he moved from the unlikely to the most sensitive. He laved her breasts with his tongue, took her fingers completely into his mouth and stroked them gently with his teeth, he even made her squirm with pleasure as he licked between her toes.

When Drey moaned softly in the back of her throat, Cyrus sucked a little harder at her nipple. It seemed that skin glided against skin for a lifetime, or perhaps only a heartbeat. She had to work to stop the tears that threatened to spill. Never before had she shared such love and ecstasy and instinct told her she would never find it again.

When he had covered her entire body with kisses, he gathered her in his arms. "I saved the best for last," he told her hoarsely as he claimed her lips in a kiss. By turns demanding and devouring, tender and sweet, he showed her how much he loved her. She felt her soul respond, opening to him and welcoming him as she hadn't before. She knew this would be her last night with him. She concentrated on savoring his flavor, the pressure of his lips and the texture of his tongue as she caressed him with hers.

When she could stand the bittersweet torture no longer, she broke the kiss, panting, "Now, love, 'tis my turn."

Following the same path he'd made over her body, she gifted him with a similar laving of his bronzed skin and kisses akin to those he'd given her. When he shivered under her mouth, she prolonged the enjoyment for him, returning again and again to those places she'd learned gave him pleasure. He gasped and shuddered when she finally closed her mouth over the head of his cock. She traced the contours of his shaft, burned them in her memory for the future, *her* future, which stretched before her in empty years. Without him.

He did not give her long enough to lap up the drops of seed that welled up in her mouth. With a sharp, indrawn breath, he shifted her until she straddled his hips and drew her down into a tight embrace. His heart pounded so hard she could feel it thundering where her thighs were pressed against his chest. His hard cock nudged her back. With his head buried between her breasts, he warned, "You will kill me, should you keep at that."

She swept the hair off his damp forehead. "I would not lose you. Not yet."

"Nor I you."

He held her like that, in silence, while his breathing slowed.

His mortal form felt so right in her arms. How would she know if she ever encountered him again or would she live the rest of her life wondering if the caress of each breeze might be him, that he still cared for her and had returned however he might to touch her again?

She tried to relax against him, trying not to weep and wondering if he could hear her heart breaking. Aye, she would miss him but surely that could wait until he was gone. Why should she feel this anguish already, long before she knew for certain that she could send him home? The grief would not leave her, however she tried to push it aside and concentrate on the moments they had left.

Finally, he mastered his breathing and lifted his head. The quirk of his lips, only a hint of a smile, was a bit lopsided beneath his stormy eyes, as if her somber mood had infected him. She summoned her will and forced herself to respond with a bigger smile.

"I love you." They spoke the words in unison.

Drey's mood lifted and Cyrus laughed aloud. In one swift, unexpected motion, he grasped her by the waist to lift her and buried himself inside her. She welcomed his cock, spreading her legs wider. He drove upward, filling her more deeply than he ever had before. They rocked in rhythm, their mouths locked in a deep kiss.

She knew she would miss him every night for the rest of her life.

He believed he would never again be unfettered and free.

In the afterglow, as they lay tangled together, he asked her to play for him. She found her pipes and tried to dispel her somber mood with a lively tune but all she blew were lonely ballads of lost love.

* * * * *

In the morning, she cleared away the remnants of their meal and gathered together what she'd need for the ritual. In the morning sky, the full moon was still visible, hanging above the horizon. A time of Power. A time for her to learn to stretch her wings.

When her bundle had been secured, she turned to Cyrus. "I have learned much during this last trip. Kelsh was right: I do indeed have great Power, both within me and around me. Whatever you may have thought of him, he has opened my eyes and led me to find my Power. In my research for him, I've come across many interesting tidbits of knowledge and lore. When you appeared, I had acted without knowing what I was doing. You were bound by my ignorance and trapped by my inexperience. I am no longer the feeble mage I once was. Today I can free you from your binding. Come."

Once in the meadow, she took her time casting the circle, as much to revel in the joy of her secret place as to prolong the pain of parting.

Cyrus watched from the place she had instructed him to stand, his face unreadable. As she worked, she was conscious of his gaze riveted on her.

Was he impatient for her to get this done? Was he apprehensive lest she not have correctly worded the spell? Was he anticipating missing her?

She hoped the latter, although she knew he had chafed under the restrictions placed on him by the binding. At least she could take comfort in his unwillingness to hold her mistake against her. He had been the best companion she could want for the time he'd spent as a man.

At last she concluded her preparations and began to raise the Power she knew lay within her. For this spell she used her own magick, as atonement for stranding Cyrus for the weeks he'd been with her.

"With the aid of wind and fire,
From the depths of my desire
Wrought of water and of stone
Springing from my mind alone

I sought to bind in human form
A creature not of woman born.

"He my greatest joy did find
As we in our love entwined
My wishes into flesh were welded,
The best of man and spirit melded
But nature must be true to form
To do the symmetry no harm.

"Where the cloud and eagle soar
His heart calls him ever more
O'er mount and vale he longs to flow
Now let him in his true form go
To roam the skies in happiness
As the Goddess and God bless.

An I will, so mote it be."

When she finished speaking, the wind rose. Rushing up the cliff and spilling into the meadow, it swept across her circle. Buffeted by the gusts, with her skirts plastered to her, she clung to the edge of the altar, closed her eyes and leaned against the force of the gale.

Silence and stillness descended as quickly as the wind arose. She straightened and opened her eyes.

The altar had been scoured clean. Weakness rippled through her. She leaned against the stone, letting it support her while she looked for Cyrus.

Chapter Eleven

ઠ૭

There was no sign of him. Her cauldron had tumbled outside the boundary of the circle, her broom close beside it. Her other implements, the athame, candles and knife, she couldn't see. Wherever they lay, they were concealed in the bracken and grasses.

Aside from her tools, the clearing was as empty as if he had never been there.

As if he never would be there again.

She shuddered at the gaping hole his absence left in her heart. A dry sob wracked her body, a cry of protest at being alone.

Wasn't this what she'd been working for, to send him back to his world? She'd known she would miss him and that it would hurt, but not so deeply — and not so soon.

Her guilt at not being able to return him to the skies paled in comparison to the pain his parting gave her. More sobs came, until she huddled in on herself, arms wrapped tightly around her ribs, letting the grief wash over her in wave after wave of anguish. She sobbed until she had no more tears, until the cries tore at her dry throat and her legs could no longer support her weight.

Exhaustion tore at her. She hauled herself up on the altar stone and curled into a heap. After a moment, Mousie leapt up and sat beside her, keeping her company with a loud rumbling purr.

She could barely summon the strength to touch him. Turning her hand over, she managed to stroke his belly fur. "I fear we'll never see him again, my friend." She wavered between a laugh and tears. "But I suppose I'm no longer a half-baked imposter. If I did just send him back to his world, I must be a full-blown mage."

Insistent fatigue weighted her eyelids. Still purring loudly, Mousie nudged her repeatedly with his head, refusing to let her sleep while every muscle in her body cried out for rest. Finally, she remembered the restoration rituals she'd memorized. Rolling onto her back, she stretched out. One by one, she ran through the exercises, mentally reaching for any ambient Power she could find as well, for she thought she might replenish herself more quickly with magick that already existed.

Before the sun climbed fully above the horizon, she felt like herself again. Mousie had moved off to a corner of the altar, eyeing her with satisfaction while he washed a large paw.

"You're becoming a nag, you know."

Unrepentant, he merely voiced a *meep* and leapt to the ground.

"I'm hungry again. Let's find my tools and go eat."

A louder cry greeted this plan. The cat stalked ahead, leading her to the missing items, one right after another.

One thing she didn't expect to find was her basket, the one that had disappeared in her first attempt to return Cyrus to his natural form. It lay empty and unchanged near the athame. Somehow, her spell today restored the balance and with that, brought the basket back from wherever it had been.

Once she'd recovered the rest of her tools, Mousie led her back to the cottage, where he demanded his fair share of the sausages and onions she fixed. The single portion looked small and forlorn in the pan. Everywhere she turned, she saw reminders of Cyrus. Laughing or serious, memories of him lingered in every corner of her cottage.

To avoid seeing him, Drey looked in on the mule and her cow and her goat. They wanted for nothing. The cottage was quickly tidied, her bowl washed and the bedding smoothed. She ran her hand over the blanket, finding it hard to swallow as she did so. She would lie alone there tonight, and all the nights to come.

Unable to bear the cottage without Cyrus, she grabbed her pipes and fled across the fields. Below the village, she found a flat rock outcropping near the river. Here the water flowed narrow, fast and deep. A stand of oak trees rose across the torrent. Spreading limbs overhead shielded her from the summer sun and bushes shielded her from the village. She settled in and played a mournful tune that made her weep. Mousie lay on his back and covered his ears with his paws.

The breeze rustling the leaves above her made her think of Cyrus. Perhaps he was listening to her now, enjoying her music. What would he think of her morose selection? She switched tunes, abandoning the drawn-out notes of the ballad for a quick, peppery folk dance.

Mousie leapt up beside her, staring intently into the canopy above. She felt a breath of air caress her cheek and thought she heard a whisper in her ear. She looked up in time to see something snag on a twig and then fall into her lap.

She caught it and found herself holding a silver pan flute. Looking up again, she laughed. "Thank you, Cyrus!"

The soft breeze once more flowed over her, and she thought she heard his voice whisper, "I love you."

She turned the pipes over in her hands. She'd never seen anything like them. The tiny pipes were arranged in the traditional manner, high to low. The brace holding the pipes, and even the pipes themselves, bore engraved runes and flowing script. Even with her magick, she couldn't decipher the individual words or their meaning.

In Kelsh's service, she'd read languages long dead. What then was this writing, to be so ancient that she couldn't even get a sense of what the writing meant? Could it be otherworldly, something never known to mortals and thus beyond the ken of even her full Power?

Lifting the pipes, she blew softly to test them.

Clear notes rang out.

Silence fell around her. Even the loud burble of the river over the stones below her perch faded to a murmur. Mousie laid a paw on her arm. "Mroul," he commanded.

And so she played.

Every note resounded with magick, every trill flowed perfectly from the pipes as she first tried scales and then a tune. Others followed as she ran through her favorites. Even the simplest songs became extraordinary when blown through the silver flute.

Mousie settled in on the rock beside her, his paws tucked into his snowy breast and his tail wrapped neatly around him. The wind stilled, only a breath of air feathering now and then across her forehead or cheek.

When at last she paused, she found herself still breathing easily, not panting as she surely would have been had she played so many tunes so quickly on her reed pipes. She marveled, examining the silver pipes again.

Barely discernable in the afternoon light, a soft glow lit them from within. When she arose, the river itself had taken on a glow as well. Even Mousie, with his snowy belly and bib, and his white feet, reflected the noonday sun more brightly.

Magick sang and throbbed in her veins, more than she had ever been aware of before. Her skin felt taut, stretched to contain it all, as though much more would cause her to burst wide open like a pod of seeds. Might the pipes be a magickal conduit, drawing magick to her when she played them? Or could it be that they enhanced the Power she already possessed?

Aware that she hadn't lost Cyrus forever—that although they might never again truly touch, he was still with her—Drey fairly danced her way back to the cottage. Mousie trotted alongside her. She thought he wore a rather smug expression.

Could he have known all along what would happen? He appeared to have sensed a significance in the breeze by the river before she did. He had been determined that she not fall asleep after the ritual of unbinding Cyrus. Why?

Had he known Cyrus would return in his wind form? Or had the cat sensed some danger to her, should she lie depleted and defenseless in sleep?

* * * * *

Drey returned to her apprenticeship to find one fewer guard to cook for. No one explained his absence. When she queried the cook's helper, she learned Rose didn't have a clue. They all just awakened one morning and Jan had disappeared.

Kelsh's previous visitors were gone but he had two new visitors. Hans was an older man, dark complected and friendly, who had visited them before. He went out of his way to pay attention to Drey, complimenting her writing when she served as scribe for him. His companion was a rough, blustering fellow that she pegged as another petty noble, ambitious and hungry for political gain. They taxed her cooking skills, devouring everything she placed before them.

Something about their oblique comments within her hearing troubled her. 'Twas as if they spoke in a secret language, nodding or jerking their heads in her direction and touching their ears or their lips in silent admonition. Kelsh had changed too, subtly but decisively. He no longer loaded her with tasks and took every opportunity to touch her. Whether on her arm or her hair, her shoulder or her back, his hands were never far from her when they were together.

He often requested her presence when he was working but most of the time he didn't have anything in particular for her to do. It was a relief when he finally dismissed her following the evening meal on the second day. The rest of his staff had retired to their rooms, for Kelsh and his guests had run everyone off their feet.

Drey sought the quiet and solitude of the workroom. It was the first time she'd been alone since her arrival the morning before. She took the opportunity to uncover her pipes, which she'd hidden in a concealed pocket in her satchel.

She lay on her pallet, eyes closed, piping a soft ballad. When she sat up, she discovered a sizable globe of magefire hovering in the air above her. Louder piping intensified the glow, while softer notes dimmed it. She played with it for a while before she tried letting the music drift into silence.

The light contracted to a hand span and dimmed a bit but remained in place, lighting the room's contents, tables and shelves, jars and boxes, in sharp relief against the black shadows. When she stretched forth her hand, the coldfire settled into her palm with a tingle. She found she could move it, carrying it around as she willed.

She settled back into meditation, seeking the source within her. She soon found it, a small part of her focused on maintaining the light, draining a very small bit of her Power.

Wearing a big grin, she pulled her focus out of herself and got to her feet. She could walk and carry the light. Making a circuit of the room, she enjoyed the play of light and shadow across the worktables and their contents, already spread out for the next day's tasks.

Darker shadows hovered at the edge of her light and she played with them, moving her hand to and fro, watching them retreat and advance. The bottle with the wisp of mist that had seemed to move on its own glowed with an unearthly yellow-green hue by the light of her coldfire globe. Several other bottles and jars showed unusual characteristics when she neared them. Others, particularly the few lining the back of the area where Kelsh had been working when she fell asleep, showed no details at all, remaining as black as the room had been when she'd awakened. They formed pockets of blackness in the room, drawing her attention by their absence, as it were. She marked their locations, for closer inspection in the light of day.

Stepping back, she noticed larger wells of darkness under the tables. Some of the boxes that she knew held scrolls showed nothing in this light, looking for all the world as though they enclosed part of an empty night sky. Under other circumstances, she might have tried to touch the darkness but something warned her that such a course of action would be foolhardy at best, dangerous at worst.

Other scrolls fairly glowed with a light of their own, shining in shades of silver or gold. He'd never guided her to any of them. Those she itched to read, sensing their call. If Kelsh left her alone in the morning, she resolved to tuck a few of those under the blanket of her pallet, to read after he retired. She was tempted to peruse them now but she was so tired she wasn't certain she could keep her eyes open.

* * * * *

The next day, Kelsh gave her the opportunity she had hoped for when he excused himself for the night well before she began to prepare her pallet. She bid him good night over her shoulder, while she concentrated on a new exercise, moving a quill from the tabletop to stand in the inkwell.

Minutes later, she hopped off her stool and whisked a few of the scrolls into her lap, ones that had glowed silver in her mage light. She waited a while longer, to be certain he was indeed gone for the night, before daring to lift them to the table and unroll the first one.

The text dealt with the nature of mages. According to the author, in general sorcerers fell into three types. The organization given by this author was by the source of their Power. The author cited another work of his as the ultimate authority in the nature of magick, from the white magick wielded by servants of the light to the foulest arts practiced by those who spread darkness across the land. Between these extremes lay magicks of every color imaginable.

According to this scribe, the most common mages were Shapers, those who manipulated the magick in the world around them. These proved to occur in varying degrees of ability and strength, from the healer who was barely aware of doing it, to the grand mages who could turn lead into gold or kill at a distance. The advantage of being a Shaper was listed as having access to a virtually inexhaustible supply of magick in those areas where magickal energies flowed freely. The drawbacks included a Shaper unable to reach or tap into external energy flows being rendered helpless.

Less common were the Makers, those mages whose magick bubbled up from within them. The advantage of Makers lay in their ability to access magick even if they should be blocked from ambient magick or stranded in an area bereft of magick. The disadvantage was the physical toll a Maker paid for drawing magick out of himself, which could leave the wielder exhausted and unable to defend against a threat.

The least common—indeed, the author had never encountered such a mage and could not be certain that they did in fact exist—was the Leech. It was widely believed that a Leech maintained or increased his or her own level of magick by consuming the Power of other mages. Should the victim perish in the transfer of Power, it was rumored that the Leech would also absorb the accumulated knowledge of his victim, thus increasing the Leech's abilities as well as his Power.

Drey sat and thought about this. Her aunt and Gran had tried to teach her to be a Shaper. She had actually managed it on a small scale when she almost lit the candle in her cottage. She had done it on a large scale when she finally managed to heal Betsy.

Was Kelsh a Maker? He'd assumed she was, teaching her the restoration exercises, which raised the likelihood that he was one as well. Was it possible that Shapers in general were women and that Makers were men? Such a division would explain why Kelsh was familiar with more efficient methods to tap into internal sources of magick.

Under his instruction she had found that the source of her Power lay within her. If she had managed a little bit of both generating her own Power and gathering it from around her, did that make her a mage unlike any other?

She realized she could easily satisfy her curiosity about the source of Kelsh's Power. Closing her eyes, she spread out her senses and searched the workroom for ambient magick.

The place teemed with it. Glittering strands lay piled beneath the benches, heaped in the corners and filled the shelves.

Kelsh had to be a Maker. He'd been shedding Power the whole time he'd worked here and so had his guests. There was enough lying about to fuel his work for months, if not years. He could not possibly be a Shaper.

Was it possible for him to detect the ambient magick without being able to use it? Could she avail herself of the ready supply here in his workroom? Would he notice if she did? There were too many unanswered questions. She couldn't risk it.

She searched the rest of the scroll for any hint of a hybrid, one who had both Maker and Shaper abilities, and found nothing at all. There were no hints that such a mage could exist but no mention of it being impossible.

Chapter Twelve

ഇ

Was that something she could ask Kelsh?

No, she decided, to ask would be to reveal her clandestine studies. He might send her away and, if that happened, she'd never learn the extent of her Power or to completely control it.

Her days settled into an uneasy rhythm of study or translation and progressively more difficult exercises that taught her to tap into and control her inner magick. At night she experimented with locating ambient magick around the head of the river.

A gentle breeze often accompanied her on her walks outside Kelsh's property. She would wander along the banks of the river, in the evening or the early morning, while the wind toyed with her hair and ruffled her hem. Often she'd play her silver pipes and relive the time she'd spent with Cyrus.

One night she felt her hair lift in the breeze as soon as she stepped across the bridge. The wind rose and stayed with her. Leaves rustled softly all around in the waning light. She sat on the bank of the large stream, above the fork where it became a river. Pulling her silver pipes out, she began to play.

As she played, the wind toyed with her hem. Sending out her mage senses, she determined that no mortals lingered in the area. Hiking her skirts up to her knees, she lay back on the soft grass. The notes from her pipes flowed up and out. The leaves trembled with their passing. Bathed in the soft breeze, she lay there for more than an hour, until full dark, playing her favorite tunes and thinking of Cyrus.

In her evenings spent walking around the river, she never thought she heard whispers of love as she had the day she'd sent him back but she couldn't be sure the wind wasn't him. In learning to develop her Power and control it, she felt she just might be treading the path to seeing him again someday, clothed in mortal flesh. The thought that she might someday be strong enough to again summon and bind him for a night fueled her late-night studies and exercises.

Her nocturnal ramblings ceased the night she read another shining scroll, one that spoke of how mages could perceive the activity and presence of other mages. She began to practice determining where Kelsh was and what he was doing and then, fearing discovery of her covert lessons, she stopped them altogether.

More visitors came and went, some lords in fine fur-trimmed garments with colored plumes in their caps, others threadbare scholars with whom Kelsh conferred late into the night. Drey was introduced to few of them. Most often he retrieved some scrolls or jars from the work shed and carried them to his great room, where he entertained his guests and carried out his own studies.

Several of them stuck in her mind. Once she caught a glimpse of naked fear on Kelsh's face as an imposing lord in fine clothing rode up with a score of guards. The man stayed for three days and Kelsh spent the whole time berating his guards and Drey. During that time, they could do nothing fast enough to suit him. She spent the entire three days in the kitchen, working alongside Rose to feed all the extra men.

Another time she was summoned to translate a scrap of ancient parchment, one that made her skin crawl just to touch it. That visitor was a stooped and gnarled old woman, with dark skin and an explosive laugh. Despite her advanced age, she came and left on foot and alone. Drey wondered what unseen protection she might have, for no one who traveled the roads alone could be confident of reaching their destination.

She never saw the other visitor, for one of the guards met her in the hall, snatching the tray from her hands and closing the door in her face. She only heard a mumbled part of their conversation when Kelsh said, "She's perfect for me and growing stronger every day." She had the uncomfortable feeling that he spoke of her.

And she *was* growing stronger every day. She could now light the hearth with a look, shield her presence from the rest of the household when she wanted no one to notice her, and calm animals, even the wild hart and the hedgehogs, enough to let her do what she wished with them. That skill would serve her well in healing, for livestock in the past had frequently resisted her ministrations.

Mayhap she could return home on the morrow.

Impatience gnawed at her to get back to her cottage and try gathering magick to shape it. The days stretched long in front of her and she dared only practice locating magick, not daring to touch it lest Kelsh know. She couldn't quite say why she didn't want him to learn of her independent studies and how quickly she was progressing on her own.

＊ ＊ ＊ ＊ ＊

The next morning when she arrived in the kitchen, Rose sent her in to the cottage's main room. There she found Kelsh sitting at the table, which was set with tea and scones.

"You have made great progress with your studies." Kelsh gestured to a chair. "Sit, and hear my proposal."

Was it time for the reckoning? She sat. Her appetite evaporated. What might he ask of her as payment for her training?

He poured tea into two mugs and gave her one. Cradling the other in both hands, he inhaled the steam as he settled back in his seat.

She sniffed at hers. Hyssop and blackberries. Mayhap a pinch of oranges. A sip confirmed her identification of the contents. The heat was welcome and the combination of flavors was delicious. Some of the tension inside her uncoiled. If her suspicions were correct, she was much stronger than he. Perhaps he wished her to teach him how she had healed Betsy.

"I won't bother mincing words. When I took you on as my apprentice, you gave me my choice of payment. You have far exceeded my expectations. You know you're a very strong mage. I believe a union of our talents would serve us both."

Her thoughts raced. She sipped the tea while she examined his words from every angle. "Union? Do you mean to promote me from apprentice to partner?"

"Nay, I mean union as in 'marry me,' as in live and work with me for the rest of your life."

She blurted out, "I don't love you!"

His mouth fell open and he stared at her for a moment. "I forget how young you are and how sheltered your life has been. Love has little to do with marriage." He stood. "I promise you, you will not be unsatisfied as my wife. I know how to please a woman—in many ways."

She could imagine that. He was a handsome man, with his neatly trimmed beard, compact build and transforming smile— but he wasn't Cyrus. She shook her head. "I cannot imagine marrying a man I don't love."

"You will come to love me, with time. I promise. Will you at least remain here for some time, no longer as an apprentice but as my partner, to see how we might fare together? I'd like the chance to change your mind." He watched her face closely. "I will not ask you to share my bed, not until you choose to."

"Then the thing you ask from me as payment for my training is the opportunity to woo me?"

He grinned. "When you put it that way, it does sound odd but aye, that is my request."

"For how long? I still have my own cottage to look after and my own responsibilities."

"Let me think." He clasped his hands and steepled his fingers, placing the tips of his fingers under his chin. "I believe six moons should be sufficient time for me to woo you."

"I must spend at least one week each month at my home."

"That is reasonable."

"No later than the winter solstice, I am free to leave and you will consider my debt to you discharged?"

"Done."

She could taste her relief. The fears Cyrus had harbored were unfounded. "Under those conditions, I agree."

The rest of the day passed as if nothing had changed, as if their conversation of marriage had never taken place.

She spent the morning translating more texts. In the afternoon she hunted wild herbs, taking along Merv and his shovel.

Past the head of the river, she realized she had roamed almost to the hidden grove where Cyrus had danced with her. She turned her steps aside. That place was special, not to be shared lightly and certainly not to be shared with the stolid, grubby and very mortal Merv.

As they made their way along one of the brooks that fed the river, she found a stand of ferns sheltering a tiny clump of delicate flowers she'd never seen before. When she crushed the stem between her fingers, the plant released a pleasing aroma. She was free to bring back whatever she wished and she wanted to examine this one. Directing Merv to collect enough to transplant, she wandered ahead along the faint path, looking for willow bark to gather.

At the stream, the trees parted to let the sun through. Rocks dotted the surface, imparting a merry chuckle to the water as it rushed over them. Drey pulled up her hem and sat on the bank. Pulling out her pipes, she began to play a lively jig.

As happened the first time, the sounds around her stilled. A wren flitted onto a branch across the stream and sat silently, watching and listening, tail cocked up. Two small trout in a pool ceased fighting and turned to face her.

Air flowed through the bushes around her, flirting with her hair, teasing it from her plait. Her heart leapt within her.

She knew that touch.

Turning her face to the breeze, she almost wept when it freshened, rising to tug at her garments. Her hem twitched this way and that, until she shifted position. Her freed hem rose with the wind, coming to settle about her hips. As the cool caress swept over her bared skin, she parted her knees. Gust after gust stirred her nether curls. In her mind, she could again feel Cyrus as he stroked her, gently parting her lips to delve inside. She remembered his words when they first met. *I liked this place best of all.*

It was tantalizing, this almost-touch, so much that she felt wet heat building within her, and desire. Beneath the linen of her chemise, her nipples hardened.

An errant current brushed a strand of her hair across her cheek. She found the breath of air so different, yet so familiar. A firm breeze shook the bushes about her. A leaf stroked the tender curve of her neck, sending a ripple of gooseflesh across her skin.

Hunger bloomed in her belly, a craving for the fulfillment she'd found so many times in his arms. She spread her legs further. The tension within her built, fanned by the light touch feathering across her most sensitive places.

Without her volition, the tone of the music changed. The notes took on a soaring, sensual quality. Her breath came faster, each rise and fall of her chest rubbing her pebbled nipples against her garments. The weight of her breasts increased, along with her desire. If only Cyrus were here now, in his mortal form!

Uncomfortable with the tension gathering in her belly, she shifted position again and a tall clump of grass sprang free from beneath her skirt. The wind seized upon it, twirling the supple leaves this way and that in a sinuous dance.

While she watched, her fingers still dancing on her pipes, the wind bent the grass, to brush across her bared thighs and trail down her cleft. She fought the urge to jerk her hips. A tremor ran through her. The wind gusted again and a firmer touch stroked the leaves more deeply through her curls.

Lightning trailed in its wake. Another rush of air plucked at her curls, a surge that cooled some of the building heat. The contrast in temperatures made her sigh into the pipes. The note came out in a gliding trill.

Again the grass caressed her and again she trembled with the force of the storm gathering inside her. She played mindlessly, not knowing or caring whether the notes followed a tune. Her awareness contracted until her world consisted of the stroking grass and nothing more. She lost the fight and her hips rose to meet each touch.

A light slap of the leaves sent her over the edge. Lightning sizzled from her toes up her spine, engulfing her again and again. She played on as she rode out the storm, soaring from peak to peak as the breeze flowed across her.

Finally she had to stop to catch her breath. When the pipes left her lips, the wind dropped. The wren flew off and other birds began to sing. She sat up and straightened her clothes.

When Merv called out to her, she rose on unsteady legs. As she turned to leave the brook, she thought she heard a whispered, "Thank you."

Her heart contracted as she whispered, "No, thank *you*."

Leaves rustled above her and a flower fell into her hand, releasing a lovely perfume. She knew the blossom came from Cyrus and had to blink hard to keep from weeping.

In her heart, she knew the truth. Kelsh did not have a hope of winning her.

Chapter Thirteen

🔖

She almost sang herself to sleep. The situation she found herself in was not as dire as she had feared.

Cyrus had not deserted her. She knew he loved her still, wherever he might roam and in whatever form. The price Kelsh had asked for training her was not as steep as she had feared. She had no illusions, however, that she might accept his offer and marry him. She would simply work here for the next six months and then return home to her cottage.

When her eyes drifted closed, she settled into the blanket on her pallet and slept.

She dreamed of lovely women, dancing in a moonlit meadow to soft music. They sang along with the tune, a song of Power and joy. A group of mages! Her toes and fingers twitched with the lilting beat. She longed to join them.

Just as she began to move her feet, she noticed a dark, cloaked figure approach on the other side of the meadow. He joined the dance, drawing the nearest woman into his embrace. They executed a few steps together. As the music slowed, she bowed backward over his arm and he bent to kiss her. The kiss began as a mutual act but then she struggled in his arms, tugging at his cloak and beating on his shoulder. Her struggles grew less and less forceful until she relaxed into limp submission. After another moment or two, he cast her aside. She fell onto the grass from his careless grip and he went on to the next dancer.

Drey looked carefully and decided the first woman was sleeping. To her horror, she looked again and realized, from the mage's unnatural pose and pale skin, that she was dead. Drey slipped backward, further into the concealing shadows.

The cloaked man by then had discarded the second dancer and was busy draining the life from a third. One by one, he worked his way across the meadow, emptying the mages, one by one, stealing their Power—and their lives.

The words she'd read in the scroll came back to her. *Beware the Leech.*

She tried to move her feet, to run, but they betrayed her, carrying her forward instead into the moonlight, straight to the Leech, who had finished killing the last of the dancers.

He held out a hand, beckoning her into his dance of death. She tried to resist but the haunting music swelled, surrounded her and pulled her forward. She held out her hand and, when he took it, his hood fell back.

She stared into Kelsh's face. His eyes bored into hers. He smiled his charming smile, saying, "You promised me anything I wish. I wish your Power to be mine." Her heart racked her frame with its pounding as his hand tightened its grip. "We made a bargain." He pulled her into his arms and whirled across the meadow with her.

His smile disappeared. His face changed. She now looked into the face of an ancient man, wrinkled and toothless. His eyes were gaping holes through which she could see his dark, shriveled soul.

He bent to kiss her. She found the strength to turn her face aside and his thin lips came to rest under her ear. She shivered at the whisper of sound, almost the rustle of parchment as he moved across her skin, before he forced her head around. She felt his lips cover hers. His fingers pressed into her jaw, pulling her mouth open. His tongue swept inside.

The only resistance left to her was to not breathe. She held her breath until she couldn't any longer. He eagerly inhaled her Power as she let her breath out.

The wind picked up around them and the wraiths from her previous nightmare appeared, howling, first in wordless agony, then pleading, "Come to us, help us, avenge us."

He sucked at her mouth and she felt her strength wane. Her Power drained into him with each exhalation.

She awakened to find herself retching, with pounding heart and clenched fists, shivering in a sweat.

Was her dream accurate? Was Kelsh a Leech? She reviewed their last conversation in light of this possibility.

An icy chill crawled across her skin as she remembered his words. He had said *for the rest of your life* and not *our lives*. There was indeed a very good chance that Kelsh was a Leech and that he only wanted to marry her to consume her Power.

That prospect staggered her, for she had never thought of herself as anyone special. After years of being considered a weak mage, she had always viewed herself as a nobody, an imposter among the accomplished women of her family. Mayhap Kelsh was playing on those insecurities.

By his own admission, she commanded much more Power than did he. Were he a Leech, that would indeed be true, for she had read that Leeches have little or no Power of their own. Through her ability to both gather and create Power, she suspected she commanded much more Power than most mages. In marrying her, he would be able to feed off her Power for years.

What had she done?

* * * * *

In the morning, she determined she would learn the truth. She packed her bag and left it tucked under one of the worktables. If her dream was accurate, she could remain under his roof no longer.

Kelsh met her as she crossed the yard. "Good morn, sweet Drey. I asked Rose to bring us our tea outside, here in the sunshine." He gestured toward the edge of the herb garden, where several chairs surrounded a small table.

She eyed him closely. Nothing about him suggested he was other than what he purported to be: a powerful mage in his own right. She searched for signs that he might be a murderer or a Leech.

He looked no different. His expression was pleasant, his demeanor appropriate for one greeting a partner or a friend. When he took her hand to lead her to the bricked area, she felt no out-rush of her Power where they touched.

"I had wondered what these were for, if they were mayhap going into storage." She sat and tucked her skirts close around her.

"Nay, the chairs are here for my pleasure. I spend more time sitting here in the winter, when no one visits, enjoying the quiet, dark evenings, than I do in the warm months." He pulled his chair closer to hers and settled in. "My life is too busy to sit idle during the long days."

"That sounds as though we shall not be idle while we break our fast."

He laughed, the sun glinting in his dark eyes. "You are quick. I thought we might discuss a journey. I'd like to take you to meet the king."

"The king?" Drey frowned. "Why should he be interested in me?"

"I work for him, as you may have heard. I know there are no secrets in villages such as this. If you are working with me, you should be known to him."

"I still don't understand why I should attract his attention. How long might we be gone? How far is it? What would I say to him?" Her mind raced.

"Ah, my Mildread. You are unique. Another woman would be concerned about what she might wear, but not you. You press right to the heart of the matter."

She didn't like the assessing look in his eye.

He stood and took her hand, lifting her to her feet. "I'd like it best if you were to tell him that you're my wife." He pulled her closer.

"I doubt that will happen."

"Oh, I don't doubt it at all. Mayhap not this trip, but eventually."

She placed her hand flat on his chest, fingers splayed. "I thought you'd not ask me to share your bed."

He met her eyes squarely. He was bold, she had to give him that. "Aye, but I said nothing about trying to persuade you. I never said I wouldn't kiss you." He bent his head. His breath fanned her cheek. "I've wanted to kiss you since you first sat across from me in the tavern."

He touched his lips to hers and she felt it. The faintest of tingles, a tiny trickle of Power as it left her. Into his kiss.

"No!" She pushed him away. "What are you doing to me?"

Rose stopped, tray poised to set on the table, mouth agape. Kelsh dismissed her with a jerk of his head. The tray clattered to the table and she fled back to the kitchen.

Drey faced him over the table. Both of them were breathing hard.

"I was kissing you."

Her hands tightened into fists. She worked to control her anger. "That's not what I mean and you know it."

The tense lines of his face softened. "I want you to marry me. I wanted to show you how I can please you."

"Then what were you doing with my Power?"

His jaw clenched. "Drey, I need you. I can make you happy. We can do great things together."

"That's not the whole truth. You mean *you* can do great things with my Power, don't you?"

In two quick steps, he had her in his arms again. "It's not like that."

"Then how is it? Explain it to me!" She stopped fighting him, made herself stand still.

"I need your Power to sustain me. Trust me. I don't need much. You have more than you need, more than enough for both of us."

Words failed her. She had no wish for a confrontation, not if she could avoid it. She wrenched free, heading for the outbuilding that housed her mule.

He followed. "Drey, you said you'd stay until winter!"

When she didn't answer, he reached out and grabbed her wrist. Before she knew what was happening, he'd pulled her against him. Looking in his eyes, she began to fear him. Her belly tightened in an unpleasant fashion.

"I would rather this hadn't happened." His voice held genuine regret as he bent his head and kissed her.

Unlike her dream, there was no transformation of his appearance, no palpable change as he held her. Trapped in his embrace, arms pinned to her sides, she could do nothing but scream in her mind while he wrested her Power from her. A steady stream flowed out of her with a twisting pain.

At last he raised his head. Satisfaction shone in his dark eyes. "You've begun to pay your debt. We could have lived in harmony for years but you chose not to share. Give me more. Give me all of it."

She found the strength to scream in earnest, kicking at his heavy boots, writhing in his arms. He made a low, unpleasant sound that raised the hairs on her neck.

The wind struck in a blast of fury.

Between the buildings it came, tumbling the two of them off their feet. They came down hard on the stones bordering the path, the impact separating them. She sprawled against the back wall of the cottage, her senses reeling.

The vortex continued on without her, whirling Kelsh along. The blur of his cloak disappeared in a cloud of dust and leaves. Over the bridge it went, along the road away from the village.

Drey shook her head to clear it. Cyrus had helped her! Staggering to her feet, she went to the work shed and found her bag. She stumbled on her way out. The ties came undone and half her clothing spilled out. She stuffed her spare shift in and secured the bundle.

She found and quickly saddled her mule. Fastening the bag behind, she hauled herself up and dug her heels into the animal's flank. Without a backward glance, she sent the beast homeward at a jog.

The breeze accompanied her, lifting her hair from time to time. She repeated, "Thank you, my love, thank you, my love," until the words ran into a single sound and no longer made sense to her.

When she reached her cottage, she quickly shut the mule in the shed. Gathering up her bag, she fled inside and bolted the door behind her. It wasn't until she lay across her bed, sobbing, that her panic began to subside.

That had been a close call. Without Cyrus's intervention, she would have died right there. Even now, alone here in her own home, she did not feel safe. She needed protection.

Pulling herself to her feet, she wiped the hair off her face. She needed to ward her cottage. Wards might not keep Kelsh out but they would give her a warning should he pursue her.

She found the tools she needed and began by the door. When she clicked the athame against the sigil she'd drawn on the doorjamb, nothing happened.

It should have glowed for an instant.

With a sinking heart, she realized she had felt nothing. No tingle of Power, no indication she was doing anything other than sketching a pretty picture and tapping it with a butter knife.

Mayhap the silver pipes would help her. They practically summoned magick on their own. They weren't in the pocket where she kept them. She turned the bag inside out, dumping the contents and spreading them out on the floor.

The pipes weren't there.

Her Power was gone completely.

Her tears began again. She gathered her tools and fled up the mountain. Alone. Mousie was nowhere around.

The meadow stretched before her in the morning light, comforting in its familiarity and its evidence of the Power she'd found in the past. Surely here she could recover that ability. She knew her magick was made of sunlight and warm breezes, not the stuff of gathering dusk and all it cloaked in shadows.

Quickly she crossed to the stone, laying out her tools of Power on the altar. A little salt was all that remained in the tiny cauldron; she couldn't remember spilling it or using it but mayhap she had in her hasty climb up the uneven path. She struck her flint to light the candles before bracing her hands on the altar and taking a deep calming breath.

Looking out over the valley, she cleared her mind of its turmoil. Her fears of Kelsh were banished. No regrets for leaving behind the silver pipes were allowed. No pining for Cyrus and his optimism—or for his touch.

The familiar motions of casting the circle soothed her jagged nerves. As she moved through the ritual, she directed her senses outward to detect Power.

Nothing.

When she finished the circle, there was no sign she'd done anything more than walk around the clearing, speaking meaningless words. She felt no snap when she closed the circle, no sensation of anything beyond the usual slight breeze and birdsong.

Had Kelsh stolen her Power? Had he absorbed all of her Talent, leaving her empty and lost?

She searched within herself, for anything indicating she still had potential.

She found nothing. No tingle, no glow, not even a trickle.

Sinking to her knees, she groaned in agony. Could she live like this? Could she tolerate spending every waking hour without the prospect of ever feeling the tingle of Power?

Knowing that she'd never again be able to wield even the small magick she was accustomed to? Losing the grand abilities the pipes gave her was one thing, for she'd only recently had that Power at her fingertips, but to lose it all was beyond her comprehension.

She'd thought she'd give anything to have Cyrus back but this void inside her was like being struck blind or losing part of her soul.

She sat with her head in her arms and wept.

Some time later she became aware of rumbling beside her. Mousie had come, rubbing against her back and knees. "Oh, Mousie, you're here!" His purr grew louder. When he patted her head with his paw, she sat up and stretched out a hand.

"You're my best friend. Even if I have nothing else, I still have you." He arched up, butting his forehead against her palm. She gathered him close and spoke into his fur. "Will it be enough? Can your love carry me through the rest of my life?"

When she ran her hand down his flank in a light caress, he gave a sharp yowl and flinched. She reached again and he dodged her. Without thinking, she closed her eyes and visualized his body, searching for an injury. In her mind, the image of the big cat glowed with health, except for a little pinprick of darkness where she'd touched him. He'd caught a thorn in his flesh, from somewhere, possibly on his climb up the hillside.

Her eyes flew open. "I could see you!"

She closed her eyes and searched inside herself again. This time, she found the glow, the tiny spark she'd missed before.

Her Power wasn't gone. Kelsh hadn't drained her beyond recovery.

Mousie danced away from her outstretched hand before he turned and made a great show of extracting the thorn. After he spit it out and returned to rub around her, she realized what he'd done.

"Mousie, I do love you. I don't care if you never catch a mouse or kill a cricket. Another cat could never replace you in my heart." She bent over, took his head between her hands and looked into his eyes. "You saved me from my own despair. If you hadn't made me use it without worrying about whether I could, I might never have realized that at least I do still have my small magick."

She relaxed into the grass, beginning the series of exercises Kelsh had taught her to replenish her strength. How ironic that he who had drained her had also given her the key to survive it.

She might never again know the great Power she'd felt while playing the silver pipes Cyrus had given her but she could, and would, practice whatever small magick she had. Never again would she complain about her abilities. Limited she might be, but she did have Talent and Power within her.

Shadows were gathering among the bushes, spreading out from the hillside when she sat up. She squinted up at the rim of the sun still visible atop the mountain. She still had time. She took up the wand and began again to cast the circle.

This time she could feel the rightness of it, the Power in the words she spoke and the intent of her motions. When she closed the circle, she once again felt the snap.

With the same joy she'd felt bubbling up within her when she first cast the circle here, in her secret meadow, she began a ritual of thanksgiving. Power thrummed through her, surging up from the mountain below and down from the dome of sky above. She could feel the immense bulk of the earth beneath her. Within that mountain, she was aware of water flowing through deep caverns and tunnels.

She hummed with it, in unison with the world around her. It wasn't until she released the Power she'd raised, back into the earth and sky, that she realized she was not alone.

Kelsh stepped forward from the dark shadows, holding something out to her, something that glinted in the fading light. Her silver pipes!

His clothing was disheveled, his hair askew. "You left so fast that you forgot these," he said. "I know how much they mean to you, so I brought them."

She feared touching him again. "Lay them on the stone." She pointed to the altar.

"No. You must come and get them."

Under his dark regard, she shifted with indecision. She'd recovered once from his draining grasp; could she do so a second time? Or would he succeed in draining her so completely that she would never regain her grasp on the Power she prized?

The pipes were a parting gift from Cyrus and she could not resist their lure. She stepped forward.

In a sudden movement, Kelsh pulled her to him, letting her have the pipes but imprisoning her within his embrace. She ceased to struggle and brought the pipes to her lips.

She played a wild melody, filled with her love for Cyrus and her love for even the smallest magick. Power spread through the clearing, thickening the air about them and pressing close. It sang beneath her skin, crackled along her spine and lifted her hair out about her head.

As the magick gathered, she felt it begin to flow from her into Kelsh, through his hands where he gripped her arms.

Let him have what he wants, she thought. Let him have as much as he can take.

She closed her eyes and pictured him as an empty wineskin. She envisioned the Power filling her, overflowing and draining into him, first as a trickle and then in a stream. When it reached a torrent, he began to strain to contain it. She continued to play, drawing far more Power than she'd ever raised before.

The Power was gathering faster than he could absorb it. She kept pushing the flow into him, gathering it from the mountain beneath them and the air about them. The pipes found it, summoned it, and molded it into a form she could use.

Finally, he could hold no more. In her mind's eye, she saw him fill and expand, his being stretching to contain it, growing thinner and thinner until he burst.

The force of it blew them apart, sending them both aloft, him falling back onto the grass and her flying toward the cliff.

She felt the backlash as an explosion, filling her vision with blinding light and lifting her off the ground once more. With a sickening lurch, the ground dropped away beneath her and she realized she had cleared the edge of the cliff. Rocks and scree fell around her as she plunged off the mountain.

A scream tore out of her, lost in the rush of the wind in her ears.

Then strong arms wrapped around her and her fall slowed. "Be still, sweetling," came a familiar voice.

Cyrus bore her up, into the remaining sunlight far above the meadow. She turned in his arms, weeping in reaction and relief.

"Hush, hush, my dearest love, you are safe," he crooned.

She hiccupped and managed a smile. Then she realized they were passing by a low cloud and looked down.

The bird's-eye view she had imagined was nothing like the reality of hovering far above solid earth. She couldn't keep her eyes open. Her heart slipped into her throat and she choked, tightening her grip on his shoulders.

"I have you," he assured her. "You are in no danger. You may not have this chance again, so take a good look." He turned around with her, sweeping one hand across the panorama below them. "This is my view of your world."

She shivered and clung to him but she did dare to tilt her head down and open her eyes.

Everything was so small. Her hillside meadow was barely visible, a smudge in the shadow of the mountain. The patchwork of fields surrounding the village might have been a plate sitting on a table that was the valley. Beyond the valley, she traced the line of the river, down to where it flowed into the sea. Oh, the sea was an immense glimmering, shifting, silver pool, stretching away as far as she could see.

She hadn't looked her fill before they were sinking down, into the shadows of evening, back to the meadow, where Cyrus set her gently on the grass by the altar.

"I am sorry I couldn't hold him. I suspected he would seek you out but the winds may not always go where they will. Sometimes we must dance to the tune of the tides and the moon. I could not hold him."

"You saved me when he would have killed me and you were here when I needed you most. I have no complaint." She ran her hand down his arm.

He was solid and warm under her hands. He regarded her with loving eyes. Partially concealed by falling night, his white hair glowed and his skin held the luminosity of a pearl. This creature of the air had somehow taken form to rescue her, through no act of her own this time.

"You can change at will?"

"So it seems. You were in need. I had no chance to choose, it simply happened. And glad I am that it did."

"And I as well." She sighed and relaxed into his embrace.

He bent his head to kiss her but, before his lips reached hers, a groan interrupted them.

Something stirred in the darkness, near the dripping spring.

"Kelsh!" Drey breathed.

"I believe he is no threat to you now."

"How do you know?"

"Use your senses. Can you not find him?"

She extended her awareness, seeking the mage, and found the man. To her amazement, the image in her mind showed no trace of magick.

Where he had been a robust center of Power, he now was nothing more than the pale presence of a normal man. Mayhap not quite normal. Where his eyes should be, her healer's Sight showed her dense pockets of charcoal.

When she'd forced so much Power on him, his senses had collapsed. Like the wheels of an overburdened wagon, they'd shattered under the strain. She guessed that his beautiful eyes, the most compelling feature he possessed, had been where he'd concentrated his use of Power. They had been the focus, so they bore the brunt of his ordeal.

He would live. Never again would he steal the essence from another mage, never again would he himself be a mage, but he would live.

She shivered. Having known Power, she could not imagine living the rest of her life denied it.

She nestled into Cyrus's arms. "He has gotten no more than he deserves."

He tucked her against his side and tickled her neck with one finger. "Forget about him. I feel no urgent need to return to the skies. Did I summon you to pleasure me this time, my great mage? You did drop into my arms like a gift from the sky. Care to stay out and play?"

"I believe I could provide pleasure for you. What do you have in mind?"

"I was thinking about this secluded grove where no one but me will see you clad in only moonlight." He kissed her and she murmured her assent into his mouth. "And should we still be there come dawn, I might yet see you clothed in naught but sunshine."

The End

Fire and Ice

෨

Chapter One
The Dark Ages
The Deep Wood

ഔ

Trina blinked the sleep out of her eyes and huddled closer to the heavy stones surrounding the fire, soaking up their faint warmth. The gesture did little good. She still ached from the cold that seeped through her woolen gown. She hadn't been truly warm since the first chill winds of winter swept into the valley months ago.

The massive granite hearth dominated the shed. Occupying the center of a cleared space in the middle of the floor, its border of rocks enclosed an area large enough for Trina to curl up on the coals, should she dare. She didn't dare, for she knew what foul things her mistress Kalidah did inside that circle.

In full roar, the fire could heat the shed almost beyond mortal endurance, boiling the contents of the largest cauldron and baking bread at the same time. Despite its huge capacity, at the moment it held a pitifully small fire that barely warmed her or the large snake wrapped around the outside of the stone border. She lifted the snake's cool, smooth head onto her lap and stroked it.

Life wasn't fair, she thought. Old Kalidah, with her dark southern skin and great age, daily strode about out of doors in her light woolen gown and no cloak, as if it were the height of summer and not the depths of winter. The sorceress insisted on calling her "Baraka of the North", though Trina knew that was not her name. She remembered almost nothing of her life before she'd been brought to Kalidah's shabby steading in the woods. One thing she was certain of was that she'd once had a family and a proper name. She might still have a family somewhere, one that knew her as something other than the harsh syllables Kalidah spat at her when her attention wandered.

Kalidah surely lied about her origins as well, for Trina was certain she must be a native of the south. She felt each breath of wind leach the heat from her body even while she sat close by the fire. The creatures in the hag's menagerie, secure in their chosen places spread about the shed, had feathers, fur or scales to protect them. Trina had only a worn linen chemise, a thin woolen gown and a threadbare cloak. She saved the cloak for the outdoors, when she really needed the meager protection it afforded.

After weeks of frigid winds and drifting snow, Trina was more than ready for spring. She knew she had weeks more of bitter weather to endure before the snow melted and the forest came to life again. For a moment, she closed her eyes and was lost in thoughts of warm sunshine on her cheeks.

The door latch rattled, breaking her reverie. Trina gave a startled jerk, stopping halfway to her feet, fingers clutching the snake's smoothness. No knock followed. No one entered.

A quick glance over her shoulder told her it was only the wind, buffeting the ill-fitting plank door on its worn leather hinges and blowing drifts of last night's snow through the cracks. She settled back into her crouch against the warm stone.

No one came from the village these days, not even the few brave or desperate petitioners who in summer would venture into the wood to seek Kalidah's aid. The sorceress' reputation, and that of her home in the forest, had spread in the decades the mage had spent working her magick in her small holding. No peasant—or lord, for that matter—wished to risk becoming stranded in the Deep Wood after dark.

In winter, it was often dark.

Trina shuddered once with the cold, then again, and rubbed her hands over her numb feet. She'd feel the sharp edge of Kalidah's tongue if she was discovered feeding precious logs to the flames, so she dared to shove only a handful of thin sticks onto the small pile of coals. With luck, she could replace them before the mage's sharp eyes noticed.

The bits of dry wood kindled quickly. The glow increased and grew to become a dancing blaze. The more she looked, the more the movement of the flames had form and rhythm. Looking *beyond* the heart of the fire, the way Kalidah had taught her to do with the scrying bowl, she let her mind ease into the cadence.

She began to sway with the rhythm she saw, and slowly the curtain of fire running along each stick resolved into small bodies. She could make out tiny arms and legs, swaying in a sinuous dance. A shiver ran through her, this time of surprise and not cold. The figures blurred into flames again as she sharpened her attention on them.

The fire was peopled with spirits? She had never heard of such a thing!

In wonder, Trina eyed the fire closely. It looked no different than it normally did. The jumble of sticks lay where she had placed them, with small flames licking at the bark. Beneath, the coals glowed red-hot on the scattered ashes. The fire looked exactly as it had on every other morning she could remember. Her years of working under Kalidah's direction had taught her to recognize the presence of magick, and she could not detect even a hint of it about the hearth.

The mage had never mentioned such beings, not even while conducting rituals involving fire. Was it possible she had somehow stumbled upon something beyond Kalidah's vast experience?

Trina could barely sit still. In her excitement, she wanted to rush to the cluttered worktable and sort through the forbidden scrolls to see if she could find any references to hearth spirits, but she didn't dare.

Kalidah's wrath at such impudence would make her anger over squandering firewood look like a summer squall compared to a tornado. Trina was not about to endanger herself, even for an explanation of this miracle. The bruises from her last beating had just recently faded, leaving behind only a little soreness.

The ancient mage slept in her cottage across the clearing. Her comings and goings were unpredictable. 'Twas far better for Trina to be found in a trance than buried up to her elbows in Kalidah's precious texts. Her mistress might subject her to something worse than a beating. She might cast a spell to remove Trina's ability to read. That did not bear thinking.

Still, she cast a longing glance at the worktable and its high hutch, crammed with scraps of knowledge in many foreign tongues. Sometimes, when she was certain that Kalidah would be gone for a long time, Trina would look through the scrolls, studying the ones she could read. Surely she had just a moment or two now, time for a quick peek at the oldest scrolls, those stuffed into the smallest cubbyhole.

As if sensing her intent, the raven shifted on his perch and glared at her. Several of the tiny animals that lived among the clutter in the hutch stirred and whispered a warning. The snake slid off her knee to resume its place coiled around the stones.

Just to see if she could see the tiny spirits again, Trina settled back again, tucking her feet against the faint warmth lingering in the hearthstones. She cleared her mind and looked into the fire once more.

A small curtain of flames still ran along the crumbling twigs. She feared they would be consumed before she found the figures again, so she pushed a few larger sticks in among them.

The bitter wind howling around the smoke hole in the thatched roof grew silent as she looked *beyond* the hearth. The whisper and shuffle of the menagerie quieted as Trina concentrated with her whole being on the leap and twist of the fire.

The tiny figures appeared again, resolving out of the flames. Fascinated, Trina examined them, making out amazingly delicate features as the shed around her faded away.

Then, in a heartbeat, she was *there*, among them, shuffling atop the charred stick. Her feet moved with an unheard beat that wrapped itself around her, throbbing in her bones. She floated in the welcome heat, feeling like nothing more substantial than shimmering air, so much lighter than her physical body.

No heavy wool, indeed no garments at all, stood between her skin and the fire's heat. For the first time in months, since the sun took its heat south for the winter, she was warm enough for comfort. As she moved atop the burning stick, the pain of her bare, cold feet eased and then vanished. Each breath of hot air warmed her inside. Eager to escape winter's hold, she inhaled deeply.

Blessed radiance! She spread her arms and raised them above her head, letting the heat soak into her. Her breasts swelled and her nipples blossomed in the welcome warmth. The spirits danced around her. Now that she saw them close at hand, she noticed some of the figures were slender and somehow softer than their companions, and decided that these must be the female flame-folk. She watched them closely and saw that they traced a different pattern in the dance. Gathering her courage, she began to emulate them, rather than the larger males. Before the flutters in her throat and her stomach became any worse, she dared to step out among them.

The fiery figures ebbed and flowed about her, giving her enough room to move but ignoring her, until one being, a slender and curvaceous one, reached out and touched her. She felt the searing heat, almost—but not quite—unbearable, as the fire-female trailed a white-hot finger down Trina's arm.

She was too afraid to shrink away, for she was in their territory now, in their world, and she knew nothing of what she was doing. Instinct warned her not to spurn them. When she didn't recoil despite the discomfort, others began brushing against her as they passed.

Each contact sent both heat and exquisite sensations shimmering through her, making her feel more alive than she ever had before. She threw herself into the dance. Sweat streamed down her bare skin. Her breath quickened and her heart beat faster. Her spirits lifted, and she began to move her feet more quickly, picking up the tempo of the flame-folk around her.

Their heated touches became part of the rhythm of the dance. She no longer noticed the discomfort. Heat from the fire seeped ever deeper into her and the delight sparked by each stroke grew. She had lived with Kalidah from a very young age and had not dreamed such comfort could come from a simple touch.

The ready acceptance of the flame-folk was a heady drug. When combined with the delightful heat of the fire, it became irresistible. She welcomed each caress, arching toward the dancers as they reached out to her.

One of the larger, sturdy beings burned more brightly than the rest. He drew her attention like a lodestone. She became vividly aware of him, aware of each movement he made. Although she watched the other flame-folk, she knew just where he stood in the pattern at every moment.

The first time the dance brought them together, he deliberately reached around her arm to run his hand up the curve of her belly. As they danced, he touched her more intimately, now stroking her thigh, now caressing the swell of her breast. A different heat blossomed deep within her wherever he touched. Greedy for that sensation, she leaned closer. He reached with both hands to cup her breasts, brushing his fingers across her nipples. First one, then the other. Need flourished under his attention. Trina leaned into him as her breasts swelled against his hands. She strained against the rhythm of the dance, seeking to close the gap between them. He held her off, forcing her to maintain the distance required by the pattern.

Her legs threatened to buckle beneath her. A new wetness grew, dampening the curls between her legs. Before the pattern of the dance took him away, he tweaked both her nipples at once, sending a jolt of molten fire racing through her. She had never experienced such pleasure. She had never even suspected such pleasure existed. Afraid to cease moving, not knowing what might happen, she forced her shaky knees to do her bidding, raised her arms into the form of the dance, and moved on.

As if following his lead, the other flame-folk became bolder, patting her where he had stroked, sparking faint echoes of his touch. The heaviness of her breasts increased. The need he'd kindled gathered there and pooled between her thighs. The touches of the others did not increase her excitement, but they kept it alive. Trina barely noticed them now, so intent was she upon him.

When they met again, she felt strung taut like a bow. Each step made her more aware of him. She could not have stopped moving if her life depended upon it. The tension building in her drove her, demanded she keep moving forward. She longed to see just where this carnal dance went. Instead of continually moving around the fire pit as the other dancers did, shifting in and out, he came to dance before her, facing her, keeping pace with her.

She relished the burn, stepping closer to touch his chest. A fever of passion blossomed in her hand, surging up her arm and down her spine. She shivered with delight, and he reached again to cup her breasts. She leaned forward, arching into his heat. Her nipples ached once more, but from growing passion this time and not the cold. There was nothing cold about this being. His gentle touch licked at her breasts, and she felt her whole body pulse with need.

She drew back a little, suddenly frightened of where she was and what lay ahead. This was not her world, this was not her place, and she was afraid of dying or being trapped here. The heat pressed close around her, stifling rather than invigorating.

His face resolved into distinct features, beneath wild hair that danced and flashed with a life of its own. His dark eyes twinkled. *Come. You have nothing to fear.* His invitation rang in her mind as he released her and held out his hand.

May the gods help her, she believed him. She clasped his hand, and together they stepped and swirled in a new dance, moving around the coals and leaping from stick to stick, following the rhythm set by the crackle and snap of the fire. He pulled her against him several times, when she would have careened into another dancer, and each time he curled his arm around her, she felt her heart swell a little. A sizzling tingle began amid the burn of his touch, where he held her hand and where he brushed against her in the dance.

To her eyes, he glowed ever more brightly. He seemed to smile at her, while the faces of the others were featureless, almost blank. She became aware that fewer dancers surrounded them now, as the sticks burned away to nothingness.

You dance the fire well, for a mortal. He spun away and immediately back, catching her in a complete embrace. *How much do you dare?*

Trina would trade anything and everything for this blissful heat. It had been too long a winter, with its endless winds and the icy stone floor under her thin pallet, for her not to take whatever chance she got for warmth.

She leaned against him in surrender. He accepted her yielding with a victorious smile before he brushed her lips with his.

It was her first kiss, over all too soon. He kissed her again, this time much more than a brush of his lips, a firm contact that fairly sizzled. She sighed, and with the exhalation, he entered her mouth, thrusting his tongue into her with an ardor she could not help but match.

Trina had seen village maidens kiss their lovers behind the market stalls and viewed the bedding of princesses in the scrying bowl, but never had she imagined the sensations that the touch of his lips brought. The heat of the fire around them paled in the face of his blazing kiss.

She shuddered at the inferno that raged through her, burning its way from her lips to her throat and straight to her belly. She melted under his onslaught, feeling the strength go out of her knees as he nibbled his way across her shoulder and down to her breast.

When he first licked the peak of her breast, she thought she might die from the wanting it sparked within her.

When he suckled her, drawing her nipple deeply into the heat of his mouth, she thought she would go mad. She felt it all the way to her core, a sharp urgent need that made itself felt in the parting of her legs, the clutch of her hands in his hair. She drew his heated kiss away from the hardened peak he'd been subjecting to such sweet torture and to her other, neglected nipple.

The door to the shed flew open. The intrusion jerked her out of the fire. She slammed back into her physical body so fast it hurt.

Kalidah breezed in on a drift of snow. She fetched up at the sight of Trina sprawled on the floor. "What are you doing?"

Trina shivered in the icy draft and stared up at her mistress. Clinging to the floor, trying to still the spinning of the shed around her, she was too shaken by the abrupt transition to utter a sound. Stringing words together into coherent speech was far beyond her.

"Tut-tut," the wizened old woman clucked and swept over to the worktable. "Shame on you for sleeping late, you lazy, worthless slave." She began to pull bottles and jars off the shelves. "Get moving! Hasten with the morning meal, Baraka."

Trina flinched at the hated, harsh name Kalidah insisted on calling her. *White One*, indeed. It always sounded to her ears like an old, sick man clearing his throat. She knew she was named Trina, had been so since before the mage bought her. Her name was the only certainty she had left of her early childhood, and what must have been her family.

As usual, Kalidah ignored her and rattled on. "We go to the village today. I must perfect this potion for Lady Nanon but I do not have everything I need. I will consult her. Come now, on your feet! Get moving."

Trina gathered her wits. Grateful that Kalidah had somehow misunderstood her confusion, she hastened to her feet and pulled her gown into some semblance of order. Her hands moved through the familiar motions of their own accord, for her thoughts still reeled from her experience in the fire.

Had she actually stood on the coals? Danced beside the flame-folk? Embraced one of them? As she moved past the hearth, Trina looked closely at the lingering coals but saw only a few small flames.

If the state of her body was any sign, she had indeed encountered the fire spirits in their own domain. Sweat still trickled down her back, making her linen shift cling to her skin. When she crossed the shed to begin preparing the porridge for breakfast, with each step she could feel the lingering wet heat between her legs. She reached up to lift the bowls down from the shelf, and her tender nipples rubbed along the inside of her rough woolen gown, right through the worn linen, sending a shaft of heat spiraling down to her belly.

Aye, she had danced in the realm of the fire spirits.

The cold reached beneath her skirt to chill the damp linen. Even though she added wood to the fire and leaned close to warm her hands at the growing blaze, still the iciness of the stone floor crept up her legs, chasing away the warmth.

In a daze, she went through the normal morning routine. Spoon up the porridge. Fetch Kalidah's jug of precious syrup and the horn spoons from the storeroom beyond the raven's perch.

Through it all, the fire's heat still burned in her mind. Even the mage's inhibiting presence could not blunt the feeling that every bit of her was more alive than it had been yesterday. She felt everything more keenly.

How could Kalidah not notice she had changed? Trina watched her mistress closely, glancing away only when the mage looked up from her porridge.

"You must have slept deeply, to be so quiet now. That is good. You need your rest." Kalidah poured more of the sweet syrup over her steaming oats. "Have you taken enough porridge for yourself, to keep you until the noon meal?"

Trina's head snapped up. She eyed her mistress with doubt. Mayhap she had heard amiss.

"You must keep your strength up, you know. I rely upon you to help me. Take another slice of bread. It is tasty this morn." The hag drew her lips back in a grimace that was the closest expression to a smile Trina had ever seen her make. Her hard eyes never wavered or softened.

When had her mistress grown concerned for her welfare? Kalidah generally treated her as an unwanted but necessary assistant, grudgingly teaching her what she needed to be of use, from reading the less-important scrolls to caring for the various animals. Never before could she recall the sorceress sparing a thought for her well-being.

Not one to pass up an opportunity, Trina grabbed a second slice of bread and wondered at Kalidah's odd behavior. Aye, she cooked and baked to meet their modest needs, but compliments did not often pass the sorceress' lips, and never in her direction.

The puzzle occupied her mind while she hitched the old sway-backed horse to the wagon. Kalidah climbed up beside her and took the reins. With awkward and uncharacteristic gentleness, the mage patted Trina's knee with a claw-like hand as she clucked the horse into motion.

Trina did not trust her mistress, not at all. She never had.

She trusted this new solicitude even less.

Chapter Two

ॐ

Trina glanced over her shoulder at the alley that led to the manor house. The trailing hem of Kalidah's best cloak twitched around the far corner and disappeared. She let out the breath she'd been holding and hefted the last box of supplies onto the wagon.

A small group of men burst through the tavern door as she tossed the rope across the load to secure it. Their voices filled the crisp afternoon air. She paused to watch them. A few of them she knew. Henri, the handsome miller. His timid little wife regularly came to the mage for amulets to protect herself from the jealousy of other women. Tam, the lord's arrogant guardsman. He was still unwed, despite having been the object of several women's love charms during the summer months. The other two men were strangers to her—a stocky man who emanated a dark aura, and a tall white-haired man with a strong but gentle demeanor. She turned back to her task when they looked her way.

The white-haired man stepped forward to take the rope from Trina's fingers. "Here, let me help you with that." His gentle voice held the singsong accent of the far north.

She shook her head without looking up, tore the rope away from him, and began tying a knot by the wagon's tailgate. Didn't he know what Kalidah would do to them both if she discovered him speaking with her?

She could take a beating, for she'd endured enough of them over the years, but he would pay far more. 'Twas possible Kalidah would blind him, or curse him. He'd come from the tavern. Being a stranger, he must not know of the black arts her mistress practiced, or he'd never have offered his assistance.

The old man's dark companion pulled him away, whispering in his ear. Trina heard the hiss of the words "slave," and "sorceress," and knew he spoke of her.

To her surprise, the white-haired man returned to her side. He did not reach for the rope again, but watched silently while she finished tying down the supplies. When she would have turned away from him, he gripped her shoulder firmly.

She tried to pull free, tasting panic in the back of her mouth. Didn't the fellow know she was the mage's property and had to be left alone? Kalidah had come across a group of children throwing rocks at her several years ago. Tight-lipped and stern, the hag had gone straight back to her workshed and conjured a plague. Several of the children died and others suffered heavy scarring from the pox that swept through the village the next day. What would Kalidah do if she found this man touching Trina?

More men filed out of the tavern to watch. They formed a half-circle around the back of the wagon.

"Please, sir, leave me alone," she whispered. "'Tis best."

Her plea had no effect. With relentless pressure, he forced her to face him. With one hand, he stopped her from fleeing while he tipped her chin up with the other.

He leaned in, thrusting his face close to hers in the growing darkness. She had never seen him before. His pale blue eyes were kind as they examined her from beneath his bushy white brows. He appeared older than she had first thought, with deep creases by his eyes and fine lines feathered across his cheeks. "You have the look of someone I once knew." He lifted a lock of her pale blonde hair and rubbed it between his fingers. "Where did she buy you?"

The question was sharp, and she spoke before she thought. "At an auction, in a large town. That's all I know."

"Do you remember your childhood?"

Afraid to admit that any memories remained, she shook her head. The scent of him was so hauntingly familiar she could not trust herself to speak. The mingled aromas of tobacco, beer and something else, something indefinable, brought buried memories to the surface, memories she would be better off without. She closed her eyes. For a moment she relived being gathered into a soft, caring embrace, hearing a musical voice soothe her child's fears.

He cleared his throat and she opened her eyes.

The men surrounding them shuffled their feet and began to mutter. She knew they were hoping for a confrontation between this tall stranger and the sorceress. Didn't he know Kalidah would come soon? Her frequent visits to the lord's household were never predictable. Sometimes she returned in mere minutes, although more often she spent hours at the manor house.

Trina opened her mouth to warn him, but he dropped his hands and stepped back. "We will speak again."

He disappeared into the bright warmth of the tavern. The men filed in after him. "Devil-spawn," one of them hissed. Before the door closed, he tossed a stone at her. She dodged it with ease.

Trina glanced with longing at the tavern. She had never set foot in such a place, had never even had a proper look inside, but the sounds and smells were too intriguing to ignore. Many of the villagers, women mingling with the men, spent their winter evenings there. Doing what? Men and women rarely worked together outside the fields. She tried to imagine hours without work, doing nothing but laughing or singing with friends and neighbors, and failed.

A glowing chink of an ill-fitting shutter on the tavern's side window caught her attention. 'Twas low enough for her to peer in, and might let her satisfy her curiosity.

She had just finished stacking the empty crates that had carried chickens to the village when the old sorceress came bustling out of the alley. No chance to sneak a look into the tavern on this trip. With a sigh, she resolved to examine the shutter on the next trip they made to the village. She pulled herself onto the wagon seat and steeled herself for the rattle and bump of the ride home.

A roughly-dressed peasant eased his way to the tavern, giving the two women and their wagon a wide berth. When he opened the door, he released a brief burst of light, laughter and raucous music from within.

Kalidah's voice sounded overloud in the following stillness. "No one gave you any trouble, did they?" The mage's tongue formed the soft, rounded speech of the south. The hard sound of magickal authority.

Trina responded truthfully, for she could do nothing else when her mistress commanded. "No."

The wagon bounced along the path through the barren forest. Under the wheels, ice and dead leaves crackled. Trina pulled her thin cloak more tightly around her and shivered. The lowering sky promised more snow by morning.

Beside her, the mage sat erect and stiff. She stared ahead with her fierce dark eyes into the growing darkness. "We must get home quickly, my child. We have much to prepare before my lady's visit tomorrow."

Trina hoped the preparations involved heat. Perhaps a boiling cauldron, to warm the workshed. She sighed at the thought of clouds of fragrant steam rising from the huge pot, warming her insides completely when she inhaled its vapor.

For the first time, she wondered what the lady had said in her audience with the mage. Kalidah had not stayed long at the manor. That was odd, for often Trina waited for hours in the dark, huddled against the old horse, while her mistress consulted her patron.

Never before had the lady visited the clearing in the forest.

Trina had forgotten that a boiling cauldron meant she must haul the water to fill it. She had just hefted another full bucket to the rim of the well when a familiar figure stepped out of the snow-draped forest by the mage's cottage, into the clearing. She grabbed the bucket and almost ran into the workshed, slopping icy water over her bare feet.

"What is the trouble with you? You're making a mess." Kalidah exclaimed in alarm as Trina crossed the threshold, brandishing her broom in reproof even before Trina spilled any water on the stone floor.

"Fletcher."

Kalidah nodded and her face wrinkled up in pleasure. "Wonderful! His mistress cannot be far behind. I am pleased that you will finally meet my patroness." She set the broom aside and gave Trina's shoulder an awkward pat on her way to welcome the lady's messenger.

Fletcher's appearance didn't warrant a smile, and Trina wondered how a slave's welfare could possibly be more important than the arrival of the lady's man. In her distrust of Kalidah's change of heart toward her, she decided it would be best to avoid attention and keep out of sight.

Trina set the bucket where Kalidah could reach it while she worked, and crept back under her table to where the huge snake lay coiled. Pulling the thin blanket over both of them despite the heat of the fire, she willed herself to disappear. Unfortunately, she hadn't gotten that far in her clandestine studies.

Fletcher had cold, flat eyes and the way he looked at Trina made her skin crawl. He didn't come often, but when he did, he stayed, sometimes for days. Kalidah spent that time redoubling her efforts to perfect one particular spell. The old mage had many scrolls and sheaves of notes bearing spells, but this one she'd been working on as long as Trina could remember.

Kalidah conducted a woman across the threshold in front of her. "Lady Nanon, may I present my assistant and companion, Baraka of the North." She paused to glance around the room. "Baraka!" she barked. "Come and meet our esteemed guest, the Lady Nanon!"

Trina eased herself out from under the table, shaking the wrinkles out of her simple gown as she stood. After one look at Lady Nanon's finery, she pulled the hem of her skirt down as far as she could, to hide her bare feet. Her dirt-rimmed toenails still showed.

The woman stood no taller than Kalidah, and they were both a head shorter than Trina. Golden embroidery weighed down the soft red wool of Lady Nanon's gown. Her darker undergown, visible at wrists and neck, glowed with the deep tones of fine silk. Brilliant stones flashed at her hem, where the toes of her jeweled slippers peeped out.

Trina looked beyond the garments, and her breath caught in her throat. This was no young beauty, no noble lass come seeking a love potion or a spell to quell a rival's attentions to her beloved. Beneath the wealth and glitter, Lady Nanon was just as old and as wrinkled as Kalidah herself.

"You are every bit as beautiful as my Fletcher has reported." Lady Nanon stepped forward and picked up a strand of Trina's hair with a hand weighted down with sparkling rings. "Such a lovely pale yellow. Almost white! So unusual, and so fitting."

She touched a cold finger to Trina's cheek and drew a trail of ice down to her jaw. Trina fought the urge to shrink away and tried not to breathe in the sour smells of old age and rotting teeth. Lady Nanon's finery could not conceal her failing health. "Your skin is so fair and unblemished. You are wise to hide it from the sun." Grasping Trina's jaw in a firm grip that took her by surprise, she turned Trina to face the fire.

Lady Nanon scrutinized Trina with hard eyes much like Fletcher's. Pulling back, she snapped, "Her eyes are blue! I thought you said she had green eyes."

Kalidah surprised Trina by adopting an almost obsequious tone. "I assure you, it doesn't matter. Her fairness is the most important thing. She will do nicely."

Lady Nanon stared at Kalidah. "You are certain there is nothing about this affair that will offend the Goddess? My son's alliances will do him no good without Her blessing."

"I assure you, there will be nothing for you to regret." Kalidah's eyes shifted and Trina knew her mistress lied. "All will be as we have planned."

Lady Nanon narrowed her eyes and considered this for a moment. "Then you may have it. We will proceed." She produced a bit of linen. Holding it in one hand, she carefully unwrapped the folds to reveal a torn portion of aged parchment.

Kalidah lifted it with reverence. Barely breathing, she held it close to the lantern on her workbench.

After a moment, she frowned. "'Tis only a fragment, just the portion we need today."

The sorceress fingered a corner and her frown deepened. "A copy as well, not much older than your son." She turned to face her patroness and Trina wondered just who served whom. She thought she glimpsed fear in the mage's dark eyes. "The master will be sorely disappointed. I do not wish to face him on the morrow and report your failure. He must have it complete, and the original. This bit is useful, but the whole is required for the ultimate goal to be achieved."

She held it backward to the lantern and squinted at it. Referring to the parchment several times, she made some scribbles on a scrap of vellum before placing those notations on top of the piece Lady Nanon had brought, and tracing a design from it.

Trina wondered at her actions, since she had never seen her mistress use such a technique. Some of Kalidah's important correspondence came written in code. Could it be a cipher, a means of concealing the document's nature should it fall into the wrong hands? This must be a very important element of the spell. She shivered and wondered just what Lady Nanon had done to acquire the little piece of writing.

Kalidah finished her drawing and set it aside. Holding the piece Lady Nanon had brought, she turned to face the lady. "'Tis odd that the part we need to aid your son is the only one you find. Have you discovered the rest of this?"

"My men have been told to locate it. I thought this was what you would need, so I saw no reason to delay. When the rest arrives, you shall have it."

Lady Nanon waved a hand in dismissal before she drew a heavy glass vial from the gold-embroidered pouch at her waist and set it on the workbench. It looked to Trina as though the vial contained some kind of living vapor, a mist that writhed within it.

Kalidah snatched it up and examined it closely, before tucking it into her bodice. All traces of deference disappeared. Pulling a chair closer to the fire, she ordered Trina, "See to Lady Nanon's horse, and then bring refreshments for our guests, and be quick about it. Bring the old bottle, the one with the red cord about its neck. We will toast our coming success."

Caring for the horse took Trina very little time. Once it was tucked into the shed with the mage's old horse and mule, she hung a bucket of feed within its reach and threw a spare blanket over its back. She paused to admire the fine lines of the gelding, running her hands over its nose, placating the old workhorse with a similar caress and lingering in the beasts' warmth. All too soon, she was back in the workshed, uncomfortable under the hard-eyed scrutiny of both Fletcher and his mistress.

"That was quick," Lady Nanon said, nodding her approval. "You are fortunate to have found so biddable a slave, Kalidah."

"She is the right one for us. I knew it as soon as I saw her, and so she has proven as she's grown." The mage's lips stretched once more in that grimace meant to be a smile.

Trina shuddered and went about her task of bringing refreshment. This whole visit unsettled her, and the mage's words, following on the heels of her lies to the lady, made the hair on the back of her neck rise. She wanted Lady Nanon and her man on their way back to the manor as soon as possible.

With an ease born of long practice, Trina ducked to avoid the raven as she pulled aside the shabby curtain and entered the storeroom. Catching up two of the finer cups and the dusty bottle of wine, she returned to hear the mage say, "After all this time, you have found it! Each time Fletcher arrives, I hope it is with this news. When you told me yesterday, I knew our time had come!"

Kalidah and Lady Nanon exchanged unpleasant, snaggle-toothed grins.

"I shall have to test the final spell and then we may begin. It will take but a moment, my lady." The mage took the wine bottle in an expert grip and opened it with a deft flick of her wrist. Fletcher ducked to avoid the cork as it sailed across the room to fall into a basket. Kalidah picked through the items on her workbench and extracted two pottery mugs. "Refresh yourself, Lady Nanon, and then I will require both of our servants' assistance in our endeavor. Master Fletcher, Baraka, you must also drink."

Stunned, Trina could only take the cracked mug when the mage handed it to her. She had never been asked to eat or drink with Kalidah's rare guests. Indeed, guests were not entertained in the rough hospitality of the workshed, but across the clearing in Kalidah's cottage. Her inclusion this time further raised her suspicions.

The mage turned away and bustled around the workbench, leaving her guests to stare at Trina. She squirmed in discomfort.

Fletcher's hungry eyes were unnerving. He looked as if he'd like to throw her on the table and feast on her. She glanced at Lady Nanon, whose bright gaze seemed to echo that intent. What was happening? Growing more uncomfortable by the moment, Trina turned her attention to her mistress's actions.

Kalidah pulled a large, bound book from a shelf and consulted it. She mixed a few pinches of this and a drop of that in a mortar, muttered something under her breath and sniffed the resulting mixture.

When the mage added a few herbs and ground them together, with her attention solely on her task, Trina began to relax. She decided it was Fletcher's presence that worried her, and the unexpected activity.

The only villagers who ventured forth to Kalidah's cottage were those seeking simples for bringing down a child's fever or a decoction for regaining a lover's regard. Summer brought more visitors than winter, when the rough track from the village discouraged all but the most determined.

Lady Nanon and Kalidah were probably bent on nothing more threatening or unusual than a magickal salve to restore youth to their complexions. They both certainly could benefit from one.

"Drink up, my dear. Don't you wish for success today?" Lady Nanon asked in a falsely sweet voice. Trina realized everyone else had sipped their wine but her. Kalidah glanced her way and lifted a brow. Afraid not to, Trina raised the mug and drank.

The wine swirled bitterly across her tongue and burned the back of her throat. She could detect the tang of magick, but there was something else, something darker and more sinister than anything she had encountered before. The liquid thickened in her throat, coating her mouth in a fashion she disliked.

The thought of having swallowed something living sprang into her mind. She worked her throat, trying to gather whatever it was to spit it out, and failed. She swallowed again, to clear her mouth. The unpleasant fullness spread down, into her belly.

Trina glanced up, past the rim of her mug, right at Fletcher. He smiled at her over his drink, a lazy smirk that didn't reach his eyes. Her heart skipped a beat, then pounded with alarm.

She squeezed her eyes shut and tried to think. The wine clouded her mind, and she struggled against its effects. She gave up, and looked to Kalidah for guidance.

The look on her mistress's face told her more than she wanted to know. She began to set the cup down and the mage moved her hand so quickly Trina couldn't follow the gesture. Despite her best efforts not to, she raised the mug and drained it in two gulps. The thick, closed sensation persisted in her throat. An unpleasant heaviness grew within her.

"I'm afraid my assistant will not be a willing participant in this ritual." Regret rang in Kalidah's voice as she set her cup aside and pulled forth a handful of herbs.

Trina watched the familiar pattern of the most common binding spell, and felt her will weaken. Several other spells followed in quick succession and her limbs stiffened, no longer under her command.

She tried to speak and could not. The wine burned in her belly, sending an uncomfortable warmth through her, heating her flesh from the inside out.

"She's a beauty, and of an age when she should have married, if not taken a lover. Are you sure she's pure?" Lady Nanon sipped her wine and smiled, swirling it around in her mouth before she swallowed.

"Aye, I've seen to that. She has no inclination to stray, not bound as she is by the spell that suppresses her desires. To be doubly sure, she's rarely been out of my sight since she came to me as a child."

Lady Nanon raised her cup in a toast. "I salute your foresight."

"I would not jeopardize centuries of work by gambling on such an important ingredient."

Trina strained against the spells that held her, trying to recall a counterspell that might free her. The wine fogged her brain, either that or Kalidah had taken the precaution of dulling her mind with one of the spells. The incantations had come so fast she couldn't keep track of exactly what the mage had done.

Such an important ingredient. What did Kalidah need her to do?

What did Kalidah and Lady Nanon plan?

What kind of ritual *was* this?

Helpless and mute, Trina watched as Kalidah readied the workbench, clearing another space and selecting jars and bottles from those filling the shelves. The creatures who lived there rustled and twittered softly as they retreated out of her way. Trina sorely wished she could do the same.

The mage directed Fletcher to move the table to the far wall and he did so, kicking aside the blankets that formed Trina's sleeping pallet. The snake slithered off to safety behind a pile of baskets. Fletcher didn't look at her as he passed close enough for her to smell wood smoke in his hair and the wine he'd drunk.

Behind her, Fletcher yelped and cursed, and Trina knew he'd stepped too close to the raven. She experienced a small amount of satisfaction. He dragged the smallest brazier into the center of the room, beside the hearth. When he straightened, he was wiping a trickle of blood from his forehead and swearing under his breath.

Kalidah shoveled some coals from the fire into the brazier and added several bundles of faggots. The dry wood quickly caught, flaring up briefly before subsiding to low flames. "You must stay on the outside, my lady, and you inside, Fletcher. Once I close the circles, under no circumstances must either be broken."

She stepped into the cleared space with a sheaf of dried herbs and a small leather bag in her hands. After dribbling flour and fragrant herbs from the bag in a wide circle with the brazier in the center, she dropped the sheaf and Lady Nanon's vial onto the coals. A smoky fire flared, and she quickly stepped back, muttering a spell in a tongue unfamiliar to Trina as she drew a smaller circle and sealed it, with only the brazier standing within. The mage, Trina and Fletcher stood within the outer circle.

Thick dark smoke, heavy-laden with the herbs, filled the room. The vial shattered with a flash of pure green light. A brisk wind began howling around the outer circle.

Kalidah ignored it, invoking various protections as she continued to pour her herbed flour from the bag into arcane patterns across the stone floor. The smoke acquired a greenish tinge and gathered in a cloud above the brazier, within the confines of the inner circle.

Straightening to her full height, the sorceress spread her arms above her head. Her wide sleeves fell back almost to her shoulders, revealing skinny arms and knobby elbows. Her ridiculous appearance should have made her look foolish, but a silver cloud gathered around her head and she acquired a powerful dignity as she swayed and chanted. The first words were unintelligible to Trina, in what she thought might be Kalidah's native tongue, but the rest she understood.

Spirit of flame, forged in fire,
Demon's shape fulfill.
Your true Name binds you to my hand,
Bend now to my will.

As the squirrel and ant labor
Gath'ring nut and date,
So shall wise Lord Roland toil
Furth'ring his estate.

As the web threads of the spider
Find and bind its prey,
His minions will seek out and kill
Those who bar his way.

All his demands those who serve him

Quickly execute.
Success and wealth, long life and health
Shall be Roland's fruit.

I wield the Power to bind you fast,
You must work for me.
In blood and fire I seal the deed,
Her life is your fee.

Trina's blood drummed in her ears and she almost fainted. She was to be a sacrifice! Panicked, straining against the invisible bonds that held her, she found she still couldn't move. The thought of her peril filled her mind until she couldn't think at all, let alone of anything that might save her.

A roar came from the fire. Since she was facing that way, Trina couldn't help but watch as the others turned to stare at the apparition that rose out of the flames.

A giant fiery head hovered above the brazier. Bushy brows of flame danced above gaping holes of darkness that formed eyes and an open, raging mouth. The demon pulsed this way and that, testing the limits of the circle that held it. The fiend's fury roared through the room again, in syllables that held no meaning for Trina.

She was the only one who didn't shrink back before the vocal assault, and she wanted to, quite badly. The spells that bound her prevented her from moving a muscle.

Kalidah recovered first, standing up to her full height, safely outside the inner barrier. From Trina's vantage point, it was like watching a mousling face down a giant cat.

"You must do my bidding before I release you," Kalidah shouted, adding a few words again in a strange language. She waved her skinny arms about defiantly.

The spirit roared again. The force of his words blew the mage's hood back, revealing a few strands of white hair plastered flat across her scalp.

"Aieeeeee!" Kalidah screeched her fury, and gestured more wildly than before.

The demon's shrieks dwindled to an occasional moan, although his features remained forbidding.

"We must act quickly. He is strong, and I do not care to test his patience."

Kalidah stepped carefully around the boundary, lifting her hem up to keep from disturbing the flour designs. She handed a large basin to Fletcher, who cast one nervous glance at his mistress outside the protective barrier before taking it. The mage gathered up a thin, double-edged knife and the mixture she'd prepared earlier.

Under her direction, Fletcher set the basin in front of Trina and stepped back. He looked her over greedily, his hands twitching at his side, until the mage waved him away. Kalidah mumbled a few words over the knife before she used it to cut away Trina's dress and thin shift, gathering the rags and carefully laying them out of the way. Again, she took care not to disturb her arcane marks on the stone floor.

The cool air feathered goose bumps across Trina's exposed breasts and belly. She couldn't close her eyes. She could only watch in horror.

Kalidah said a few words in another tongue and Trina's mouth opened. The mage took a fingerful of the herb mixture and smeared it inside Trina's cheeks. Kalidah gestured, and Trina swallowed.

Fueled by the herb mixture, the wine heated her blood once more. Fire spread through her veins, burning its way to her breasts and her thighs, pooling into a hot and urgent need. She tried to shift her legs and felt the moisture flow as she struggled to move, to no avail.

Unlike the desire she'd experienced in the fire, this burned with an uncomfortable edge, a fierce thorn that pricked her from within. She longed to spread her thighs to ease it, to massage the ache away from her engorged breasts. The need roaring through her was tenfold, nay, a hundredfold stronger than her response to the fire spirit's heated kiss.

Fletcher made a questioning sound.

"That begins to release her from the spell that has held her desires at bay for all these years. With the magick in the wine, she will be more than ready to aid me."

Over the mage's shoulder, Trina saw Fletcher stare and lick his lips. He took a step toward her, craning his neck to see past the mage. His pupils had dilated. She could sense the magick of the wine pulsing in him.

Kalidah did not turn, but ordered him, "Enough! Do not rush. There is time for looking later, when your turn comes."

Using the very tip of the knife, she sketched a line from Trina's throat down the center of her chest. Warmth trickled in its wake, and Trina knew the mage was drawing magickal symbols in blood. She tried to concentrate, to decipher the pattern, but could not maintain her attention on Kalidah's motions.

As the mage worked, desire surged free, buffeting Trina with its needs. She simply had to slake the raging hunger coursing through her. Her chest burned with it, her nipples fiery points of mingled pain and pleasure. Her breath came faster. More moisture gathered between her thighs, enough to trickle through the hair and run down her leg.

Pain grew from the designs, focusing her attention away from the growing hunger. She could almost envision the pattern, was on the edge of understanding, when Kalidah set the knife down and began rubbing the herbal mixture into the cuts. Numbness set in under her gnarled fingers, followed by a renewed glow of pain and heat. One knuckle brushed a nipple and red-hot sensation knifed through her. Trina lost track of the pattern in the flash of pleasure, and inwardly groaned.

The demon in the brazier turned to her, its gaping eyes reflecting a need that matched her own. Flames licked at the confines of the inner circle, probing, seeking a way out. She felt the demon's attention shift to the mage, its fury palpable in the closeness of the shed.

I want her.

The thought rang in Trina's head, although no words were spoken.

Kalidah spoke without turning. "She's not for you. Not now."

I will be first.

"No, my lord demon, you will not. Her life is yours. Her virgin's blood is mine."

Trina's knees would have trembled, if she could have moved.

The fire rose again, threatening the thatched roof. Kalidah gestured and it flared once more before sinking again to simmer along the top of the brazier.

"Fletcher, it is time. You may have her. Be sure the first blood flows into the basin."

Trina steeled herself for his unwelcome touch and found her traitorous body, in thrall to the wine, the herbs and the magick, pulsing with anticipation. May the Goddess help her, she wanted his hands on her breasts, his mouth on hers. She wanted him to spread her legs and plunge his hard shaft into her. Anything to satisfy this gnawing, painful hunger.

In Fletcher's haste to get past the mage and reach her, his foot caught in Trina's cast-off garments and he stumbled. He flailed his arms, reaching outside the circle to grab first at the table to regain his balance, then at a chair. He finally seized a walking staff that leaned against the wall.

He fell anyway, dragging the staff across the outer circle. The tip crashed to the floor. It broke the inner ring of flour.

The demon rushed from the brazier in a gout of fire, engulfing the helpless Fletcher. He burst into flame with a hideous cry. Collapsing to his knees, he writhed and obliterated more of the protective symbols and the circle containing the demon.

The inferno grew. Kalidah stood in the center of the maelstrom, chanting in a language unfamiliar to Trina. The old woman's hands flew, tracing sigils and commands.

A clear area formed about her, the fire licking and testing the boundaries. She redoubled her efforts, reciting spells in an unintelligible rush of syllables. The fire retreated before her efforts, but not without a struggle. The mage took a step back to avoid the demon's advance before she gained a measure of control.

Finally the flames withdrew, almost to the confines of the brazier itself. The mage breathed deeply, a grim smile contorting her features. Lady Nanon shifted closer. Kalidah waved her off.

"This demon is strong, and may be gathering himself for another attack."

No sooner had she spoken than the flames again rushed in her direction, taking the shape of a giant hand. Once more she threw magick in its way.

The hand skipped aside to wrap fiery fingers around Lady Nanon, setting her aflame as it had her manservant. Lady Nanon did not succumb as easily. She raged and fought the grip of the flames, uttering her own spells.

Her limited Power failed at the task. Her rich garments burned as quickly as Fletcher's livery. At the end, she stumbled toward Kalidah, who backed into the worktable and could recoil no further.

Confined and cornered, the mage was unable to make full use of her abilities. Trina held her breath as Kalidah gathered her Power, the glowing orb of it visible in the smoke that filled the shed. She was torn between her desire to be free of Kalidah's service and dread at what the demon would do to her should the sorceress lose the struggle. Would she burst into flames and be consumed? In this magickal battle of wills, so far the mage had proven to be weaker than the demon she had summoned. Trina feared that, no matter the outcome, she was bound to die.

Flames fed on the ancient parchment and vellum scattered on the worktable, running from item to item until Kalidah was ringed by her enemy. Her voice grew weaker along with the glow that surrounded her. The fire arched over her head and stole the breath from her lungs. The glow subsided until the fire overwhelmed it, quickly creeping up from the hem of her robe to engulf her fully.

Trina knew the moment her mistress died. The raven screeched and flew out the window. The owl followed on silent wings. Freed of their bonds by Kalidah's death, the birds were only the first. Trina found herself able to move but penned in by a furred and feathered tide that flowed off the shelves and out of the shed to safety.

When she turned to flee, she discovered the entire hut ablaze. The roaring flames fed on old parchment and dried herbs. Chairs and tables and shelves were consumed. Even the flour patterns on the floor burned.

Barefoot and naked, spurred by fear, Trina hastily picked her way across the shed, trying to avoid stepping on anything burning. The tail of the old snake slithered over the threshold in front of her.

The lintel fell as she reached it, knocking her back into the conflagration. The last thing she knew was the white-hot embrace of the flames.

Chapter Three

❧

She came to her senses lying in the sunshine by the well.

A cloud of thick smoke wafted over the clearing from the charred ruins of the shed. She tried to sit up and could not.

Her head spun and her skin burned. An attempt to breathe deeply made her cough.

"Wait. You must rest." The deep voice rumbled against her ear and she realized she lay cradled in a warm embrace.

Naked.

She was *naked*.

Her skin burned at the contact with his. On the heels of her realization came the heated tingle of wine and magick, sizzling through her where she touched him. She stirred, resisting the urge to move closer.

They were *both* naked.

He leaned over her. It wasn't Fletcher, or anyone she'd ever seen.

His hair and thick beard were red-gold, the color of flame. His eyes glowed like the most prized dark amber. Brown freckles sprinkled across his ruddy skin, right down to where she lay against him, the milky white of her arm a stark contrast.

After the fire in the shed, her skin should be reddened and blistered.

She should be dead.

"You are well. The others are dead." 'Twas as if he read her mind. He lifted a hand to turn her face to his, rubbing his thumb across her lips. The wine burned in her breasts and belly, fanning the magick back to life where he touched.

Trina tried to speak and found her tongue thick from the wine, the herbs and the smoke. She swallowed and tried again, finally croaking out, "They would have killed me."

"I know. Fortunately, the clumsy one freed me."

Fear surged through the desire, clearing her head. She clawed at his hand to free herself, ready to flee. "You are the demon?" How else could he know what had occurred in those last seconds before the fire?

He grinned and winked at her. "Aye, I am, when foolish mortals Call me to be. When they dare."

Her breath caught in her throat. His words echoed those of the fire spirit in the dance. She could not help the shiver that ran through her.

He ran his finger down her skin and she knew him. There was no mistaking his touch.

Her fire-dancer, the demon and this man were one and the same.

This made no sense. The sun picked out golden highlights in his hair and cast his eyes in shadow. Intelligence shone in those eyes, and kindness. His flesh felt real beneath her hand, albeit a bit warmer than she expected. Her dancing in the flames in spirit form was one thing, but to have a spirit take mortal form, become solid flesh and blood, was something else again.

She swallowed hard before she could speak. "Then what are you now?"

"I am not certain. I have never before taken this form. It is…different." He frowned and rubbed his thumb across her lips again, sparking desire within her. "It is unusual, this urge I have."

Urge. She too felt an urge, born of Kalidah's meddling. What urges might a demon have? The image of the bundle of herbs Kalidah had dropped onto the brazier rose in her mind. She'd wager the misty vial had held some magick in its green vapor as well. After the magickal rite Kalidah conducted, their urges might be born of the same source. She summoned her courage and asked, "An urge to do what?"

"This." He bent his head and kissed her.

She surged up into him, opening her mouth for his questing tongue, meeting him halfway, twining hers with his as molten desire thrummed in her veins.

He broke the kiss to trail his mouth across her face to her ear. He licked the skin there, then breathed softly, and she discovered another new sensation. Wonder of wonders, she felt a dampness between her legs and an urge to thrust her hips against him. Surely this was evidence of his magick, his Power as a fire demon. The effort of holding still made her tremble. Her response seemed to entice him, for he repeated his actions, slowly moving down her neck and across her chest. The heat of his tongue, followed by the coolness of his soft exhalations, made her nipples pucker in anticipation and focused her attention on where his mouth caressed her. By all the gods, she had never experienced anything like this. He lifted his head and she held her breath. What enchantments would he show her next?

The sparks of excitement that kindled as he progressed were overpowered by a blaze of delight when he captured her breast. Teasing the tight peak with his tongue, he wrung a sigh from her. He suckled and she sighed again, followed by a gasp of pleasure as he nipped at the tender flesh with his teeth. His hand sought her other breast, stroking and stoking the hunger sparked by the wine.

She stretched against him, reveling in the feel of his heated skin against hers. Lingering fear nibbled at her and she thrust it resolutely aside. He might yet kill her as he had the others, but she wouldn't die without taking what pleasure she could.

He growled low in his throat. Something in her responded to that sound, filled with mastery, laying his claim to her. She wanted him to possess her, the magick wine and the herbs demanded from her no less than complete capitulation. She loosened her grip, relaxing into his embrace. He moved up to nuzzle the sensitive skin of her neck and gently pulled her hair with his teeth, sending a tingle sizzling through her.

The final remnants of the binding spell ripped away, releasing years of pent-up desire held at bay by the mage's will. A flood of yearning filled her. Her years with Kalidah had been bereft of physical contact. With his touch, her fire spirit offered her the comfort she only now realized she craved.

She wanted to fling wide her legs and engulf him with her body. She wanted to embrace him so hard he melted into her and they became one. Trina gasped at the force of unaccustomed emotions and sensations coursing through her.

"Have I hurt you?" He pulled away, concern for her showing in a small frown.

All remaining fear fled. She would live, and enjoy whatever pleasure he might give her. "Nay, you have set me free!" She took his face in her hands, drew him back and pressed her lips to his. He responded by picking her up and carrying her across the yard, into Kalidah's cottage. They found the feather bed in the back alcove, sinking together into such softness as she'd never known.

He knelt between her knees, holding her hands away from her sides, and looked his fill. She was beyond beautiful, this young mortal who dared to dance the fire. She gazed trustingly up at him, her blue eyes glazed with passion.

Running a hand down her arm, he marveled at the paleness of her hair and the perfection of her ivory skin, now marred only by a tracery of thin dark lines where the black mage had cut her evil signs. He let go of her hands to trace the main pattern across the center of her chest. Fury burned within him, anger that such an innocent should fall into the hands of one so foul.

She reached for him, and anger was quickly replaced by desire. The suddenness and intensity of his feelings took him aback. How did mortals tolerate these surges of conflicting emotions? That was his last coherent thought, before passion eclipsed all else.

He could feel her need and he could feel the magick she'd swallowed clamoring for release. The herbs the old mage had fed to his flames pulsed in answer, and once again he felt the urgent need take hold of him. It thrummed through him, until every fiber of his being focussed on one goal.

He must possess her.

Reaching forth, he gathered her breasts in his hands. Was he mistaken, or were they a bit larger and firmer than before? She arched against his grasp, pressing against him as he massaged her softness. The heady scent of her, the silken slide of her skin against his, enticed him. When he squeezed her nipples gently between his fingers, she whimpered and writhed beneath his touch. He liked the sounds she made and the way she felt when she moved against him, so he did it again, and again.

His mortal body amazed him. He had never experienced such exquisite torture as he did now, viewing her welcoming body stretched out, inviting his explorations. She spread her legs, revealing a cluster of pale curls. He bent his head to inhale the musk of her desire and his cock hardened in response. There was no question what she wanted, and what he would do.

Magick could not be denied.

The herbs and magick drove him, roaring through him until his head swam with their combined force. Blindly, he lifted her hips and surged forward into her, bursting past the fragile barrier of her maidenhead to impale himself fully inside her. The sensation of being buried within her tight channel almost overwhelmed him. This was precisely what he needed, where he was meant to be.

She cried out, pulling back, and his vision cleared. He sensed a distancing on her part as her pain overrode the effect of the wine. She stilled for only a moment before she wrapped her legs around his waist, drawing him even deeper into her. He followed the movement, leaning down to kiss the taut tip of one breast while his hand found the other peak.

He sucked and nibbled on one nipple and let his fingertips strum and rub and pinch the other. Both tightened to hard little nubs beneath his attentions. The globes of her breasts grew heavier as he tongued and tasted her.

An irresistible aroma of woman mingled with magick and passion grew and surrounded them, filling his head and fueling his ardor. Small sounds filled the room, the slap of his ballocks and the wet murmur of her cleft as he drove home. She moaned and moved beneath him, twisting up into him. He continued to possess her as the magick urged him, with his hands, his mouth and his cock.

She felt heavenly beneath and around him. He could not have stopped for anything and so he continued driving into her tight passage. She clenched around him like a hot glove, welcoming his cock with each plunge of his hips and squeezing as he withdrew. His toes curled with the force of his passion. Sparks glinted in his vision.

Trina clutched at his head, pulling his mouth back to her breast. He obliged her, nipping and tonguing the taut peak until the magick engulfed her again, this time sweeping him along with her. He roared as she contracted around his cock, sheathing him in ecstasy, until the power of his climax robbed him of sense. He collapsed next to her as everything went black.

* * * * *

Dawn tinted the morning sky with faint light, sparking early birdsong. Trina stirred and snuggled into the softness, pulling the heavy covers over her. The warmth felt wonderful. So did the tingle she felt in her left breast, much like the touch of the fire spirit when she'd danced on the coals. The events of the day before came back to her.

The covers shifted, and she realized it was *exactly* like the touch of the fire spirit. She rolled over, and found herself face to face with her savior from the fire.

"Good morrow, my sweet beauty." He smiled and something within her stirred. Not like the magick, but not unlike the heat of the wine.

He pulled away and stood, sweeping the covers off her with one deft motion. She began to follow but he waved her back. "I must be sure you have fully recovered from yesterday's ordeal."

She tried to cross her arms once, but he impatiently pushed them aside to examine her chest. With great effort, she lay still under his scrutiny.

He traced a pattern lightly across her breastbone and around each nipple. Her skin contracted and chilled in the wake of his fingers. "I fear these marks are permanent. You must never become entangled with another sorcerer, for you already bear half the spell needed for the mage's foul ritual. You will not survive another such ceremony." He regarded her gravely. "I have not saved you forever. Whether you are a virgin will be of no matter, now that you bear these marks."

He stopped touching her, and she almost begged him to continue. When he stood and left her, crossing the cottage to open a large wooden chest and sort through it, she felt bereft and opened her mouth to call him back.

For what? She could hardly say, *I need you to touch me and comfort me, for no one else knows or cares that I'm alive.*

For all she knew, he didn't care. He was a fire spirit, after all. What made her think he might have any tender feelings for her, a mortal?

Before she could decide whether she should speak, he returned with a cup and a cloth. With scant regard for her ability to move herself, he arranged her with her feet on the floor and her hips almost hanging off the bed. She flinched as her pubic hairs stuck together and pulled as he parted her legs. He began to wipe her clean with warm water.

The sting of the pulled hairs disappeared. Comforting warmth spread with the pressure of the cloth. Trina leaned back into the softness of the mage's feather bed. "Mmmmm. That feels good."

"I thought it might. One of the mage's spells made you bleed more heavily than you would have otherwise. Her rite required a full ladle of virgin's blood."

He had to care, she decided. He might cleanse her even if he had few feelings for her, but she doubted he would consider that she might enjoy the sensation. The gentleness of his touch bolstered her belief.

He wiped away the last of the blood and the remnants of his seed. The sight of her, spread before him, brought back echoes of the sensations he'd felt while buried inside her. She'd been so tight and hot around him. Nothing in his vast experience could rival that feeling for intensity and wonder. His cock jerked and stiffened at the mere thought. He took pleasure in the unusual sensation. He had always thought mortals to be fleeting and insubstantial beings, incapable of standing against his spirit's strength. Now that he had taken their form, felt the frame of solid muscle and bone encasing him, he wasn't so sure.

He took a deep breath and blew it out in a sigh. The simple act of filling his lungs stunned him. Odors wrapped themselves around him. He could smell the lingering smoke from the fire, cheese stored somewhere in the cottage, the bundles of herbs hanging overhead, the male tang of himself and overlaying it all, the wonderful, alluring female spread before him. The heavenly perfume of her cleft rose to tease him and he inhaled deeply.

Gods, but she smelled good enough to eat. He pushed aside the growing need he felt to bury himself in her. He knew how delightful that was. Other sensations, other experiences beckoned.

Bending down, he parted her soft curls with his tongue. Her outer lips swelled under his breath. She spread her legs further and lifted her hips in invitation. The petals of her inner lips unfurled before him, releasing a slightly different perfume. One more deep breath, and his surroundings ceased to exist. He smelled nothing but her lusty fragrance. Closing his eyes, he could detect several different layers to her scent. Pungent arousal overlay them all. Beneath, not quite masked by her desire, was the lingering scent of their previous joining, her climax and his seed. Gods, but the combination was thrilling.

His cock strained, distracting him. His eagerness to bury himself in her was almost as strong as the call of the magick had been. With difficulty, he mastered the urge and concentrated on learning more of these mortal bodies.

He slid his hands up along her, enjoying the silky skin of her belly as he reached higher, stroking her as he leaned closer. She shivered beneath his touch, found his hands with hers, urged him to massage her softness, led him where she willed. He discovered her breasts filled his hands perfectly.

When he parted her nether lips to touch her with his tongue, she gasped and bucked, pushing into him. She tasted divine. He lapped the full length of her cleft with his tongue, probing and exploring the different qualities of her folds. Here he found she was wet and slick beneath his tongue, there more velvety in texture. Her soft curls tickled his nose. Her breath quickened, coming in small gasps and whimpers. The bud of her passion grew larger, peeking out at the top of her lips. Yielding to temptation, he lapped around it, and she moaned. He made certain he touched it with each stroke of his tongue, and began timing the squeezing of her nipples with that touch.

As her breath began to come in ragged pants, she cried out. She buried her fingers in his hair. Her thighs pressed against his ears and she tried to pull him away. He was strong enough to resist her and she soon abandoned her efforts to clutch the blankets in both fists.

He enjoyed the taste of her, and the feel of her soft breasts as they swelled within his hands. Her flesh grew firmer and more of a solid handful under his touch. He noticed a change in her taste as she cried out, flooding his mouth with a rush of fluid as she writhed and spasmed against him. The nutty flavor of her climax pleased him. Her small heels beat upon his back. He drank deeply of her, reveling in the power he had to give her pleasure.

Trina lay against the pallet, gasping and winded. This man, this spirit, this demon, whatever he was, had given her the most intense pleasure she had ever dreamed of, nay, even beyond that. The wine and the magick no longer throbbed in her blood, although the heat she'd felt in the fire sizzled beneath the surface of her skin, promising more to come.

Was it possible she might yet die? Could one perish of pleasure?

He released her, running his hands down her ribs, and came to lie beside her, staring at her naked body. He trailed a finger across her heaving belly. She ought to feel self-conscious but she could not. She felt feminine and almost sated. She thought she could easily grow accustomed to these new and strange feelings.

She examined his face, taking in the small laugh lines at the corners of his amber eyes, the generous mouth visible between his beard and mustache. He licked his bottom lip and she thought about the wonders he had just shown her, using that mouth.

"Your blush is beautiful."

Suddenly shy, she ducked her head. He lifted her chin with a finger, and kissed her again.

She tasted herself on his lips and beard as he gathered her close. He kissed her more leisurely this time, with none of the urgency and haste he'd shown before.

"What is your name?" she murmured between kisses.

He paused and drew back. "I will not give you the Name that binds me."

She was horrified that he would even think she might seek that kind of power. "I don't want it. I've seen what you can do when it is abused." She touched him gently on the chest. "I only want to know what I am to call you."

He considered that. "You may call me Brand."

"And I am Trina." It felt good to speak her birth name aloud, and not have to dread the mage contradicting her. "Trina," she repeated. Not Baraka anymore. Never again.

She could feel his desire, where his hardness pressed into her thigh. She rolled atop him and he pushed her up to sit at his waist. She had a marvelous view of his broad chest with its sprinkling of freckles. Reaching out, she ran her palm across his skin. The soft curls of his red-gold hair sprang to life as her hand passed over them. Her fingers feathered over his nipple, and he shivered beneath her touch. Intrigued, she would have explored this, to see if she could give him the same delights he'd shown her in this manner, but he forestalled her.

Grasping her shoulders, he pulled her forward until her breasts swung right above his mouth. He captured one nipple, and she sighed, arching forward to allow him better reach. He sucked, drawing deeply, and she had to lean her hands on his shoulders for support.

Desire blazed through her as he massaged her breasts and suckled her. Her elbows shook with the effort it took for her to remain upright. He grazed her with his teeth and pinched her nipples until she threw her head back and lost rational thought.

She became aware of her hips sliding around on his torso, slick with her juices, and then he grasped her waist, lifting her up and back until she hovered over his shaft. He seemed to hold her there forever, right on the edge of heaven, while he probed her cleft, finding the right angle. He released her, and she took her own weight. She slowly started to settle onto him and then stopped, frightened lest the second time be as uncomfortable as the first. This time there was no magick to heal the hurt, no herbs to urge her past the pain.

He returned to admiring her breasts, laving her with his tongue and rolling her nipples between his fingers, pinching and pulling lightly. A deep longing grew from his caresses. She felt herself loosen, expand to encompass him, and knew she could relax, that there was no pain to come. She lowered herself onto him, reveling in the sensation as he filled her.

Brand panted and thrust into her, while she gasped and pushed down to meet him. He gripped her head, bringing her down to kiss him, plunging his hard tongue into her as he thrust his hard shaft into her, and her world exploded into fire and light.

"Trina!" He roared her name as he joined her in her flight, filling her with his seed. Again and again he pumped into her, and Trina soared with him.

Chapter Four

ဢ

Brand held her close for a moment longer, then gave her a gentle push away from his warmth. "We have much to do. You must leave soon."

"Leave?" How could he speak of leaving when she had just found where she wanted to stay forever? To hide her confusion, she concentrated on flattening the rumpled folds of the blanket beside her, smoothing them all the way to the edge of the mattress.

He used her chin to turn her face to his. He wore a stern expression and she began to comprehend. "Do you not think the wealthy old woman will be missed? She was garbed in finery that indicates wealth and importance. Someone will come to seek her, perhaps not today or tomorrow, but soon. What will you tell them of her fate? If you are the only one left alive, you must make explanations. Whoever hears your story will not choose to believe the truth."

The rightness of his words sank into her, lodging in her chest with the weight of a millstone. How many times had she heard Kalidah complain of the inability of most mortals to accept magick? They must needs have something or someone to condemn. No one would believe her, whatever story she told. She would be blamed. She would be punished.

Trina scrambled from the bed. Hesitating, she stood in the room while the chill seeped into her naked flesh. Her sole possessions, her thin and worn clothing, had gone up in smoke with the workshed. She had no idea of what to do, where to go. She had often longed to be free, but suddenly realized that freedom carried the price of taking care of herself.

She didn't have the faintest idea of how to begin. Life with Kalidah had meant never having to make a choice. Her clothing, her food, her activities, had all been restricted to what the old hag permitted. Suddenly, myriad decisions about every aspect of life faced her. She would have to learn to make choices every minute of every day. With so many options before her, how was she to choose? She looked to Brand for guidance.

He watched her from the tangle of blankets on the bed. She could read the hunger in his expression, and knew she ought to be self-conscious about her nudity. For some reason, with him it didn't matter.

When Fletcher had looked at her like he wanted to swallow her, she'd felt only revulsion. When Brand had tasted her most private flesh, she'd only felt rightness and wonder. She felt it again now, as he devoured her with his eyes.

Dampness and heat flooded her belly under his gaze, chasing away the chill of the morning air. When Brand rose, she went to meet him but he held her at arm's length when she would have embraced him.

"There is no time for more pleasure. We must prepare."

He wouldn't leave her on her own! Relief swept through her, sweet and golden. He *did* care what happened to her. The thought made her a bit dizzy and she grasped his arm for balance. Again, she felt that tingle where she touched him. To distract herself from his nearness, she asked, "How?"

"We should make it look as if all four of you perished in the fire. Gather a few things from here, but leave the most valuable."

"Valuable to me or to the villagers?" She began to understand who it was important to fool.

"The villagers. They are the ones who will discover and report the destruction of the shed." He nodded and grinned at her, a wonderful expression that warmed her to her toes.

Delighted, she smiled back at him. No one had ever approved of her as he did. With his encouragement, she knew she could make the decisions she needed to start life on her own.

Some of her fear drained away. With his counsel, they would be the right decisions.

Brand continued, "It should not appear that the cottage has been ransacked. You will be safer if the villagers report that the shed has burned but there is nothing unusual about the cottage."

She envisioned the villagers picking through the mage's things, and her smile grew wider. Kalidah would have had a spitting fit at first her slave and then the village peasants handling her prized possessions.

Swiftly, Trina searched the cottage. From a row of hooks by the door, she took the mage's second-best cloak, a bit worn but still much warmer than her threadbare garment that had burned with the workshed. In a heavy, ornately-carved chest, she came across a folded pile of assorted clothing. Why on earth had the old mage collected so many different sizes? She found a few garments that would fit her fairly well, two undergowns and a sturdy woolen gown, and set them aside with the cloak. They were plain but finer than anything she'd ever worn. Among the assorted footgear stuffed under the bed, she found a fine pair of soft leather boots that fit her perfectly.

In the very bottom of the chest, she found two small leather pouches. They both chimed when she lifted them. Opening the worn laces, she saw the glint of gold. She put one with her clothing and returned the other to the depths of the chest.

"No," Brand ordered over her shoulder. "Leave the gold where it will be found more easily." He crossed to a shelf and took down a dusty beaker. "Here."

She slid the pouch into the vessel, and Brand placed it in a more prominent position.

He touched her shoulder in a soft caress. "Much as I enjoy watching you dance around in nothing but your beautiful ivory skin, you must dress. I will gather other supplies for you to take."

Trina dressed slowly, knowing that he watched her from the corners of his eyes, when he wasn't outright staring. She enjoyed every moment, stretching her arms high to pull one of the soft linen shifts over her head. Her breasts swayed as she let it fall to her waist. Brand was still naked. She caught sight of his growing erection and felt her nipples tighten in response. She shimmied her hips and the hem fell to her ankles.

He groaned softly and returned to his task. She waited until he'd stuffed a sack with food from the cupboard, smoked meat and foreign cheeses and spices. Wide-eyed, she gaped at the pile of luxuries, food she'd not known the hag had. Resentment flared briefly, for Kalidah had only fed her plain porridge and boiled meat. She thrust the thought aside, telling herself rebelliously that now she could eat her fill of the mage's private stores.

She turned to concentrate on Brand. When he turned again, she lifted the woolen gown, feeling her breasts strain against the linen as she did so. She smiled into the fabric as she pulled it over her head. Teasing was fun.

Firm arms clasped her without warning and Brand's mouth found a nipple through the linen. She gasped as he bore her back to the bed and tossed her in a heap.

"Beware your behavior. Act the harlot, and you will find yourself living outside the bounds of society, with ruffians and thieves for companions." She tore the gown off her head to glare at him. He stood over her, his face set in a harsh frown. "Do you wish to be forced to seek the protection of one such as Fletcher? Do you long to have a different clumsy oaf warm your bed each night?"

She stared up at him in dismay. Tears stung her eyes. She'd thought *him* a tease for a moment, until the truth of his words struck home.

"Life is not a game." He turned and strode over to the cupboard, extracting a large knife. Ignoring her, he tested its sharpness before jamming it back into the sheath and then into the bulging pack at his feet.

Swallowing hard, she wiped the back of her hand across her cheek. She would *not* cry. She wouldn't. To conceal her embarrassment, she turned away and finished dressing in silence.

Wordlessly, Brand scooped a handful of coals from the hearth and filled a brass coal carrier. He fitted it between two felted wool forms and placed it in the pack.

Scrambling to her feet, she began to plait her hair with angry tugs. "I'm sorry." Why was she apologizing? "I've never before had anyone who cares what happens to me."

"Never?" He turned to face her and his expression softened.

"Not that I can remember. I've been with Kalidah since I was very young."

"Then where will you go?"

Her heart tumbled through her chest and lodged somewhere beneath her stomach. "Me? By myself? Alone?"

Brand gave her an odd look. "Of course. I cannot accompany you. I am what I am, which is not mortal. You belong with your people. I must return to the spirit realm."

"But-how-why can't we at least travel together?" Trina heard the plea in her voice but couldn't stop it. Being in charge of her destiny was frightening enough. The prospect of facing the strange world beyond the mage's clearing alone terrified her. She put a hand out toward Brand in entreaty. When she saw how it trembled, she thrust it into the folds of her skirt.

He crossed to where she stood. "I have more than enjoyed your company, but I have no knowledge of how or why I took this form." He grasped her hand and rubbed his thumb over her knuckles. Just his touch eased her trembling. "What if I suddenly disappear? I cannot predict how long I may remain in this shape, and I would see you safely on your way before I leave you."

Trina swallowed her disappointment. For all she knew, he had to remain here, in the mage's hearth. It sounded as if neither of them understood just what he could and could not do. If only she'd taken the risk of looking through those old scrolls!

He repeated his question. "Where will you go?"

She marshaled her thoughts, casting aside regrets from the past to focus on the present. When she did, she could only see one course of action, and that was finding the man whose scent had evoked warm childhood memories. "There was a man in the village two nights ago. He approached me while Kalidah was with Lady Nanon and I was loading the wagon. We only spoke briefly, but he said I resemble someone he knows."

"Then you must ask him."

Trina thought about the man from the tavern who threw a stone at her. The peasants all knew her, and would report her survival to Lord Roland. Kalidah's reputation might have protected Trina, but without the mage's daunting presence to counter the reward the lord would be willing to pay for information concerning his mother's fate, Trina had no hope of ever leaving the village should she be seen there. "I dare not go to him."

"I agree. That is too risky. Did he say where he was from?"

"No, but he had the accent of the North." Realization dawned as two pieces of the puzzle of her heritage fell into place. "That must be why Kalidah called me Baraka of the North! She knew that was where I'd come from when she bought me."

Trina followed Brand's stare, out across the courtyard, past the well to the remains of the shed. "It's a shame the parchment burned so quickly. She might have saved the bill of sale." He shrugged and turned away. "So we must get you to this man, somehow."

At least he included himself in this portion of her journey. She breathed a sigh of relief and repeated, "I dare not enter the village."

"No, you must go north on your own." Brand looked her over thoughtfully. "You must hide your hair, at least for now.

Once you are away from all the people who might recognize you, your appearance will not matter." He set the bowls back on the shelf and came to twist her hair up on top of her head. "Have you pins for your hair?"

She shook her head. "I have nothing. My sole possessions were the clothes I wore, the ones Kalidah cut for the ritual." The memory of how close she'd been to death still chilled her. She rubbed her arms to warm them.

"And she had so little hair, I'm sure she had no need of pins. I wonder, though…" Brand let her plait fall to her shoulder while he went back to the cupboard and drew a box from the shadowed depths. He placed it on the table. She saw that, like the chest that held it, the lid was richly carved, decorated with twining ivy and absurd little faces peering between the leaves. The lid resisted his efforts to lift it, finally giving way with a small squeak to reveal the glitter of gold and jewels.

Trina hastened over to stand beside him and stare at the heaped pearls and gold with a sigh of awe. She stirred the gems with her finger. "There must be a king's ransom there."

"Perhaps," he admitted. "You must take some of this with you and I will hide the rest. A purse of gold coins is something one might expect a mage to have. If jewels are found and rumors spread about the mage's treasure, no one will believe this is all she had. It will become a legend and there will be constant searchers here. Mortals are gullible creatures, who like to believe in the impossible. In their quest for treasure, one of them may find something we've overlooked, some evidence you are still alive. Lord Roland will want answers about his mother's death. He will not rest until he finds you."

Brand spread a handful of the jewelry out on the table, and picked up three gold pins. They were as long as her hand, blunt on one end and tipped with a jewel on the other.

"Here. These will keep your hair up under your hood." He handed them to her and sorted quickly through the rest of the treasure, dividing it into two piles. One he swept back into the box and one he wrapped in a linen napkin. Tying the corners of the cloth together to make a neat bundle, he tucked it into the pack on the floor, shoving it to the very bottom.

With hasty motions, she managed to coil her plait as he had done, and began to secure the soft loops of hair with the pins. He nodded his approval and she pulled her hood up to hide her fairness. With her fine new clothing, free of holes and stains, and her hair concealed, who would recognize her as Kalidah's threadbare slave?

"Now darken your brows with soot from the hearth. You do not wish to draw attention to yourself." He hefted the pack, tucked the treasure box under his arm and vanished into the sunshine.

Did his steps falter? Trina watched him closely, and indeed his gait held a slight stumble. Was he vulnerable in this form, here in the mortal world? Did she endanger him by delaying his return to the fire? He was correct. There was so much she didn't know or understand. She decided to trust his judgment in this as well as the preparations for her journey.

She did as he bade her. Once she'd run a sooty fingertip lightly across each of her eyebrows, she followed him into the courtyard.

Brand awaited her by the well. "Look." Two sets of footprints, from his large bare feet and her trim boots, showed clearly in the snow, leading from the threshold of the cottage to where they stood. "This is what we must avoid leaving for the villagers to find."

He knelt and passed his hand over their tracks. The snow melted into a puddle. "Soon that will freeze, leaving no trace of our presence." As she watched, the edges began to thicken in the frosty air.

The aged horse trotted past her into the forest, trailing a broken halter. Lady Nanon's gelding followed. When Trina looked up, Brand stood by the trail to the village, holding the mule on a short rein. "I broke their leads, as if they had torn them in terror at the flames. The horses will turn up somewhere in the woods, and the mule will disappear with you. If you ride him on a meandering course to the road that leads north, no one should wonder at it."

He helped her clamber onto the mule's bare back. "It won't be as comfortable as the saddle, but it will be far more comfortable than answering the questions Lady Nanon's family would ask. Begin with a straight trail north, then wander a bit, as if the beast calmed down after its initial fright. I'll melt signs of your passage through the snow, and tidy up here."

Trina clung to his arm after she gained her seat on the mule's broad, bony back. More than anyone she'd ever encountered, this spirit, this man who was not a man, had shown her nothing but kindness and affection.

Their parting could not be so casual, after what he'd made her feel. She placed her hand over his. "Will I ever see you again?"

Brand shrugged and cupped her cheek with his hand. He smiled tenderly and she tried to memorize his face, from his glowing amber eyes to his ready smile.

He leaned close enough for his breath to warm her. "I never expected to see you at all, either in the fire or in the mage's circle. I certainly never expected to take this form, to taste the human joys you have shown me." He pressed his mouth to hers in a brief but thorough kiss. "You are the most amazing being I have ever encountered. The gods have blessed me beyond what I deserve, and I dare not ask for more."

"I dare." Trina voiced her innermost wish, though the words were soft and threatened to choke her. She reminded herself that no one controlled her now, no one would punish her for speaking. "I dare to ask for your company on my journey. I dare to ask for more of you, to warm me at night and guide me by day."

"We must be content with the miracles we are given and not make demands. You are my miracle, Trina."

The simplicity of his statement and the truth that rang in his words brought tears to her eyes. "You are my miracle as well, for you have set me free, and saved my life. I owe you more than I can say."

Brand wiped a tear from her cheek. "You owe me nothing. Whatever I have done for you, you have repaid thrice over."

He gave her one last, lingering kiss. The tender sweetness of it made her tears flow freely. She would have held him longer but he pulled away.

"I will never forget you, Trina of the North. May you safely reach your home and your family. May you find where you belong. Good luck!" With a wink, he shoved the pack into her arms and slapped the mule on the rump.

She didn't want to leave him.

To stay was to die.

She wiped her eyes before she turned to look back, and saw him blow her a kiss.

Would she ever see him again? Trina tried to turn the mule, to go back and ask, but the frightened animal appeared bent on getting far away from the mage's clearing in the woods. If it hadn't been for Brand and what she'd shared with him, Trina would have been in complete agreement.

Their frantic progress finally slowed. Trina kicked the mule with her heels to keep the beast moving north. As they lumbered along, she prayed Brand would finish clearing their tracks and disappear before the villagers arrived. She let the mule have its head while she scrubbed at the tears on her cheeks.

She was on her own, for the first time in her life.

* * * * *

Brand straightened from his task and stared in the direction Trina and the mule had taken. Something tugged at him, a foreign sensation, stronger than all the other new feelings and experiences she'd shown him. She was such an innocent, all too ignorant of the world and its dangers. He longed to follow her, to guide her on her way, shield her from whatever harsh events the future might hold.

Fortunately for her he hadn't, for he felt himself weakening with every step. He would never want her to become dependent upon him, for he knew nothing about his ability to maintain this form. Right now, he'd wager he had very little time to erase their footsteps in the snow before he collapsed.

He realized with a sense of shock that he wished to remain longer in this human body. He'd grown accustomed to its feel. He'd never realized there were so many scents in the world. He enjoyed using this body, stretching his legs, picking things up and feeling their weight and texture. Trina suited him. She felt right within the shelter of his arms. He already longed for her presence, the feel of her soft skin pressed against him, the curve of her shy smile.

The curiosity he'd initially felt had grown into a desire to protect her. The fascination he'd approached her with when he first saw her standing on the coals, mustering the courage to step out into the dance, had blossomed into something stronger.

He felt responsible for her.

Satisfied that the clearing and cottage were as free of signs of their presence as he could make them, he stumbled to the remains of the workshed. His knees threatened to buckle under him. For a moment, he thought he might not make it back to the fire, then the dying embers amongst the wreckage touched his feet with welcome warmth. He sought the warmest regions of the debris, looking for a portal to the fire spirit realm.

His foot struck a coal and he began to shrink into it. In the last sight he had of the clearing, a pair of roughly dressed peasants shuffled out of the woods.

* * * * *

Trina worried about Brand until she realized she had no idea which direction was north, and then she began to worry

213

about herself. She was unable to halt the mule, and after a moment she thought that might not be a bad thing, since she wasn't sure she could get the lumbering beast started again if she did.

The forest of bleak trunks and angled limbs, devoid of leaves, stretched away from her on all sides. No sign of Kalidah's cottage and clearing remained when she turned and stared back in the direction she'd come. The sky had grown overcast while she wasn't paying attention and there were no longer shadows to guide her northward. After biting the inside of her cheek and coming up with no solution, she decided at least she would be with the mule and the pack Brand had put together for her, wherever she wound up.

The mule splashed through an ice-rimmed stream and up the opposing bank. She thought the animal might have found a path of sorts, from the way the undergrowth was thinner where it walked. The snow lay undisturbed between the bracken and saplings. After the second low branch slapped her face, she decided it must be a trail made by some of the smaller woodland animals.

Another branch tore at the folds of her mantle. She managed to free it and barely avoided being swept from the mule's back. Concerned that she might tumble off and be left on foot without the supplies Brand had packed, she sketched a quick but effective binding spell. As long as it held, the mule would not leave her.

The beast turned onto another path, free of overhanging limbs. Settling into the rough cadence of the animal's walk, Trina relaxed and let her mind wander. Although she wished to know her future and tried to concentrate on what lay ahead, her thoughts kept turning back, to the mage's cottage and Brand.

The memory of his smile warmed her almost as much as his heated kisses had. She repeated in her mind every word he'd said, every gesture he'd made. Every touch he'd given her, every caress. Reverie claimed her and she no longer felt the chill of the forest. A flush crept over her, warming her as she recalled the pleasures he'd shown her. She rocked gently on the mule as she relived her all-too-short time with Brand.

Her lover. The words lingered in her mind, and when the mule's ears twitched, she realized she'd said them aloud.

The afternoon had faded into twilight. She had to find a place to camp. Soon, before the waning light left her stranded.

Not long after, she tussled with the mule to make it follow a branch in the track. Not long after that, a narrow clearing appeared ahead in the growing darkness. As she grew closer, she realized it was a road, closely hemmed in by the trees.

Pulling on the mule's halter with all her might, she managed to turn it onto the broad path, in a direction she hoped was north. It wouldn't do to wind up right back in the midst of the village she most wished to avoid. Around the first bend in the road, a narrow stone bridge stretched over a river. Trina marveled at the slow deep stream of wide water, wider even than the mage's holding. Peering over the edge, she couldn't see the bottom, just dark, sluggish, cold water. This river resembled nothing she'd ever seen. The narrow, swift stream through Lord Roland's village flowed fast enough to power his grain mill.

On the far bank, a steep hill rose up behind the remains of several scattered hearths. This must be a common stopping point for travelers. She thanked the gods that today it was deserted. No one would notice her. She bullied the mule to the back of the area, choosing an old firepit almost out of sight of the road. A shallow cave would provide enough shelter for them both, as long as there was no storm.

The mule followed her under the overhang. She pushed the beast away and felt the chill as it moved off. The animal's warmth might help her sleep through the cold night. She let it huddle against the rock while she gathered odds and ends of wood from around the other hearths. Two logs by the hearth she'd chosen were huge, too big for her to move. Someone in the past, with more strength than she possessed, had burned a similar log. Its sizeable remains lay between the stones, the bark still intact on one side, ready for her to rekindle the fire around it.

The other hearths had small stacks of unused kindling and faggots. She placed some in her hearth and stacked more close at hand to feed to the fire as it burned down. Satisfied that she had enough wood to last through the night, she pulled the coal carrier from her pack. It took little time to light a small fire between herself and the gathering night.

She had nothing to feed the mule. Neither she nor Brand had thought of packing any grain. To her wonder, the mule ate the bread she offered. She dined on cheese and hard sausage, staring into the growing darkness. The mule lowered itself to the ground and she leaned against it, grateful for its warmth at her back.

Had she ultimately traveled north or south from where she started? In the morning, if the sun shone, she would be sure to start north again.

To what? The promise of a distant memory, of a family that might have died long ago or forgotten her? What if they'd moved to a different village and she couldn't find them?

She had no way to earn her keep. She'd seen too many of the women in the village toil long hours for a crust of bread or a small coin, barely enough to keep their children fed and clothed, let alone themselves. The lot of a woman on her own was hard under the best of circumstances. Without skills to provide for herself, survival was questionable.

She stared into the flames.

Was *he* there? Could she lose herself among the flame-folk, remain with Brand? No one here in her world even knew that she lived. Certainly no one cared whether she died. In the hearth, among the flames and coals, lived the only one who'd ever shown her kindness.

She fed most of the wood into the fire and stared *beyond* the growing flames.

Tiny bodies appeared atop the sticks, dancing in the heat. Trina released a breath she hadn't known she'd been holding and relaxed.

In a heartbeat, she was *there* again, enveloped in heat, sweat already blooming on her skin, shuffling above a flaming log. She stepped forward, her feet finding the rhythm and taking up the familiar pattern of the dance. The flame-folk closed in, stroking her arms and shoulders in welcome.

She searched their ranks. Were these the dancers she'd seen before? Their ready acceptance of her made her think yes, they knew her, but the one she sought was nowhere to be seen. She moved her feet, one before the other, but took no joy in it. Her heart grew heavy within her. Disappointment slowed her steps and the dancers whirled past her in a blur.

She'd been a fool to think she could find him again. She sighed and tried to take herself back out of the fire, into her body.

Nothing happened.

The coals shimmered beneath her feet and the dancers flowed by. Bending her head back, looking up, she could just see through the haze of smoke to where her body was, propped against the mule. It was an eerie feeling, looking at herself sitting that way, eyes wide and staring back. A shiver ran through her despite the fire's enveloping heat. She was a soul without a home, watching a body beyond her reach.

What if she failed to find her way out of the spirit realm? What if Brand never appeared? Would she remain here, and her physical body wither away, an unoccupied husk of flesh and bone? What would happen when the fire burned down? Would she die?

She broke away and returned to the dance, this time in a frenzy to lose herself in the ebb and flow of heat and fire-folk. For the sake of her sanity, she couldn't afford to let the *what-ifs* intrude.

Her feet found the rhythm and her mind calmed. She danced until the flames began to die down around her and the flame-folk drifted off, one by one.

Chapter Five

ೕ

Trina sighed and stretched her stiff limbs, wincing as cold air washed over her face.

Cold!

Her eyes flew open. The remains of the fire crackled before her, not much more than coals glowing low in the pit. The empty clearing lay beyond the fire. The road was out of sight, hidden by the curve of the forest.

She was alone once more. Disappointment settled heavily in her stomach. So much for spending an eternity with Brand. She breathed deeply as the realization took hold that she had survived. Relief swept through her, replacing the loneliness. She was no longer trapped in the spirit realm. The mule was a comforting, warm presence at her back.

She found a small log beside her, one that she'd overlooked before, and dropped it onto the bed of coals. Small flames sprang up around the wood. She stared over the fire pit, out into the other campsites that lay dark and deserted in the night.

Across from her, at the edge of the forest, a pair of iridescent eyes gleamed yellow-gold. As she watched, a second pair appeared, then a third. The first creature approached until she could see the wolf's snarling mouth, its shaggy black and gray pelt. The mule behind her struggled to its feet, braying in dismay. The trio of wolves paced back and forth beyond her puny fire. They eyed the mule with hunger and anticipation. She imagined she could see them planning their attack, communicating silently with each other. The small pack moved closer, ringing the fire, hemming her in.

A fourth pair of eyes gleamed in the darkness, back in the woods.

Her fire, already so small it wasn't a deterrent, would not last long. Carefully, not moving too quickly, Trina groped about for any remaining wood. Her hand grasped another small log, and she thrust it into the fire.

It was not much more than a large twig, one end still bearing leaves. The flames flared up, driving the closest wolf back. To her horror, the leaves quickly burned to nothing.

The wolf gathered itself and leapt.

Fire blazed around the stick Trina held across the pit. Higher and higher the plume of flame rose, engulfing the wolf. She cringed, bracing for the impact of the burning animal. Belatedly, she tried to weave a spell of protection around herself and the mule.

Strong arms materialized out of the fire to embrace the wolf. The words of the spell died in her throat as Brand towered over her. Twice the height of a man, he rose in splendid nakedness from the flames. Glowing muscles rippled across his shoulders as he tossed the smoldering carcass back at the rest of the pack and turned to her.

"I cannot conjure flames from nothing, I can only consume what is here. You must add wood to the fire. Quickly." He already was shrinking down, smaller and smaller. Trina hurried to obey his command. There were no more small logs or pieces of kindling left. She threw her weight behind the first of the large logs.

Brand thought she would take forever to roll the two huge logs into the pit. From behind him came the snarls and growls of the pack as they tore into their former leader. The wood had hidden a pile of smaller logs and faggots stacked neatly against the side of the shallow cave. He watched with approval as she clawed and raked the kindling onto the logs. Her hands trembled but she persisted until a goodly mound covered the coals.

When it all caught, he resumed his normal human size and stepped from between the hearth stones. She threw her arms around him and sobbed.

Tenderness stole through him and he clasped her to his chest. "Hush, hush, you are safe now." He sat down and shifted her onto his lap. Petting her hair as he had seen farmers do in settling frightened livestock, he held her close and let her cry. Something hitched inside him when he breathed, something warm and comforting. He searched within himself and found nothing of the furious passion that had consumed him before, just satisfaction at being with her once more. Simply holding her like this felt right.

"I didn't think I could move those big logs."

He stared into her tear-streaked face, confused for a second, lost in experiencing the moment. With his thumb, he wiped the tears from her cheek. "You have more Power than you think."

Her smile was weak and wavered, like her voice. "More likely panic gave me strength."

"Whatever it was, you now know what you have within you. Do not doubt yourself again."

She laid her head against him. He settled her there, in the shelter of his arm, and felt her relax into him. Beyond the fire, the tumult of the wolves subsided into an occasional grunt and snarl.

"Where did you come from? I went into the fire and tried to find you before, but you weren't there."

"You looked for me?" She nodded against him and yawned. "I was—elsewhere. I came here because it felt as though you Called me."

Her eyes gleamed in the firelight as she twisted to look up at him and protest, "How could I do that? I do not have your Name!"

"I know you don't, but I felt the pull. Somehow, we have been linked. I believe a bond formed between us when I found you in the firedance. Mayhap the herbs and drugs combined in the mage's black ritual strengthened that bond. Whatever it is, I knew you needed me."

He pressed a gentle kiss to her brow. "I have no idea how we are bonded. It is unknown to me. What we have done together, from dancing in the fire to our physical joining, has never been done. Such a joining is unusual, too physical for a spirit. We were not aware of such things. Had it not been for the mage's spells, and you, I would never have known it." He gathered her close.

She rested her head against his shoulder and tried to make sense of his words. It seemed a barrier of some sort had been broken by Kalidah's attempt to bend the fire to her will. "Have other mortals come to dance the fire?"

"Aye, sometimes. Never has a spirit traveled to your realm."

"But you have."

"Aye, and I have to wonder . . . why?" He threw back his head and laughed, the sound rumbling under her hand on his chest. "I always thought mortals were foolish, endlessly asking questions and agonizing over the meaning of things they simply ought to accept." He sobered. "Perhaps I am meant to learn why mortals think the way they do. Now *that* is a frightening idea."

"Why?" She asked the oh-so-mortal question before she thought.

He laughed again and kissed the tip of her nose. "You prove my point. Many things are best not understood. All mortals are foolish, some more than others. "

The fire burned low before them. Did he mean she was foolish? She waited in his close embrace for him to say more. A twig cracked apart and crashed to the bed of coals. She shut her eyes, content to bask in Brand's presence, come what may.

He didn't continue, so she asked, "Will you stay?"

"I do not know if I can. Now rest, while I keep watch for as long as I may."

He held her as she drifted into sleep. How had he appeared in the nick of time? What was this tie between them? How had it come about, and why? It troubled him, for not only had he never encountered anything like it, he had never heard even a whisper of the possibility it could happen.

Another thing he found troubling was how he became weaker the longer he remained outside the spirit realm. He wondered if there could be some way to sustain himself in this mortal body.

He had come close to expiring back in the mage's clearing. He had pushed himself almost beyond his endurance because it had been important to him to see Trina safely on her way. Even now, he could tell his strength was not quite what it had been when he'd surged forth from the hearth. Returning to the fire restored him, but what if Trina needed him when he had lost too much of his strength?

Chapter Six

ಬಂ

Trina awakened in mid-morning to find herself alone, curled against the mule's warmth. The fire had burned down to a heap of ashes and a few coals. No sign remained of the wolves. Swallowing her disappointment at Brand's disappearance, she ate a cold meal before packing and resuming her journey.

From shadows cast by the weak winter sunlight, she determined the four directions, and turned north. She settled into the depths of her cloak and prepared to ride until the mule tired.

To her consternation, she had not gone far down the road, not more than several furlongs, when the beast stopped, standing stock-still in the middle of the road. Why had the mule chosen to stop here?

The forest stretched cold and empty around her, offering no welcome expanse of grass or sign of habitation. The bridge and her camp lay behind, concealed by a curve in the road.

She searched the treetops for anything that might indicate the presence of a cottage or farm. From the corner of her eye, she thought she saw a puff of dark smoke against the gathering clouds, but when she turned in that direction, whatever it was had disappeared.

The only sign of life was an eagle, hovering on a current of air far above. With a sigh, she wished she had learned more in her years with Kalidah, so that she might see through the bird's eyes and know the lay of the land. This sort of magick was forbidden to her. Kalidah had shared only what she found tiresome to do herself.

Trina closed her eyes and tried nonetheless. The clip-clop of horses approaching on the road behind brought her back to earth.

Aware that she might be wise not to meet other travelers, Trina looked around for shelter of some sort. A large thicket stood back from the road. She tried to turn the mule off the road and into the scrub toward it. Tugging on the rein on that side did no good. The stubborn beast refused to obey her, first leaning in the opposite direction and finally staying right where it was as a compromise.

The thought that she might abandon the mule and hide in the thicket occurred to her, but she rejected it. The travelers were bound to look for the mule's owner, or worse yet, steal the mule and all of her belongings.

Unable to turn fully and view the road behind her, she waited, shrinking into the mage's second-best cloak and muttering the few spells of protection she could pull from her scattered thoughts. She tried to think of a plausible reason to be here on the road in the woods by herself, and could imagine none.

Before long, the sounds of the travelers grew louder. Voices called out in foreign accents, hailing her. These were no rough peasants. She heaved a sigh of relief.

She waited patiently until the first riders reached her. The heavy creak of wheels told her wains slowed the group's progress, and indeed, when the first men came into her view, they were the armed escorts typical of the trading caravans she had seen on occasion in the village.

One wore more armor than the others, heavy leather studded with iron. The captain of the guards, she guessed. He stopped his horse by her, demanding, "What are you doing out here by yourself?" His fellows fanned out to peer into the surrounding undergrowth. "Do you think to lure us into an ambush?"

"Nay, good sir," Trina began, adopting her most subservient air.

Before she could begin to make up a story explaining her presence, a familiar voice interrupted, "Ah, we have found you. When you didn't join us at the tavern, I wasn't certain if we would meet you on the road, or where you might be."

The kind, white-haired stranger from the village appeared, pulling his spirited roan up next to her mule. He turned to address the guards. "This is the young woman I mentioned. She is traveling with me."

The guard gave her one last glance, nodded and moved off. The white-haired man caught her eye and winked as he stretched down to grasp her mule's bridle. Under his hand, the beast obediently jogged into motion. Trina stifled a curse. She should have expected the stupid animal to obey a stranger.

"These are my traveling companions, and now yours." Under his breath, he added, "I recognized your voice. Play the role of niece with me, and we will not arouse suspicion. Address me as Uncle Juhan."

With a groaning of its axles, the lead wagon lurched forward once more. On the box, the driver and the woman who sat beside him began to argue. The nearest guard commented and they all laughed. As the heavy wagon gathered speed, the mounted guards fell in behind it.

Trina's companion identified the people making up the traveling party as they passed. "Melusine and Heyward, the merchant and his wife." A stout couple, mounted on fine horses and dressed in elegant wool mantles, nodded in their direction. "Their daughter Lyse." A white-skinned beauty, who had pushed her hood back to let her masses of curly, dark red hair fall free, smiled at Trina. "The others you will have time to meet later." He led her into a space in the group as it swept past. "Come. Let us take our places."

Trina glanced around. She recognized none of the folk in the caravan. "You were with a friend in the village. A stocky man, with dark hair. Do you not travel with him?"

"Gregor? He's no friend of mine, merely an acquaintance, someone who traveled the same road for a time. He had business first with Lord Roland and then with a merchant to the south. We parted company last evening."

Trina kept silent about the dark aura that had surrounded Gregor. She felt safer knowing there was no one around but Juhan to connect her with the village or Kalidah. For some reason, she trusted him. Pleased at the thought that every minute carried her further from danger, she sat a little straighter on the mule's back.

Juhan waved a hand at the road ahead of them. "With luck, we will be in Bridgeford by dark."

Trina struggled not to gape at his words. "Bridgeford?" she whispered in awe. She had heard the place mentioned often enough by travelers in the village, but never expected to see it herself. The town boasted a cathedral, a castle and a huge marketplace every week.

"Aye, we are bound north, to your homeland and mine," he explained.

They jogged along, the mule now content to keep pace with his gelding. "Heyward concluded his business with Lord Roland yestereve. We departed the village early this morning. Bridgeford is the next town with an abbey where we may pass the night in safety. Our plan is to reach Fishkill within a se'enight. From there, we will have a short sea voyage and then a few days' more travel before you are home. I imagine your family will be thrilled beyond belief to have you back among them, Katrina."

She gasped. "You know my name?"

"I guessed." He reached out to pat her hand where she held the reins. "You bear the look of your family."

Warmth kindled in Trina's heart. She did have a family, and they wanted her.

This kindly gentleman would see that she reached them. She took a deep breath and let it out slowly in a sigh at the wonder of it. In all her years with Kalidah, she had never dared to hope that she might someday find herself free of her servitude, let alone be reunited with her parents. Now it appeared that all of this might come to pass. The pent-up tension in her shoulders relaxed all at once and she let herself smile, first hesitantly, then in unrestrained happiness. Her face felt strange, her cheek muscles tight, unaccustomed to a joyful expression.

Her companion smiled back, a crinkling of his face that framed his mouth with wrinkles and lit his eyes in a friendly twinkle. "Call me Uncle Juhan."

A lump formed in Trina's throat. Could this kind man be part of that family?

She swallowed hard, and managed to ask, "Are you truly my uncle?" Questions tumbled about in her head. Did she have brothers and sisters? Aunts and uncles? Grandparents?

"Not by blood, but certainly by affection and habit. I've been best friends with your father since we were small lads."

A faraway look came into his eyes and his smile became softer. "Your grandfather died the same winter as my mother. That was a very bad year in the valley. I was ten. The next spring, my father married your grandmother." He gave Trina a sharp glance. "Can you keep this straight?"

"Oh, I understand." Trina nodded. "Tell me about my mother."

"Inge, your mother, was four that year, and a fearless whirlwind. She would climb anywhere, stick her little nose into anything she could find. I was given the charge of keeping her out of trouble. The task took more than I expected. No one could predict where she would go next."

His words conjured a picture in Trina's mind. She could see her mother, a tiny flaxen-haired child, racing around the holding. The girl's high laughter rang across a pond as she fled ahead of a tall, dark lad who struggled to keep up with her despite his longer legs. When she reached the stand of trees, she swung up among the leafy boughs, pulling her feet up just in time to elude her pursuer's grasp.

"She led you on many a chase. There was a pond, and a stand of willows." The words were out of her mouth before she thought.

Uncle Juhan stared at her. The sounds of the caravan filled the silence between them with the clip-clop of the horses' hooves and the creak of the wains. Laughter flowed from somewhere behind them.

Time stretched out and still he didn't speak.

Trina wondered if she shouldn't have spoken so freely. She'd opened her mouth and was about to apologize when he stopped her with a raised hand. "I forget. You have spent years in service to a sorceress. I should not be surprised when you show a bit of Talent yourself."

Trina blushed and shook her head. "I have no Talent. What Kalidah taught me, anyone can learn. She often told me so."

"Do not fool yourself. She chose you for your abilities, however small they may be. Your mother did indeed run from me, often. There *was* a pond, and four willows beside it. They stand there still, behind the house, where the small stream flows down from the hills."

Trina's mouth fell open. "I have never known such things before."

"You have never been out in the world before. I'm sure your mistress did not encourage you to develop your magickal skills."

"Kalidah never encouraged me to do anything but heavy household tasks." She thought of Brand, and dancing on the coals among the fire-folk. "What do you know of magick? Might I truly have Talent?"

"We can find out. There is a young woman knowledgeable of such matters who recently came to the hills above our valley. You and she are much of an age, and I know her to be gentle and kind. We will seek her opinion. Mildread, she is called." Uncle Juhan leaned over to pat her hand. "Expect many things to be different now, Katrina. Your mistress was an evil woman who served none but her black heart. You will find our valley filled with light, not darkness."

Trina rubbed her chest through the wool of her gown. The pain of the arcane patterns as Kalidah carved them was still fresh in her mind. As was Brand's warning. "Is Mildread very powerful?"

Uncle Juhan shook his head. "I do not believe so, although she may have grown in Power over the months I have just traveled. Not like some, and certainly not like your mistress. She's young, as I said. I think you will like her."

A shout from behind caused the caravan to slow. Uncle Juhan turned in his saddle. Trina strained to turn far enough to see, but finally gave up, waiting for the commotion to reach them or resolve itself.

Unlike the accented speech of her companions, the cries from the back of the caravan had the familiar, rough sounds of a peasant, one she knew from Lord Roland's village. The warmth turned to ice in Trina's chest.

As Tam the guardsman approached, she tried to hide her face within her hood, holding the heavy folds together.

"There! That's her, the sorceress's slave!" The few people within Trina's sight all stared at her as Lord Roland's guardsman twitched the hem of the cloak she wore. "That's the cloak my sister made and bartered to the mage so she'd heal my nephew last winter. Now the mage's dead, along with our lord's mother and his man Fletcher." He crossed himself, as did a number of the travelers.

Tam could not have followed the mule's meandering path through the woods, else he'd have caught up with her long before now. Sheer bad luck had placed him and Juhan in the same party of travelers. Trina trembled in her cloak. That same bad luck had brought her to this place just in time to join the group.

One of the guards barked, "What is your business, fellow?"

Tam drew himself up to his full height and stated, "I am sent to deliver word of Lady Nanon's death to my lord's sister, Lady Giselle, who lives in Bridgeford. She is the wife of Lord Berold."

The guard flinched at the mention of Berold, and shoved his way through the gathering crowd to grab the mule's reins from Trina's hands. "Let's see what she's got to say for herself." He yanked Trina and her mount forward, brushing aside Juhan's effort to stop him. "Come, tell your story to the captain."

Tam followed, still clutching the fabric in his hand as they approached the front of the caravan. Trina sneaked a look at the guard. Where his face had been severe before, he now wore a forbidding, stony expression.

The captain of the guards stopped his mount at their approach. She'd been right, he was the one wearing heavier armor. He frowned as the lead wagon ground again to a halt. "What's this? We have no time for more delays. If we do not keep moving, we'll find ourselves still on the road at nightfall."

Tam took a deep breath. "Two days ago, this creature here, this spawn of hell," he spat the words out as if they would poison him, "killed our Lord Roland's mother and her guard. Bind her well, for she's a powerful mage."

"See here, fellow, you cannot go about denouncing innocent women!" Juhan protested as he forced his horse between Trina and her accuser. He turned to the guard holding the mule's halter. "You cannot know what he says is true. Do you know him to be who he says he is? This fellow could be anyone! For all you know, he's a rogue who wants to lure us into an ambush!"

Everyone looked from Tam, in his polished leather armor, to Juhan, who sat tall and proud and indignant on his trim gelding. A few crossed themselves again. Some glanced uneasily into the dark forest that leaned over the road on both sides. The guard captain hesitated in confusion. Either could be right, from the looks of them.

Juhan pressed the guard's hesitation to his advantage, "This young lady and her noble family are well known to me, from her childhood and even mine. This fellow is mistaken." He reached out to tug the hem out of Tam's grip and fingered the cloth of her mantle. "He bases his charge on the cloak she wears. This plain twill is not so uncommon a weave and walnut hulls are always walnut hulls, wherever they may be harvested and mulled into such a brown dye. The color is unremarkable. There must be many ells of such fabric, woven in many places, and some will have been made into cloaks. Any similarity is chance, nothing more."

A rustle in the undergrowth caught Trina's attention and the forest came alive around them. A multitude of men in tattered clothes rose from the scrub and ran forward.

"Ambush!" the captain cried, drawing his sword.

Bows twanged and arrows flew. The first one took Tam in the throat. The second felled the captain. The third one skewered the nearest horse. The mule reared in fright, slipped on the ice and fell in a welter of legs.

Trina found herself sprawled on the ground, partly pinned beneath the thrashing beast.

Uncle Juhan threw himself from the saddle to lie beside her. Wedging one foot behind her on the animal's spine, he pushed on the mule, timing his tugs on her with the animal's movements. He wrenched her free, then covered her with half his cloak as the ambushers swept across them.

"Hush," he warned her, whispering in her ear. "Feign death."

Aware that if she did not, she would soon be dead in truth, she went limp. Around them, animals cried out in terror. People screamed, the high shrieks of a few women continuing long after the cries of the men had ceased.

Had she escaped bondage to Kalidah only to die here, so soon after? Would Brand look for her? Would he miss her? Would he ever know what happened to her?

What would he advise her to do now? He had appeared from the fire to battle the wolves when she'd needed him. If Uncle Juhan's ruse didn't work, might Brand be able to help her?

She'd packed the coal carrier near the top of the satchel on the mule. Risking a glance through narrowed eyes, she could tell that despite the snow, much of the brush lining the road appeared dry and brittle. Just right for starting a fire.

Trina kept still, holding her breath when a boot pounded the road a scant hand's breadth from her face. She managed not to whimper when her friend and savior jerked and groaned. She groped between them for his hand and squeezed it.

He made no response.

She kept her eyes closed, feigning a faint if not death.

All sounds died away, save the soft rhythmic sobbing of a woman.

Another boot crunched on the road, near her. She bit back a cry when she was grasped by one arm and jerked to her feet.

"Here's one we missed." The man who held her pulled her close enough for her to see thin red veins around his bulbous nose and smell his foul breath. He was missing three teeth. A thick white scar puckered his face from one eye to his chin. "Take her, Jacko. Your turn to go first." He tossed her casually toward one of his companions, a tall thin man with long, matted hair and a hooked nose.

As Trina spun out of his grasp, time slowed and a kaleidoscope of colors passed before her. Huddled piles of dark cloth, brown and black, a stark contrast to the red pools spreading around them. The creamy thighs of the wagon driver's wife, where she lay, legs splayed wide, and the doughy white buttocks of a man grunting up and down over her. Long copper tresses drifted in the breeze, mercifully covering the merchant's daughter's staring, empty eyes.

The mule stepped toward her. Trina reached out and clawed at her pack, trying to reach the coal carrier. She fumbled with the drawstrings. Her fingers refused to obey her commands. She tore at the knot, willing it to part.

Jacko jerked her away and half the contents of the pack tumbled out. As he yanked her roughly to him, she punched him in the face, hard. In the moment that bought her, she saw the bundle of felt part and the copper coal carrier fall free.

The two halves of the metal container split apart on impact with the hard-packed earth. Instantly, fire sprang up in the dry weeds bordering the road. The crackle of flames surrounded Trina and her attacker. She found herself spinning away again, this time to freedom. She fetched up against a horse and clung to the saddle, braced for another attack.

Behind her, one of her captors screamed. She turned to face whatever new danger there might be.

Brand stepped from the fire.

He was magnificent. Muscles rippled along his powerful arms, back and thighs. As before, he wore no clothing to interfere with his movements.

With one hand, he threw fireballs that expanded as they reached the ambushers, engulfing the brigands in flames one by one. With his other hand curled into a fist, he threw forceful punches that easily found their mark. None escaped his blows and where each landed, flames took hold.

Jacko tried to fight but a swift blow to his chest sent him to the ground, beating at his flaming garments and choking. The man who'd pulled her from the ground attempted to throttle Brand from behind. The fire spirit flickered and appeared to melt before her eyes, becoming solid once more facing the fellow. It took but a moment for Brand to wrap his hands about her attacker's throat. Fire swept along his very skin, igniting his hair and clothing from within.

The remaining brigands fled in disarray. Brand pursued them where they ran, felling each one in turn. When no more remained, he returned to Trina, sweeping her into his strong embrace.

"Are you hurt?"

"Nay." She shuddered and huddled against him, turning away from the horrible fate of her companions. "In another minute or two, I would have been. Thank the Great Cauldron you arrived in time!"

"If you hadn't dropped the coals—" A moan interrupted him.

Trina turned, hoping at least one of the travelers still lived, that someone else had escaped the carnage. She listened but it did not come again. She looked to Brand in a mute appeal for help.

He hesitated. "It is not my concern."

"I must know if there are any survivors. I have the skill to save them. Please help me," she pleaded.

For a moment she thought he would refuse, then he nodded curtly and they began to move through the group.

Trina was aware that Brand moved much more quickly, only touching each person briefly before he moved on. Having to search for the rise and fall of a breath, or find a pulse, slowed her progress.

The driver's wife had crawled to her husband's body before she collapsed. Trina rolled her over with care, but drew back when she saw the protruding hilt and the flood of scarlet staining her breast. The brigand had buried his knife deep before he tried to make his escape.

While Trina watched, helpless, blood stopped pumping from the wound. She had no need to touch the woman. She knew of no spells that that could raise the dead.

The woman's killer, hampered by his breeks around his ankles, had not gotten far before Brand dispatched him. She skirted his smoldering remains to reach another traveler stretched full-length in the road. If she'd had the time, she might have cursed the raider's soul but the living, however few there might be, were more important than the many dead.

That man, too, was beyond her help.

"Here!" Brand called.

Trina rushed to his side, and found that Juhan still lived. An arrow stuck up out of his upper arm. From the looks of his back, he had also been kicked if not stepped on by a horse.

She gently explored the area under the dusty hoofprint on his cloak with her fingertips. There was one place where she believed a rib had splintered, but nothing more serious. The pieces of the bone lay together in place, in no danger of causing him further injury.

When she leaned close, she could hear each breath rattle in his throat. "Turn him over, gently." Together she and Brand eased him onto his back, taking care not to jostle the arrow. Trina wadded up her cloak, the mantle that had caused so much trouble, and stuffed it under Juhan's shoulder, so that his weight rested comfortably on it rather than the shaft.

Once settled in that position, he breathed more easily.

Trina stood and looked Brand straight in the eye, silently willing him to help her. There was no way she could accomplish this on her own. "I must have fire, to heat water to wash his wound and to cauterize an iron to seal it."

To her relief, Brand grinned. "That I can supply."

"And please check the others, to see if any live." She held her breath until he gave another short nod and moved off.

Trina found a skin of water and another of wine. She gathered and sorted the herbs that had fallen from her pack. By the time she returned to Juhan's side, Brand had lighted a torch from the wagon. He positioned it against a small iron pot filled with water. While the pot heated, he held a blade in the flame.

"No one else survived," he reported. She nodded briefly herself in acknowledgment before turning to the task of treating her protector.

She cut away the fabric on Juhan's shoulder and split his sleeve, pulling the fabric apart to reveal the wound. The rest of his clothing could wait, for she needed to work quickly. The sooner she cleansed the wound, the less the chance of infection setting in. The less the chance of infection, the greater his chance of survival. Aware that her fate was linked to his, she took a deep breath, steadied her hands and concentrated.

It took but a few minutes to strip the fletching from the shaft, push it through and then wash the small hole the arrow had made. Trina was aware that Brand watched her closely as she filled a bladder with hot water and worked it against the man's arm until the water flowed freely out the other side.

Brand made a sound in his throat and she looked up. He'd blanched visibly, his freckles standing out in stark contrast. "Must you do that?"

She nodded. "Aye. As much of the thread from his clothing must be cleansed away as can be. The water will carry away any dirt from the wound as well. He will heal more quickly, and there is less likelihood of festering." The man shuddered beneath her hands. "'Tis a blessing he is not awake."

"I would not like to have such done to me." Brand turned away to stare into the forest.

"Then it is a good thing you are a spirit and not a true man." Trina strove to keep the smugness from her grin and failed. "It is the lot of men to fight, and when men fight, they cannot escape being wounded at some time or another."

Brand rubbed his knuckles. "As with the wolves, killing your enemies gave me satisfaction. I can see why men fight." His voice grew husky. "Another thing for which this body is perfectly made."

Trina looked up from mixing her herbs. From the smoldering look in his eyes, she knew exactly what he meant as the first thing for which his body was perfectly made. She had to agree with his assessment. Heat suffused her cheeks and she dropped her gaze.

Two pinches of this and a small handful of that. She strove to control her breathing, for she was not unaffected by his nearness, to say nothing of his nakedness.

If she would save the man who held the key to her future, she needed to concentrate. With Brand standing close enough for her to feel his heat, staring at her in that way, she could think of nothing but him.

To distract him, she said, "Thank you for saving my life once more. Three times now you have pulled me out of danger. I liked the fireballs you threw this time."

"They are useful, aren't they?" He sounded quite pleased with himself.

She began to pat the wound dry with a clean cloth from her bag. "Can you teach me to do that? The roads are not safe. I might have need of them before I reach my family."

"Your family? You know where to find them?" Brand reached out with his bare toe and nudged the man who lay sprawled before her. "Is this the man you described to me?" He didn't wait for a reply. "Has he told you who you are?"

"Just that my name is Katrina and I resemble my family." She paused to brush wisps of her hair, which had come free of the plaits, off her face. "He is an old friend of my parents. There was no time for more before that self-important fool Tam accused me of murdering Fletcher and Lady Nanon. Uncle Juhan defended me, and then the brigands ambushed us."

She packed the wound with her mixture, smiling to herself as Brand looked away. "For a spirit, you are squeamish. I would not have thought it."

"And for a mortal, you dare much to criticize me."

Trina glanced up at him. He wore a frown but she detected a flicker of humor in his eyes. "It is no criticism, merely an observation. There are many men who cannot abide the sight of blood."

"I cannot abide the sight of him lying there, for it makes me think of you in his place, wounded or dead. What if you had not freed me from the brass vessel in time?" His voice shook a little.

"I didn't know you would come. I hoped you would, but I was also trying to reach the blade you packed for me." She placed folded linen strips against the wound, covering the poultice.

"And do what? Would you have killed the lot of them?" He chuckled.

"They were not well-armed," she pointed out. With the small knife from her belt, she sliced through the clothing that remained around Juhan's neck and his chest, baring his torso to allow her to anchor the dressing.

"Oh, and you would have been, wielding that short blade in your little hands, against all those strapping men?"

He was laughing at her!

She tied the last knot in the bandage and drew herself to her full sitting height, tipped back her head and glared up at him. "Do not underestimate me. Remember, I lived with Kalidah for many years, and learned while I helped her in her mage's studies. I am not without resources."

"Then you have no need for fireballs." He grinned at her.

She spoke before she thought. "I'll wager you don't know how you summon them."

She bit her tongue at her audacity. Brand might be fond of her but he was not mortal and she should not expect him to respond to her as a mortal man might. He was now her only companion and she did need his help, not only for herself but also for Juhan. What if he took offense?

"Oh, really?" The light in his eyes was teasing, not insulted.

She sighed in relief. "Really."

"You do dare much, for a mortal. A small mortal, at that." Brand towered over her for a moment, then turned and flung a small fireball at a spindly scrub pine by the side of the road. In an instant, the tree was fully aflame.

She sketched him a courtly bow as best she could from her seat in the dirt. "Sir, I stand corrected. You do know how to summon them." She watched the pine tree burn. "I still want to know, can you teach me to do that?"

Brand shook his head. "That is a Talent you cannot acquire. You are only a mortal. As such, you must be a powerful mage indeed to command the flames in such a manner. You are not so powerful and never will be, for you do not have the heart for it."

The finality in his tone stung. Who was he to say what she could or could not do? "What do you mean, I don't have the heart?"

"Such Power comes with a price. You are not ruthless enough to pay what it would cost you." His grin faded. "Kalidah was older than she seemed. Did you know that?" Trina shook her head and he continued, "She abandoned her family and friends centuries ago. They are all long dead by now. Do you think she hesitated to leave them behind? Did the thought of them deter her from coming to this wasteland and living alone, with naught but a slave for company? Do you think she ever wavered in her resolve to bend spirits, magick, everything she encountered, to her will? It suited her to advance Lady Nanon's son, and thus create a more powerful patroness for herself. After years of living with you, sharing her life with you, working alongside and instructing you, she was more than ready to sacrifice your life to her ambition. Could you do the same?"

"No." Trina shook her head and sighed.

He was right. She could not choose ambition over her family as the old mage had done, forsake her desire to live among folk who loved her. She would have to make do with what she had, a large knife and a few spells, mostly for the confusion of her enemies and the protection of herself. As a would-be mage she was pitiful, for her reaction to danger was to forget what little she knew. She resolved to remember to use the spells she possessed more readily.

The mule had scrambled to its feet some time before, and now walked over to nuzzle her arm. Pleased that her hasty binding spell had held through the chaos of the brigands' attack, Trina absently scratched the beast's forehead.

There was nothing more she could do for her uncle here. She looked beyond Juhan's feet, and saw that buzzards had begun to gather on the road, a stone's throw away.

The birds faded behind a sort of haze. She glanced up, and realized that a very fine snow had begun to fall.

The clouds hung dark and low, promising more to come. She took a deep breath. The air felt heavy and thick in her throat. This was no ordinary snowfall, this was a major storm gathering. She had to fight the wind to hold her hair out of her eyes.

"It will be several days before Uncle Juhan can travel, if his wound does not fester. We must find shelter until then. Mayhap there is a cave nearby, or some other place we can stay until the storm blows over and he recovers."

Trina found she was speaking to no one but the mule. Wrapping her arms around herself to try to keep warm, she peered through the thickening snow, across the wreckage of what had been the large party of travelers, searched and finally located Brand, up to his elbows in the nearest wain.

While she watched, he pulled a variety of colorful garments out of the depths of the wagon. He cast them aside, letting them fall to the road in bright splashes of crimson, topaz, midnight black and grass green. Three mismatched boots joined them in the gathering snow. A few weapons landed amidst the clothes. Several large leather bags struck the ground, one of which spilled a river of gold.

Juhan groaned and stirred, and she spent several minutes settling him, brushing the snow from his face and hands. He did not regain his senses.

Brand showered an armload of goods on the road next to her. He had gathered some more practical garments, found mates for two of the boots and, from somewhere, had gotten a warm woolen cloak to replace the troublesome one now shielding her patient from the chill of the road. "You will need these, and gold is always useful."

When she shook out the mantle, a pair of heavy wool mittens, patterned in flame-red and black, tumbled out of the folds. She might have wished for gloves, the better to tend her patient, but she would take what she could get.

The cloak was finer by far than the walnut-brown twill, and no glove would be as warm as the knitted mittens. When she shrugged into it, the cloak covered her completely, cutting off the icy wind. She tied the embroidered bands under her chin before pulling on the thick mittens.

"Where shall we go? This storm has the feel of a blizzard." She glanced at the heavy clouds and then down at her patient. "Uncle Juhan must have shelter from the elements, for several days at least. I do not want to risk moving him far."

"I will find a place."

Trina looked around at the carnage. None of the others stirred, neither travelers or brigands. Snow was settling in a thin white blanket over the scene, robbing it of some of its horror, but Trina knew what lay beneath and shuddered. But for the chance fall of the coal carrier from her pack, she might well lie still and silent among them.

Despite her confident words to Brand, she had little illusions that she might have fended off the brigands with her few spells and the knife. "What shall we do with the bodies, and the remainder of the merchant's goods?"

"Leave them."

"But—"

He was gone, plunging into the forest, leaving her alone with the dead and the dying. She sighed. Thank the Great Cauldron, everyone else may not be his affair but she seemed to be his concern. She knew he would not abandon her voluntarily, but what if he weakened as he said he had in the mage's clearing?

The smell of death had begun to gather on the road, rising from the charred remains of the brigands Brand had dispatched. Crows now wheeled overhead, screaming their claim to the waiting feast. The buzzards had moved to the far side of the carnage and approached as close as they dared. One sidled closer and risked a peck at the nearest body.

To her surprise, Trina felt no dismay at the bird's action. She searched herself for some kind of emotional response, and found she felt this was right and meet. These people's souls had departed, leaving behind their mortal remains. The scavengers were part of the natural cycle of things, making use of what the souls no longer needed.

When she made no move to chase the buzzard off, others closed in for their meal. Silently wishing them well, she turned her back and addressed herself to the task of her own survival, and that of her Uncle Juhan.

Trina concentrated on making her companion more comfortable. His pallor had not changed, nor had his breathing. As long as he remained the way he was, she believed he would live. The cold crept up from the road, chilling her through her warm boots. If she felt it, so must he. She placed another folded cloak under his head and shoulders, then tucked his hands beneath his garments.

In moments, Brand returned, crashing through the undergrowth. His appearance startled her. She had forgotten that he still wore no clothing. Snowflakes melted as they struck him, streaming across his broad chest and down his muscular legs in steaming rivulets. She tore her attention away from his exquisite physique, and saw that he wore a delighted grin.

"It is perfect. I have found the brigands' hideout, an old cottage near a stream. Two chambers and a large hearth. Come." He carefully gathered up the unconscious man, cradling him in his arms. "Bring what you can carry. I will come back for the rest."

Wordlessly, Trina picked up some of the things he had taken from the cart as best she could with the heavy mittens she wore. He'd gathered blankets and garments, some that would probably fit her and others that might fit her uncle. She slung them over her shoulders and threaded each of her arms through a basket, packed full of things Brand had decided were valuable. She hoped he had chosen well, for before her journey was over, she might have need of things he would disdain. However, except for the oversight of grain for the mule, he had provided well for her from Kalidah's hoard. She had to trust him now.

There was no path beyond what Brand had trampled. She stepped in his footprints, clearly defined where the snow had melted under his heat. She'd only gone a few steps off the road when a twig snapped behind her.

The hair on the back of her neck rose. A tight knot of fear chilled her belly. Had a brigand somehow survived?

Whirling to see what walked behind her, already starting to utter a spell of protection, she came face-to-face with the mule. In her start of surprise and her gesture to form the spell, she lost hold of the baskets.

The mule's soft brown eyes seemed to question her before it pushed back the folds of the cloak to nuzzle her elbow. Beyond the beast, the road stretched white and silent as the snow blanketed everything. With a shaky laugh, Trina rubbed the animal between its ears. "So, you're still under my binding spell. Come along, we've got to catch up with Brand before the snow fills his tracks."

The sharp tang of cheese rose from one basket when she hefted it and a loaf of bread almost tumbled to the ground. Her stomach growled as she restored the food to a more secure position. The morning's meal lay many hours in the past. She hoped the cottage wasn't far as she set out, her boots crunching in Brand's deep, melted footprints, which were already turning to ice.

A short distance into the forest, a brook ran through a deep rocky ravine, blocking the way. Brand waited for her there, and together they walked upstream along the high bank. The sure-footed mule followed. After a short climb, the thick forest gave way to a small clearing.

An old ramshackle cottage filled most of the space. Once roses had softened the walls and humped roof, but now only a few brown twigs clung to the mud and thatch. Trina could make out where, in the distant past, someone had tended a garden. The weeds in the space had been ground into the dirt by the brigands' comings and goings.

They would not lack fuel. A stack of firewood outlined the near border of the old garden plot, and a thin ribbon of smoke rose from the squat chimney. She studied the pale gray vapor for a moment, and with satisfaction saw that the wind tore it to shreds before it rose above the trees. Good. There would be little chance of anyone noticing the smoke and discovering them.

"Open the door and quickly! He needs to be inside." Brand stood before the cottage, scowling at her. Snow still fell thickly around them, gathering on Juhan's garments and melting as it touched Brand's head to stream down his face and neck.

Trina hastened to lift the latch and swing the door wide for Brand while she surveyed the room. A long table cluttered with filthy bowls, empty beakers, moldy crusts of bread and odd bits of this and that occupied most of the space, surrounded by assorted rude stools and chairs. The cottage reeked of beer, old food and unwashed bodies.

Brand strode to an alcove near the fireplace and laid Juhan down. Trina pushed a few stools together and dumped her burden on before seeing to her patient. Once she satisfied herself that Juhan had a reasonably clean pallet to cushion him from the hard, packed earth floor, she took a moment to establish a healing sleep spell over him before she set to cleaning and tidying up what would become their temporary home.

As she worked, she fretted over whether such a simple spell would suffice. Kalidah had often worked on constructing spells for hours or days, seeking the precise words and elements to evoke the response she desired. Surely Trina's limited knowledge meant she could only create a rudimentary spell. Would such a weak effort actually hasten her uncle's healing?

She made short work of the mess, gathering it in what must have once been a tablecloth. Bearing her squalid bundle, she almost pitched headlong over the sill when she opened the door to find the mule waiting just outside. The beast followed her when she went to dump the jumble of debris into the woods behind the cottage. The wind whipped her skirts about her as she fought to fold the cloth into her arms.

Brand joined her, saying, "You must go inside and eat. I'll bring the rest of what we'll need." He gestured behind them and she peered through the swirling snow at a shelter that had been tacked onto the rear of the cottage. "That lean-to has housed livestock, probably goats, in the past. The surviving horses and your mule should do well there for a few days."

With that he was gone, striding into the woods once more.

The mule nuzzled her arm. Hasty her binding spell might have been, but it certainly had produced the desired result. She could only hope her healing spell would be as effective. Sighing, Trina sketched in the air the signs to release the spell that bound the animal to her, and herded the mule into the dilapidated lean-to. Although the manger smelled fetid, the mule buried its muzzle deep in what little fodder there was and began to eat. She filled the empty bucket with snow before she ducked under the ramshackle eaves and back into the driving storm.

Trina's heart lifted as she returned to her cleaning. Brand had said "we" when he spoke, as though he might now remain with her at least until Juhan could travel, if not accompany her all the way to her family. She spoke to herself sharply, telling herself not to read more into his words than she should.

It was no use. By the time she had built up the fire, hung a pot of fresh snow to heat and prepared a plate of bread, hard sausage and cheese, she had convinced herself Brand would stay. Why else should he take the trouble to gather supplies for her, and help her care for the only person who knew of her family? The thought that Brand might be saving Juhan so there would be someone to look after her once he was gone crossed her mind, but she chose to reject it.

Sitting at the table, she thought over how much help Brand had proven to be. He seemed so knowledgeable about the world that she had difficulty remembering he was not a well-traveled human scholar. Curiosity filled her. Where had he learned what he knew? How did he know what magickal Power cost, and why she would not be willing to pay the price?

She looked up in mid-chew as Brand blew in the door on a blast of icy wind. A heavy wool cloak now shielded his shoulders from the weather, indeed a layer of snow began to melt and drip onto the floor as soon as he was inside. He carried more supplies, a small cask, bags of food, wineskins.

"Here. This should keep our bellies filled for a while." He spread out his bounty. He had found smoked meats, more cheese and some dried fish. "I have removed all the worthwhile items from the caravan. No one coming upon it will think anything other than that it was attacked and looted. The snow will cover any sign that we were there. I found more gold, and stuffed it all into a hollow tree downstream. I will show you where it is before we leave. Should you need it later, you may always return to find it."

"I already have more than I will ever need. Enough of money. How do you feel?" She was half-afraid to ask, for fear he might disappear before her eyes.

"I am strong enough to finish the task of settling you in." He turned away and undid the clasp, letting the cloak slide from his shoulders to the floor.

He certainly looked strong and healthy. Trina swallowed as she eyed Brand's nakedness. He walked away from her to the alcove, oblivious to his nude state, but she could not help staring. He was so well-formed, from his strong feet all the way up, past his tight buttocks to his broad shoulders. She was glad for the stout stool supporting her, for her knees went weak with wanting at the sight of him so displayed.

A wench could lose herself in his wild beauty. The thought of repeating their lovemaking weakened her knees further and set her hands to trembling with anticipation. If he stayed, she had no doubt what activities would occupy them during the storm. Her healing sleep spell would keep Juhan from awakening before she wished it.

He turned and asked, "Is he resting well? Did your rough treatment of him do any good?"

Trina tore her attention away from Brand's splendid torso to consider her patient. "He now rests easily. Time will tell how well I cleansed his wound. I have put a spell on him, to increase the restorative quality of his sleep. I hope he will grow stronger through the night."

"And when will he be recovered enough to travel?" He placed his fists on his hips and Trina had to force her hands to keep still. She longed to trace the gleaming contours of his body, feast her touch on him.

She swallowed again. "I have no idea. Much depends upon his wellbeing to begin with, about which I know nothing. He appeared healthy enough, but he may have hidden weaknesses."

"Can you not tell?" Brand looked at her curiously. "If you can cast such a spell, you should be able to determine its success."

"I know only what Kalidah permitted me to learn," she confessed. She hated to admit that the spells at her command were few and paltry. To her consternation, her cheeks heated.

"So despite your ability to enter the fire, you are not the skilled sorceress I believed," he stated with a sigh. "I suppose I will have to help you further."

Just what did he mean by that? Better to know than to not know. "Are you going to come with me?"

"Aye." Humor flashed in his eyes as he crossed the cottage in two strides to lift her from her seat and pull her close. "As often as possible."

She would have groaned at the poor jest but his mouth claimed hers, and she could only murmur encouragement. He tasted like the cold wind and snow, not like a fire spirit at all.

He drew back his head and whispered, "The taste of you makes me hunger for more."

A shiver of anticipation ran through her. "Help yourself," she invited.

Tucking her under his arm, he grabbed a wedge of cheese from her plate. The taste of the cheese, his first experience with food, struck him with a force he did not expect. The sharp bite of it stung his mouth, bringing forth a flood of moisture from the inside of his cheeks. It reminded him of how Trina had flooded his mouth with her nectar when he'd licked her cleft. He wondered if this sensation even approached what she'd felt then. He closed his eyes to savor it, a feeling almost painful in its intensity. How had he once thought these mortals to be simple?

He chewed furiously and managed with a little difficulty to swallow. Trina held up her mug, and he took a sip. The dark ale sizzled in his mouth. He drank deeply, feeling how the drink warmed his belly. His gut contracted, demanding more. He bit into the cheese again, and again he felt the exhilaration. 'Twas something akin to the ecstasy he found buried in Trina's body, but different.

The truth hammered into him. This was what he'd been missing.

He knew, with a certainty he couldn't question, that as long as he ate enough to sustain this mortal body, he would not falter. He took a bite of cheese, together with a small piece of bread. The combination was even better than the cheese alone. Already, he felt his strength increasing.

"Mmmm. Heavenly." As he chewed, he ran his hand over her back, through her hair and along her jaw.

"Me or the cheese?" She snuggled into him.

He heard warm contentment in her voice, with an undercurrent of passion. His response was immediate and physical. Fortunately, the caravan had carried all kinds of stores, and he'd cached the rest of the less perishable foodstuffs not far from the cottage. They had a lot of everything, from clothing to food and drink. He suspected he'd need quite a bit of food to maintain his strength, shut in here with Trina and his desire for her. "Both."

"I had no idea you needed to eat." She looked up at him and cocked an eyebrow.

"I never have had food before. When you ate in the mage's cottage, I had no desire to taste the bread or the cheese. Now it seems right. Just like touching you, and exploring your softness."

He kissed her again, softly and gently. She tasted of sharp cheese and smoke. He hoped the storm lasted a long time, so he could not only sample more of her delights, but all of the different foods he had retrieved from the merchant's wagon. He kissed her more deeply, and decided the food could wait.

"But—"

"You mortals talk too much. It is the source of all your problems. Just feel." He took her head in his hands, and tipped her face up to his. "Just feel."

She closed her eyes and did as he said.

His lips were alternately soft and demanding. She gave herself up to the craving his kiss engendered.

He shifted her onto his lap, and wrapped his arms around her in a warm embrace. She slid her hands into his hair, running the damp curls through her fingers.

Touching and kissing him but not seeing him was different than anything she'd ever experienced. In her mind, she pictured his actions, as though she saw him in the scrying bowl, fondling another woman.

The sensation of feeling his touch while she watched his movements was incredibly exciting. Heat trailed in the wake of his hands. She kept her eyes closed and leaned into him.

Brand touched her everywhere, smoothing his hands over her back, cupping her buttocks where she sat on his strong thighs. She could feel his arousal through her skirts and moved her hips a bit to tease him. He groaned and plucked at her garments. Cupping her breast and finding a nipple, he pinched her gently through the fabric. A tendril of fire spiraled through her.

"You are wearing too much," he broke the kiss to complain. He bent his head and nuzzled her neck, finding a most sensitive spot behind her ear.

She caught her breath in a gasp. Who would have thought a small patch of skin could be so susceptible to pleasure? Desire almost choked her. She had to clear her throat before she could speak. "The fire in the hearth has not yet warmed the room."

"It has enough for you to no longer need this." He unfastened her cloak and let it fall behind her to the floor. "Are you still cold?"

She gasped as he rocked her backwards, lifting her foot and running his hand up her ankle to her calf. She clenched her eyes shut as he tipped her back farther, until her foot pointed at the ceiling. Her head hung down and the jeweled pins tumbled out to let her hair trail free onto the floor. Her skirt tumbled to her waist, revealing her completely to him.

He kept her there while he licked his way up her leg. Or was it down her leg? She tried not to think, still picturing the two of them in her mind.

She both saw and felt him find the back of her knee and bite her gently. Hunger for him burned in her, turning her insides to molten desire. She whimpered as he trailed kisses down her thigh, toward the juncture of her legs.

Then he suddenly swung her up, letting her leg drop to the other side of his lap, so that she sat astride him. He gathered her chemise and gown in both hands and pushed them both over her head.

Cold air washed across her heated flesh, puckering her skin into gooseflesh and her nipples into hard, almost painful, pebbles. He left her garments bunched on her shoulders, pinning her arms behind her. His hot, wet mouth closed on one cold nipple and she gasped with the force of the heat that blazed through her.

Unable to see him, unable to touch him, she felt her world contract to the feel of his mouth and hands as he fed the flames of desire. He nipped first one taut peak and then the other, holding the bud tightly in his teeth while flicking his tongue across the tip. She shuddered as waves of heat flowed from his mouth, spreading deep into her belly to lick at her womb. Evidence of her desire flooded her cleft and she squirmed on his lap.

"That's perfect. Just feel." His hot breath fanned over her breast. She arched into him, craving the sensation of his mouth on her bared flesh.

Reaching behind her, he placed her hands on his knees. When she supported her own weight, he pulled her close, so that the hard ridge of his erection nestled along her nether lips. She snuggled closer and spread her legs. Her nether lips opened to his cock.

She imagined the view from above, seeing them fit together but not joined. They were so close, the head of his cock might have belonged to either of them. Then he gathered her breasts in his hands and covered her mouth with his, and she lost all rational thought. There was just the reality of his touch, his taste, his feel. She burned with his kisses, opening to him, welcoming him into her mouth.

Her hips jerked, for she wanted more. She wanted everything. She wanted him to fill her, devour her, consume her.

Then he pulled away, but only long enough to lift her and glide into her in one smooth motion. She slid down his shaft, seeing in her mind and feeling how well he filled and stretched her. Watching him disappear into her wetness while she felt the hard heat of his erection enter her sent a shiver through her.

"Yes," he hissed as she came to rest against him. "Perfect."

"I—" she began.

"No thought. No talk. Feel me." He clasped her to him for a deep kiss that brought another rush of heat to her belly. "Feel us."

She felt him jerk within her. He rocked her back toward his knees, bent to kiss her neck and pulled her forward again, angling his hips to meet her. He didn't move much within her, but it was enough.

The soft curls of his beard brushed across the place he'd kissed, and she let her head fall back. In her mind, she saw him bend to reach her breast, licking her areola and nipping at the taut peak. She felt the tug, felt the need that spread through her, slowly consuming her, like flames devouring a pool of oil.

She moaned as she watched his hard shaft pull from her, gleaming wet in the firelight, only to feel him thrust and fill her. She braced her feet and moved to help him slide in and out of her in a timeless ritual of passion that fed the flames, until she felt she would explode with it.

When he claimed her mouth, entering her with his tongue in time with the thrusts of his hips, she did.

Chapter Seven

✖

Morning dawned dark and silent. Not even the wind made any sound. Trina pushed open the front shutter and found a world of white.

Snow piled up against the cottage wall to the level of the windowsill, and still fell in thick flakes. So thick it obscured everything. So thick she couldn't tell just how deep it was.

Had it drifted that high, or had so much fallen overnight? Was it even morning? Had they dozed and loved until it was now late in the day, or could it be a whole day later?

One thing was certain. They were snowed in. Whatever Juhan's health, it would be days if not weeks before they could travel.

Her patient required her attention. His wound showed no signs of redness or irritation when she changed the bandage, indeed she could almost see the edges drawing together cleanly. The skin had been torn and ragged where the arrow entered, gaping open after her ministrations to cleanse it. His flesh now showed signs of healing.

Did her uncle possess Power of his own, to recover so quickly from such a wound? If he believed she held magick at her command, mayhap it was common in the people of her birthplace.

Could that be why Kalidah had bought her—beyond the desire for one of her coloring to use for that awful ritual? That speculation led her thoughts deeper along the path. Could her Power be why she was stolen? Kalidah had shown herself to be cunning. Trina wouldn't hazard a guess to her age. With the Power she'd wielded, the old woman might be literally as old as the hills. Was it possible the old mage had sent her minions to find a child who met her demands? She had too many questions, and no answers.

She was impatient for her uncle to recover. He seemed stronger and regained his senses while she tended him, not enough to speak but his eyes were clear and understanding while she got a little broth into him and changed his clothing.

With Brand's help, she washed what she could reach, from a bowl of heated water. After Juhan lay back again, as clean as she could make him, with his belly warmed from the broth, she let him sleep naturally, to see how he would fare.

While she fried sausages and onions, Brand plowed his way through the snow to the animals in the shed at the back of the cottage. He returned just as she scraped their breakfast from the heavy iron pan into bowls patterned in twining vines and colorful birds. She had to laugh at the idea that she, not so long ago a lowly slave, now dined on sausages flavored with exotic spices, served in fancy carved and painted wooden bowls.

She and Brand sat across the table from one another and ate. He reported he had brought enough hay and grain from one of the wagons to keep the beasts hale and hearty until the storm subsided and Juhan healed enough to allow them to resume their journey.

Trina cast a glance at the huddled form of her uncle, still and silent in the alcove. His chest rose and fell with each steady breath. She knew he was resting as comfortably as she could make him, and wished she could do more.

She returned to her seat beside Brand, wondering what would come next.

He smiled that knowing smile of his. "You must begin to learn of the world outside your woods."

"I'd rather learn more of you."

"Sassy slave." She couldn't take offense when he said it with such warmth.

He pushed the dishes aside and began to draw on the table with a stub of charcoal from the hearth. "This is your woods, and this is the road north."

She interrupted him with a hand on his wrist. Ignoring the seductive heat of his firm flesh beneath her fingers, she asked, "How do you know this?"

His eyes burned into hers. He shook his head slightly. "I have been in many hearths, and seen much in my time. I have done many things you would not understand. Do not ask me to explain. Some I cannot put into words, and some you simply could not comprehend."

She swallowed and withdrew her hand. "Is this like making the fireballs?"

He considered that for a moment before answering. "Yes and no. The ability to control fire is part of me, part of what I am. The knowledge I have gained over the years comes from observation, and from digesting maps and journals."

"Digesting?" She stared at him, realizing he was right. She was unable to fathom what he might mean.

"Precisely. Of all I destroy in my frenzy, some things stamp themselves on my mind as I consume them. I learned much from your mage and her papers, although nothing of your origins." He trailed a finger across her breast, where the dark tracery of Kalidah's evil patterns lay beneath the wool and linen. "That is how I know of your marks, and what another sorcerer might achieve should you fall into his or her hands. You would not like what I have done to learn what I know."

Trina gulped. His answer was not what she expected, and she would not ask again. Uncomfortable with this information, for it reminded her that he was so different from herself, she cast about for something to distract him.

"Are you still hungry? We have plenty of cheese and the bread will grow stale if we don't eat it."

"So like a proper housewife. I believe I could eat some more." He grinned at her and nodded at the piles of loot he had brought on his trips from the wreckage of the caravan. "There are so many things I wish to taste. Didn't I see a small crock in one of those baskets? Let's see what it is."

She told him, "A small crock might contain anything from horseradish to honey or mustard."

"I have never tasted honey and mustard."

Trina had to laugh at the way he lumped them together so. "Honey and mustard are not the same thing." She rummaged in the basket and in triumph held up two small pottery crocks, one short and squat, the other taller and curved like a lyre. They bore different stamps on their corks. "We have both. Do you want to taste something sweet or something spicy?"

"What is the difference?"

"How do I explain this?" She hefted the crocks and considered. "Mustard is best with meat, or smeared on bread to accompany a meal. We might have eaten it with our sausages. Honey can also—" She broke off and chuckled. "Now that I think of it, they *can* be thought of as the same. Both can be served with meat, or spread on bread. Honey is also wonderful in porridge. Mustard would not be."

"No?" A smile lurked in Brand's beard. "Are you sure? We might like it."

"*You* might. Do not expect me to try it." Trina slapped the bread on the table between the crock and the jar. "You have a lot to learn about mortal tastes. Try each in turn on the bread, by itself. See if you like each by itself before you begin mixing flavors."

Juhan groaned and shifted. Trina flew across the cottage to kneel by his pallet. Pain creased his forehead and deepened the furrows by his mouth. She reached into a basin of cool water nearby to wring out a cloth and mopped his brow.

His eyes fluttered open. He tried to rise, made a rasping sound, licked his lips and managed to croak, "Katrina?"

"Aye, it is Katrina." She smiled in delight. Regaining his senses meant he was recovering. Mayhap her simple spell was helping.

"What hap—?" He broke off and dropped his head back onto the pallet with a gasp.

"We were attacked by bandits. The caravan was destroyed. You and I are the only ones left alive."

Her uncle sighed and closed his eyes. After a moment, he opened them and looked questioningly up at the ceiling.

"We are in a cottage nearby, and safe now." Trina spooned some willow tea into his mouth. He grimaced and she reminded herself to sweeten the next pot she brewed with honey. When he swallowed, she gave him more. "You were injured and must rest. We will be fine until you are ready to travel."

He relaxed. She continued to spoon-feed him, more tea and then some weak broth. When he'd fallen asleep again, she renewed the healing spell and left him to sleep under its benevolent influence. She fairly danced back to Brand. "He's going to be fine."

She stood looking at him for a long moment, while he sat and munched on cheese and bread, slathered with mustard. This man who wasn't a man had become her lover and her friend. Her smile faded as sadness suffused her. At any moment, he could disappear into the fire and she might never see him again.

"I like both honey and mustard but you are right. They do not belong together." He cut another large hunk of bread and slathered it with honey.

Trina strove to maintain her calm demeanor. It would do neither of them any good for her to dissolve into tears, as she longed to do. Instead, she needed to make the most of her time left with him. Summoning a smile, she sat beside him and carefully kept her tone light. "You certainly do have a hearty appetite."

"Never have I experienced such appetites." He swallowed the bread and pulled her to him. "Never have I experienced such a riot of feelings."

She knew exactly what he meant.

Gently, he lifted her hand to press a kiss to her palm. A shiver of need ran through her, a spiral of fire that threaded its way from her palm to her heart. She too felt a riot of emotion, as lust and love mingled within her.

"Part of me longed for the sight of your sweet face while we were apart. You make me hunger and thirst for you. You make me crave your touch and your taste." He touched his lips to her neck in a soft kiss. "I think I may have been wrong. You do wield great magick, for you have bewitched me, sassy slave."

With a pang, she acknowledged that she had grown to love his strength, his good humor, his wisdom and his kindness. Her breath caught in her throat. May the gods help her, she loved him — and he wasn't mortal.

They had no future together.

He would never dandle their babe on his knee by the fire while she prepared their supper. He would not grow old with her. She knew little of spirits, but she'd wager all the dead merchant's gold that Brand was already older than she could imagine. Most likely, he was older even than Kalidah. She determined to make the most of whatever time they had left together. Whatever it took, she would never let him guess how sad the thought of their parting made her.

When he kissed her, she flung her arms around his neck and opened herself to him. She would see to it that, long after she'd crumbled to dust, he would remember the lonely mage's thrall who once loved him.

Trina pulled her gown over her head and unlaced her shift. Now, what had he done that had proven to be such sweet torture? Ah, yes, prolonged anticipation, if she remembered aright. Of course, when he'd held her on the edge of rapture, she hadn't been thinking clearly, much less marking his technique.

While he watched, she eased the neckline lower. He followed the progress of the descending linen over the swell of her breasts with his eyes, licking his lips as though he longed to taste her.

When she paused just before baring her nipples, he made a sound deep in his chest. She hesitated, only the barest hint of pink showing above her shift, and the groan became a roar. "I am not made of stone, wench! Why do you tease me?"

"Because you teased me." She moved the linen back up a bit.

"I never!" He reached out and ripped the shift from her, casting it aside. His strong arms gathered her close for a deep, swift kiss. His hands smoothed over her curves, tracing her hips and cupping her backside.

"Never?" She snuggled into his nakedness, reveling in the feel of skin sliding against skin.

"Perhaps once or twice," he conceded. His mouth found hers and he claimed her, branding her with his passion. All her intent to tease him slipped away as she lost herself in his blazing kiss.

He picked her up and laid her across the table.

She stretched before him, raising her arms and then running her hands down her sides. With a small smile, she cupped her breasts. "Are you still hungry?"

"Aye, sassy slave, hungry for you." He parted her knees and stepped between them. Bending over her, he growled, "Two can play this game."

His warm hands touched her everywhere but her breasts. He stroked her ribs, caressed her thighs, ran his fingers along her arms. Each caress heightened the sensitivity of her skin. His thumbs traced the line of her jaw, feathered touches down her neck. Her breathing came ragged and fast, as she waited for the next touch. Where would it be? He skimmed his hands along her inner thighs, then flattened both on the table beside her. He waited a moment and she almost cried out with the tension building within her. Then his tongue found one nipple. She writhed in need, barely able to stand the sensation of his wet massage without any other stimulation.

Unable to stop herself, she whimpered.

"Had enough?" He transferred his attention to her other nipple, while his hands remained idle.

"Aye," she gasped.

Swiftly, he engulfed her breasts with both hands, and drove into her. His thick cock filled her completely. She gasped again at the thrill of sudden contact in all the right places. Hard and fast was exactly what she wanted, to wipe out the sadness she felt. She needed to lose herself in him, in his touch and his taste.

He swallowed her moan of pleasure in another kiss. As the sound escaped her, he took advantage of the opportunity and swept his tongue inside. She sucked, relishing the now-familiar taste of him. He tasted of passion and pleasure.

She raked her nails over his back as he filled her, mouth and belly, welcoming his hot possession. This time, he alternated the thrusts of his tongue with the thrusts of his hips. She moved her knees higher and tipped her hips, increasing the depth of his thrusts. The angle changed the sensations within her womb. The head of his shaft reached a new spot, a place that made her shudder with the intensity of the pleasure he gave her.

Trina thought she might expire from the ecstasy of him plunging into her depths, stretching and filling her as she'd not thought possible. Small spasms pulled her tighter around his cock. She surged up to meet each thrust, wrapping her arms around his chest for leverage.

It felt as though a glowing cord connected his tongue and his shaft, sawing molten heat through her with each thrust. The heat within her grew with each rhythmic pass of the cord. Her belly and breasts burned as molten desire expanded and spread.

He placed her hands on her breasts, cupping her fingers around their fullness. She understood, and began to fondle herself. Was this what he felt, when he caressed her? His hands were larger and warmer, although she did her best to imitate his touch. Each stroke of her hands, each gentle touch on her skin, sent shudders rippling through her. How could she feel a touch on her chest both up and down her spine, all the way to her toes? She pinched her distended and aching nipples, seeking relief from the mounting tension. Once she opened her eyes to stare into his approving amber gaze. All the sensations raging through her promptly increased in intensity. Her hips jerked helplessly against him. His lips curled against hers in a smile. She closed her eyes again.

The cord of fire in her chest expanded. She dimly heard the suck and gurgle of her increased wetness each time he penetrated her. A new sensation began when he reached between them, to stroke her *there*, where she encircled him. An inferno roared to life beneath his touch. The conflagration grew as his fingers caressed her, pushing her ever upward, closer to the pinnacle. He suddenly increased the tempo of his thrusts and touches, pounding into her. Her breath came faster and faster as she matched him move for move. Sweet gods, this was what she wanted, what she needed. The growing cord of fire exploded, engulfing them both in a blaze of ecstasy.

He roared wordlessly as he drove deep again and again, pumping his seed deep within her womb. She held him close as she spasmed under his thrusts, welcoming the sizzle and burn of their mutual release.

Whether he would remember her, she couldn't know. She would remember him for her lifetime. Of that, she had no doubt.

They lay together on the table, limbs entwined, until Trina's feet grew cold. She pushed at him, gently, and he moved to let her rise.

After tossing another log on the fire, Brand gathered her into his lap, pulling the table and his stool closer to the hearth. She huddled into his warmth and he rubbed her feet.

"I have never known such bliss." He nuzzled her hair. "The gods truly blessed me when you embraced the fire."

Trina's stomach rumbled. Embarrassed at such a rude noise at such an intimate moment, she wrapped her arms around herself and ducked to hide her face behind her hair.

He threw back his head and laughed heartily. "You have a great appetite, for such a small mortal." Pulling the discarded dishes in front of him, he tore a hunk of bread from the loaf and slathered it with honey. "Eat."

Trina obediently took a bite. When he held the mug to her lips, she drank the dark, pungent ale.

"I, too, have a great appetite." He took a large bite, swallowed and repeated, "I have a great appetite—for a small mortal."

Trina stared at him over the rim of the mug.

"In case you missed my jest, for you are not laughing, that would be you, sassy slave." He grinned and swallowed a large amount of ale. "That is why I will try to stay with you."

She stared at him, thinking furiously of some other meaning she could put upon his words. There was none. Her heart leapt within her. "You will?"

"You have but puny resources to defend yourself." Brand waved his hand in dismissal of Juhan. "Your friend there will be of no use for weeks. I would not have you harmed."

She quirked a brow at him, feeling light as a bubble and ready to overflow with joy. Unaccountably, tears pricked at her eyes. "You wouldn't?"

"Nay, you have become dear to me."

"And can you remain in this form for weeks, if necessary?" She blinked away tears. Why should she cry when she was this happy?

"I believe so." Brand lightly brushed his thumb across her cheek, wiping away a tear. "Do you remember me telling you I had no idea how long I could maintain this form? When you left the mage's cot, I was already weakening, quickly. I feared I would expire before I found the coals still glowing beneath the debris of the shed. I despaired of ever enjoying this mortal body again, at least for any length of time."

He took a sip of ale. "Tasting the cheese, the first food I ate, was a revelation to me. Food and drink give me strength, replacing what I expend in using this body. If that fails, I find that merely returning to the spirit realm restores my strength. Last night, while you slept, I tried changing my form. Going back and forth from the fire is not without effort, but I can do it. Perhaps it will become easier the more I travel between here and there. With food and revisiting the fire, I believe I can stay with you until you reach your family. In this mortal body, I feel good." He nuzzled her neck. "You feel good."

A new emotion, one of rightness and abundance, stole through her, lighting the dark places in her soul. She had always felt alone before. She no longer did. Now, through whatever magickal circumstance he had come to her, she had a lover. She knew her future would be fine, whether their time together was tallied in weeks or years.

He rose and held out his hand. "Come. Your friend is resting, and I would dance with you."

"Here?" She looked around and saw little room among the stools and baskets for dancing.

"Nay, in there." Brand nodded toward the hearth. "Where we met. In my world."

"Oh." She had no fear of the fire, especially not with him at her side. Still she hesitated. When last she'd managed it, she'd almost been stuck in his world. "I'm not certain I can do it again. The last time, you weren't there and I wasn't sure I could get back here."

"I am with you now, and you need not be afraid. You will not know until you try. I believe you can."

She drew back slightly. "But you said I am not willing to pay the cost of learning magick."

"I meant that you do not have the cold ambition that is needed to wield great power. I do not know how you first joined us on the coals, but that is no great power, it is merely a magickal skill." He stepped toward the fire, drawing her with him. "See them? They await us."

Trina steadied herself and looked *beyond* the fire, as she had before. After a moment, she could indeed make out tiny, fiery forms moving on the coals.

"I will wait for you. Settle yourself, but don't be long." Brand pulled her close for a searing kiss. "I will miss you, my love," he whispered as he released her and stepped into the fire.

He grew thin and almost transparent, flickered once and disappeared. Trina sat on the floor close to the fire, resting her arms on a stool in front of her. Looking into the hearth, she could see no sign of the fire-folk.

Could she do this again? Her heart pounded. What if there were something special about Kalidah's hearth, and only coals from there would permit entrance? The mage had lived there for untold years and surely she must have imbued the stones, perhaps the fire itself, with her powerful magick. This fire had not been kindled from those coals, but from the embers that lay beneath the ashes when they arrived at the cottage.

If Brand believed she could, then she would try to recreate her previous feat. She shifted the stool aside and sat with her back against the legs of the table, her hands crossed in her lap. One deep breath and then another relaxed her. She cleared her mind and let her vision drift into the distance, looking *beyond* the flames.

The more she looked, the more the movement had form and rhythm. She let her mind ease into the cadence.

Slowly the curtain of fire running along each stick resolved into small bodies. She could see tiny, distinct arms and legs, swaying in a sinuous dance.

The transition occurred so swiftly her head spun. In the heat, above the coals, she stood atop a stick, watching the fire-folk sway and spin, flowing around her as they swirled by.

She searched the dancers, and found him.

Brighter than the others, large and powerful, Brand approached her in the pattern of the dance. The fire-folk parted to let him through.

Come. The word rang in her mind.

She took his hand, and stepped out into the dance.

Chapter Eight

The next morning, Trina leaned over the bowl, staring intently *beyond* the reflection of the cottage rafters above her. She relaxed as best she could, given the attention Brand focused on her.

"Do not stiffen so. You are fighting the magick." He ran a hand along her spine.

"I am afraid I cannot do this," she confessed. A lump threatened to clog her throat. She kept her eyes fastened on the bowl. If she looked at Brand, she would burst into tears. "I am afraid I will never do aught but perform the simple spells Kalidah taught me. If Juhan were not recovering so quickly, I would believe even those are worthless."

"There is nothing wrong with simplicity. It might be a mistake for you to strive for complexity."

"Why is that?" Her gaze flew to his face in astonishment. His statement challenged everything she'd learned working for Kalidah. Surely everything the sorceress did was very difficult.

He smiled reassuringly. "Just as every woman has her own way of cooking, every mage has her own way of commanding magick. If you excel at making simple, tasty and filling dishes from the foodstuffs you have at hand, why would you waste time and money experimenting with exotic ingredients? Do what you do best, and be content."

"I do not have to craft complicated spells?"

"Nay, you do not. Remember, simple is often quick and you may need speed at some time in the future." He laid a hand on her cheek, turning her face back to the bowl. "Now, try again. You saw the flame-folk in the fire, which is much like seeing anything in the scrying bowl." She took another deep breath, heavy with the herbs Brand had steeped in the water. "You make me nervous."

"I did not realize I was such a distraction." He grinned. "Would you prefer that I leave? I could tend the mule and horses, and give you a little time alone."

It was a tempting suggestion but she hesitated. "What if I need you?"

"You worry too much, sassy slave." He tweaked her nose. "Should you have a question, you may call out. I will hear you. These walls are not as thick as a sheet of parchment, for all they do hold out the snow."

A blast of cold air accompanied his departure. Trina did not look up, concentrating instead on achieving the relaxation that eluded her in his presence.

As had happened before when she used the scrying bowl, all at once the rafters disappeared. A pale gray fog covered the water.

While she watched, the mist rose to the bowl's rim. *That* had never happened before. She shuddered and strove not to blink.

Images of her family as Juhan had described them occupied her thoughts. She wanted to see what they were doing, to see if she could sense anything from her home. The images she'd seen in the flash of Juhan's childhood stayed with her, the brook bordered with willows and the yard outside the kitchen.

The fog began to clear, subsiding into the water, leaving a cloud-studded sky in its wake. She tried to picture her mother, a woman Juhan said in her youth had looked much as she Trina did now.

The sky became grass, nay, trees, as the focus sharpened. A clearing came into view. Stools and logs surrounded a large fire in the center. Only a few were occupied, and those by rough men who bore no resemblance to Juhan or herself.

She sighed in disappointment and prepared to end the exercise. She tried to pull her awareness back into the cottage.

Nothing happened. Nay, that was not correct. The scars on her chest flared with pulsing pain.

The scene changed again, moving to one side of the clearing. A fine tent stood beneath the spreading arms of a huge fir tree. While she watched, a figure seated inside rose to its feet. The vision moved into the tent, showing her not the man's face—that remained in shadow—but the heavy pendant he wore.

The design on it made her scalp tingle. She couldn't make out details, for it shifted and blurred when she tried to sharpen her gaze on any portion of it.

Within the heart of the dull black stone, a pinprick of light appeared. As it grew, it gained shape, becoming an eye. Unlike the lines of the pendant, every detail of the eye was clear and harsh. Its lidless gaze bored into her.

She felt the probe of its attention like a physical touch, reaching into her mind. Drawing her hands up, she tried to push the bowl away, and found she hadn't moved.

Every effort to disengage, to turn away, was futile. Much as the potion Kalidah had fed her, the eye rendered her helpless.

Pain lanced through her head, eclipsing the burn of her skin where the sorceress had marked her. Dear Goddess, what was this demon—for it could be nothing else—doing to her? Bits of early memories rose up before her.

A man standing beside the brook she'd seen in Juhan's thoughts, but in a landscape changed by years.

A cookpot bubbling over a hearth.

A striped gray cat snuggled in a pile of hay nursing a litter of kittens.

Her mother, aye, looking just as her uncle had described, as Trina had last seen her, bending down to kiss her goodnight.

The well in Kalidah's clearing, rimed with frost.

She watched in horror as the invader examined them, plundering her mind. More images of her service with Kalidah appeared.

The mage teaching her to read. Her struggle to decipher foreign words in cramped script.

The proper handling of fragile vellum and parchment.

Lady Nanon's finery.

A splash broke the demon's spell.

Trina wiped broth from her eyes and face. Her vision cleared in time to see Brand strike the scrying bowl. It flew across the cottage and crashed into the hearth. She took a deep breath, pleased to find the pain had subsided in her head and her chest.

"Are you free of it?" Brand demanded. He knelt beside her, still holding the ladle. Behind him, the contents of the broth pot spread across the table.

She collapsed into his arms, her breath coming in gasps. "Did you see it?"

"Nay, only the glow from the bowl." His arms wrapped around her. "Truth be told, I did not wish to look. The stench of its presence was enough."

She buried her face in his shoulder. Overlaying his unique scent were the faint smells of hay and manure, the combination comforting in its wholesome normalcy. The only sounds in the cottage were the crackle of the fire in the hearth, their breathing and the measured drip of the broth onto the floor. She breathed deeply and some of the tightness in her chest eased. "Wha-what was it?"

"It was a pryer, I believe. A nasty charm, usually set into an amulet or other small item, dormant until it is triggered by a touch of Power. It then releases a demon instructed to delve into the mage's memories, absorb knowledge and relate what it learns to its master. Some are tuned to an individual mage's touch. The worst destroy the mind as they draw forth knowledge. Some dark mages will use both aspects to eliminate a rival."

Her life with Kalidah, although she had learned much, had sheltered her more than she knew. Of all the things the demon might have been, she would never have guessed such an evil intent. "Sweet Lord and Lady, what else is there to fear?"

"More than you wish to know about, my love. Far more." He pulled back to look at her and wiped a drop of broth from her nose. "Did it harm you? What was it seeking?"

"I think it didn't hurt me." She shook her head and tried to remember.

Tamping down the terror she'd experienced, she made herself look back at the images the demon had viewed. "I don't know. I saw scenes from my childhood, from before I was with Kalidah. It may have done me a favor by breaking those free. I saw my mother. She looks just like Uncle Juhan said she would." She absently rubbed her chest and flinched when the scars once more flared to life—and pain. Sucking in a breath, she fumbled with the laces of her shift.

Brand pushed her hands aside. "Allow me." With a deft and gentle touch, he unfastened the ties.

When he drew back the linen to reveal the scars, he frowned. "Your marks are inflamed, fairly pulsing with Power. I suspect that charm was tuned to this pattern or to your former mistress's magick. Mayhap even your own."

Eyes wide, Trina stared at him.

He watched her gravely. "Tell me what you can. Did the demon see any of this area, where we are now? The merchant's caravan, the brigands, this cottage?"

"Nay, only my very early life. A few scenes at Kalidah's holding. You interrupted before it looked for anything recent."

"I was fortunate. The broth still held the remnants of your healing spells. That was enough to turn aside the demon's regard, long enough for you to break free." He gathered her close again. "It knows about your family. I fear we may encounter whatever or whoever seeks to use your scars once we reach your home. Mayhap before. You will keep away from standing water, and only risk the fire when I am near."

"Yes, master." Her tone was serious, no longer sassy.

"Would another mage know of Kalidah's plans? Did she correspond with anyone? I expect she had many enemies."

"The lord's mother brought her a bit of parchment she needed, and from their words, Kalidah was assisting her with something. Kalidah wasn't pleased that it was only a small piece, and she claimed it was a copy as well. I know Lady Nanon had sent out men looking for the parchment, and they were still seeking the rest of it."

Brand stroked his beard. "We don't know if those who seek it know Kalidah's name."

"Wait a moment." Trina frowned and tried to remember the conversation between the sorceress and her patron. "When Kalidah complained about the bit being a copy, she mentioned she didn't want to disappoint someone she was going to see the next day. She called him the master. That's the only time I ever heard her mention him."

This news met with a groan. Brand ran one hand through his hair and grimaced. "That means she was serving Lady Nanon and another mage. We have no way to tell who it might be, and I'm sure he's both stronger and fouler than she was."

Brand took her gently by the shoulders. His expression was grim. "We have to learn what we can from that man. Did you see where the pendant was? Anything that might tell us how far away it is or who might have created it?"

"There was green grass and a huge fir tree. The man who wore it was in a fine tent. Servants accompanied him, but they were not well-dressed. Not as rough as the brigands who attacked the caravan, but not a great lord's retainers."

"How heavy was their clothing? Winter leather and wool or spring's linen?"

She frowned. "I think 'twas light wool, a bit of leather here and there, mostly short vests. I saw no cloaks at all."

"South of here, then. We have a bit of time to prepare. We cannot assume that the demon acquired no knowledge of our whereabouts. It is also possible that the man you saw was

272

merely a servant. His master mage could be anywhere, and no doubt has servants in many places."

Kalidah's potions and spells had only immobilized her. The demon had done far worse when it entered her mind. Its hold was so strong she'd been unable to summon any means of resistance. The thought of how easily it invaded her thoughts and memories wrapped icy tendrils of fear about her heart.

"You will not venture outside without me." Brand continued his instructions. "You must ward the cottage. Mayhap it would be wise to set wards out in the forest. At least that would warn us of anyone approaching."

"Set wards?"

"Aye, a protective spell to guard an area from intruders." He frowned. "Hearth and home, did that mage teach you nothing of use?"

"She taught me only what she didn't want to waste time on doing herself."

"Can you construct spells?"

"She had me transcribe some, and I've watched and listened to enough of hers. I can try."

"Then begin. I will clean up this mess." He gestured at the broth, congealing on the tabletop and floor. "Should you need a focus for your spell, mayhap there is something appropriate among the merchant's wares."

Trina rummaged in the baskets and boxes until she came across the merchant's records. The bound accounts ledger proved to be full, all pages used on both sides, but she found a few scrolls with one surface completely covered but the other blank. It took but a moment to scan the neat script. She could use both sides if she needed, overwriting the thin, spidery hand. The merchant now had no need to contact the Jews in some place called Venice, or for the loans they offered. Had it been a letter to family, she would have preserved it, making sure it reached his relatives.

What might she use as the anchor for the protective shield? There were all sorts of things in the caravan's stores. Various casks and pottery crocks, some empty, some sealed. Her imagination ran free, but she couldn't figure a way to easily employ any of the items as protection. Grain and wool were abundant, clearly what the merchant dealt in. A small carved casket resisted her initial efforts to open it. She persisted. When the lid sprang open, she was rewarded with the sparkle and fire of gems.

She held up a chunk of polished amber. Through it, the flames danced and shone brighter. Perfect. Picking through the pendants—she shied away from looking directly at those, turning each facedown—and strands of stones, she found enough pieces of amber to make a large handful.

The assorted containers held no ink. She had to make do with a thin bit of charcoal from the hearth.

Brand shooed her from the table. "You don't want grease on your work. Away, and let me mop this up."

Settling on the floor near the hearth, she smoothed the parchment across a stool in front of her, spread the amber atop it and began to compose a protective spell.

Firelight in amber bright,
Hold vigil from the corners
Spread your web
About our heads
Alert us to invaders

Keep watch though the darkest night
From dawn to dawn protect us
Let no one intrude upon
Our privacy and shelter
Or pass you by unseen

As Trina wrote the words, she kept forefront in her mind the mage who put the charm in the pendant. What had Brand said of the warding spell? *At least that would warn us.*

She idly stirred the amber with one finger while she thought what she required of the spell. A large piece rolled away from the others, closer to the fire. While she watched, it picked up the flames and glowed so brightly it almost hurt her eyes. Trina snatched up the charcoal and began scribbling.

This nugget I will keep at hand
As herald of your warning
Should the sinister approach
Let the flames caught deep within
Burn brighter, glowing with alarm

When our enemies come near
No cottage shall they see
Conceal us from their quest
Let them choose another path
That leads them far afield

As fire burns in amber's heart
Like shall pair with like
I who know the fire-folk dance
Ask protection from all harm
As I will, so mote it be

She read it over. It wasn't the finest of spells, but she thought it would serve.

Brand agreed. "'Tis not a complicated spell, but effective. You have mentioned everything, as well as what binds the necessary three elements together."

"*Three* elements?" Trina glanced at the spell she'd written. There were only two, as far as she could see.

"Aye." Brand ticked them off on his fingers. "The fire, the amber, and you. Without the affinity you have for fire, do you think you could command the fire and amber's cooperation so readily? Some sacrifice would be required, some offering to bind you to them so that they work your will. Remember what I said about paying a price for magick?"

Trina nodded. She was beginning to understand.

"You have paid the price for this by venturing into the fire, and relating well enough to survive. You did not offend my folk or try to take advantage. You trusted me. You look upon your ability to enter my world as a blessing, not as a right." He touched her lips. "And this is not much that you ask in your spell. The natural response of amber in the presence of fire is to glow. You are giving it that opportunity, just defining the circumstances. Did the sorceress teach that to you?"

Trina shook her head and permitted herself a small smile. His praise gave her a warm glow of happiness. Mayhap she knew more than she gave herself credit for. "She taught me nothing of why and how magick works, only to do what she required of me."

"Your uncle was right. You do have Talent. Whether great or small remains to be seen. Listening to your inner voice is an important skill, and one that many mages, no matter how great their Power, never master." He gathered up the amber. "Let us waste no time in setting the wards. Although you say the pendant was in warmer climes in your vision, distance is but a small barrier for some mages."

She bundled up and they trudged through the snow to erect the ones outside first. Together they walked the perimeter of a large circle, enclosing much more than the cottage. Trina used a stick to draw a huge circle in the snow. She closed it and felt the tingle of Power as she recited her spell, following Brand's instructions to imbue it with her will. She closed her eyes and envisioned a glowing bowl of light, the color of flames, covering the entire clearing.

When she opened her eyes, her jaw dropped. She gaped at the faint shimmer of the barrier, stretching overhead to meet above the chimney. Turning to Brand, her eyes wide, she found him grinning proudly.

He picked her up and twirled her around. "You *are* a mage!"

She worked another set of wards, to further guard the cottage itself. There, she drew the glyphs Brand showed her, on the corner posts of the structure. Inside, she drew similar signs on either side of the door and the lone window. The process of linking them in her mind, imagining the protective barrier stretching between them, was just as effective as physically tracing the circle. When she finished the spell, the glyphs flared with light before disappearing.

Trina's heart was lighter than it had been. Satisfaction filled her. For the very first time, she felt confident she could make her own way in the world. Aye, there were dangers and she had yet to discover the extent of her abilities but, with Brand's advice and Juhan's company, she would learn.

* * * * *

The next day, Juhan rose to eat at the table for the first time. His skin was still a bit pale. He sat and stroked his growing beard while Trina prepared a bowl of broth with a little meat for him.

"I am grateful indeed that you learned those healing spells, my dear. 'Tis nothing short of incredible that I am recovered so soon." He moved his arm gingerly and winced. "On my own, I would be dead now."

"On our own, we would both be dead, uncle." Trina set the bowl before him. "Had it not been for Brand, the brigands would surely have killed us as they did the others."

He cast a glance over at Brand, where he rearranged the casks and baskets. "Then I must be grateful to Brand as well." Juhan sipped a bit of soup. "Ah, that is delicious. I am also grateful to your mistress, for teaching you to cook so well."

"Do not waste your gratitude on that evil woman," Brand snarled. He came to sit across from Juhan and leaned forward as he spoke, punctuating his words with a slap of his hand on the tabletop. "She was ready to sacrifice your niece's body and life for her vile schemes."

Juhan raised a brow. "I can still express my thanks. No one is entirely evil, just as no one is entirely good. We all begin in the middle, before we choose which side of the road we walk. Even those with foul intent bear some small reminder that they were once balanced, buried though it may be."

"There are some who have smothered that benevolent spark and that sorceress was among them." Brand and Juhan eyed each other over the few feet of table. "You have not tasted their foulness, unleavened by even a particle of good."

Juhan broke into a laugh. "Katrina, I knew your young man was special. I believe I have figured out why." He took her hand. "You are indeed gifted with great Power. I have only heard rumors of those who talk with spirits elemental and none who walk with them. Or lie with them, as this case most likely is." When she pulled at her hand, he tightened his grip. "No need to be shy or coy. I may have been weak while I lay upon that pallet under your healing spells, but I have never been deaf. Aye, I heard enough to figure out the truth, and I'm proud that you do not shrink from your abilities but embrace them. And him."

Juhan then regaled them with tales of his travels. For many years he had served as a courier of sorts, carrying messages and small items from manor to manor, court to court, valley to valley.

"The life of a traveler suits me. I have always been restless. Even as a youth, I was ever curious about what lay beyond the next hill, the next valley."

"Have you a wife, children?" Brand asked.

"I have never stayed in one place long enough to put down roots." He chuckled. "My mother used to tell me that my horse was the closest thing I'd ever have to a child."

"Better treat the beast as a child than a wife." Brand leered suggestively.

Both Trina and Juhan burst out in laughter.

"Your fellow has a fine sense of humor!" Juhan marveled. "I'd not have thought it of such a one as he."

Trina gazed up at her lover. "He is full of surprises."

"Aye, I can imagine."

Brand asked, "Do you know what you carry for these men who hire you?"

"Sometimes I do, but not always. Some things are best not known. There are matters I do not wish to become entangled with, beyond my part in delivering a message." He paused while he chewed a bit of meat. "And those I serve are not always men. In my early days on the road, I did carry items and information for only men. Lately, I find more and more women are active in their husband's affairs or trade. The world is ever changing."

Trina savored the moment and relaxed in the comfort of Brand's arm as her uncle spoke. She had a family, she had Brand, and her ability to erect the wards had shown her she had Talent.

"On this trip, I carried a series of messages between two powerful lords who, through my efforts, have arranged a truce and cemented it with a marriage between one lord's sister and the other's nephew."

She smiled. Of course *her* uncle would never work for less than the most powerful, would he?

"Things almost fell apart when my room was searched one evening while I ate. Thanks to my counsel, the thieves did not find what they wanted to."

"And how did you save the truce, uncle?" Trina relished the title as she half-listened to his answer.

"I had advised them to conceal the nature of their correspondence by couching it in terms of a trade agreement, one that benefited them both. 'Twas only when a particular word in each sentence was pulled out, and those words copied out in sequence, that the true message could be read. One of the lord's sons improved upon my idea, and suggested that a faint tracing be made upon the document, such that when the parchment were held backwards to the light, the means of finding the right words would be revealed. With his refinement, should something have happened to me that I could not personally deliver the scroll, the message would still have been received."

"That was clever."

"Aye, and that is why the man and his son are lords, and I am a mere courier." Juhan sipped his broth.

"I meant your idea. His contribution would be of little use without your development of the scheme." Trina protested before she saw the glint of humor in his eyes.

Trina told him of her life, from her early days with the old mage to her discovery of the flame-folk. She and Brand took turns telling of their travels. The story of Trina's experiment with the scrying bowl caught Juhan's attention.

"That was indeed a pryer. They are filthy, nasty charms." He grasped Trina's chin and turned her face to the light. "You did not resist, did you?"

"Nay, I couldn't. I didn't know how."

"Good. The worst harm is done when the victim forces the demon to rip out the memories." He turned to Brand. "I have never heard of pryers instructed to destroy the mind they plunder. Mayhap the victims you know of were damaged in the struggle."

Trina looked up from her pondering and asked a question that had long troubled her. "Uncle, you know much of these things. Are you a mage? Do mages run in my family?"

A wistful smile crossed his face. "Sadly, nay, child, I am no mage. Power runs strong in our families, but no man in our valley has aught beyond what one might consider strong instinct. The Power lies in the women alone. 'Twas how your mother knew you still lived, and why, even after all the intervening years, each month more queries go out for news of you. She has never given up hope of holding you again, although you are grown too large to climb in her lap."

Juhan handed his empty bowl to Trina with a trembling hand. She looked at him closely. His pallor was better than it had been and, when he spoke, his voice was firm.

"I am quite fatigued this evening. The walk across the cottage, even with your help, sapped what little vigor I had. If you will excuse me, I will retire to my pallet early."

Brand offered his arm for the old man to lean upon. "You are gaining in strength, but are not yet fully recovered. We must get you outside each day, but not for too long a time."

Juhan grimaced. "Katrina's wonderful healing charms have fortified me, but the recovery of my endurance must be earned."

"It is my pleasure to help you, Uncle." How wonderful it felt to say that! She had a family, after all her yearning. In truth, she had begun to hope more out of habit than out of any expectation to find and return to them.

Trina grinned and followed her uncle's progress across the cottage. His steps were sure but slow. His recovery would take time, but he was on the mend.

When they reached his bundle of blankets, he sank onto them with a sigh. "If you would be so kind as to enhance my sleep tonight, I would appreciate it." He winked at her, where she still sat. "I wish to sleep soundly."

Trina's skin fairly burned. How kind of her uncle, and how thoughtful. She composed herself to recite the spell, crossing to make the proper gestures over where he lay.

With a smile, he pulled his covers over him and closed his eyes. Before she made it back to the table, gentle snoring drifted from his corner.

Brand carried a stack of bowls to the area they used for cleaning up. "Alone at last," he murmured into her ear as he passed her.

"Aye." She grinned at him. "Alone indeed."

"I've missed you since this morn." He wiped down the table. With a gesture at the dirty dishes, he said, "Those can wait until tomorrow. The clatter might disturb your uncle. He needs his rest."

Trina didn't miss the suggestion in his tone. "Aye, and the light might bother him." She blew out the candles and extinguished the lantern. The dying embers from the hearth lit the room with a soft glow.

"Come to me, my love. I think your sweetness is the perfect ending to the meal." The promise in Brand's eyes warmed her heart. "Have I told you today how much I love you?"

"Only nine or ten times."

"Really? So seldom? I must rectify that." He drew her close and enfolded her in his embrace. "Sometimes I have trouble believing that this is real, that you are real. But it must be, for we fire-folk do not dream."

"I'm surprised that my uncle recognized you for what you are."

"He is a wise man. In his travels, he has seen things you cannot imagine. I doubt much surprises him." He tilted her face up to his. "You, however, continually surprise me. The ease with which you pulled together that spell, using your own style and following your instincts, is an indication of what you shall one day be capable of. It will be interesting to see how your skills develop."

His eyes gleamed with the soft glow of the coals as he lowered his head and kissed her. She met him eagerly, opening for the sweep of his tongue, twining hers with his. The heat of his kiss matched the warmth of his admiration and pride. That he expected great things from her made her eager to prove him right.

One touch of his hand to the pulse in her neck and lightning rocketed through her, quickly surpassing the intensity of her gratification and driving all thoughts of spells and magick from her head. There was only the two of them, brought together by passion and heat.

He tasted of the stew they'd eaten, and ale and cheese. His smoky male scent filled her head. She pressed against him, seeking greater contact, seeking the fulfillment only he could provide. She suckled gently on his tongue and he moaned into her mouth. She captured it with a sigh of her own.

For a quick moment he thrust his hips against her, the hard outline of his cock evidence of his excitement. She reveled in the power she had over him, that she could give back to him some measure of the intense pleasure he'd so often shown her.

He kept his lips sealed to hers while he quickly divested them of their clothing. Her gown and chemise fell around her ankles. He broke the kiss and pulled away, leaving her to shiver in the cold.

Scooping up the pile of linen and wool, he arranged all their clothes on the tabletop. When he turned back to her, his hands brought welcome heat to her chilled skin.

He rubbed her all over, warming her to the point that where moments before the cold air had pinched her skin, sweat now arose. When she was rosy and breathing fast beneath his touch, he indicated the padded table. "Come, let us try a different way."

She stood before him, her back against his chest. His hands roamed across her belly and breasts, sparking thrills as he brushed her nipples and caressed the soft globes of her breasts.

His hard shaft came to rest between the cheeks of her ass. She shifted against him, rubbing without hesitation, exploring the sensations of cradling him in a new way.

"Do you like this?" He whispered into her ear as he dipped his head to nip at the tender skin beneath the lobe.

"Aye." Her breath came in pants, matching the accelerated pulse beneath his lips. "And you?"

"Aye, indeed. It is well that your uncle is bespelled, for I want to hear you scream with pleasure this evening. I only wish that I were two, so I might possess you completely."

"Two?" She pushed the word past her trembling lips. Did he mean—? The thought sent her heart to pounding against her ribs.

"Aye, two, one in front, one from behind." A pinch of both her nipples as he spoke made her gasp as much as his declaration.

She twitched under his touch and wetness flooded her cleft. His hard cock burned into her back.

"Lean forward." His voice held the magickal note of command.

Trina found herself obeying, sprawling across the mound of fabric he'd built to cushion her from the hard wood of the table. 'Twas just in time, for her knees had begun to tremble so hard she doubted she could have remained standing.

"Ah, this is the perfect height." Brand parted her thighs, pushing her knees aside and stepping between them. His cock probed above her cleft. Sweet Goddess, was he planning to penetrate her there? The thought was exciting, but the reality might prove to be less so.

Nay, with relief she felt him slide the head of his cock down and around her cleft, slipping in the wetness of her arousal. His hand stroked her nether lips once and then his fingers slid inside her. With soft touches, he stroked her there, until she was writhing and thrusting back against him.

"Aye, you are ready for me." He followed the words with a slow, steady thrust into her, expanding and filling her as only he could. He felt larger than usual. She had never asked, but did he have the power to alter his size and shape?

She shuddered as he began to slide in and out, pushing against her until she slid a bit on the clothing beneath her. Sweet goddess, he had placed the rough wool of her cloak so that her nipples scraped against it with every movement. Sensitized by the initial contact, they began to throb with a pleasurable fire with every breath she took.

Enough of the various garments folded over the edge of the table to provide her with stimulation there, as well. In taking her from behind, he had ensured she would not lack for any pleasure.

His strokes remained slow and steady. The heat built in her breasts and pooled in her belly. As the anticipation of an incredible climax grew, Brand began to massage her ass. His hands worked to assist in pushing her down against the wool, increasing the tension inside of her.

Almost without her noticing it at first, he began spreading her cheeks with each pass of his hands. When he ran one finger around her anus, she jerked in surprise. He persisted and, as she grew accustomed to the sensation, began to press into her.

Slick with her juices, his thumb slid easily inside. She froze for a moment but he soothed her with soft words and she relaxed under his touch. He started working his massage in time with the thrusts of his cock. She nearly came as he worked a second finger in.

Both of them were breathing raggedly but Brand kept a fairly constant rhythm going. Trina became mindless with pleasure, as her world contracted to sheer sensation, the double penetration Brand was treating her to, and the scrape of her sensitive clit and nipples across the rough weave of the fabrics. She thrust back against him, pushing her thighs against the edge and scrabbling with her fingers for purchase on the smooth table.

He gave up any semblance of timing and drove his thumb as deep inside her as he could, flexing it slightly as he speeded up his thrusts, his cock hammering into her.

White-hot and sizzling, her climax surged through her from her womb to her breasts, burning its way along her spine. Her toes curled and her scalp tingled as she cried out and clenched around his driving cock.

Brand showed no mercy as he continued to thrust home, through her tight passage. She shrieked his name as another, even more intense surge shook her. She screamed wordlessly as she shattered into brilliant shards of light, and then into darkness.

Brand collapsed, panting, atop Trina's limp form. Hearth and home, he'd never dreamed of such ecstasy. He gathered her into his arms and rolled over, cushioning her against his body instead of the table. Her heart beat fast and steady under his palm.

Much like his.

For some time, he'd been considering the possibilities presented by a mortal's body and wondering about exploring those with Trina. He'd not dreamed that she would be so willing or that the results would be so astounding. He spent a few moments in happy thoughts of other explorations they could conduct together.

He may have dozed off, or he may just have been lost in his happy anticipations. He came fully awake when Trina stirred in his arms.

The interior of the cottage was lit brightly, as if by sunlight. A chill swept through him as he sat up, shaking her into wakefulness.

She leapt to her feet, exclaiming, "The wards!"

The glow came from the large amber nugget. Firelight danced and twisted in its depths, a warning that was unmistakable. How long did they have before danger reached them? He uttered a curse, that he had missed the onset of the beacon.

Chapter Nine

కు

They struck swiftly.

A string latch and leather hinges were no match for the shoulder of a fully-armed guardsman. Or the heavy boots of his companion. The two of them hit the door together. The aged planks splintered under their onslaught. Brushing the bits aside as if they were no more troublesome than flying leaves, they strode into the cottage.

A fireball sprang to Brand's hand, unbidden but welcome. Suddenly aware of their nakedness and Trina's vulnerability, he stepped in front of her and faced the enemy.

Confronted by a naked man holding a growing ball of flame in one hand, the intruders hesitated. Brand wasted no time in hurling the only weapon he had at hand.

The fireball passed completely through the men, leaving them unharmed, to soar through the now-empty doorway and disappear into the darkness beyond. The figures—armor, weapons, clothing and all—shimmered and wavered in the wake of its passage.

The only sound in the cottage was a gentle snore from Juhan's pallet by the hearth. The two figures remained half-transparent, milling about, their lower legs disappearing as they walked through several stools and a stout wooden strongbox.

"By the Great Cauldron!" Trina came to stand beside Brand. She hugged her cloak about her shoulders and shivered. "What are they?"

He stepped up to one and thrust his hand into the gleaming outline of its form. A slight chill spread up his arm, but there was no resistance, nothing to indicate that there was a demon present, or an actual entity of any kind.

"An illusion, I believe. A figure created of magick and will. Some mages use them to go where they cannot or prefer not to travel." Even as he spoke, the guards were dissipating, thinning into nothingness.

Trina gaped at the remains of the door. "How could they break down the door if they weren't really here?"

"I imagine it was done with a concentration of the mage's will, focused to coincide with their entrance." Brand went to peer outside, stepping over the shards of wood littering the floor. "That it was done so completely, and timed so well, indicates a mage of great Power, or mayhap several working in concert."

Outside, the sputtering remains of the fireball revealed smooth, unbroken snow across the clearing. The only visible tracks were his own, from earlier in the evening when he'd trudged around to the shelter in back to feed the horses and the mule.

No one had trodden the path from the road and no one had come from the road to the cottage's door.

Trina turned to Brand, her eyes wide with fear. "We must leave this place, tonight. Whoever sent those things knows where we are."

He nodded gravely. "Help me pack and then we will awaken your uncle. The next visitors will be all too real."

* * * * *

The cathedral loomed above the surrounding structures. Its spire was visible for leagues, long before any other sign of habitation could be seen.

Juhan and Trina rode the horse and mule, while Brand trudged along beside, leading the other horse and all of their supplies. Their flight from the cottage had taken its toll. Juhan was barely ready to travel, but travel they must.

They stopped on an overlook, where they could see down into the town. High stone walls, more worked stone than Trina had ever seen, sheltered most of the town. How long had it taken? How many men had worked on this?

Outside the walls, hedgerows and ditches framed a neat patchwork of fields and pastures. Inside the town, shops and houses and warehouses crowded together. Trina wondered if it was possible to walk from one end of the town to the other, never leaving the rooftops. A few small figures could be seen in places where the rooftops left the narrow streets and alleys open to view.

"Here we shall be safe, for a night or two," Juhan declared. "The enemy shuns large groups of people, preferring to work unnoticed in the shadows. The presence of the holy order of monks and their cathedral will also help."

Trina raised her eyebrows. "Why?"

"Most people fear demons as characters in stories to scare children, or from legends. The Christian holy men, priests and monks, believe as most do not. That belief gives them strength."

"What is a Christian?"

"One who follows the teachings of the Christ. Many of them are good-hearted and honest but, like any group of men, there are those among them who take their instructions to extremes. Your gifts would earn you death by fire and a stake, I fear. Conceal your abilities while we walk among them."

Trina looked down into the town with a wary eye. Who would have guessed that the world beyond Kalidah's holding would be so complex or hold such dangers? "Aye, that I will."

Uncle Juhan turned his horse back onto the trail. "I know a tavern where we may find welcome." He cast a glance up at the evening sky, streaked with red and blue by the setting sun. "Hurry. The gates close just before full dark. We will be safe within the walls, but until we reach them, we are vulnerable."

Picking their way down the hillside took longer than they expected. The path was old and poorly maintained. In places rockslides had obliterated the solid footing and they had to cross one by one, careful lest their passage dislodge more scree and stone.

Once among the fields, they found the road that led them in a roundabout way through the fields. By the time the gate came within view, Juhan was glancing all around. His unease infected their mounts, making them difficult to control. They reached the gates in a rush, all of them eager for the safety of the crowded town.

* * * * *

The two guards at the gate waved them inside, to a small area bounded by the guardhouse, the barracks, the wide outer gate and an inner gate. There, another pair of guards stopped them.

"Who are you and what is your business?"

Juhan maneuvered his horse so he could see the guard's face. "We are bound northward, and seek the shelter of your walls for the night. We were traveling with a merchant and his guard until brigands attacked."

The guard's interest heightened. "When? Where?"

"Days ago. I took an arrow in the shoulder and spent time recovering in an abandoned cottage off the road in the woods. 'Twas, oh, mayhap a half-day's hard ride south. We have the merchant's records, to deliver to your care. His family and heirs should be notified. We are the only survivors."

The guard nodded. "Our Lord Gilles and the abbott will do what is necessary. These are perilous times." He hesitated.

Trina understood when her uncle reached into his saddlebag and pulled out a bottle. Slipping it to the guard, he asked, "Where can we find the best lodging? Clean with good food, and not too expensive?"

The bottle disappeared into a fold of his clothing and the man's face split in a grin. "My wife's sister keeps the best kitchen in town at The Bubbling Bog. Two streets down, second tavern on the right. Tell her Ronnie sent you, and that she's to treat you right. Try a mug o' the house dark. It's beyond excellent."

"Thank you for your kindness."

"Thank you, sir." The guard sent them off with a wink and a slap on the mule's flank.

"Come." Juhan led the way into the town.

Trina was glad he'd taken the mule's reins, for there was so much to see that she couldn't keep her attention on where they were going.

Even at dusk, when one might expect the townsfolk to be winding down their day, the streets were bustling with more people than she'd ever seen in one place.

Young men in aprons rushed between goodwives carrying baskets laden with bread, meat and vegetables. Carts and foot traffic clogged the way. Street vendors called out, hawking their few remaining wares.

The Bubbling Bog was everything Ronnie had said. Mention of his name brought a big smile to the groom's face and he jerked his head toward the front door. The guard's relatives were welcoming and appreciative of another flask, which Juhan slipped into the landlord's hand.

The huge establishment was nothing like the tiny tavern in Lord Roland's village. The entrance led to a hallway with a large, open taproom on one side and several closed doors on the other. The public room stretched out from the double doorway, with room for many tables. Loud diners crowded the benches and chairs, clearly enjoying their meals.

"Nice and clean. Good customers," Juhan muttered to Trina as the plump maid led them up the wide stairs. "We shall be safe here."

The maid's face was rosy by the time they reached the third floor. "We got nothing private fer the lass, I'm sorry. Just this one room for you all, unless you want a cheaper place. You kin have pallets in the taproom, once it's closed. We've got a few men what prefers that. No stairs at the end of the night, if you knows what I mean." She winked at Trina and flung open a door. "There's two beds and I kin have the boy bring a pallet for the third."

The room was tiny, with one wall sloping steeply from the ceiling. Two narrow beds left little room for the pallet. Juhan glanced at Brand before he assured the maid, "We will need only the two beds. My niece and her husband won't mind sleeping snug together."

The woman chuckled and elbowed Brand in the ribs. "Aye, 'tis sometimes a little chill up here at night. I'll send the boy up with your other bags."

Again, a small flask changed hands. Once she had made her way back down the stairs, Trina asked, "Why do you give away the things we got from the merchant's stores?"

"Little gifts guarantee that we make friends. Everyone here will go out of their way to make us comfortable. We may not be the wealthiest customers but we can still be among the most generous. This is not where I usually stay but at some time my usual lodgings may become unsafe. You know that I work as a messenger of sorts, carrying small goods and information for pay. Much of that is sought by my employers' enemies. I may need to lodge here again in the future. It behooves me to plan ahead and cultivate friends in many places. Gratuities like the ones I have given to the guard and the staff here will ease my way should I need to seek shelter in haste."

Trina stared at him, absorbing this. "I had no idea that's what you were doing."

"You thought I squandered our goods." Juhan smiled. "Nay, I am looking far into the future. Which is why I also took the liberty to keep most of our more valuable items with us, rather than entrusting them to the stable hands. That's another lesson of the world at large. Trust no one."

"Not even family?"

"Only family you know well enough to trust. A difficult lesson to learn but if you heed and believe me, you will never pay the price of betrayal."

"You want me to trust you?"

Juhan's grin was rueful. "Aye. Do you know me well enough?"

"Aye." Trina reached up to kiss his cheek.

"May we eat now?"

* * * * *

The morning dawned bright and clear. Brand threw open the tiny shutter, letting in light and cool air.

"Was the maid correct? Did you find the night held a chill?"

"Not that I noticed." Brand grinned at Trina. "Were you cold?"

She blushed. "Nary a bit."

"Then let us break our fast and apply for an audience at the cathedral. Brand, you might want to wait here. It would be dangerous for us all should anyone recognize your nature."

"If we had secured a room with a hearth, I could rest in comfort. I suppose I can pass the day in the taproom, learning what I can of the town."

Juhan looked at him askance. "I wager you're eager to try the local food."

Brand smiled and replied easily, "And the drink. Did not Ronnie recommend the house brew? I shall ascertain his accuracy and report upon your return."

"Don't run up too large a bill. We have far to go before we reach home."

"I make no promises." Brand winked at Trina. "Just be sure you don't linger."

* * * * *

"The bishop's secretary will see you now." With a bow, the priest ushered them into a small office.

Another priest rose from behind the cluttered table with a smile. "Juhan! It is good to see you. How have you been?"

"Fine, Father James. And you?"

"I am well. Not getting any younger, but that is a common complaint about which we can do nothing. Any word on your search?"

"Aye, good news. Father, I am delighted to present my niece, Katrina."

The priest engulfed Trina's hands in his. "I too am delighted to see that our prayers have been answered. My child, many of us have prayed daily that you might be restored to your family." He turned back to Juhan. "Where did you find her?"

"Of all places, I found her on the road, searching for her family even as I searched for her." He settled in one chair and indicated Trina should take the other. "As I have pieced it together, she was taken from her cradle and carried south, to someone who wished a babe like her. She's grown up as a slave, serving a most evil woman. How she avoided the taint of her mistress is a mystery to me."

"Only by the grace of God," the priest offered. "Another thing for which we must be thankful."

"Indeed. We are bound for her home, to restore her to the arms of her parents. There are disturbing occurrences, however, about which I wish to consult you. When I say her mistress was evil, I mean that in the most basic sense." In a few words, Juhan described the destruction of the caravan, Trina's experience with the pryer and the later intrusion by the apparitions and their hasty flight from the cottage. He concluded by expressing the concern that they had not outrun their pursuer, whoever it may be, and that he did not wish to endanger Trina's family by leading the threat with them.

"You have no idea who it might be?" At Juhan's denial, Father James turned to Trina. The twinkle had disappeared from his eyes as he asked, "Child, may I touch you?"

Wordlessly, she held out her hand.

Once more, she met his warm grasp. He crossed himself and gazed into her eyes for a moment. She felt the slight tingle of magick and fought not to show any reaction. At length he released her. "Relax, my dear Trina, you need not fear discovery. I too have Talent, although not many here are aware of that aspect of my service to the Church."

He went to sit again in his chair behind the table. "I can find no lingering effects from the pryer. As for who set it and sent the illusions, I can't begin to guess. We who serve the Light face many enemies. When it comes to why the illusions were sent, I have a few ideas. Tell me about the attack."

Trina described what little she'd seen, substituting a knife for the fireball Brand threw that went right through the image.

The priest pursed his lips and narrowed his eyes. "And there was no sign of a real intruder?"

Trina shook her head. "The snow was unmarked."

"Then what alerted you? Are you skilled enough to have set wards?"

Astonished, Trina could only gape at him. How did he know?

"It is no mystery. You were burdened with an injured man and fearful after being subjected to the pryer's scrutiny. Prudence would dictate taking whatever precautions you could. What puzzles me is how an illusion could trigger the wards." He steepled his fingers and rested his chin on them. "Tell me about the cottage and the surroundings."

"There is an old garden in front, trampled by the brigands. In the back, there is a shed built up against the cottage."

"How do you reach the shed?"

"There is a path from the front, between the trees. Not wide enough for a cart, but fine for a horse."

"Could there have been anyone in the shed while you were distracted by the illusory attack?"

Juhan sucked in a breath and frowned. "I never considered that possibility."

"I have seen the combination used before. What we must do now is examine the tack and whatever else you have with you that was in the shed at the time. Did you store the saddlebags or any containers there?"

"Aye. We did not have much room in the cottage's main room, so we left as much as we could in the shed."

"The more to search, then." He pushed back his chair and stood. "We must discover if you have led your enemy here, and see what we can do about it. The sooner we begin, the sooner we can avert their attention."

The priest left the office for a moment, speaking in low tones to someone outside. Juhan took the opportunity to lean close to Trina. "You see, nowhere do you find everyone to be as you expect. I had not known until today that Father James had Talent. Do not take this as a sign that everyone here is like him. He is unique among clerics, as I am continually learning anew."

"Then I am to conceal what he does not know?"

Juhan laid his finger on his lips. "Trust no one."

Father James returned, put aside the parchment he'd been reading when they arrived, and rubbed his hands together. "Shall we return to your lodging?"

Trina and Juhan rose.

"And just where are you staying on this trip, old friend?"

"The guardsman recommended The Bubbling Bog, and we have found it acceptable."

A frown creased the priest's brow. "I am unfamiliar with that establishment. Does it lie near the docks?"

"Nay, 'tis hard by the south gate. Not a savory neighborhood, but a clean and honest place, from what I can tell. The taproom does not appear to host many altercations."

Father James smiled and suddenly he looked years younger. "I remember a few altercations we were involved in, once."

"Aye." Juhan fisted one hand and looked at it. "We did make an impression on those idiots, didn't we?"

"And a costly impression on the publican's furnishings, as I recall."

Outside, Father James took a bag from his assistant. Without further comment, he gestured for Juhan to lead the way.

Trina followed, eyeing her uncle with a new perspective. Clearly he and the priest had been friends for a long time but they had been in a tavern fight together? A courier and a priest? How long ago? Where? Why?

She pondered this while they made the short walk to the Bubbling Bog. For the first time, the bustling streets held less appeal than her speculations. A courier and a priest? Or did the friendship go further back, to before they were in their present positions?

When they entered the tavern, Brand looked up from his trencher. Waving a tankard, he grinned and called out, "Could you not have stayed a little longer?"

"We have urgent affairs to attend to." Juhan glanced around at the group near Brand. They drifted off, back to their benches and stools. "Are you coming?"

Brand gulped the last of his ale and slapped the tankard back on the bar. Wiping his mouth, he rose and followed. The priest awaited them at the corner of the building.

"The stables are around back." The priest led the way. He nodded to a boy raking straw over a puddle. "How's your gram, Hans?"

"Better, Uncle James." The lad grinned and tugged at his cap.

"I'll come see her in the morning."

"Aye, sir. She'll be waiting." Hans turned back to his chore.

"I didn't know my nephew was working here." Father James strode through the open archway. "In here. Your tack will be hung near the stalls. 'Tis there we'll most likely find your tracker's token."

From a pouch at his side he withdrew a cloth. "Stand behind me. If I am correct, it will show you to your enemy. Let him see me, a stranger, instead."

"I do not understand," Trina ventured.

"The polished surface of the ornament that has been added to your bridle or halter will act as a scrying surface, but in reverse. He need only gaze into whatever he uses as a viewing medium to see where you are, and what you are doing. Let us hope he is at rest, or busy in his pursuit of you. Now that you have stopped, he may be riding hard to catch you."

Trina gasped and glanced at her uncle. He, too, had blanched.

The priest walked cautiously down the wide aisle between the stalls, his handkerchief held at his side. They watched as he hesitated for a moment, then unerringly found the stalls that housed their horses. He casually turned and leaned back against a post hung with assorted tack. Keeping his shoulder firmly against the tangle of leather, he motioned Trina over.

"Here, take this." He thrust the cloth at her. "Wrap it over your hand. Open your senses, and feel behind my shoulder, low, below my armpit. You should feel a warm spot. That is the polished disc. Cover it with your palm and the cloth."

Trina obediently covered her hand and worked her fingers between the heavy cloth of the priest's robe and the straps. She took a deep breath and tried to recreate the way she felt when she could see the flame-folk in the fire. Closing her eyes helped shut out the rustle and stamp of the horses in the straw and the chatter of the yard.

The heat from the magickal disc almost burned her fingertip. She hissed in surprise and the priest blew out his breath. "Fine. That's it. Keep your hand over it while I move away. Be sure to conceal it completely."

As he shifted his weight, she slid her hand around until she felt the burn on her palm and cool leather or air all around. "I have it." She nodded and he stepped back, turning and holding the cloth by wrapping it around the post.

"Well done. You may release it."

Trina eased her hand away, surprised there was no mark or visual evidence of the heat she'd felt radiating off the device.

Father James bunched the cloth up and pulled at the disc. With a click, it came free and he pulled it off the halter. Folding the linen over and over to form a thick pad around the thing, he stuffed it in his pocket. "I worry that this may not be the only item of his you bear. He has planned well thus far, and we must not underestimate him. Let us return to my office, and discuss what we can do to confound your pursuer."

Together they turned to leave the stable, Father James in the lead. Brand brought up the rear, close behind Trina and her uncle.

Trina put her hand to her chest and rubbed the slight ache of her scars. The ache flared into a burning sensation that rippled along the pattern. The ache rapidly grew into searing heat.

"Father! Uncle!" She pulled on Juhan's arm. "Something is wrong."

The priest stopped just short of the doorway. As he turned to face her, a blast of wind blew in and sent him reeling.

Icy air swept through the stable, knocking over feed buckets and swirling straw and tack into flying tangles. The bright morning light waned to twilight, as though a big storm approached or heavy clouds obscured the sun. The stable hands scrambled to flee into the depths of the stable. Brand grabbed Trina and her uncle and pulled them into the shelter of an empty stall. Father James followed to crouch in the straw.

As suddenly as it came, the wind died away. An unsettling silence descended in its wake.

No one moved. 'Twas as if even the horses held their breath.

Chapter Ten

છ૭

The hair on Trina's neck rose. She glanced at Brand. He didn't speak but motioned her to stay where she was.

Outside, a heavy boot struck the slates of the yard. Then another. With slow, measured treads, someone approached the stable.

The burning of her scars grew until she thought her gown might burst into flames. She shifted uncomfortably. A shot of pain from the gentle rub of linen across the pattern brought tears to her eyes.

In a burst of light, the sun returned and outlined a man's large figure in the doorway.

Father James rose to his feet in one motion and stepped into the aisle between the stalls. Grasping the crucifix on his chest in one hand, he held it forth. His mouth opened and he began to chant in a language Trina had heard Kalidah use.

The man took two steps forward before the first sentence was done. His hand shot out in a pushing gesture and Father James fell to his knees. A strangled gasp passed the priest's lips and the chanting ceased.

The air around the man shimmered and his form blurred. Unsure if she was watching a real person or an illusion, Trina blinked several times and tried to look *beyond* him the way she had the hearth and the scrying bowl.

A heavy fog obscured his figure and she realized what she was seeing was actually there. The darkness was his dark aura, a true indication of his nature. Within the cloud, an area of absolute black hovered on his chest.

Her breath caught in her throat. Could this be the man she'd scried, who still wore the pryer's pendant?

As the thought ran through her mind, the man began to speak. His words and gestures made the scars she bore flare to life and greater agony.

Brand claimed the arcane pattern could be used by another mage. Whoever sent the illusions to the cottage had been powerful indeed. Unless there were two powerful mages seeking her, the man who stood before her was her enemy as well as a very powerful mage.

Father James lay still and silent, crumpled where he fell. Her uncle was frozen in place. She couldn't see Brand to know if he could help her.

The lines Kalidah had carved on her chest pulsed with the man's words. She recognized a few but could make no sense of them, nor could she figure out the intent or meaning of the spell. Without knowing that, she could not begin a counterspell. She lacked the ability to craft any spell quickly. For even such a simple task as setting the wards, she required a lot of thought and time.

Time was what she didn't have. The mage spoke faster now. He leaned forward intently, eyes closed beneath his creased brow and hands sketching signs in the air.

How could she thwart his spell? Could she somehow reverse what he was doing, turning the tables on him?

Turning the tables.

The image of Kalidah working on her last spell came to mind. She had turned the parchment over and traced the wrong side because the true meaning of the image had been concealed in that fashion. Might a reversal of the pattern Kalidah had made do the same?

Brand maintained that simple was often best. Strengthened by that memory, and knowing she must do something or she would die, Trina struggled to move.

'Twas as if the mage had thickened the air, trapping them as in cooling wax. No wonder her companions had done nothing to hinder the man's actions. Her limbs were leaden, too heavy to force to her bidding.

A basic counterspell came to mind, one Kalidah had used to banish lingering traces of magick from a previous ritual before she started another. Her lips refused to move, so she screamed the spell in her head, over and over.

After repeating the spell so many times she lost count, Trina found she could shuffle her feet a little. The air thinned a bit. Her lips began to move, permitting her to mumble the spell aloud. She doubled her efforts to counter the mage's spell.

She finally managed to turn her back on the mage and his incantations. There was Brand, caught in the same sticky web as the others. His hand rose slowly to her. She tried to lift her hand to take his but failed. The effort exhausted her, and she could do naught but wait and see if presenting the mage with a reversed pattern would affect his spell. Fatigue and pain overwhelmed her. She strove to keep uttering the counterspell.

The mage's voice rose and the pain of her scars escalated along with it. Tears streamed down her face. She thought it could not hurt any worse, and then it did. She opened her mouth wider to scream and found she made no sound.

No matter what happened, she would welcome the end as a relief from the burning ache on her skin. This was worse than being branded with the design all over again.

The mage finished his chant and a flare of bright light engulfed her. Something behind her exploded. The force of it struck her in the back, throwing her into the stall to land face-down on a pile of straw.

Around her, the world came to life.

A babble of voices filled the air. The shrill tones of the stable lads asked what had happened. The booming voice of the landlord demanded an explanation for the noise that had cleared out the taproom.

She couldn't move.

Close by, she heard a groan. A weight shifted off her back and she was free. Hands grasped her shoulders and gently pulled her to her feet. The painful burning of the scars on her chest had subsided to an ache and her back was cold but, other than that, she felt normal.

"Are you hurt?" Brand plucked a piece of straw from her face.

"Nay, I am fine. A bit shaken, but unharmed."

Brand and Uncle Juhan supported her in their arms. Both appeared fine, although their hair was every which way and bits of straw clung to their disheveled garments.

"He tried to banish me!" Brand exclaimed in outraged tones. "He came far too close to it for my comfort."

Juhan took her hand in his. "I am unsure what he did, precisely, but I could not move so much as a muscle."

Someone draped a cloth across her shoulders. It settled across her bare skin and she realized the back of her gown was gone.

She turned to face the priest. He gestured toward the doorway, where a smoldering figure lay sprawled across the threshold.

"My dear child, I do not know what you did, but we have all survived." He spoke with a painful rasp in his voice. "Your enemy failed rather traumatically, 'twould seem. Might the charred remains of your clothing be somehow related?"

"Charred?" She moved her shoulders gingerly but felt no pain on her back.

"Aye, niece, your garments are burned, although the skin beneath is unmarked."

"I know I failed to help." Father James ran a hand over his throat. "I will bear a reminder of his Power for some days, I believe. You have my deepest gratitude."

"Nay, 'tis my uncle and—whether you believe me or not—Kalidah we must thank." Trina smiled at his dubious expression. "I once saw her trace the wrong side of an image to use, and Uncle Juhan explained to me how sometimes a map is partially reversed to conceal its meaning. I could do nothing to counter his spell other than turn my back, to reverse the pattern I bear. 'Twas the only means I had of possibly thwarting him."

"I'd say you thwarted him completely. I'd like to claim responsibility, but I just told you of my work. 'Twas you who remembered and thought to act on it." Juhan eyed the mage's remains. "We may never know who he was or what he wanted."

"Never have I seen a mage of his abilities align himself with another or work for the benefit of someone else. We may be confident that your troubles are over." He indicated them all with a wave of his hand. "Will you remain a day or two, to gather your strength before resuming your journey?"

Trina glanced around the stable and exchanged looks with her uncle. Juhan said, "Nay, I think we will be happier to have seen the last of this place. Once we have packed, we will be on our way."

The priest shook his hand, holding tight while he placed his other hand atop their clasped hands. "You are always welcome here, old friend."

"Thank you, for your friendship and your willingness to help us. I will always remember."

Chapter Eleven

ɛɔ

Juhan grabbed the mule's bridle and pulled it to a stop. He smiled broadly. "Are you ready?"

Sunshine warmed Trina's head and shoulders. Around them, green meadows dotted with wildflowers were filled with buzzing bees. Her uncle and Brand rode beside her. Just over the crest of the hill before them, her family awaited. Her family. Her mother. Her father. Brothers and a sister. Assorted aunts, uncles and cousins. She even had a grandmother.

"I cannot believe I'm here! After all these years, not knowing if my family remembered me, not even knowing if they were still alive, it doesn't feel real." She took a deep breath and blinked back a tear. "I'm as ready as I'll ever be."

"Then come along." He jogged their mounts into motion. As they crested the hill the family holding came into view, spread out before her. There was the stream that fed the pond and the four willows she'd seen in her vision. And the people! Someone called out and they came from outbuildings, from the main house and from the shade of the willows. Young and old, they gathered, until a chattering crowd had formed just beyond the footbridge. Waiting for her.

Juhan waved to the assemblage and received a cheer in response. "Welcome home, Trina," he said. He held Brand back and let her cross the bridge alone.

As the mule reached the ground on the other side, a woman broke loose from the crowd and ran to pull her down into a tight embrace. "Katrina! My baby!"

"Mama?" Trina could barely see through her tears. What she could see proved that she did indeed resemble her mother.

"Aye, I'm your mama. And I am so glad you've come back to me." Her mother released her. She traced Trina's cheeks with her fingers before gathering her close once more. "By the Goddess, I worried I'd never see you again, but I never gave up hope. Not for one moment did I stop praying and searching. Never," she said fiercely. "Never think you were forgotten."

"Uncle Juhan told me you wanted me."

"He was right. Every time he came back without you, I badgered him and gave him grief until he left again. I always sent letters with him, to go to cities where he didn't have time to travel. I can't wait to send the good news that you've returned!"

"Inge, let us have our turn." A burly man with a kindly face shouldered his way through the throng to them.

"I've waited years and years for this moment, so don't rush me." A smile softened her words. "Katrina, this is your father."

"Welcome home, daughter." He stood at a slight distance and looked her over soberly. "Inge, she's got your eyes and hair, but I think that's my chin." He cocked his head to one side. "Your height and slim build, thank the Goddess. Her sister Anna is stout enough for them both." His eyes twinkled and the corner of his mouth twitched up. A wave of chuckles swept through the assemblage.

"I am not, Papa!" A tall, slender young woman slapped him on the arm.

"Katrina, lass, 'tis good to have you home." Her father swept her up into a hug, along with her mother who still clung close.

Her mother never let go of her. As they moved from person to person, she would stroke Trina's hair or whisper words of love and prayers of thanksgiving.

Trina met so many family members her head swam. She couldn't keep them straight. Although she'd heard the names from her uncle, they came to her so fast she couldn't keep track of which faces matched what names.

Soon the press of family members waiting to be introduced or to see Trina, touch her and hug her eased. Only her parents and Anna remained close.

"I imagine you are tired." Her mother patted her cheek.

Anna spoke up. "If what Uncle Juhan says of your solitary life is true, you must be overwhelmed by such a crowd. Do not worry if you cannot remember everyone's names. That will come in time, sister." Her pretty face broke into a grin. "How odd it feels to say that! Although you have lived in our thoughts and prayers, having you here in fact is strange. Wonderful, but strange."

Trina looked around at all the people. "Does everyone live here?"

"Aye, on the manor or in the village. We've always been a close family." Her father gestured toward the river. "All of your brothers have wed but none went far from home. Baldwin is now the miller and Gerhard took over the butcher's trade after he died two summers ago. That's Gerhard's daughter Mara, there with his youngest boy, Tadd. Young Henck, your oldest brother, helps me run this place." He shook his head. "If I had another son to train with the old smith, one day I'd rule the valley in its entirety!"

Inge smiled and patted his arm. "You've no need to control all trade in the village. Everyone will always regard you as the village patriarch."

Trina watched her parents smile into each other's eyes and wondered that she was now a part of such a loving group. In all her imaginings, she had never thought she would find such a perfect family. With Brand, she now had everything her heart could desire.

Where was Brand? She searched among the small knots of people around the yard and found him in the deep shade, deep in conversation with her uncle and a man she thought was the father of one of her brothers' wives. She envisioned the family trees she'd seen among Kalidah's paper and decided that made the man nothing to her, but he was her brother's father-in-law.

She realized that she had introductions of her own to make. "Come, I want you to meet someone."

Her mother kept her arm around Trina's shoulders and her father stayed close. Anna took her hand as they moved between people, finally ducking beneath the trailing branches of a willow.

"Mama, Papa, er..." Trina found shyness thickened her tongue. "This is Brand, who rescued me from the fire and traveled with me."

"I am truly grateful to you for saving my daughter." Her mother let her go to embrace Brand. She quickly released him and stepped back. Examining him at arm's length, she exclaimed, "Oh, my. You are not what I expected."

Brand smiled at her. "But you are precisely what I expected. Trina looks exactly like you. I see the same intelligence in your face, and the same wealth of kindness."

A twinkle grew in Inge's eyes as she pulled her husband forward. "This is beyond wonderful! Stan, I think you may well control the village trades, sooner than you think."

He looked from her to Brand and then to Trina in question. "I do not understand."

"Trina's young man here is no man."

"Do not speak to me in riddles, Inge. Spit it out for me in plain words."

"You will have not a son but a son-in-law to work the forge. Brand is not mortal, he is of the fire."

Her father's eyes bulged. "He's what?"

"An elemental. A spirit in mortal form. I'm certain he can take on the job of smith, and mayhap with work that exceeds any smith there has ever been."

"If he will. He only traveled with me to be sure I reached you safely. I beg you, Mama, do not presume too much. He is not of this world."

"Tsk-tsk. He can do what he wants, and I'm certain he wants you." Inge reached up to run a hand across his jaw. "Am I not right, Brand? Do you not wish to remain with my daughter above all things? Take her to wife, then, and find a welcome in our midst."

Trina took a deep breath and held it. Goddess, but her mother was a brazen woman! To ascertain and accept his nature so easily, and to boldly pledge her daughter to a man not mortal.

"This I had not expected."

Her father muttered, "Neither had I."

Juhan placed a hand on his shoulder and whispered, "It was destined from the start."

Brand shifted his gaze from her mother to Trina. "I would indeed remain here, but there is another to be consulted and if need be convinced. Trina, love, what say you?"

"I say yes. Stay and live with me. It is my heart's desire, with no need for convincing. You have done that every day since I first met you."

Her mother broke out into a huge grin. "What a feast we shall have! My daughter restored to me, and a marriage as well. Juhan, you bring miracles with you this time. Come, Stan, let us decide when to celebrate." She tugged on his hand, ducking under the willow to stride across the yard.

Trina had to laugh at her father's words as he trailed behind her. "From the sound of it, my love, you've begun already. The question is more when to call a halt and return to our daily lives."

Uncle Juhan sketched them a bow and followed her parents, pulling Anna with him.

"Alone at last. I fear living here means we will have to work to find time for the two of us." Brand pulled her into his arms.

Trina snuggled into his embrace. He was right. Her family was wonderful, but there were so many of them. "Do you not mind?"

"Mind what? Being commandeered like a soldier by your irresistible mother? 'Tis like trying to turn aside a tornado."

"But you might not want to remain here."

"Why would I not? I suspect the job of smith is something I can do with my eyes closed. Playing with fire every day, bending metal to my will, is a small price to pay for spending my nights with you." His chuckle shook his chest beneath her hand. "Do you suppose the village folk will object if I do not wear clothing? Should I have need to go into the fire, I would not want to have to stop to remove my shirt and braes."

"I do not think the women would mind."

They both laughed as he captured her lips with his. She opened her mouth to him, sighing as his tongue joined hers in a dance.

"I promise we shall continue this later. Here comes your sister, along with a band of children."

"I'll hold you to that promise."

Why an electronic book?

We live in the Information Age—an exciting time in the history of human civilization, in which technology rules supreme and continues to progress in leaps and bounds every minute of every day. For a multitude of reasons, more and more avid literary fans are opting to purchase e-books instead of paper books. The question from those not yet initiated into the world of electronic reading is simply: *Why?*

1. ***Price.*** An electronic title at Ellora's Cave Publishing and Cerridwen Press runs anywhere from 40% to 75% less than the cover price of the exact same title in paperback format. Why? Basic mathematics and cost. It is less expensive to publish an e-book (no paper and printing, no warehousing and shipping) than it is to publish a paperback, so the savings are passed along to the consumer.

2. ***Space.*** Running out of room in your house for your books? That is one worry you will never have with electronic books. For a low one-time c ost, you can purchase a handheld device specifically designed for e-reading. Many e-readers have large, convenient screens for viewing. Better yet, hundreds of titles can be stored within your new library—on a single microchip. There are a variety of e-readers from different manufacturers. You can also read e-books on your PC or laptop computer. (Please note that Ellora's

Cave does not endorse any specific brands. You can check our websites at www.ellorascave.com or www.cerridwenpress.com for information we make available to new consumers.)

3. *Mobility*. Because your new e-library consists of only a microchip within a small, easily transportable e-reader, your entire cache of books can be taken with you wherever you go.

4. *Personal Viewing Preferences.* Are the words you are currently reading too small? Too large? Too… ANNOYING? Paperback books cannot be modified according to personal preferences, but e-books can.

5. *Instant Gratification.* Is it the middle of the night and all the bookstores near you are closed? Are you tired of waiting days, sometimes weeks, for bookstores to ship the novels you bought? Ellora's Cave Publishing sells instantaneous downloads twenty-four hours a day, seven days a week, every day of the year. Our webstore is never closed. Our e-book delivery system is 100% automated, meaning your order is filled as soon as you pay for it.

Those are a few of the top reasons why electronic books are replacing paperbacks for many avid readers.

As always, Ellora's Cave and Cerridwen Press welcome your questions and comments. We invite you to email us at Comments@ellorascave.com or write to us directly at Ellora's Cave Publishing Inc., 1056 Home Avenue, Akron, OH 44310-3502.

THE
☥ ELLORA'S CAVE ☥
LIBRARY

Stay up to date with Ellora's Cave Titles in
Print with our Quarterly Catalog.

TO RECIEVE A CATALOG,
SEND AN EMAIL WITH YOUR NAME
AND MAILING ADDRESS TO:

CATALOG@ELLORASCAVE.COM
OR SEND A LETTER OR POSTCARD
WITH YOUR MAILING ADDRESS TO:

CATALOG REQUEST
c/o ELLORA'S CAVE PUBLISHING, INC.
1056 HOME AVENUE
AKRON, OHIO 44310-3502

MAKE EACH DAY MORE *EXCITING* WITH OUR

ELLORA'S CAVEMEN

CALENDAR

www.EllorasCave.com

erridwen, the Celtic Goddess of wisdom, was the muse who brought inspiration to story-tellers and those in the creative arts. Cerridwen Press encompasses the best and most innovative stories in all genres of today's fiction. Visit our site and discover the newest titles by talented authors who still get inspired - much like the ancient storytellers did, once upon a time.

Cerridwen Press

www.cerridwenpress.com

Discover for yourself why readers can't get enough of the multiple award-winning publisher

Ellora's Cave.

Whether you prefer e-books or paperbacks,

be sure to visit EC on the web at
www.ellorascave.com

for an erotic reading experience that will leave you breathless.